GUTIAN CODE

Love & Dark Series
Book 3

HINA MCCORD & BECCA C. SMITH

Published by Red Frog Publishing, a division of Red Frog Media

Visit our website at www.2nerdgirls.com

First published in 2020

The characters and events portrayed in this book are fictitious. Any similarity to real persons, living or dead, is coincidental and not intended by the author.

ISBN 9781949877304

Printed in the United States of America

Dedications

Hina:

To Tom Mccord, my grandpa and my inspiration for everything that is good and healthy. You taught me to love myself because you loved me unconditionally. You are brave and strong, and whatever world or universe you are in now, they are lucky to have you, just as I was. Sending you hugs that are as close as my arms and as far away as the cosmos.

Love always, your Pooh Bear.

Becca:

To Ed. You may not have been my grandfather by blood, but you were my grandfather by love. You filled our days with tons of laughter and love. My grandmother once told me that when she met you at the age of seventy-two, she knew you were her soulmate and that it had been worth the wait. I love you to pieces!

PROLOGUE
MOLLY

"Are you afraid of me?" I asked Bohe, who sat quietly in the corner.

"I stopped fearing death long ago," he replied calmly.

I wouldn't have blamed him if he *had* been scared of me. *I* was scared of me. And currently, I was scared *for* me.

Grandfather wasn't going to like this.

Father's last two children, Bohe and David, were *my* responsibility. I was supposed to keep them safe for whatever Grandfather needed them for. I was relatively sure it was to make Father happy, which only made what I had done worse.

I'd drained David.

There was no way to tell if just a drop of Grandfather's blood was in his system, because that would be enough to revive him.

And I got scared Grandfather would be angry if he told on me . . .

So I'd decapitated him.

Afterward, I felt horrible. He actually seemed like a good person, if vampires could be considered good. And now my fear of David telling on me for draining him was replaced by my fear that Grandfather would torture me for *killing* him.

And a very small part of me hated to admit it, but I'd never tasted anything so delicious.

Bohe smelled divine as well, but my fear of Grandfather stopped me from taking a bite of Lucian's last living child—well, not quite the last. Jeff, Ur-Nammu, and I were his children as well.

Jeff.

My heart squeezed with longing at the thought of my husband. Why wasn't he with me? Why was he with *her*?

Shea.

The Vessel. Claiming she was my daughter! As if I'd have kids.

But I did.

I had Shea.

I loved her.

What was I thinking? Was this a trick from the Vessel? Was she that powerful?

No.

These thoughts were coming from me. They grew stronger the longer Grandfather was away. I used to tell him every time I had that kind of thought, but I stopped because he'd always feed me his blood after. And I didn't like it. The taste was mind-blowing, the power indescribable, but . . .

I didn't like it.

I didn't like forgetting *her*.

My little girl.

No.

She was the Vessel. She was evil. She was the enemy of Grandfather and of me. She'd destroy us all, she was so powerful.

Confusion overwhelmed me.

What was happening?

"Is the Vessel trying to brainwash you again?" Grandfather's voice sounded from behind.

I knew he was going to give me more of his blood. I almost longed for it at the moment. I didn't want to remember anything. I didn't want to feel this pain. I nodded.

He was alone, but I could hear Father in the next room, struggling against the chains. Grandfather had made me secure him to his bed. He'd said that Lucian would be honored to be tied with the bones of Ashliel. I didn't know Father all that well, so I'd done what I'd been told, but from the sound of Father's angry screams, I didn't think Grandfather was correct in his assessment.

"I need to be with Lucian. I don't have time for your weakness," Grandfather scolded.

I glanced briefly at David's dead body, feeling guilty.

Grandfather nodded. "His blood made you vulnerable. It's how the Vessel reached in and probed your thoughts, filling them with lies."

But I thought David's blood had made me stronger.

I didn't know what was real anymore.

"Make me understand," I begged.

Sighing, Caelius pricked his finger with one of his fangs and drew a single drop of blood. He never gave me more than that. It wasn't enough, but I'd take it, even if it only allowed me to think

3

clearly for a short while.

I drank, and before I could utter a response, Grandfather left to be with Lucian.

I waited for the blood to take hold.

Where was I?

I looked around and saw Bohe in the corner, sitting next to the headless corpse of David.

I tried to remember what I had just been thinking, but nothing came to mind.

I felt a twist in my gut, but it had no meaning.

Maybe it was the fact that I had killed one of Father's children.

I looked at Bohe and asked, "Are you afraid of me?"

He only answered me with silence.

CHAPTER 1
SHEA

Was I Dream-Walking? Had I died? Where was I?

Looking around, all I could see were miles of white. There were no walls or floors. My feet felt like they were on the ground, but no matter how hard I searched, there was no surface beneath me. It was as if I was floating.

My instant reaction was one of panic, but every time I thought I would go into full-on anxiety mode, a sense of calm would wash over me and I'd relax again. It was a strange cycle that kept repeating until I thought I'd go mad.

Seriously. Where was I?

I did a complete body check. I could feel my legs, arms, head . . . Yup, everything was real and *here*. Wherever *here* was.

Before this place, I could remember pieces of what had happened. I had used my elemental powers to take Caelius down. I'd shredded trees into spikes, pinning Caelius to the ground so Lucian and the others could hurt him enough so we could all escape.

But it had been too much.

I had expended every ounce of power I had, and my body had finally given up. I must have passed out.

Helena.

She had betrayed us. That, I remembered.

Caelius had said he'd jumbled up her brain. We'd thought Lucian's necklace was our superweapon, that it would destroy him. Unknowingly, she had turned it into a device that had given him immense power and he'd gloated that it had also taken my soul.

Yeah.

Feeling a little stupid.

And looking around at all the white surrounding me, it was a good bet that I'd croaked.

Maybe with no soul I was in some kind of afterlife waiting room, as if the universe wasn't quite sure what to do with me. And since I was completely alone, it looked like I was the only one.

I didn't *feel* soulless though.

But what would not having a soul feel like? I needed to take some kind of morality test.

Did I still love Lucian? Yes.

Did I still want to save the world from Caelius? Yes.

Did I still want to rip Caelius apart until all that was left was a gooey mess of skin and guts? Yes.

Wait. That sounded pretty soulless.

"You have your soul," Aidan's voice said from the ether.

"Aidan?" I called out, feeling a surge of hope.

A shape transformed in front of me, but it definitely wasn't Aidan's.

I should have been terrified by what I saw, but the figure was stunning to look at. His lion's head, with hundreds of eyes, stared at me with kindness. His torso was that of a man, perfectly muscled like a Michelangelo statue, but his bottom half was ox, thick and powerful. On his right side was one giant wing in the shape of an eagle's, and on the left side, where another wing was supposed to be, was only a nub.

Gazing into the hundreds of blue eyes before me, I saw . . .

My Aidan.

It *was* him.

I'd know those baby blues anywhere.

His lion head and expression looked unsure, as if he didn't know how I'd feel about seeing his true form.

He could have been in the shape of a razor blade for all I cared. "Can I hug you?" I asked, not sure what the protocol was for embracing angels.

And that was what he was: an angel. It was easy to forget that when Aidan was in human form—the only way I had ever known him. Since he was an earthbound angel tied to the Vessel, it meant we'd been born on the same day, minute, and second. Having been raised together in Phoenix, Arizona, I didn't know anyone as well as I knew Aidan, but I felt like I was seeing who my best friend truly was for the first time.

And it was glorious.

"Of course you can hug me." Aidan smiled.

It was a little strange to have a lion's head with hundreds of eyes smile at me, but I fell into the embrace like he was my savior. Because in that moment, he was. These arms would feel the same on any plane of existence—strong, powerful, and cozy like a teddy bear. I never wanted to let him go.

But after a long moment, Aidan pulled away. "I had to bring you here. We need to talk to my brothers."

Okay, I knew it was Aidan, but lion's head . . . lots of eyes talking. Very surreal.

Aidan seemed to sense what I was feeling and laughed. "Is it weird, talking to me this way?"

"More so when you laugh. It's like talking to your Animoji on the phone. Is that why you always choose a lion?" I asked, and we both cracked up.

With a wave of his hand, Aidan's angel body shimmered in front of me until he was back in human form. Though Aidan's angel form was beautiful in its own way, his human form rivaled it. Wearing a simple white T-shirt and jeans, Aidan looked like he had just worked out for fifty hours in a gym somewhere. His swoopy brown hair was perfectly messy, and his giant blue eyes sparkled at me like they always had. My best friend. Nothing would break our bond.

"Better?" He smiled.

"You don't have to do that. You're making me feel like an angel racist." I felt like a jerk for teasing him before.

Aidan's easy smile was about the best thing I'd seen in a long time, then he said, "Yup. Shea Harper: angel bigot."

I smacked his chest, laughing. I suddenly wished we could stay like this forever. It was easier to forget everything that was happening with our loved ones when we were isolated up here in this land of glowing white.

8

Speaking of which . . .

"Aidan, what happened in that last battle?" I looked around with doubt. "I'm assuming since we're here that Caelius is still on the loose, but . . . who made it?"

His face showed what I feared the most. He didn't want to tell me. That was bad.

"Lucian?" I could barely speak his name, I was so terrified of what Aidan would say.

"He's alive, Shea." His voice cracked as he continued. "Lucian sacrificed himself to save the rest of us: you, Meky, Nefertiti, Ur-Nammu, your dad, and Sherit."

"What do you mean *sacrificed*? You said he was alive!" I stood in front of him as if I was a wall trying to break a storm.

"He gave himself to Caelius . . . willingly." Aidan's voice was quiet.

Oh, God.

My entire being froze in agony. Lucian *gave* himself to Caelius. All Caelius had ever wanted was Lucian, and now he had him. What was Lucian enduring while we stood here in this place? We needed to save him! We needed to get him back.

I hadn't thought it was possible to hurt this much. I was crushed by the excruciating weight of helplessness and guilt. Lucian was probably being tortured and ravaged by Darkness itself.

And my mom . . .

"Aidan! My mom is there too, isn't she?" I felt another surge of panic.

Aidan nodded and took my hands to calm me. "She drank Caelius's blood. She worships him now, so she's probably safe for the time being."

I wanted to believe that, but how could I? This was Caelius we were talking about. Two people I loved with all my heart were in his grasp. It was excruciating. I looked up at Aidan. "We have to help them. We can't leave them there."

Pulling me in for another tight embrace, Aidan's words rang in my ears. "We will. That's why we're here—for help, and to get some answers. We have to do everything we can to stop Caelius so that we can get them back."

It didn't feel like enough, but I knew it had to be. Lucian had given himself to Caelius so we could escape, and I didn't want that to be in vain. We needed the inside scoop on Caelius and the Light, and the only way to get it was through Aidan's brothers.

Pulling away from the hug, Aidan kept his grip on my hand like he used to when we were kids. "It's time to talk to my siblings."

I nodded and motioned for him to lead the way.

Closing his eyes, Aidan concentrated.

The whiteness around us grew brighter and brighter until I shut my eyes, afraid I'd go blind from the intensity.

"You can open your eyes now, Shea." Aidan's voice was soothing.

I looked at Aidan, and his three brothers stood before us. I'd seen them before in our first epic battle against Caelius. They were in their man-shaped bodies, which was probably Aidan's idea. All joking aside, Aidan really was making me feel like I was too fragile to see angels in their true form. We had bigger problems to worry about though, so I didn't say anything.

Sabrael, Harahel, and Gavreel were well over ten feet tall.

They looked like they were sculpted out of marble, skin smooth but perfectly muscled. They were wearing simple white robes. If I saw them on the street, I'd think they were three very tall supermodels going to a toga party. I kind of wanted to see their true forms, since I couldn't seem to get the image of them making fashion poses in a photo booth out of my head. I had only caught glimpses of their true form when we had fought Caelius: wings the size of a dragon's and even more of a mishmash of the animal kingdom than Aidan.

Maybe it was better to see the beautiful toga boys in front of me after all. I'd probably stare too long if they were in their real bodies.

Which, of course, Aidan had likely guessed because he knew me so well.

It was Gavreel who spoke first. "Welcome, Vessel."

Sabrael and Harahel echoed Gavreel's words. "Welcome."

Awkward.

It felt so formal, like I was in some kind of movie where I was at the pearly gates and everyone suddenly spoke like they were in a Shakespearean play.

Harahel interrupted my thoughts by saying, "We have much to discuss, Vessel."

"Can you call me Shea, not Vessel?" I looked at Aidan for support, and he gave a slight nod to his brothers.

Sabrael replied, "To us, all Vessels are the same, made from the drippings of Light. But if you wish for us to call you by your *human* name, we will do so."

"Uh, thanks." Smooth. I was definitely representing *all* Vessels with my eloquent speaking skills.

Gavreel continued. "Your soul is made from the Light, and Caelius still needs this to regain his full strength. If he is to succeed, he will destroy everything in his wake, *everything*. The three of us cannot leave the Light to help you. If it's left vulnerable, Caelius could abandon his mortal form and consume the Light completely."

Harahel finished his brother's words. "If this were to happen, all of creation would be lost."

I almost couldn't comprehend what they were saying. Caelius had the potential to destroy the world, but now they were declaring that if given the chance, he would consume *all of creation*.

Yeah. I didn't want these guys to leave the Light either.

I was by no means a martyr, but I suddenly understood why Aidan had been willing to kill all the Vessels before me and then die himself. It was the Vessel or all life on Earth. Kind of a no-brainer.

What he had done still hurt like hell, both physically and emotionally. But I understood it now more than I ever had before. And that was just stopping Caelius in *human* form. If Caelius were to return to his "natural state" and the Light wasn't being protected by the angel squad? That was it. Game over. No more life in the universe.

"So, we should make sure he stays mortal?" I asked. Darkness incarnate on the loose seemed a lot more dangerous than mortal Darkness. Maybe Aidan's brothers could tell us how to capture him again or how to defeat Caelius once and for all.

Gavreel shook his head. "No. Caelius needs to go back to his true form. The Light gave him a chance to live the life of a mortal, to experience what it was like to be human. He was to observe but not to interfere with human life. When he gave his blood to the first human, Lucian, he broke his promise to the Light and had to be imprisoned. Caelius's blood will turn a human into what you call a vampire; it's like a sickness made of Darkness. If a human has even a drop of Caelius's blood inside them, they will remain a vampire, feeding on life itself."

"Blood," I said, clarifying what "life itself" meant. Blood was what made people live, so it made sense that the only way for a vampire to stay alive was to drink it from a living, breathing person. But my brain still wasn't comprehending why the angels didn't want Caelius to stay in a mortal body. "Isn't Caelius more dangerous in his true form, as Darkness?"

"As long as we protect the Light, Darkness cannot win," Sabrael answered. "It's a balance between the two. Clearly, Caelius doesn't like this. It's his nature to destroy. The Light thought that putting him in a human body might give him more empathy, maybe even allow him to understand what it means to create. But even in Caelius's desire to create something of his own, he made beings that want to ravage all living things, like he does."

"Not all of them do," I blurted out. Lucian wasn't like that, and neither were Nefertiti or Meky or my dad. The angels stayed silent, neither agreeing nor disagreeing with me, which in angel-speak meant they thought I was mistaken.

I wanted to argue more, but I knew it was pointless. I knew the things Lucian had done in his past, and they weren't exactly peachy. And Nefertiti had been a warrior *before* she'd become a vampire. And how well did I really know Meky? She'd claimed that Caelius had never let them drink from a living human, that

13

he'd only let them have leftovers from all the male vampires, but what if that wasn't true? What if all vampires were killers just like Caelius was? It meant that Caelius's blood turned anyone who had it in their system to the "dark side," whether they wanted to or not.

"Is there any way to remove Caelius's blood from someone who's turned?" I wanted to rip him out of every vampire I knew and cared about.

"We do not know," Harahel replied. "But if the blood *is* removed, the vampire would become mortal again. Most creatures with immortality would not give this up easily."

Aidan finally spoke. "Lucian would give up immortality in a heartbeat if it meant being with Shea."

My chest squeezed. Lucian and I would both be human then. We could have a family. We could just be . . . us. I needed to get him back from Caelius's clutches. I needed to get my mom back. I felt so useless at the moment. What could I really do? Caelius needed my soul in order for him to be at full power. Was I really thinking of walking into his *lair* like a meal on a platter?

Yes, I was.

Sabrael's voice cut through my thoughts with anger. "The Light does not care for Caelius's creatures, and as the guardians of the Light, neither do we." Turning to Aidan with scolding eyes, he said, "We will give you all the powers of the Light we can so you may fight Caelius in battle. But Adnachiel, Caelius *must* return to his true form. If he drains the *Vessel's* soul, he will destroy *all* life on Earth."

Why aren't they killing me then?

I couldn't help it. My brain heard their words, and that was

14

the first thing that popped up.

If the world would end by draining me, why wouldn't they end me right now?

I decided to keep that little revelation to myself.

They obviously had their reasons, and if I was being honest, that was what worried me the most.

And we were back to *Vessel* again. I knew Aidan had chosen to protect me, but his brother's words about not being able to kill Caelius still hit me hard. He was going to take down the world if we didn't somehow force him to give up his human body.

Damned if we do, damned if we don't.

"How can we get Caelius to give up his corporeal form?" I asked. "There's no way."

"You must find a way," Harahel said with authority.

Then without warning, Sabrael, Harahel, and Gavreel reached out and each placed a hand on Aidan's chest and mine.

Our bodies glowed white, and I could see both Aidan's human and true form all at once, as if I were seeing double. Before my eyes, Aidan grew back his missing wing until both of his wings were over twenty feet in length.

I could feel the Light coursing through me, strengthening me, making me feel invincible.

Then their hands left our chests, and so did the glow.

Gavreel spoke for all three brothers. "Aidan, your wing has been restored. You can fly again—you always could. It was your shame over Moses that kept you grounded all these years. You must toss such petty things aside and use flight in this battle. We have filled your blood with Light so that you can heal, so that you can burn and pull energy from the sun."

Then he turned to me. "And to you, Vessel, we have given our power. We hope it is enough to return Caelius to his true form when the time comes. But you must not run to confront Caelius. If he takes your soul, all is lost. Only attack him when the timing is in your favor and you're sure you can turn him back to Darkness. You'll have one chance. Use it well."

Thanks. Could they have been any more vague? Attack, but don't attack? Which one was it? I decided I'd leave strategy up to those of us who were left fighting.

After a moment, the light died down, and I turned to Aidan. He was fully in human form, but he looked like he'd just drank ten energy drinks in a row. I imagined I must have looked the same because he gave me one of his goofy grins.

"It's time to leave now," Aidan said, and everything went dark.

***

I slowly opened my eyes to see my dad, Jeff Harper, sitting in a chair next to me. I was lying in a somewhat comfortable bed in an empty room I didn't recognize.

Dad's eyes lit up when he saw that I was awake.

"Shea, oh thank goodness." He took my hand and squeezed it. "We were so worried."

I looked around at the empty room. "*We?*"

Dad shrugged. "Well, you know, Nefertiti and her family show worry in their own way."

I supposed that was true to a certain extent, but my guess was that Nefertiti wanted me alive not for any feelings of friendship,

16

but because I might be able to help her rescue her daughter Setepenre. And probably Lucian, but I didn't want to think about Nefertiti's feelings for my boyfriend.

Dad let go of my hand and stood up. "I'll go get everyone." He left the small room, and I got a better look at where I was. There were no windows and just one door leading out to a hallway. It made me think we were somewhere underground.

I didn't want to wait for the others to come to me, so I stood up from bed and tried to follow my dad. As soon as I was in a standing position, a wave of dizziness hit me. Luckily it passed after a few seconds, but I was still unsteady.

How long had I been out?

Carefully watching my steps, I walked out of the room and into the hallway beyond. I had no idea which way my dad had gone, seeing as the floor was the same linoleum tile as my pseudo-bedroom, and it wasn't like he'd left any footprints. From the stucco on the ceilings and the army-green paint covering the walls, I was pretty sure this building had been built in the '70s. Or if it hadn't been, the interior designer needed to join this decade. Left seemed like a good idea, so I headed down that way, hoping I'd catch up with my dad.

Nope.

It must have been forty-five minutes of me walking down endless hallways of green tiles and white walls before I finally heard Aidan's voice. "Shea? Where are you?"

And so began our game of Marco Polo, where eventually I found Aidan in the middle of one of the numerous hallways. I sighed in relief. "This place is insane. I've never seen so many freaking hallways in my life."

Aidan's smile instantly warmed me as he hugged me tight. "Crazy, right? I guess it's some kind of underground bunker. Nefertiti says it was built by some rich guy in the '60s in case there was a nuclear war. Helena found it abandoned in the '80s and kept it on her list of hideouts. Nefertiti wants us to be in a place that Helena can find. Hopefully when we see Helena again we'll know if she's . . . you know, not on our side anymore."

It was sad to not be able to trust Helena. We all knew she had been brainwashed by Caelius, but was she still?

Looking at me, Aidan shook his head. "And Vessel or not, your body has been in another astral plane. You should be resting."

"*You* should be resting." I really had nowhere to go with that. I just didn't want to lie down again, not when Lucian and my mother were with Caelius.

Chuckling, Aidan pulled away and nodded in the opposite direction of where I'd come from. "Come on. This way."

We eventually passed the room I'd woken up in, and by taking a right instead of a left, we entered a large study with several couches and chairs. I wanted to smack myself in the head; I had been so close. Leave it to me to go the opposite direction.

Ur-Nammu and Sherit sat on a couch together talking while Nefertiti and Meky stood by a giant fireplace that looked like it hadn't seen fire in decades.

Dad leapt up from an armchair and walked toward me. "There you are. I told you I was going to bring everyone to you. Why did you leave?"

"I thought it'd be faster if I came to you."

Dad, Aidan, and I all laughed.

Then Dad said, "Yes, you got here *much* faster."

18

Nefertiti walked over with Meky by her side. Meky gave me a slight wave while Nefertiti eyed me like I was a disappointing boxer she'd have to train for the championship.

"We were discussing strategies on how to get Lucian and Setepenre back, but Aidan says you have to sit this one out." Nefertiti watched me carefully, gauging my reaction.

I whirled on Aidan. "What are you talking about? I'm the best chance we have of getting Lucian, Sete, and"—I turned to Nefertiti with slight annoyance—"my *mom* back." Only mentioning Lucian and her daughter had been expected, but a part of me wondered if the reason she hadn't mentioned my mom was because she didn't think Molly Harper was saveable.

"Yes, of course, your mother," Nefertiti added as if she were placating a child. "So you *do* plan on helping us?"

Aidan stepped in. "Shea, you heard my brothers. You can't be anywhere near Caelius yet. We're not ready for the big takedown. If he drains your soul, he'll be at full power, and we'll have no chance of getting him to give up his mortal form. He'd destroy the world first."

"Can't he do more crap when he's Darkness again?" I asked what I thought was an obvious statement. I hadn't been satisfied with Aidan's brothers' answers. Being all Darkness sounded way more sinister and dangerous.

Shaking his head, Aidan sighed. "No, Shea. With my brothers protecting the Light, he will be put back into the cosmic balance of the universe when he becomes Darkness. Here on Earth, as a human, he can physically destroy anything he wants. It's one of the perks of being human, remember? Free will. Ever heard of it?" His sarcasm was not lost on me.

"Don't give me attitude." I looked at him with pleading eyes. "Don't bench me when my mother is brainwashed. She has no memory of her own daughter because of your brothers. And Lucian is probably being tortured as we speak!" Tears welled in my eyes. "I just can't. I have to do *something*. I have to."

Nefertiti nodded. "It's settled then. When we attack, Shea will come with us. Sherit, Meky, and Ur-Nammu will stay behind, of course."

Aidan laughed, annoyed. "So everyone who matters to you stays behind, but all the rest of us are expendable?"

With an edge of fury, Nefertiti said, "I lost *three* of my daughters in that battle, and Caelius made it very clear that he plans on taking the rest of my family if given the chance, so yes, *Beast*, my girls and father will stay behind."

I joined in at that point. "Okay, no more of this *beast* talk. We're all friends here . . . kinda. Can we at least come up with a plan? Because if your strategy is to just 'storm the castle,' we're screwed."

Nefertiti had no response, which meant that was exactly her plan.

"We need someone on the inside to get to Caelius so we have eyes and ears on everything he's doing," a woman's voice said from the doorway.

All heads turned.

Helena walked in.

With everything that had happened, no one knew how to react. Caelius had confessed that he had controlled Helena. Lucian's necklace had been our greatest weapon, but Caelius had compelled Helena to turn it into a full-blown battery to juice

20

him up instead.

No one could blame her for having been mind-controlled.

But no one could trust her either.

Helena continued. "I have someone with me who may be able to help us."

Motioning to the doorway, Helena signaled.

Everyone stood dumbstruck as a man we all thought dead walked into the room.

Duncan, Lucian's Second-Born who had been murdered by Caelius and had died in Lucian's arms, stood before us with a half smile.

"Hullo. Lang time nae see," Duncan said in a thick Scottish accent.

What did he just say?

CHAPTER 2
LUCIAN

I stared vacantly at the endless white above me. If I wasn't a vampire, I would have thought it flawless. But there were specks, dirt from age, and a hairline crack that ran from one corner of the ceiling to the other.

I tried to move but couldn't. Aidan's devoured brother's remains had been reshaped and now formed bone chains at my wrists and ankles. Even in death, Caelius would make use of Ashliel. Even in death, there was no escape from Darkness.

I looked around the room. It was an elaborate hotel . . . in Paris. The subtleties in the air gave it away. Paris had a scent I had relished long before I'd met Shea, a scent that now made every part of my body ache and long for those nights we'd spent here.

Of course Caelius would pick Paris. His jealousy knew no bounds, and I'd been as imprudent as ever, thinking I could fool him for long. I ran through Caelius's relentless lovemaking in my mind. I had fought back every urge to resist, every grimace and ounce of Gutian pride, all to give them a chance, not to hide, but to *live*. I'd thought I could distract him with my body, at least for a few thousand years or more, at least for Shea.

I wanted her to love someone else, to experience the world, to see beauty and to find happiness, to laugh, to feel *anything* before she felt Caelius's cold desire carve out the soul from her flesh. I wished he'd never found out that the necklace hadn't worked. I would die to spare her that fate now. In fact, what I valued most inside of myself already had. Even still, Caelius was Darkness, and he was right to call me a *boy*. Of course he would see through me. I had been foolish to think otherwise.

I hated his icy hands running over every inch of my body. I hated the idea of making love to anyone who wasn't Shea. And it wasn't making *love* with Caelius. That was the problem. I had tried to convince my mind that it was just sex, that it didn't matter, but in all my years with Nefertiti, I had never once cheated on her. Then, out of all the centuries that had passed in the shadow of remorse after Nefari's presumed death, it was only Shea who had pulled me toward love again. And because of that, my severe loyalty to her had instinctively outwitted my reactions. I didn't love Caelius, and I couldn't fake it.

I sighed. "How long are you going to sit there, watching me?"

"Grandfather can't look at your face right now." Molly sneered in disgust. "And stop talking!" she spat, her words full of malice and desire. Bloodlust was pulsing in her tone like the shadow in Caelius's black heart that had covered her own.

She had finally answered audibly. I had been trying to convince her for days on end that Caelius was a monster, that he had manipulated her. It was no use now. She was restless and angry. Mostly she mumbled and argued with herself, as if I wasn't chained three feet from her.

I'd thought I could exploit her obvious conflict to my advantage. Yesterday, she'd paused as if my words had broken through, and for that instant, I thought I saw compassion fill her gaze. Then he'd beckoned, and she'd run from the room. When she'd returned, she was in ecstasy. That's when I knew: Caelius was giving her *his* blood. Not the blood of Second-Borns, but his own. No amount of convincing was going to break the brainwashing that liquid Darkness could have on a vampire.

Looking at her now, it was hard to believe she was related to Shea at all.

That sweetness, honesty, and sense of humor, if only I could see a glimmer of it, a piece of Shea in this new hell. Instead I was reminded of my mistakes. Killing her parents and turning them had been *my* doing. It was only fitting that the vampire version of Molly torment me now.

"At least you smell like Shea." It slipped out.

I closed my eyes.

In an instant she flew to my bedside, her hand extending like talons as her nails hovered over my neck.

"If Grandfather hadn't commanded me not to *touch* you—" Small specks of saliva landed on my face, her mouth open, baring teeth as she spoke. "I am nothing like the Vessel! I won't believe your lies!"

"Now, now, La-Narru. Don't provoke her." Caelius stepped into the room, and everything went cold. His voice usually carried a childlike whimsy with an undertone of vindictive contempt. But now? There was no humor to it. It was a mixture of rage and tenderness. If I didn't know him so well, it would almost sound like he was heartbroken.

"Leave," he commanded.

"Of course!" Her hands moved away from my throat as she obediently made her way out the door. "But, Grandfather . . ." She hesitated. "I know it's not time yet, but since I've held back and behaved so well, can't I have another drop of your blood? I can't stand it, the time in between feedings! I need it, Grandfather, please!"

He growled, and the walls shook around us.

"Obey." One word, and he didn't make eye contact. Instead, his gaze burned into mine.

She deflated, slinking out the door like a child who'd lost their security blanket.

Obey? Usually he had more style than that.

"You're losing your edge, Caelius. If you're not careful, I'll turn Molly to my side. I've always been good with women." I let a half smile slip.

"No, you won't," he mocked. "One drop of my blood will keep her subservient for weeks, and I won't give useless human cowhide more than that."

He wasn't taking the bait.

I swallowed.

He stood at the edge of the bed. His determined gaze was worse than Molly's hand hovering over my throat, threatening to choke the life from my body.

"Are you just going to stand there?" He didn't move. There was no banter, no snide Caelius-like remarks. "I don't know why you're keeping me here. As soon as I convince Molly to get me

25

out, I'll be back with Shea. And we'll *kill* you this time. And I'll laugh! I'll laugh over your pathetic ashes, you perverted piece of sh—" He covered my mouth with his hand.

"You want to provoke me so that I will end your life." He paused, and I held my breath. "I would ask *why*, but the answer you gave me days ago was enough. I'm sure it's still the same. Because you love *her*."

My eyes bulged, and I screamed obscenities into his palm. Despite my outburst, his vision seemed so clear. I realized now how cloudy it had always been when he'd looked at me. Still, if I could just exploit that lingering tenderness he was feeling toward me, I could protect Shea. And if I couldn't, he was right, I would spit curses at him until he cut off my tongue and ended my life.

"I'm going to keep my promise, boy. It seems I'm the only one who will." He took his other hand and pulled it through my hair. Over and over he repeated the motion, staring at me with those burning auburn eyes. "You fear I will use you against Shea, so you prefer death. But you already *died* in Egypt under Nefertiti's window."

He moved the pad of his thumb over my bottom lip. "And with this same mouth you promised me your afterlife. As a boy by the river in your homeland where we first met, you promised to be mine, calling me God. *Your* god. Just like you unconsciously did again when you surrendered to me. Pity, I thought being in Gutium had made you remember . . . but it was all a lie!"

He pulled my lip down, running his index finger along my bottom teeth. "I was omnipotent, wasn't I? I watched over you. I didn't interfere with your life until it came to its natural end in Egypt. I let you have your free will." He pulled his hand away

26

from my mouth, staring at the fingers now coated with my saliva. "Unlike the pathetic mortals in your life, I will *make* you keep that pure promise you enticed me with." He moved his fingers to his mouth and licked the wet slowly, his eyes never leaving mine. "As you have ensnared me throughout time—again and again, tempting me with your words and body—you will ensnare Shea Harper, destroying her with your own hands . . . as you have destroyed me. As you destroy *all* who care for you."

He half smiled to himself, but it wasn't the Caelius smirk I had known over time. It was a grimace, a painful thing. He placed his hand back over my mouth. "Even though you do it so fluidly, turning love into hate is no small feat. So first, let's start with something easy, shall we? I'll have you hold something tender against you, something tender that you will come to despise."

I knew before he walked in, his scent reaching me as soon as the door opened: *Camellia sinensis*. My mind thought of the Latin first, but I had memorized it in every language because he had taught it to me. He had drawn out the words like painting long strokes with ink as he spoke its praises.

He had told me its origin once, holding the hot cup and serving it as tenderly as one would present a newborn to its mother. He'd explained that in 2737 BC, Shen Nung had been sitting beneath a tree while his servant boiled drinking water for their journey. Some of the careless leaves fell inside. Shen was known for herbalism, and instead of punishing his servant for the chaos of nature's whim, as most nobles were inclined, he'd decided to try the concoction.

Now everyone just called it *tea*. It was prepackaged in tiny contained bags, all that was wild, mysterious, and raw now bleached and dried for the world to consume at its thoughtless leisure. But back then—the passion for it and the aliveness when he'd told me the stories, beaming with pride of his rich heritage—it had seemed so much more to me than just a tea leaf. It was an art. *His* art.

"Liu Xie." I spoke the words into Caelius's palm.

He nodded at the muffled sound. "Yes. Emperor Xian of Han. The last in the Han Dynasty. The failure you adored so perversely that you even gave him a pet name. It was Bohe, if I'm not mistaken."

I swallowed, unable to speak. Even though Shen Nung was eventually despised by the people, Bohe had idolized him in his youth, so much so that he always smelled of tea. Drinking it, bathing in it—it was one of his greatest mortal pleasures. I remembered long nights in China smelling the hair at the nape of his neck, the herbal infusions there having a calming effect on my tormented mind. And here it was again, that calming scent, this time filling me with agony.

"Finally silent, darling? Are you surprised?" Caelius stroked my hair one last time before sitting in the corner of the room, where Molly had been.

I took my eyes off of Bohe, looking back up at the ceiling. In that glance, he'd looked as innocent and frightened as he had been when the warlord Dong Zhou had killed his older brother. He'd forced Bohe to become emperor at eight years old. In the years that followed, he became an ornamental finger puppet, a lapdog for that vicious war-hungry murderer.

How many centuries had passed since he'd had to play the part of a lonely marionette? How long had I protected him from re-experiencing anything from his childhood? And yet, here it was, having come full circle. Because of me, his strings were once again pulled, and he would be forced to play the puppet.

"You turned this doll after Pompeii, no?" Caelius clicked his fingernails on the wooden chair, leaning his head casually on the heel of his palm. "After you dug yourself out, of course." He smiled, but the tenderness in his gaze was giving way to fury with every word he spoke. "Does your pet know that you *watched* him, and how long you watched him for? You and I are not so different, are we, Son?"

My mouth felt dry, and I swallowed as shame cast itself over my senses. I met Bohe when he was a boy. He'd been kind to me, this *thing* walking the night. The fresh ache of Adnachiel and the madness of being trapped in cooling lava and clawing my way out inch by inch over a hundred years had made me more animal than man. And there he was.

I closed my eyes, remembering that moment as if living it again for the first time.

He had been small, and his cheeks were round and soft—a chubby boy in silk robes hemmed with gold. I had never eaten a child before, even at my lowest. But I was still burning with the scars of Pompeii, and I despised royalty because of Akhenaten. The idea that any man thought he was above another because of birth or station disgusted me.

I had thought that the little ruler would grow up to be a monster like all the rest I had known and seen throughout the ages. I was close to devouring him whole, to losing the only boundary I had left. But then he had asked if I was hurt, concern filling his blameless face. He had taken me into his private chambers. His small hands had trembled as he'd tried to mend the blood spilling from my gut. It was an open wound I hadn't noticed. I had been numb for so long then.

He'd bandaged me tenderly. Then he gave me food, the garnet ring adorning his finger, and some of his favorite tea that he had kept hidden under his bedding. I thought it strange then, for the son of an emperor to hide something so meaningless. But when he spoke of the herbs and smells, I could see how precious it was to him, more so than the bejeweled ring he willingly stripped from his pinky.

But most surprising of all was when he'd bowed and spoke into the innate carpet at our feet. He had asked that I sell the ring and live a safe, honorable life free of violence. Then he pleaded with me to leave in haste and to never return, that it was a dangerous time and if anyone found a vagrant on his grounds, it would mean their death or worse.

I watched him silently, bent in submission. And for the first time in a long time, I felt something beyond the pain of Pompeii. I willingly obeyed the little ruler. It was only as I staggered through the open doorway, back into the gardens that I had clawed my way into, that a violent wind shifted the loose silk robes from his shoulders. I paused. There, half naked before me, was the reason he had shown kindness to the rabid dog that wandered into his palace. How else could an emperor's son know how to properly mend an open wound?

He had been beaten.

Wrapped in white, pressed with herbs, I saw that his back was bleeding from fresh shallow cuts. His wounds were something I had known all too well as a young slave in Egypt. Even as a boy after my mother's death, as the honored son of Onack the Great, I had publicly endured the lash from my own father's hands.

I stared at the would-be emperor. I didn't have to know *who* had given him those wounds; I knew what they meant, and in that moment, I saw myself—the part of me that I hated the most. He was unwanted, and he would suffer greatly for it. I had to know just how helpless he would be to fate's twisted plans for him, if his life would mirror my own, if he would become the monster he now set free back into the world.

It was only then that I'd started observing him.

At that time, I *needed* to turn someone; even in my stupor I'd been aware of that much. There was a pattern: around the time the new Vessel would arrive, or not long after, I would get this deep, unquenchable ache for company. I called it many things, but in truth, it was loneliness and despair.

Turning a new Second-Born temporarily kept me from acknowledging those erupting feelings. When they were first turned, they'd worship me. The adoration, the bond, it was unbreakable . . . for a while, at least. Even if the soothing was a placebo effect, their comfort would usually see me through for a decade or more. But with Bohe, because he was just a child, I had waited. And I had wanted to. A sick part of me needed to see what kind of man he would become.

It was the first time I had stalked someone I knew would one day be mine.

"Look at him, La-Narru." Caelius's voice grew impatient. "I've dolled him up for you; the least you can do is appreciate a pig wrapped in fine garments."

I bit my bottom lip and looked again at Bohe. His long black hair was looped delicately like the inside of a nautilus. Decorative sticks protruded in every direction, breaking the perfect Fibonacci sequence that had become his dark tresses. His face was powdered white, save for the red paint drawn on his lips and the pink blush painting the apples of his cheeks moving upward to dust black-lined eyes—eyes that implored me to do *something*, anything but lie there helplessly.

I pulled against the angelic chains. It was more of a gesture for Bohe, by now I knew it was useless. I'd thrashed while Caelius had ravaged my body in every position for months.

There was no escape from this for either of us.

My eyes traced over his petite frame. When he was alive, he had been more delicate than the men of his region, and the vampirism cast him even more profoundly in a feminine light. I focused on his minute hands, hands that were now trembling under Caelius's watchful gaze. It wasn't the first time I had utterly failed Bohe, but it might have been the last.

I strained further, trying to lean my torso up from the mattress. "He's dressed in a Hanfu? And he's wearing stage makeup." I feigned a sarcastic laugh. "What are you playing at?"

"Quiet!"

I could feel the energy surging off of Caelius like black waves flowing over my body.

"He looks like a doll like this, so I prefer it for my fantasy." He licked his lips and stood up. He walked slowly until his large towering frame stood behind Bohe. "You're going to do just as I asked, aren't you, little Liu Xie?" Bohe's face flushed, and he nodded in obedience.

"Don't!" I gritted my teeth. "Don't touch him!"

Caelius growled. The room trembled, and it vibrated the white sheet that had been carelessly covering my naked torso. Bohe eyed the bruises and bite marks littering my frame in horror.

"And what would you have me do instead, lover?" The room grew still as Caelius relished his handiwork.

"Let him go; feed off of me instead."

Bohe's eyes warmed. If he had been one of my Second-Borns who could cry, I might have seen it then.

Caelius's eyes, in contrast, were cold as stone. "I've already *tortured* you. Now I need something *more*." He paused. "What do you expect your little emperor to do? Should he fight me? Run? Beg?"

What would I ask from him? To resist Caelius like I always did? And for what, for my benefit?

I stared into his dark brown eyes. Bohe had suffered so much in his mortal life; his own mother had tried to abort him before she was poisoned. He'd been hated, tormented, and used. The more I had observed him, the more I had come to want him. But still I had waited.

Caelius eyed me as he looked down at Bohe. "You know, *Emperor*, he watched you. He let you be that warlord's puppy. He watched as you fled your captors only to be captured again and again. He watched until the end of the Han Dynasty was official, until you were forcibly made to give up your title. It was the only thing you had left at that time, if I recall. How many times did he stand by while someone more powerful made you *theirs*, to use as they needed? Now I'm giving you the chance to make him *yours*. To use him as *you* desire, little emperor. Aren't I kind?"

Bohe's eyes were pained as they looked down on me.

"It wasn't like that, Liu Xie!" I called in desperation.

"Oh, but it was," he whispered into Bohe's ear. Caelius's eyes met mine, but he left his lips where they were. "He thought he was being patient, letting you have your sad little mortal life before he gave you a new one, before he gave you bliss and eternity. All so that you would adore him. I understand—I made the same mistake. We are alike after all, aren't we, La-Narru?"

"I'm nothing like you!" I lunged forward. My wrists were already raw, but I pulled harder at the restraints. "I know what you're doing! You're trying to convince me, to show me how you feel through some twisted game of comparison!"

"Oh. Is that what I'm doing?" His hands fell idle at his sides.

My chest twisted. It was true. In the beginning I was watching, waiting to turn him when he was old enough. I was desperate and cruel at that time, but I had grown to care for Bohe. I had never been conflicted about turning someone until then.

"I didn't *want* to turn you!" I shouted.

He winced. With my words the hurt in Bohe's brown eyes seemed to cut even deeper.

"It's not that I didn't want you!" I reached out to him, but the shackles held me back, the white sheet finally falling to the floor as the chains clanged against the stone tiles. He had been unwanted his *whole* life.

I sneered, looking at Caelius. I was playing right into his hands, giving him the drama he longed for. "Bohe . . . before you, I turned Gracuri."

Caelius's head jerked back, the fury in him returning. "Even now you bring up *Gracuri*!" He spat out the name like a curse.

I ignored him, looking only to console Bohe. "I enjoyed

Gracuri's company, and our lazy walks by the river. We were friends before I turned him. And because of that affection and mutual respect, after he became a vampire, I left Gracuri to live out his life as if he hadn't been turned. As a mortal with power, he was a Greek god among men. The tales of his heroism mark history books, even today. We would meet, and I would bring him treasures from my travels, and he would tell me stories of his latest triumphs. But when I returned to Thebes . . . when he . . ."

"Yes, yes." Caelius laughed. "Though they don't call him *Gracuri* in the books, do they? Sophocles was too much of a coward to use his *real* name. But you can read about that little swine everywhere, can't you, La-Narru?" Caelius looked around the room, placing an exaggerated hand on his hip. "Where did I put that suit of his? I lost track of it after I stuck his head on a spike."

I pulled uselessly against the chains. Gracuri—*my* Gracuri—tortured and impaled by this *thing's* hands.

"Oedipus." Caelius turned and whispered into Bohe's ear. "What a tragic tale. A tale that should have ended there. You see, I commanded La-Narru to kill him for overexposing our kind, but he didn't *obey* me, and Gracuri suffered just as you will suffer, Bohe. All because he won't keep his promises."

"Why—" Bohe's voice was soft, and it carried with it the musical tone it had always had in youth.

"Go on, Duke of Shanyang," Caelius said. "Talk to your daddy."

Bohe swallowed, looking down at my chest, his eyes not meeting mine. That was the title he'd been given *after* he was finally dethroned. It was a polite title that carried with it all the weight of his defeat. "Lucian, what does Gracuri—"

"Oedipus. Let's call him by his historical name. Since La-Narru is so offended by such things, we should really stick to the history books from here on out, as fallible as they are. The history and titles of piglets are so important to La-Narru, aren't they, *Duke*?" he mocked, his gaze darkening further.

Bohe cleared his throat. "Yes. Of course, Grandfather. As you speak it."

I winced at hearing him say that word. Caelius was no grandfather, nor was I a father. All of this twisted dialogue around vampirism, all of this corruption, because Caelius was Darkness in human form but no better than a spoiled, ignorant child.

"Because of Oedipus . . . you didn't want me?" Bohe's voice was smaller than before. The way his tone shifted at the end—half question, half acceptance—was agony.

"No." I leaned back onto the bed, sighing. "Yes." I swallowed. "Because of Gracuri."

I hesitated. This was a memory I'd never wanted to return to. "He'd been pure and noble, even after he was turned. He refused to eat humans and survived on animals alone. And he laughed, laughed with the coming of dawn, laughed at the stars blinking in the night sky. He was an abandoned, starving orphan, and still, I thought there was nothing that could take the smile from his lips." How many years had I spent hiding from that smile, the memory of it, a ghost that I couldn't bear the sight of?

"He turned every misfortune and dark idea into a philosophical question that ended in the hope for a better future, not just for himself, but for all of mankind. He *believed* in the good in everything and everyone. He reminded me of Adnachiel

36

in so many ways, but he would never betray me. He would never kill . . ." I paused. "The innocent." This was a painful conversation that wasn't meant to be had with Bohe, but with Gracuri himself. It was a conversation I had wanted to have a thousand times over, but I'd never had the courage to face myself, to face him.

And now it was too late.

"You didn't want me because you wanted someone like that angel who betrayed you? The one you loved so much, who was like a brother to you and Moses?" Bohe clenched his jaw, his small hands forming fists at his sides. It was a rare sight. Bohe had never been a fighter.

I blinked. He didn't understand what I was confessing to. "No, I . . ." Taking in another long breath, I damned my own lips. If it wasn't so painful, I could tell him quickly, but every word was like unearthing splinters hidden deep inside bone. The burden of my guilt was a heavy, ancient wooden box that I had packed away a long time ago, never intending to open.

Caelius had to be enjoying this. If he'd had his fill of causing me physical pain, then emotional pain was the next item on the menu, and using my own words to hurt Bohe only amplified my misery and added to his delight.

"I let Gracuri go. I traveled and put distance between us. We would meet every summer, once a year, by the river. We would talk and walk until nightfall, then I would leave again, even if he begged me not to. I thought I was protecting that smile I'd come to rely on. But he was still newly turned, and I was careless because he was dear to me, giving him the freedom I had once craved in Egypt, to live as he wanted to in Athens."

My jaw clenched. If only it had stayed that way. If his

37

honorable heart had been left intact, I could have visited him over the centuries and *never* turned another. His laugh would have given me the strength to hold on after every Vessel died and Aidan disappeared from existence. How ignorant and dangerous thoughts like that had been.

"It was my fault." My chest seized, and I could see the corners of Caelius's mouth start to rise in amusement. "Because Gracuri was a *vampire,* when he discovered that his wife was his biological *mother* and that he had killed his real *father* . . . had he been just a mortal, all those people wouldn't have died." I remembered the smell of it. How long had he been there by himself in that infected filth and decay before I'd arrived?

"He laid waste to the whole kingdom—children as well. You know it's something I forbid, the only rule I have for our kind, and he broke it a hundred times over. Their small bodies, twisted and broken." I cringed, wishing I could burn the image out of my mind.

"When I found him, he had gouged out his own eyes. His body was in a pool of dried blood surrounded by rotting corpses. He didn't feed on them, just butchered them, wasted in a fit of madness and rage. He cried and screamed and wailed for days without ceasing, refusing to be comforted. Every time his eyes grew back and he saw what he'd done, he would rip them out again." I'd never seen anyone mutilate themselves like that, over and over . . .

My body shook with the memory. I had loved him, and seeing him in a pool of red, his body growing thin from blood loss, starving and mad, his beautiful smile twisted in inconsolable grief . . .

"His agony and the sound of his wailing stay with me, even to this day. When the wind shrieks through empty streets, I can still hear it."

Nightmares.

I'd had my share of them after my mother died when I was mortal and actually slept. As a vampire, I was thankful we didn't sleep or dream, at first. But over time I realized that vampires dreamt in a different way. Our minds could act out memories in the dark–haunting echoes, regrets that followed us because our shadows did not.

"His screams . . ."

Bohe's soft hand reached for me, but Caelius grabbed it at the wrist. "Let's not interrupt such a fine memory, *Duke*."

I swallowed. Gracuri's eyes, crushed in his own hands . . . He'd been one of the rare children I'd made who could still cry. Even as an immortal whose tear ducts should have dried with the change, what twisted irony to make a boy that could only laugh, weep. "I consoled him for a long time."

"Just to be clear, I had sent La-Narru to kill him. But instead, he *consoled him for a long time*." Caelius's tone was like ice, the hand around Bohe's wrist tightening painfully.

"I finally persuaded him to live on and let his eyes grow back." I remembered his surrender to my coercion, his limp body falling into my arms, the light in his newly forming eyes, dull.

"He changed after that. He never again cared for human life, for anyone, other than me. And I . . ." This was that splintered box I hadn't wanted to open.

"Continue. Don't keep us in suspense," Caelius jeered.

My words creaked as Caelius forced open the lid. "I

abandoned him. I couldn't look at him the same, and he was so observant. He kept remarking on how my glances weren't like they used to be." I thought of my cutting words to him, how I hadn't known how to mend what I had broken. "Eventually, even I blamed him outright, calling him a monster. He moved around after that. It was a lonely life, I'm sure. I'd always meant to tell him that it wasn't his fault . . . to apologize. Instead I separated myself and made it seem like a punishment, but in reality, it was only I who had failed. The true reason I couldn't look at him the same wasn't because of what he'd done, but because I missed his smile. I missed who he'd been, and I couldn't rectify what I had turned him into. He was *never* to blame, *I* was. And now he's gone. He'll never laugh again, like he did by the river. I'd always hoped to hear it one more—"

"Boring." Caelius pushed Bohe's wrist behind him, into the small of his back, resting his chin on top of his head. "Who cares about that incestuous cow? We want to know how that relates to *us*, don't we, Bohe? We're jealous and tired of hearing about your love for that dead Greek tragedy. Does he even love you at all, Liu Xie?" Caelius twisted Bohe's wrist further. "It's always someone *else* he talks about, isn't it? The Vessel, the angel, Gracuri, Nefertiti, blah, blah, blah. When is it *our* turn?" he growled, and for a moment Bohe did too before he caught himself.

His face reddened with embarrassment, and Caelius smiled. "Did I hit the nail on the head, Duke of Shanyang?"

"Caelius, stop!" I smacked the chains just for the sound, to draw Bohe's attention to *my* words and not his. "I was afraid to turn *anyone* after that, even though I still craved it for my own selfish reasons. I thought, 'What will become of him if I

40

turn him now?' I didn't want to *ruin* you like I had ruined him. Gracuri was a *good* man with a lion's heart, and he was *never* the same. Without all of that blind power, he could have remained an orphan and happy, smiling by the river, a mortal who would have lived and died with the laugh of life still inside of him!"

My lungs squeezed. Every time I remembered his laugh, it felt like a knot in the center of my chest was pounding against that buried box of guilt, and I couldn't breathe. "After he gouged out his own eyes, I felt responsible for him in a way I wasn't responsible for any other child prior. I still feel responsible, even now. His death hasn't changed that."

"Us! We don't care about your regrets! You should have listened to me and killed that fake-smiling swine!" Caelius's nails grew, and the tips left indents in Bohe's skin that pooled with blood.

"Gracuri's the real reason I watched you, Bohe! That's what I'm saying!"

Caelius relaxed. "Finally. Out with it, boy."

"I was afraid to do anything that would change the course of your life, afraid to turn you and ruin your light. But after you gave up your role as emperor, after your final submission, you fell ill. The doctors in that region were barbaric and ignorant. I killed them after they covered you in leeches. I tried to mend you with the herbalism of my own people and what I'd learned through my travels. Nothing worked, and your body grew still and cold, your breath rattling in a cage of ribs, like your soul was trying to claw its way out of your body forever."

I looked at his full lips. They were now painted red, but then they had been blue and dry. "In the end, I couldn't lose you. I

41

gave into my selfishness, hoping it would be different." I reached for him but couldn't touch the cheeks I had stroked then. "And it was. You were not Gracuri. Bohe, you are beautiful and unique. Because of you, I turned others. I was able to move forward for another century. The regret I now feel for turning all of you is because of Caelius's blood and torment, not because of who you *are*. I have always been proud of the man you became, Liu Xie. I have *always* wanted you."

"I have always wanted you." Caelius chuckled miserably to himself. "You so easily say the words I long for to this worthless dynasty boy." A chill ran through the room as he laughed. "Unbelievable." He ran a hand through his hair. "That whole story, just so you could prove he was worthwhile. You care for him that much."

I swallowed hard. Caelius's tone was not bemused. It was angry. My eyes left him and jerked to Bohe. I was surprised to see Liu Xie's face looking elated. His body sagged in relief, even as Caelius's hands held him firmly in place.

"I'm glad, Father," Bohe said quickly.

His words were lost under the growl of Caelius's heavy voice. "Don't flatter yourself, *Duke*. He's good with words, but he's terrible at following through."

My mouth fell open, but I was silent.

This was not the time to provoke him.

Caelius relished my silence, and for a moment I could see his old spark return, the pleasure in my agony. "*In the end, I couldn't lose you.* How poetic, La-Narru, almost like you were in childhood. Perhaps if I had spouted those same words you would have forgiven me like you are expecting this doll to forgive you now. As if forgiveness means anything."

He laughed, looking toward the ceiling. "He watched you suffer all those years, *Duke*. Just like I watched him become a slave in Egypt. He thinks me cruel, but we are the same. And I do not need his forgiveness, and you won't pardon him so easily, will you?" he jeered. "The Light speaks often of forgiveness. I still think it's meaningless, but your fragile kind clings to it so desperately. I wonder why. Is it mortals who forgive? Is it because you're weak? Or is it because you're desperate?"

Caelius grew the nail on his index finger and traced the sharp tip of it down the red paint on Bohe's lips, cutting a deeper red into it. "Say it then, doll. Say it for Gracuri and *all* his children who never had the chance. If my lover needs to hear it so badly, let's have you appease him this one time, for me." Caelius tightened his grip around Bohe's arm, and he flinched from the pain.

"Don't say a word, Bohe. You don't have to do anything to appease me. I've never been your master. I've never done to you what those throne-stealing bastards did, and I won't now. You're not my puppet. Hate me if you like. Just . . ."

Escape. Just get away from here, and I'll handle Caelius.

I pulled on the chains again.

I had said a million things in an attempt to provoke Caelius after he had discovered my betrayal, useless words that had fallen flat on the ears of Darkness. There was nothing I could say or do now that I hadn't already. What did I have left to give?

I took a deep breath. "I'm sorry, Bohe. I'm sorry that I turned you and now you're in the hands of a warlord worse than any you experienced in China." I couldn't meet his gaze. All of this failure was stacking on top of me and crushing my will to fight.

"Good boy, La-Narru. Knowing when you're beaten is the first part of the process when you're breaking a pet." Caelius yanked the Hanfu down so that Bohe's shoulder was exposed. I looked at the deep teeth marks. Caelius had already fed on him, which meant most of his mind wasn't his own anymore.

I let out an exasperated sigh. "Nothing I said matters now."

"Nope!" Caelius laughed jovially to himself. "He's already mine. I have been beating and feeding on the emperor, and trust me, what little willpower there was in this doll is no more."

He pulled the large sash in front of Liu Xie, untying the knot. "Isn't that right, puppet?" Bohe's lips tightened, and he nodded. The yellow sash slipped to the floor. "I don't know why you would use these *things* to console yourself, La-Narru. My grief was inconsolable after I found out you'd lied to me, and breaking him brought me no pleasure whatsoever."

"I'm going to destroy Paris this weekend. Shea ruined my lovemaking, so I'm going to ruin the memory of yours. But I don't want my precious La-Narru to get bored in my absence. Today I will watch, but tomorrow and the next I will leave you alone with him, and he may do as he pleases." He grabbed the back of Bohe's neck. "You are going to spend the next three days with my precious La-Narru. But you're not to take a drop of his blood, do you understand?"

"Caelius!" My mouth dropped open. "Don't! Isn't it better to have a powerful, willing vampire at your side? You could accomplish so much more with a brilliant strategist like Bohe. Don't abuse him, and he'll be loyal. You'll have an invaluable asset, just don't make him do what those generals used to—"

"What is this concern for *my* safety? As if I need a strategist when I myself am a master at the craft." Caelius smiled. "What, you'd prefer your son sacrifice his pride rather than have him take yours?" He shoved Bohe by the neck so that his face was inches from mine. "No such luck. Enjoy how done up he is for you. Enjoy his little chubby cheeks because in a moment his actions will erase every sweet memory held between you. And I'm going to watch. I think I will quite enjoy watching this doll play with you."

Remorse filled Bohe's gaze as much as it echoed in my own. There was nothing I could say, and I knew how this would end. Still he waited, as if I could give him the words he needed to hear. I should have said, "Caelius will hurt you anyway; you don't have to do anything he says. Run, fight, but don't obey." It was true, and we both knew it. But I couldn't give up on Bohe now, just like I couldn't all those years ago when he'd fallen ill in China. I still wanted him alive, and if obeying Caelius meant that he could live, then I didn't care what he did to me. Even if he became loyal to Caelius, even if I never saw him again, it would be enough if I knew he was *alive*. All these years, just knowing he was out there in the mountains—studying, drinking tea, living in peace—had brought me some comfort during long nights when I feared insanity would take me.

Even now, I still couldn't lose him.

"See how selfish your maker is, even after his flowery words of confession? He has nothing to say to you now that you're the one in a position of power," Caelius said. "Remember that in the days of my absence."

I looked at the tension running through Bohe's body, the

terror every time Caelius spoke. I hated seeing it: his obedience to the now-reigning warlord. It was an old wound, and Caelius was exploiting Liu Xie's traumatic childhood, using him like he had been used his entire life as a mortal. After I turned him, he'd made me promise that I'd never let anyone make him a puppet again, that even I would resist the temptation.

And I had kept that promise, until today.

I looked at the fear in his dry eyes. "I never wanted this for you, Bohe."

Caelius pulled the chair from the corner of the room closer so that it was right next to the bed and sat down. "How sweet." He wet his mouth as his eyes took in my helpless exposed frame. "Now, now, *little emperor*, dance for me like the marionette you are."

CHAPTER 3
SHEA

I sighed a breath of relief as everyone's attention turned to Duncan and Helena. Nefertiti had been pretty set on putting together some kind of kamikaze rescue mission that would have most certainly ended in our deaths and me getting my soul sucked. What would that even feel like, anyway? I really didn't want to find out.

Duncan nodded to me, and suddenly I was the center of attention again. "Gracuri told me to stay away from ye since ye were Lucian's. Ye have to be pretty special to make him kill an entire line of vampires just to prove a point. I'm sorry, the last time we met, I was being killed myself." Duncan laughed.

And I found that I instantly liked him.

He reminded me of Aidan, with his warm smile and pleasant demeanor. Thinking about it, Lucian had probably turned Duncan for that very reason. I'd realized pretty quickly that Aidan and Lucian's bromance might even rival the love Lucian and I had for each other. It made a kind of odd sense that he'd turn a guy who reminded him of Aidan. And now that Duncan was talking a bit more, I found it much easier to understand his accent.

"I didn't realize Caelius had been controlling me until *after* the necklace had been used." Helena broke my train of thought with her remorseful tone. "I got all my memories back at once. Somehow I was able to rig the necklace to power him up without stripping Shea of her soul, though I have no idea how I managed that."

Nefertiti answered for her. "Because you have the strongest mind of anyone I've ever known." She walked up to Helena and placed a hand on her arm in support. It was very unlike her; she wasn't exactly the touchy type. Or was she? The more I thought about it, the more I realized that I didn't really know Nefertiti or any of her children. I knew Aidan, but I was still in the dark about his past lives. So really, all I had was *Dad*. But now that he was a vampire and had almost eaten me when I'd had accidentally cut myself on a rusty nail, I felt like I couldn't really trust anyone.

I didn't even know if I could trust Lucian. That thought scared me more than anything.

Helena looked relieved at Nefertiti's touch and continued. "I appreciate it, but I wish I could have done more. Caelius knew what we were doing, and I wasn't aware of it, even though I was *living it* side by side with the devil himself muddling my brain." Her eyes were haunted, then she focused on Duncan. "I went back to Lucian's prison, trying to find anything that might help us, and that's when I saw him. His body should have been desiccated, but he still looked alive. When I went over to him,

I realized that Caelius's blood had touched his lip. It must have fallen in when Lucian was crying, some of the splatter washing off into his open mouth. I had no idea his blood was powerful enough to do that."

Duncan chimed in. "It brought me back te life, but I had a wee crush on ma grandfather because of the stuff."

Helena nodded. "Thinking about it rationally, I now realize that it's possible. Caelius's blood is what gives vampires life, whether it's a drop or a hundredth of a drop. Duncan had just enough to bring him back and to be loyal to Caelius."

"And now?" I asked, suddenly worried about these two.

"Duncan was still weak, so I was able to chain him down," Helena replied. "It took a few days, and luckily it was just a tiny drop of Caelius's blood. I gave him an entire hospital's shipment of blood bags to clear his head. Now he no longer feels an obsession for *evil incarnate*."

Shrugging, Helena added, "I didn't know I was being controlled. Now that Lucian has been taken by Caelius because of my failure, I just . . ."

I felt the need to intercede. "You saved my *soul*. I'll always be grateful for that."

Nefertiti's eyes were distant as she said, "We all know how strong Caelius's blood compulsion is. He's made us do things we never thought possible, and he's erased memories we never thought he could."

Whoa.

That sounded like drama I wasn't sure I wanted to hear or not. I didn't need to be reminded how evil Caelius was, but I still needed to know what I was up against.

Before I could form a question, Duncan said, "Whatever we decide we should do, we need to do it quickly. Have ye seen what Caelius and his little army have done to Paris?"

Gulp.

Paris?

Aidan walked over to a small boxy television resting on an end table and switched it on. The TV was black-and-white and should have been in a museum. When there was nothing but fuzz, Dad joined Aidan's side and pulled up two metal antennas to get a local signal. I thought they were called rabbit ears, but I couldn't remember. I'd only seen old TVs like this on . . . TV. After some serious finagling and turning a knob a few times to go through the stations, a news channel finally came in clear.

My heart thudded in my chest.

The footage we all stared at was terrifying. It looked as though Paris had been hit by a nuclear bomb. Destroyed cobblestone, bricks, and broken glass littered the ground. Not even the Eiffel Tower stood; it was just a twisted heap of metal that had been bent into a million different shapes. The strength it must have taken to literally destroy every building in Paris astounded me. If this was Caelius at half power, then I didn't want to imagine what he'd be like at full power.

I could barely hear the anchorman as he listed the number of fatalities, which currently was over . . .

A million.

People.

Dead.

I couldn't breathe.

I was having a panic attack.

I'd had them before, but recognizing what it was didn't help me break out of it.

I felt like I was dying.

Strong arms held me up as I crumbled to my knees. Aidan's voice was soothing and strong as he said, "Shea, are you okay?"

No, I was not okay. None of us were okay with Caelius out there. He was going to destroy the world, and I wasn't sure if we could stop him. I wanted to say all of these things, but my voice wasn't working.

Through my panicked haze, my eyes focused on the television, and suddenly Caelius's evil grin was there, laughing as he stood on a pile of dead bodies while thousands of bullets bounced off his skin. A tank, a bazooka, a grenade—all attacked him, but he stood unmoved, only laughing harder, calling the humans ants.

The anchorman was scared out of his mind. "We don't know what he—what *it* is. But it can't be stopped!"

My dad switched off the TV, and no one argued.

Without the horrors of what had happened in Paris playing, I was able to breathe again. Aidan's arms never left me. He was my set of human crutches.

"I didn't see Lucian or Sete in that newsreel," Nefertiti said with a tinge of hope.

My dad lashed out at her. "But Molly was right there with him! We just saw her kill thousands with her bare hands!"

I hadn't seen that. I wanted to vomit. I still couldn't speak. This wasn't happening. This wasn't my life. It was a nightmare I needed to wake up from.

I pushed away from Aidan and finally found my voice. "Caelius picked Paris because of me, because that's where Lucian and I were, together, after Caelius escaped. We were happy there."

Meky crossed her arms. "Caelius is nothing if not predictable."

Nefertiti directed her words toward me. "He must know by now that the necklace didn't drain your soul, and Lucian can't truly hide how he feels for long. Caelius will see through him, and when he does . . ."

"Caelius won't compete with you, Shea," Ur-Nammu said. "He'll simply erase you from Lucian's memories."

My mind came into focus at that.

"What?"

Then Nefertiti stood before me, her expression oddly soft. "Caelius's blood compulsion was powerful before he was released from his prison, but now? He's probably shoving his blood down Lucian's throat. Caelius will be able to create any memory he wants, and Lucian isn't strong enough to fight it."

"Lucian is stronger than any of us!" I was immediately defensive. "He can fight it! He won't fall for Caelius's lies!"

Nefertiti, Ur-Nammu, and Meky all shared a look of . . . what? It was as if they were remembering something.

It only made me angrier. "What?"

"Shea, Caelius has done this to Lucian before, and he never remembered what Caelius compelled him to forget." Meky's tone was kind, but it didn't help soften the blow.

"It's true," Nefertiti said with absolution.

"Don't even try it." My defensiveness knew no bounds. "I know you're about to say something like he compelled Lucian to forget his love for Nefertiti or something stupid like that, which is bull-crap. He completely confided in me that he loved you. It's obvious the way you two look at each other . . ." What was I

52

saying? I was so scared of Caelius erasing me from Lucian's brain that I was arguing a case for Nefertiti to be with him again? All of this was making my head spin.

Nefertiti held my arms until our eyes met. "Shea, listen to me." When she was sure I was paying attention, she continued. "Lucian never forgot our past, that is true, but Caelius never wanted him to. Caelius did make him forget that we *reunited* once, a thousand years ago."

"Maybe Lucian did remember," I said weakly, but I knew it wasn't true. If Lucian had thought for an instant that Nefertiti and her children were still alive, he'd have searched for them until the end of time. He never would have given me a second thought. Finally, I asked, "Why did Caelius make Lucian forget? I thought he wanted you two to be his Adam and Eve or something." My chest and heart ached. I didn't even know why I was asking the question.

Meky stepped in. "It was my fault, really."

Aidan shook his head. "No, it was mine."

Nefertiti rolled her eyes with annoyance and pulled her hands away from my arms. "It was Lucian's fault, and his alone." She eyed Meky. "He beat you to a pulp! If he had decapitated you, you really would have died!"

The realization hit me: the Gunnhild Viking era, when Aidan and Meky had fallen in love. Lucian had "killed" Aidan's lover to hurt him, not knowing that it was Meky and that she couldn't be killed by normal means.

Nefertiti almost growled at the memory. "I was furious. The deal I made with Caelius was that my family would keep to the shadows in exchange for his protection, but when Meky almost

53

died? Even he couldn't stop me from confronting Lucian. In Egypt Lucian had made a Gutian vow that he would protect my daughters' lives even if it meant losing his own. And he put hands on Meky? His favorite! Beating her for the sake of hurting"—she nodded disdainfully at Aidan—"*him?*"

Yeah. That would piss me off too. I was about to ask Nefertiti how the confrontation went, but I was pretty sure I knew already. Lucian would have been devastated. "He never would have forgiven himself, so Caelius wiped the memory of you confronting him," I guessed aloud.

Nefertiti nodded. "Caelius only wanted our reunion to happen when he was *freed* from his cage, so he sent Ur-Nammu with his blood and compelled Lucian to forget. Caelius still let Lucian hold on to the memory of killing Meky because he was happy that the act of hurting an angel brought Lucian so much joy." She barely glanced at Aidan. "He really felt betrayed by you."

Aidan didn't argue.

No one did.

"So not once did he remember seeing you?" I just couldn't believe that Lucian's brain wouldn't remember *Nefertiti*. He had loved her so much. I was still jealous of their history, of what they had. I was feeling so insecure.

When Nefertiti shook her head, confirming that Caelius had succeeded at wiping out that memory of her, I knew with certainty that if Caelius used his blood to compel Lucian to forget me, it would succeed. We had only been together about a year—what was that when Lucian had been pining over Nefertiti for thousands? I was a blip. She was eternal. If he forgot her, he'd most definitely forget me.

The pain was too much to bear.

Leaving the small group of vampires and an angel, I walked over to one of the couches and sat. Millions of people were dead because Caelius was jealous of my relationship with Lucian. Of course he'd compel me from his brain! Why wouldn't he?

If he could erase me, then Lucian would be *all his*.

Surprisingly, it was Duncan who sat next to me. "I know I should be leavin' ye to your thoughts, but I have to tell ye, Lucian's heart is strong, stronger than I've ever seen. Try to have some faith even if it's none ye see."

It didn't help a lot, but it did help. "Thanks, Duncan."

"We're going to be good friends. I can see it already." Duncan's crooked smile was small, but it was genuine.

And weirdly, I felt the same way.

"Besides," he said, "let's figure out a way to get him back so ye won't be worryin' about the possibilities that may or may not happen."

Feeling a surge of hope, I slowly nodded my head. He was right. The fact that Lucian wasn't in any of the footage indicated that he wasn't Caelius's lapdog yet, which meant he was still Lucian and we could save him.

Nefertiti's plan of blindly breaking in suddenly seemed a lot more appealing.

"Now what is this plan of yours?" Ur-Nammu asked Helena. "You want Duncan to go in as a spy?"

Duncan whispered in my ear, "They're talkin' about me when I'm sittin' right here. Something yeer used to, I suspect?"

"Considering I'm the Vessel, yeah. It's my soul on the line, and everyone wants to make decisions for me, but all I want to do is get Lucian and my mom back." I didn't know why it was so easy to open up to Duncan. Maybe it was because I didn't know him. He couldn't judge or tell me what to do. Or maybe it was because he was just a nice guy that genuinely wanted to listen. Either way, I appreciated his company.

"For it's a man, he spoke. I told him not to," Helena suddenly said, a surprised expression on her face.

Duncan and I exchanged confused glances as Helena continued to spout gibberish.

Goose bumps instinctively rose on my arms.

Duncan noticed and stood. "Trouble," he said.

I nodded and stood up with him.

We both walked over to the group. As we approached, I could see Helena's eyes darting back and forth as if she were caged inside her own body. Then she said, "He will to for a name. I found the her for you."

Nefertiti placed her hand on Helena's arm. "Helena. Breathe deep. What's happening?"

Ur-Nammu said, "I'll Dream-Walk inside her mind. Maybe I can see what's going on."

Helena pulled away from Nefertiti with a jerk, her eyes still wild. "For to me a child."

Ur-Nammu's eyes closed, and I knew he was astral projecting inside Helena's head.

Helena's eyes stopped moving when they suddenly focused on me, but it was almost as if it wasn't her. She went from terrified to . . . furious. Helena stared at me with a hatred that radiated off her body.

Quicker than I could follow, Helena ran the distance between

56

us and pinned me to the ground. Sharp fangs pierced my neck as she drank deep and fast. Aidan and six powerful vampires tried to rip her off of me, but she was like a pit bull, jaws clamped down and not budging.

I was losing consciousness, but I had to make my blood liquid sunshine as I had in the past. It required a lot of concentration, which I didn't have.

I grew weaker by the second.

Was this how I was going to die? I couldn't seem to summon the Light inside of me. I kept reaching for it, but it was just out of my grasp. I called out to Lucian in my head, knowing full well he couldn't hear me, but I wanted my last thoughts to be of him. Then maybe he'd know I was with him, that I loved him and that our souls would always be connected.

For just a second, I thought I heard him call back.

Even if it was just my imagination, it somehow gave me strength. I connected to the Light inside me as if it were the easiest thing in the world. I filled every blood cell in my body with the pure Light of a Vessel.

Helena screamed as she pulled her teeth out of my neck. It was enough for the others to drag her free of me completely. I sat up, gasping for air, suddenly realizing that Helena's body had been pressing so hard on my chest that I hadn't been breathing.

Nefertiti took charge of the attack, being the warrior queen that she was. The others circled Helena like backup bodyguards, giving Nefertiti the space to attack Helena fully. But I could see by the way Nefertiti held Helena's arms down that she wasn't trying to hurt her; she was trying to snap her out of whatever had caused her to attack in the first place.

"When I Dream-Walked, I saw nothing but black!" Ur-Nammu shouted over the commotion.

We had underestimated Caelius's mind control.

He'd left some kind of brain-bomb in Helena, making her attack me. The gibberish had probably been Helena trying to fight it. It made me realize just how strong-minded Helena truly was. I wished that I could fix her, that I could take away any kind of control Caelius still had on her. If I could fix her, then I could fix Lucian if I needed to.

Helena tried desperately to gain her freedom, her eyes still focused on me. But Nefertiti was Helena's maker, and the longer she held Helena down, the weaker she seemed to become.

"Helena, listen to my voice," Nefertiti commanded. "You are safe. You are free from Caelius."

At the mention of his name, Helena thrashed, but Nefertiti's hands might as well have been iron.

"Helena!" Nefertiti boomed.

The sound of her name jolted Helena to tear her head away from staring me down, and she looked up at Nefertiti.

In a voice just above a whisper, Helena pleaded, "Nefertiti, please . . ."

It hurt my soul in a way I couldn't describe. I could see the terror in Helena's eyes; she had no control over her body or mind.

I had to try *something*.

Knowing I might aggravate Helena more, I crawled toward her anyway. Her eyes glossed over with rage again, and she renewed her struggle to break free. Aidan and the wall of vampires blocked me from her.

"Shea, get out of here!" Aidan cried out.

At this point, Helena was a rabid dog that no one wanted to put down, but the situation was growing dire enough that I suspected everyone was considering it.

"I can help!" I yelled back, not knowing if it was true or not. The Light had healed Lucian's wounds when he'd been burned to a crisp by the sundial in Egypt. I had to see if I could heal Helena's brain. It was worth a try.

Aidan moved aside, and I felt a wave of love for my best friend. He trusted me, even if he shouldn't. I crawled past him and touched Helena's leg to form a connection with her. Helena shrieked in a kind of crazed glee at being so close to me, and Nefertiti looked downright pissed at me for being there.

"Do what you're going to do!" Nefertiti screamed. "Just do it fast! She gets stronger when she's near you!"

No pressure.

Closing my eyes and Dream-Walking inside Helena's mind, I could instantly feel that Nefertiti was right. Caelius had made it so Helena would grow in strength when near me, which explained why no one had been able to pull her off of me before. How he could do that, I had no idea. I just needed to find Caelius inside her. It wasn't his blood though, like Nefertiti had suggested. I could feel that right away. It was something *else*.

A shadow with . . . instructions?

There were words and thoughts burned into a black mass floating through Helena's entire body, constantly moving so it would stay active and impossible to eradicate.

But I was made from the Light.

And Light casts out shadow.

I mentally chased it while hearing Helena scream viciously

59

on the outside. That was when I knew: she wasn't screaming—it was the shadow, knowing I was coming for it. It was crazy racing through her body. It felt like a movie I'd watched in middle school where a scientist had found a way to shrink and travel through blood vessels. I was able to go everywhere, through her heart, lungs, arms, and legs. It was like a crash course on the internal workings of the human body, except I was chasing something dark, something evil . . . and it was terrifying. The banshee shrieks alone made me want to run away, but I knew the only way to help Helena was to track Caelius's shadow and annihilate it.

Using all the strength I could muster, I mentally leapt toward the shadow and grabbed it, infusing it with Light. I could feel my hand on Helena's leg heat up to the point where I thought it was on fire. It burned badly, but I kept holding on, pushing my Light into Helena and surrounding the cloud of darkness that was Caelius's mind control.

My ears rang from Helena's intense cries, but it was working. I could feel it.

Whoosh!

And just like that, it was gone.

I searched her body one last time, but there was nothing, no darkness.

Opening my eyes, I noticed that Helena had stopped screaming. Nefertiti held her in her arms, and Helena desperately clung to her. I pulled my hand off Helena's leg, and we both let out a grunt of exhaustion. A perfect gooey handprint was on her calf, and it looked *nasty*. She dug her head in and cried in Nefertiti's arms.

Aidan waved his hand over mine, and my pain was instantly gone. Shaking his head at Helena, he said, "The Light inside me will only burn you more. You'll have to heal with blood."

Helena didn't seem upset by this at all. She just looked relieved to be herself again.

Nefertiti let Helena use her body for support as she stood up. Meky stayed a step behind in case she fell. Helena hobbled weakly toward me. "Is it gone? Can Caelius take me over again?" Her expression was terrified.

I shook my head. "No. I saw what he used to control you, and I chased it away. I didn't see anything else."

Relief flooded every feature on Helena's beautiful face. "Thank you, Shea. I owe you."

Then I threw it out there. "Maybe I could do the same with Lucian if Caelius mind-controls him?"

The look in Nefertiti's eyes made my heart squeeze with disappointment. Shaking her head sadly, Nefertiti said, "Caelius will control him with his *blood*." Then she said with slight hope, "But if Caelius uses both blood *and* his shadow, then yes, you may be able to break one at least. It could mean the difference between life and death for him."

"It's too late for Lucian," a familiar voice said, making my heart stop.

Mom.

I turned around to see Molly Harper, my mother, holding a small box in her hands.

She stood about twenty feet away. There was something different about her. She looked . . . sad? I couldn't tell. She was so unlike the mother I knew and loved. When her eyes met mine,

61

there was no recognition. They were just empty and horrifying to look at.

Then her attention turned to Dad. "Hello, Jeff." Her voice was thick and pained. "Are you ready to come with me yet?" It was almost a plea, and my heart ached for her. Even if she couldn't remember me, she remembered Dad and loved him deeply.

Dad stood next to me, placing his hand on my shoulder, and said, "I'll never leave *our* daughter."

"She's *not* our daughter!" she screamed, shaking her head as if warding away some kind of evil.

Aidan stepped toward her. "Molly, let me give you back your memories—"

"Take one step toward me and I'll be gone before your next breath!" Mom's eyes darted toward me. I wished Aidan could leap across the room and fix this, but she could fly like Lucian and Nefertiti, so it was useless to even try.

It took a moment for Mom to compose herself, but once she did, her face turned sad again. "Lucian felt the Vessel's presence moments ago, and that's how we found you. Grandfather likes the chase, so you'd better run far and fast because he's going to come here next." Then she tossed the box at Nefertiti's feet, her tone colored with even more sadness. "You're to come with me, Nefertiti. Grandfather sent that as an incentive."

Nefertiti tried to hide the terror from her features, but I could tell she was scared to open that box. Ur-Nammu, Sherit, and Meky stood rooted as well, knowing that whatever was in there would most likely devastate them too.

Kneeling down, Nefertiti slowly pulled back the lid.

Her daughter Merytaten's severed head lay inside. Caelius had killed her in their last battle, and her flesh had already decayed to the point of seeing the skull beneath.

"You're a mother!" Nefertiti hissed at Molly. "How could you do something like this?"

Molly stood silent. It almost seemed like Nefertiti's words had broken her. She wasn't yelling that she wasn't a mother. If she was struggling like this, maybe she could fight Caelius's compulsion. Maybe she could remember . . . me.

After what seemed like an eternity of silence, Mom finally spoke in a monotone voice. "I'm sorry for your loss, but Grandfather says it's time to make a new deal if you want to protect the daughters you have left."

"Why did Caelius send *you*?" I asked before Nefertiti could respond.

Molly paused, unsure, then said, "Caelius wants to torture you. He despises the Vessel."

The fact that she paused gave me hope. I took a step forward. "If you truly believe you're not my mother, then how would seeing you be torture for me?" I tried to reach her with logic, then a thought suddenly occurred to me. "And if Caelius really wanted to torture me, why wouldn't he torture me through Dream-Walking? I have no defenses when I'm asleep."

I had a theory that had been rolling around in my head for a while now, and I hoped my mother would be able to confirm it. It was a conversation I'd had with Nefertiti, when she told me that she had Dream-Walked with Gracuri to keep him and the last of Lucian's Second-Borns hidden. She had been cryptic and careful during her Dream-Walks, but she expressed her doubts about Caelius having the ability. I knew she, as a warrior, could never fully trust that it might be true. It would leave her too vulnerable. But the more I thought about it, the more I felt that Caelius would have gone straight for Gracuri and probably tortured Nefertiti for trying to hide him in the first place. But Caelius never brought it up.

I reiterated what I had said before, trying to reach that part of her that remembered she was my mother. "With Dream-Walking, Caelius could torture me as long as he wanted, never allowing me to wake. I'd be in torment forever."

Molly stood there for a long while, staring at me.

"He won't hurt you. Grandfather is kind," Molly said, unsure.

"Of course he will. He wants to take my soul. He wants to kill me." Then I pushed further. "All he'd have to do is Dream-Walk with me, and he'd be able to control me to do anything he wanted."

Molly shook her head. "No, Caelius can't compel you because of your Light, and he can't Dream-Walk. Darkness can't *create*, and walking through dreams is building a true connection with someone and the scenery and . . . it's not just about control, it's . . ." She trailed off, talking as if in a daze.

I was in shock that not only was I right, but that I had gotten my mother to admit it.

If Caelius couldn't Dream-Walk, then we had an open line of communication with no fear of Caelius listening in.

This was huge.

I exchanged looks with Nefertiti and Ur-Nammu. They were trying to hide their surprise from Molly.

Then her eyes cleared. "I don't know why I told you that."

"You told her because you trust her." Dad stepped forward.

"Because she's *ours*."

A flash of emotion illuminated Mom's eyes. There was definitely something there.

My heart squeezed.

But the moment erased itself as soon as it had come, as if she'd been fighting some inner battle and had lost. She nodded toward Merytaten's head with true sympathy and said, "We should leave before he kills any more of your family."

There was a moment where nobody moved.

Then finally Nefertiti set the small box down and walked toward Molly.

Ur-Nammu held her back. "Please, you can't go. Caelius will kill you."

Nefertiti shrugged him off. "Then he'll kill me. As long as my daughters are safe, I don't care. It is our code, after all."

Ur-Nammu had no argument. He knew that, to her, only her daughters mattered.

As she reached my mom's side, she said, "Let's go."

Before they left, Nefertiti stared at me. She was giving me a message. Helena's original plan had been to have Duncan act as a double agent, but Nefertiti was going instead.

She was going in.

And she was coming back with information, or she would die trying.

CHAPTER 4
LUCIAN

Bohe took the blade Caelius gave him and hovered over my torso, biting his bottom lip.

It was painful to watch, but I couldn't take my eyes off him. Sweat covered his supple skin, and every muscle was taut. He was trying to resist, as if a force, and not his own compulsion, was pressing his hand down.

His arms trembled as he finally stopped. "I'm sorry, Lucian. I defied him for days, but I–I'm not myself. I'm not strong like you are."

My eyes squinted as I felt the knife on my throat. "Liu Xie, you are one of the strongest people I know. This doesn't change that."

"You'll hate me after. What he wants me to do to you—"

"It's all right." I tried to make my tone comforting. "He's already done the worst to me himself." From the corner of the room, I could see a faint smile cover Caelius's lips from the sentiment. "Whatever you do, Bohe, it's already forgiven."

"It's so important to your creations, isn't it, Light? This *forgiveness*. How childish," Caelius taunted.

Bohe clenched his teeth as his breath hitched, and he finally met my gaze. "Even with your forgiveness, it's painful to hurt the one I love. I won't forgive myself as readily. I know I have no right to ask, but please, remember me like I was before." He closed his eyes, and so did I.

Like he was before . . .

I thought of the days that passed in China, of our long conversations over tea. The smell of his skin had always brought me comfort. Now the delicate fragrance of *Camellia sinensis*, however, was overwritten with the strong scent of fear. It was like a lotus pulled back down into the muddy pond that had birthed it. I sighed. Bohe—who had kept his delicate light, even when subjugated by warlords—was drowning in the mirth of Caelius's darkness.

And I was helpless to save him.

All I could do now was honor his request and remember him like he was before.

I felt rough skin on my lips.

Rough and cold.

It was strange. He had always been so soft to touch.

He didn't move, as if frozen in place, embracing me one last time as he had done the night I turned him.

Then the texture on my lips struck a disgusting chord of familiarity.

They weren't lips pressed to mine.

My eyes flew open.

Caelius's hand was between our mouths, his irises ablaze like fire. My eyes darted back and forth from Caelius to Bohe. He pulled his lips from Caelius's palm in shock. I jerked my head away from his hand and yelled, "Bohe, run!"

"Grandfather, what's going on? I thought before I cut him, I could say goodbye in my fashion—"

Caelius pulled him back by his hair.

I knew that look. "Caelius, don't! It was nothing! He'll only do what *you* ask from now on! He's loyal, you can keep him alive, he'll tortue me, he'll serve you and I—"

He elongated his nail and slit Bohe's throat.

Blood rained down over our bodies.

My mind froze in horror.

Liu Xie gagged for breath, his hands desperately grabbing his throat, trying to close the gash. Caelius wrenched them away, pulling the yellow sash from the floor. He ripped it into four pieces and tied Bohe's arms and legs to my own. "Now, now— stay in place, or I'll tear off your arms next."

His slick red chest convulsed as he writhed on top of me. "Bohe! Hang on! It's okay, it's just pain, your body will heal! It will pass!" I looked up at Caelius brimming with hate. "You monster!"

Caelius's hands balled into fists as he looked at the two of us. "He'll heal, the pain will pass? That's a problem, isn't it, darling?" He pulled a bone from his pocket and shoved it in the open wound at Bohe's neck. "Problem solved."

I lashed out, the chains shaking both of our bodies, trying to loosen his knots so that he could move his hands. "You crazy bastard, let him go! He was doing what *you* wanted!"

Caelius reached down, running a hand through my hair. "That's *angel* bone, boy. He won't heal. Your body will be his immortal grave. How romantic."

Bohe's frame jerked, his head thrashing as more blood spilled over us. I could feel the hard pounding of his heart, its erratic rhythm in time with mine. "Please, Caelius! What do you want? I'll give you—"

"You."

My mouth fell open. Bohe wheezed, his torso trying to push away from my blood-soaked chest, but the knots were too tight, and he was weak.

"Fine! Have me! Have whatever you want! Just let him go," I begged.

Now the hand in my hair gripped into a fist as he tilted my chin up. With his other hand he ran the pad of his thumb over my bottom lip. "No, I don't. I don't *have* you." He looked down at Bohe in disgust. "But that doesn't mean I'm going to let anyone kiss you, either."

His hand relaxed, and he stepped away, looking at the bloodied mess.

"This isn't the view I was hoping for." He moved the back of his hand over his lips, kissing the spot where mine had been. "I thought seeing someone else torture you would help diminish you in my eyes. I hoped it would lessen my desire for you. But the idea of this swine kissing without my permission what I know is *mine*—" A low rumble quaked the room as he scratched his nails down Liu Xie's back. He cried out, thrashing again, his blood now splattering the walls as Caelius flung it whimsically about the room.

Bohe's heart started to slow, his motions less exaggerated but all the more desperate. I stared at his wrists wrapped in the yellow sash. They were burning where they touched my angelic shackles, burning and keeping him weak. Because he was a Second-Born, anything made of Light was like poison. My lips trembled as I heard the scream of flesh around the bone in his throat, sizzling with every moment that passed.

"Caelius . . . don't do this," I pleaded.

Emperor Xian, the last of the Han Dynasty, my lifelong friend Bohe, degraded to this monster's plaything . . . because of me. "I get that you're jealous, but it's *my* fault for turning him in the first place. Punish *me* for wanting anyone other than you!"

The auburn of Caelius's eyes burned even brighter. "You care for him that much." He tore a new line down Bohe's back.

I paused.

My pleas were making it worse.

My mind turned and turned, but I didn't know what to say. How could I negotiate with Darkness? What card did I have left to play?

Bohe's heart slowed further, no longer in time with my own. His body twitched, the strain of his muscles giving in to exhaustion.

Caelius turned and walked toward the door.

"Wait! Don't leave him like this! Caelius, please! Father!"

His back hunched. "Father? Please? Words that mean nothing to me now."

I remembered what he'd said when he was deep inside me, the longing in his eyes as he spoke. He didn't want to be called Father—that was always meant to be a stepping-stone. He told me that as a child in Gutium, when I had thought him more than mortal, I had moved him with my words then. I could move him now.

"God, spare him. Aren't you more than human? Aren't you *better*? Only a human would do something this cruel to someone he desired, but not a god. Be merciful. Caelius, be *my god*."

I could hear his breath hitch as he turned slowly. There it was again, that tenderness I had seen emerge in the time he had thought I was his. I had given my body over to him, lying with words of praise, all to buy Shea and the others time to heal and hide.

His gaze softened.

I'd found it, his weak spot.

He stepped back toward me. Bringing his hand down, he stroked the back of it against my cheek. "Even though I know you are saying this for *him* and not me, I will be merciful. I will be *better* than human. After all, everything I do is for you, La-Narru. Remember that."

He reached down to Liu Xie's neck.

I held my breath as he grabbed the bone and pulled it out.

Instantly, I could see the wound start to heal itself. I could also see the deep black burn its presence had left.

My blood was all that I had left to give him, and if I could convince Caelius to leave, I would gladly give Bohe all of it. Killing me would help Shea, and the strength in my blood would make Bohe strong enough to get out of this place. His large brown eyes rose to mine. Relief flooded his features and reverberated through my bones as well. "It's okay, Liu Xie," I whispered, kissing his forehead. "My precious *Camellia sinensis*."

71

I looked up. "Caelius, thank you. I—"

He sank his teeth into the still-pink flesh at Liu Xie's neck and, with one violent inhale, drank him dry.

Bohe's emaciated body fell back to my own, limp like a wooden doll whose strings had been cut. The tears that had been at the corners of my eyes fell down and into my open mouth. I stared at Caelius in horror.

He grimaced seeing my expression. "I don't understand. Are you not pleased?" He tilted his head to the side in confusion. "You were asking for mercy, were you not? A quick death? Surely you weren't expecting me to let him *live*? Not after you all but confessed to loving him."

My mind reeled at his words.

"You disgust me." I spat into his face. It landed just below his eye. "You're sick . . . you . . . you're—"

"Careful." His expression hardened, the tenderness shifting from confusion to rage. "If I'm not mistaken, you still have one Second-Born left, besides the Vessel's parents. Ur-Nammu is one of your favorites as well, is he not? If I were you, I wouldn't put my *maker* into such a foul mood. For *his* sake, of course. Because that's all you do things for, right? For someone else? How selfish of you."

I clenched my jaw. Hate radiated from my every pore—every pore that could feel Bohe's cold dead skin resting against it.

Caelius moved his thumb over my spit, wiping it off his cheek. He stared at it a moment. "A parting gift for the Duke of Shanyang." He smeared it into the long black tresses of Bohe's now-uncoiled hair. His eyes matched the fury in my own. "I'll remember this, and next time I won't show mercy, no matter how hard you *beg.*" He turned and moved toward the door, lifting a hand and waving it as he passed through. "See you in a few days, handsome. Like I promised, Bohe will keep you company in my stead while I continue to destroy Paris. Enjoy the fruits of your pleading."

He slammed the door behind him.

I screamed.

I screamed as loud as my lungs could stand, and then I screamed more. I could feel him, could feel Bohe's delicate wrists and ankles tied to mine. His chest, molded to my shape, his head resting under my chin as if in sleep. We had done this before. I'd held him like this, his body slack in my arms, when I had drained him of his mortal life. The fever that had wrecked his body had left him, along with the last warmth of human blood. I'd hesitated then, remembering Gracuri, worried that I'd destroy the beauty of Bohe more than any mortal had in his lifetime.

I struggled against the chains, wanting to touch him.

I needed to hold his head in my hands, to stare at his lips, his soft cheeks, like I had then. In doing so, I had convinced myself that I couldn't live without him, that the world was better for having Liu Xie in it, even as a vampire. But I was not Lucian the Merciful. The longer I had stared then, the more I had felt my own selfish desperation. The loss of Adnachiel had been renewed by Pompeii. The loss of Gracuri was fresh. In that moment I had felt all the losses over my lifetime: from Moses to childhood, the death of all of Gutium, the loss of my own mortal life.

Now here, with his body against mine, I felt it all again. It was like a wave that had been held back by a low tide, filling in all the crevices of my grief.

Why was it always like this? One domino and my mind relentlessly connected all the times I'd felt this way before. But it was so much worse now. Now that Shea had revived my heart and I couldn't bury the pain under thousands of years of well-developed callousness, I was raw and open to my feelings. Tears streamed from my eyes, and I screamed again. I couldn't fill my mouth with the sands of Egypt. I couldn't stuff my self-hatred with dirt. I couldn't bury the pain with my own hands in the blood or life of another, and I couldn't bear it.

"*Wǒ ài nǐ*," I cried out.

He and I should've been dressed in white. The dirt I despised should've been under my feet as I walked a traditional funeral march by his casket. There should've been a ceremony and an offering. Had he still been a ruler in his own time, the complex funeral rights of China had tombs that rivaled ancient Egypt. There would've been provisions left for the deceased, provisions to carry them into the afterlife like Qin Shi Huang and his nine thousand statues, his terra-cotta army meant to protect the first emperor of China.

In his burial, respect would've been paid to his ancestors as a sort of filial piety. He had decided to become Buddhist in his later years, and Buddhist ethics dictated, to some extent, that it was a virtue to respect one's elders, parents, and descendants. It was a sort of last respect given, even upon death. The family was also expected to take vigil, watching over the casket of the beloved deceased for days, ensuring that the soul had support as it journeyed into eternity. Unless . . . unless you were an unmarried bachelor. Unless, of course, you weren't human anymore.

Moreover, Bohe had already had a funeral.

Though it wasn't as elaborate or as honor bound as it should have been. At that time, his title of Emperor had been stripped, and he'd been reduced to the Duke of Shanyang. No one visited his grave to offer incense or flowers or to tidy it up when time destroyed it. Not that any of that mattered to him. But it mattered to me, just as it did now.

When he'd opened his eyes then and looked at me, the dark brown almost black, it had been the happiest I'd seen him. Instead of instantly craving blood, he had kissed me. It had been quick and soft. When he'd pulled away, all he'd said was, "I'm home." As if that was what my arms were to him.

I gritted my teeth. Was I now a fitting casket to hold him? If he could awaken now, would he look at me like he had then? Would he be relieved to know that he died in his home?

I gasped for breath.

This was agony.

"I won't leave you, Bohe," I whimpered, choking in air to steady my breath. "It's tradition to stay by your side until you pass over. If your spirit *is* here, I'll pray for you—I'll chant so that my words may light a path to your *true* home. I was never really home for you. In the end, I used you like I used everyone else. I'm sorry."

I closed my eyes, feeling the weight of his body on mine. I whispered into his hair, cupping his head under my chin. It was the only way I could hold him now. I uttered a small blessing in his native tongue. Not traditional, not any chant I had heard him spout over tea, but it was the closest translation I knew for the blessing in Gutium for fallen warriors on the battlefield. It was something that was mine, that I could still give him.

I didn't know what or whom to pray to. Would I need to bargain with Anubis for his safe passage down the Nile, or the Steed of Oknah to carry his spirit to the stars? I didn't deserve either. I deserved Caelius and his endless black oblivion. But Bohe had deserved so much more in life . . . and in death.

I whispered into his dulling hair for the last time. "From my home to yours, Liu Xie, Emperor Xian of Han, the last of the Han Dynasty, my *Camellia sinensis*, my beloved Bohe." Tears rolled down my chin, leaving splotches on the drying blood at my chest. "If you find no home for you in the afterlife with the emperors of China, I am the son of Onack the Great, leader of Gutium. I consider you one of my own. If your people will not have you, mine will. You are welcome there. I cannot hold you anymore, but surely the arms of my mother, Anna-Steen, will." I choked on my own words. "You may have my home, my place, if you still need somewhere to belong."

I wept.

This was useless.

I had given up on believing in gods and the afterlife a million times over when I'd been mortal, and then more so when I'd become this. And yet when I could not escape my pain or desperation, it was to some invisible force that I prayed. Did that make me a fool? I tried to breathe in deep, but it came out in jagged gasps. I would give anything to run from this place, to bury him properly. I would give anything to hide from these feelings.

Alone.

Why do I always end up alone?

The weight of it, and Bohe's body, crushed me deeper than

when I'd been buried in the fiery mountains of Pompeii.

I was alone then.

I would always end up alone.

It ached.

I couldn't breathe.

"If there's no afterlife," I gasped, "if my mother is not there to hold you . . . if you are truly gone, I will burn your memory into the existence of all things. You will be everywhere I look, as with my other children. I will never forget you. As long as I exist, I will be a living tomb for the memories of your life. But please, *Mother*, if you are there . . . hold him." I panted for breath. The pain was incredible. I couldn't bear this, having his dead body tied to mine for days. I would go mad. I felt the chaos in my mind seeping in like thick black smoke. Better to go mad than to remember this gruesome end, than to have it forever carved into my soul as some pawn in Caelius's useless game.

"La-Narru, don't."

I blinked and searched the room.

Am I really losing my mind?

"It's just a body."

I smelled a rich herbal blend of earth and leaves all around me.

"I'm not there."

A light kiss brushed against my lips.

My eyes widened, and I jerked up. "Bohe!"

I looked down as his body half slid from mine. "Bohe, you're still alive!"

I moved again. "Bohe!" His face shifted up.

Dead eyes frozen in anguish stared back at me.

They were empty.

I looked around the room. Was this an illusion, a trick, a hallucination? I stared at his petrified body. "Bohe, *please*. Kiss me again, like you did the day I turned you. *Live* again. Don't leave me."

A silence as cold and as dead as he was filled the room.

I stared at his sunken cheeks.

He was gone. There was no reviving him now.

Just as the realization broke me, I felt a strange lightness there. Words echoed off the bloodstained walls. "I'll see you when you come home. That's where I'll be waiting."

My mind fought the peace attempting to overcome my mourning with facts about Darkness always winning and nothing being sacred. Still, the room *felt* different than it had before. Was this the peace I had heard mortals speak of? Humans said they had felt their loved ones say goodbye, but I had known only grief. I bit my bottom lip. It felt warmed by the lingering sensation of touch. Was this really the taste of Liu Xie? Was it possible, or was this a waking dream because I didn't sleep and my mind couldn't cope with reality?

Bohe.

He had become spiritual as the centuries passed: secluding himself in the mountains, in temples, studying enlightenment and trying to forget his time as a young puppet emperor. It was why I'd seen him less and less. He had changed, and I had remained much the same: scared, alone, and savage. That peace he'd found, that evolution . . . was that why I could hear *something*? I swore it was his voice that'd spoken, that it was his smell, his taste.

An overwhelming feeling of light covered me for a moment,

and I felt another presence.

"Shea?"

Was Shea reaching out to me?

Was it her heavenly Light that had touched me and Bohe because his body was tied to mine?

Was that why I could hear him?

"Shea!" I reached my hand forward as it was caught by the chains. "Shea, where are—"

I stopped myself.

I growled, hardening my emotions.

No.

I'd sacrificed my dignity and pride so that she could escape, so that she would be safe. Reaching back to her now would only guarantee her death. Even though I wanted her comfort—even though the Light that touched me and Bohe now was nothing but divine, and underneath it was Shea Harper, real and flesh and blood—I had to protect her. She was a piece of Light that I could never touch or hold again. My soul mate. My world.

I fixed my gaze back on the ceiling.

I had to reconnect with who I'd been before I'd met her. This vulnerability would only cause her death, and I would lose her like I'd lost everyone else.

She had to stay away from me.

I had to be the one lost in battle this time.

Though there would be no words spoken over my corpse. I prayed only that she could let me go or kill me if she had to.

I guess I have one more card to play after all.

I didn't know if she could hear me through the wall of Caelius's Darkness, but if she could, I sent my thoughts to her one last time. *End me, Shea Harper. End me before Caelius does to you what he's done to Bohe, what he'll do to everyone and everything I love.*

***

Five days passed. The horrid stench of Bohe's rotting body was only matched by the smoke and ash pouring through the crack in the door. I had no need to scream—all that I felt was being voiced for me in the slaughtered sounds of what had once been Paris. Would there be anything left of it by the time Caelius finished? Would the Eiffel Tower at least stand?

This was what Shea had tried to stop. This was why, even before Shea, I had kept Caelius locked in his cage, only feigning to take the Vessel to hurt Adnachiel. I winced. If only I had talked with Aidan sooner about Moses, if only we had spent decades working on a way to kill Caelius rather than my childish obsession with revenge, this might have all been avoided.

But he'd pierced my heart when he'd taken Moses.

The pride of the Gutian people was that we lived by a code that was governed by the ideals of loyalty and love. My father used to say that you couldn't really kill a Gutian; our souls would fight beyond the grave. Our code was etched in the existence of all things. Only when my mother died, alone in the dark holding her cold body, had he commanded that I look.

"This is the only way to truly kill a Gutian," he'd whispered, "to pierce them directly through the heart, to take away what they are fighting for, leaving nothing in their hands but remorse. She will live on, mounting the Steed of Oknah to rest with our kind in the stars, because her soul was made to *fly*. But look closer now, La-Narru, for today you have not lost a mother, but a father."

It was hard to breathe, remembering his words. It was no wonder I'd eaten her ashes after that.

Now, at the end of the world, when I had done all I could to save the ones I loved, I understood his words more than ever. I'd lost so many; they'd died in my arms as my mother had died in his. If I lost Shea too, I would truly be dead.

The door flung open.

"Look who's feeling more himself!"

Caelius sauntered over, soaked in fresh blood. "Did you miss me?" The tips of his hair dripped crimson onto my cheek. "Oh?" He stared a moment longer. "And here I was referring to myself, but look at you." He smiled. "You have that cold callous look in your eyes." He traced his bloodied hand down the length of my side. "What's wrong, La-Narru? Did Emperor Xian not entertain you enough while I was gone? Did you get bored like I used to in my cage, longing for you and you alone?" He leaned forward and grabbed the back of my neck, forcing my lips open as he kissed me hard.

I jerked my head away. He laughed, wiping his mouth. I spat, trying to get the blood out of my throat.

"What's wrong, darling? Not hungry?" he jeered.

"I don't know where it's been," I shot back, hardening further.

He placed his hands at my wrists and pulled the yellow sashes free. "You don't want the blood of the innocent to taint you?" He smiled. "Oh *please*, don't act so virginal." He walked to my feet, untying the knots there as well. He pulled him off. The loss of his weight was replaced with an inescapable emptiness. I almost asked him to leave the body with me. I wasn't ready, even after he had started to smell, to let Bohe go. In truth, that was why I'd turned him. I would never be ready to lose him.

He threw Bohe over his shoulder like a doll. The look of it cemented the reality aching in my chest: he was gone.

Caelius moved his thumb over my mouth. "If their swine blood has touched the lips of a god, then trust me, it is purified enough for *you*." He adjusted Bohe on his shoulder. "Isn't that what gods do, La-Narru? Purify. In history, Paris will be an example like Sodom and Gomorrah. The desecration of those cities was seen as the Light's holy glory, just as taking Paris will be my glory. I brought them brimstone and fire, after all." He touched the creases by my eyes. "And it looks like you've done enough crying to be my symbolic pillar of salt."

My muscles coiled as I clenched my jaw. My tears were not for him to relish; they were for Bohe. "All that I have and am is not yours and never will be. And you are no *god*. You're just Darkness that needs to know its place—"

"You're the one who needs to know his place, boy." His playful grin subsided, and he paused, taking in a long drawn out breath. "It took a whole city to get the bounce back in my step, and one minute with you to remove it. Why is that?" He scrutinized the hard lines on my face, as if looking would procure some sort of answer. He sighed again, uncertainty moving over his features.

"Well, onward and upward, or so they say." He tossed Bohe's body through the open door. It hit the wall with a thud and crumpled into a pile like trash.

"Don't treat him like that! Have you no respect for the dead?

No honor?" I stared in abhorrence at Liu Xie's now-concave face.

"How cute that you still care after days with that *filth*." He laughed, low and long. "That puppet won't dance for you anymore. Its strings are cut. Best to throw it out."

Caelius ran his hand over my face. "If nothing else, you are my favorite plaything, but more than an empty puppet, I'll make you *mine* without the strings. I'll make you keep your promise, La-Narru. It's all I've ever wanted since I became flesh. And the point of life is to get what we want, isn't it?"

I bit the inside of my lip, hatred boiling over. "Don't call me that. My childhood name isn't yours to use so candidly."

"I will use you and it as I please!" He slammed his fist next to my face. It punctured a hole straight through the mattress. "I gave you the name Lucian! It was *mine*!" He ripped his fist out, cotton spilling in tufts, the fibers floating through the air like snowflakes. "And until *you're* mine, I'll call you by the name of the boy who begged for me to be his god by that river in Gutium! I'll taste the sweetness from your lips as you call me it over and over! And *this* time you'll mean it, like you did then! This time when I create your name anew, you will treasure the name Lucian like the gift that it was!"

"I'll die before that happens."

"Maybe." His irises blazed like rubies. "But not until I've tried *everything* to keep you." A sort of sadness filled his gaze as he wiped the mattress stuffing from his hand onto my chest.

"You're wasting your time—we both know that." I leaned forward, as close as I could before the chains pulled me back. "Just kill me now and save yourself the trouble."

He drew his face closer to mine, then licked the side of my

cheek. "Oh, it's no trouble." He straightened up, humming to himself, savoring the taste of my sweat.

I gawked in disgust as he motioned toward Bohe. "I want some privacy. Close the door, but do pick that puppet up and dispose of it, dear. The sight of it seems to be troubling my lover."

I scowled, looking toward the doorway. "It's sick how you've made Molly your errand boy."

"Molly?" He laughed. "Does it exhaust you, being wrong all the time?" He squeezed my cheek and patted it. "Not the brightest, but at least you have your looks."

A shadow moved from the dark hallway. She stepped forward. I didn't need light to illuminate her face. I knew who it was. I had made clay sculptures of that shape for years.

"Nefertiti."

She refused to meet my gaze, gently picking up Bohe and slamming the door closed.

"What have you done to her? Why is she *here*?" I pulled furiously against the chains.

He covered my mouth with his hand. "Look at you squirming like a fish on a hook every time there's new information." He moved his other hand down Bohe's dried blood, caressing my torso. "It's enough to make a god want to take you all over again." He slid his long fingers down between my thighs, pulling on the meat of them. "But there's time for that later, time when you'll give it up to me without resistance. You'll be supple and willing."

I hardened, trying to close any lingering vulnerability inside.

"Nefertiti was part of the original game. It's frustrating to plan something for so long and not have it work out, don't you think? You must have felt that a million times by now." He laughed, squeezing my inner thigh harder. "I want to see how it would have worked, you and Nefertiti reunited at long last. You have a child together, after all."

He placed a hand over his forehead in feigned despair. "And that whore, Shea, killed some of Nefertiti's children and almost all of yours, attacking us without provocation. It's really Shea who's ruining your life, she and that Adnachiel you hate so much, the one who betrayed you and killed Moses.

"I'll rewrite everything for you so that you can finally forget your strange obsession with her and be happy, like I'd planned for centuries. I'll take care of you, darling, and you'll appreciate me for it. With a little work and time, you'll be mine eventually."

My eyes widened. It wasn't possible, was it? He'd driven me mad before, I had killed Shea's parents unknowingly because of it, but I was stronger now, and I had eventually come back to myself. There was no way I would think that Shea had killed anyone. He couldn't take her from me. She was all that was left in my heart, all that was keeping me alive. She was burned into a part of my soul that even he couldn't remove.

I swallowed. Darkness had limits. Everything did. He couldn't remove love. He could hide it for a while, but he could never remove it. I was about to tell him just that when I thought of Molly Harper—Shea's own *mother*, someone who loved Shea more than her own life, who'd birthed her . . . and now she hated Shea with every fiber of her being.

Caelius slowly removed his hand from my mouth. "Do you understand what I'm going to do to you?"

"It won't work," I choked out.

"Well, well, you've given more convincing speeches from the

other side of my cage." He licked his lips. "What's this doubt I smell past your perspiration? Come now, if even Nefertiti was willing to allow me to do this to you, Gutium's strongest warrior, surely you know that this truly is the end."

"I'll die, Caelius. Without Shea—"

He laughed. "We'll see."

"You're using Nefertiti's children against her. I know she wouldn't—"

"*Your* child in particular, La-Narru, let's not forget. The one she cared so much for that she found me in Egypt, begged me to turn you, and promised me her life and her children if only to save you, so that her precious Setepenre would know your face." He smiled. "Nostalgia. Of course, she never knew that I was going to turn you anyway, that even then I desired you more fiercely than she."

I shivered. Guilt, shame, fear—this helpless feeling I had spent lifetimes trying to run from—swelled all around me. Ever since I'd watched my mother's fevered body grow still, I'd known it was my fault; all of this was because of me. She was my first loss, and every loss after was mine to bear alone. My father was right. I was no one's son now, except this monster's. I brought nothing but pain and death to all who knew me.

Caelius leaned forward, kissing my cheek. "Don't despair, dear one," he whispered into my ear, cupping my face. "I'll rewrite your mind, and you'll be happy once again, as you were in Gutium before the wars. And you'll worship me in return, and we will have our Eden. You and I. Forever."

"You're going to make me be with Nefertiti?" My voice quivered. "In front of Shea. To hurt her."

He kissed my cheek again tenderly, moving down my jaw, kissing in small breaths as he spoke. "Yes." His voice was soft. "You'll finally be freed from the guilt of Nefertiti's death. The reunion will be a happy one. She's not to sleep with you, but I can tolerate a few kisses here and there. Maybe. We'll see.

"Then she's to convince you that she is *not* your salvation, *I* am. Not that you'll need much convincing after I give you everything your heart truly desires." He ran his teeth along the side of my neck. I braced for the pain, but it didn't come. He closed his mouth, pressing soft lips to my throat instead.

He leaned back. "I give Molly a single drop of my blood and it lasts for weeks. It's enough to keep her *hating* her own daughter. Her mind and her loyalty are mine completely." He scowled. "I hate it. My blood is too precious to give to any human pig. But for you, darling La-Narru—"

He cut a long line down his wrist. With his other hand, he forced open my jaw, holding it in place, pressing his elbow into my solar plexus, opening my throat in a gasp.

I thrashed as he poured his blood into my mouth like emptying a jug of water down the sink.

I choked trying to resist, trying not to swallow, but it was still getting in, seeping into my very being.

My body instantly felt like it was on fire.

I writhed in agony, but he didn't stop.

It was too much.

My mind jumbled.

I could smell everything, see everything in the room on a microscopic scale like it was being torn apart, broken down into atoms. Time slowed. Stronger than any drug, stronger than my will, his blood moved with an unholy power inside of me.

No.

This was what he meant.

My mind, my memories, my heart.

Shea, please, no.

I couldn't lose her too, not like this.

I tried to hold on to that one word as everything went black.

Shea.

I felt myself, my true self, sinking into an endless pit of mud, blinded by all-consuming Darkness.

Shea.

Further and further down I sank.

My soul was being ripped, torn from every vein, every muscle. Torn from skin and bone and pushed deeper into blackness.

Sh—

What was that word I was holding on to?

What was that feeling?

It was all for something.

Or for someone.

What was it?

"Come now, boy. Say my name."

"Caelius, I can't breathe!"

Was that the name I was looking for, alone in the dark?

"Call me God."

"God, I'm dying, save me!"

"Of course, darling. Always."

Caelius, my god.

Caelius, my savior.

That was the name.

The only name I needed to reach out for in the darkness, to never be alone.

CHAPTER 5
SHEA

I stared in shock, and a little bit of awe, as Ur-Nammu decapitated one of Caelius's vampires with his hand.

His freaking *hand*!

It was like Ur-Nammu had transformed it into a butcher knife, the head came off so clean. I was in the middle of trying to connect to the wind, to create some kind of hurricane or something, but watching Ur-Nammu fight was mesmerizing.

Here on this strange battlefield, an abandoned playground outside of Toledo, I could truly see the warrior he'd once been. He no longer looked like the grandfather figure I had grown used to. He was in his element and had been born to fight.

And he was terrifying.

He was currently protecting Meky and Sherit, not that they needed it. Nothing registered on his radar except his grandchildren, not even protecting me, who was supposed to be a superweapon against Caelius. Though at the moment, Ur-

Nammu did *sort of* inch his way toward me when another vamp got closer.

Luckily, there were no witnesses to see this epic battle. The playground was next to a condemned elementary school in a neighborhood that had been demolished in favor of a slew of McMansions. Construction hadn't begun yet; there was only dirt and debris for a half mile in every direction. Whenever Aidan's angel-sense picked up that vampires were close, we'd book it to the nearest unpopulated place. The last thing I wanted was for any innocent bystanders to be killed.

This was the tenth attack so far.

Mom hadn't been kidding when she said Caelius would come after us. Luckily, he'd sent what Ur-Nammu called "lesser vampires," which were no match for a group of Second-Borns, an angel, and a Vessel. As if to prove my point, Duncan easily ripped one of the vampires *in half* before decapitating them.

We had killed thirty already. My dad had taken out the first two quickly, and Helena had used some kind of device to take out the next three. The rest were a joint effort with Ur-Nammu and Duncan doing the heavy lifting.

Now there were only five left.

Suddenly, a particularly vicious vampire made a mad dash for me, her red hair flying behind her like some kind of comet with teeth. Without thinking, I connected to the air around me and, in a flash, there was a ten-foot tornado wrapping itself around my attacker. I couldn't tell who looked more shocked, me or her.

Another vampire took his chance and leapt toward me, completely clearing the eight-foot parallel bars between us, but Ur-Nammu was on it. He grabbed him by his head in midair and squeezed with his hands and—

Pop!

Gross.

I think I just swallowed a piece of brain. Nope, scratch that—it was skull.

I could feel the tiny piece move down my esophagus like a half-eaten tortilla chip.

What was Ur-Nammu's obsession with heads? He was either decapitating them or popping them like grapes. I wasn't complaining, but it was pretty disgusting. Thinking about it a little more though, taking out the head was most likely the quickest way to kill a vampire.

Three left.

Meky jumped on the back of a large vampire who must have been a linebacker before he was turned. Her petite frame looked like she'd be no match for him. But Meky was a Second-Born, not to mention the daughter of a badass warrior queen, which kind of made her a princess warrior in her own right. With no effort, Meky ripped off both the large vampire's arms at the same time, held them like trophies, then tossed them to the ground. Before the vampire could react, she easily ripped off his head and tossed it next to his arms. What was left of the vampire's torso slumped over, hitting the end of a slide.

Two more.

Duncan snapped another vampire's spine, breaking her in half before ripping off her head. Everyone had their signature move.

The last one was all Aidan. Placing his hand on the vamp's chest, he poured Light into the woman until there was nothing left but a black husk of charcoal.

"Is that tornado girl coming back?" Sherit asked.

"I really don't know," I answered honestly.

"I don't sense her. I think she ran." Aidan walked over to me. "You okay?"

I wasn't. But I nodded. "Yeah, we should get going though."

Dad leapt over a broken seesaw, landing at my side. "I killed those first two *vamps*. Did you see?" He looked at me for approval.

I still wasn't used to my parents being immortal, but I was glad he could take care of himself now. And he wasn't killing people, he was killing vampires, which was good . . . even though *he* was one, and so were all these other people, and my mother, and ugh.

"Yes, good job, Dad," I answered. "You killed some *vamps*." I couldn't help but tease him. He was my dad—it was my job. And shortening vampires to vamps was very *dad-like*.

He laughed. "Would you prefer bloodsuckers? Leeches? The Vampeer?"

Aidan and Duncan nudged each other, both appreciating the humor. They had become fast friends. Their personalities were so much alike that it had proved my theory correct: Lucian had turned Duncan because he reminded him of Aidan. Duncan didn't seem to mind though. He actually seemed honored by the fact, calling Aidan his brother-from-another-mother.

Walking toward the minivan we'd rented, we all smooshed in and drove away. To where? I had no idea.

Twelve hours later, we pulled up to a small motel outside of Duluth, right on the water of Lake Superior. Driving for that long had made me more than a little stir-crazy. At least if we got into a fight here, I could use the water to our advantage.

It had been a while since Nefertiti had left with Mom, and we were exhausted from the constant cycle of running and fighting. Looking over at the motel, I noticed that the building itself was run-down and appeared to only have ten rooms. There were two cars parked in the lot, so at least it was empty-ish.

"Please tell me we're going to book a minimum of three rooms this time," I complained from the back of the eight-seater van that squished Dad, Aidan, Ur-Nammu, Meky, Duncan, Sherit, Helena and me together. With the speed all vampires seemed to possess, I'd thought we'd travel by supernatural means, but I guessed that method was the easiest for Caelius to track. Since the guy had been trapped underground for the last three thousand years, he didn't know much about technology, hence the deluxe minivan we were all currently crammed into.

Everyone, including me, felt better with Dad at the wheel. He had the most experience driving, and with the amount of road trips he'd done over the years, he knew his way around the States.

"One room," Aidan called back from the front passenger seat, his tone leaving no room for argument. Since I was the only one who needed sleep, we'd been renting a single room and paying cash, for safety's sake. We didn't want any detective-vampires to track us the old-fashioned way like the diner vamp had with me and Aidan when all of this had just started.

"I'll order an extra cot so it won't look suspicious," Aidan announced, as if that would somehow make me feel better.

"Yeah, because four grown men and women renting a single room isn't suspicious at all. That extra cot will totally make us seem legit." I didn't bother to hide the sarcasm in my voice.

Duncan laughed and gave me an approving nod from the first row.

Aidan ignored me, but I could see the remnants of a smile as he left the van and headed to the lobby.

"Can we get out now?" Meky was losing patience as well. I couldn't blame her. Since we were the smallest, we had both been designated to the middle seats in the van. With Duncan on her right and Ur-Nammu on her left, the girl was pancaked. At least I had Helena and Sherit next to me, which gave me a lot more elbow room.

Duncan jumped out and slid open the side door so everyone could leave. Only Dad stayed inside, ready to park the car in front of our new temporary abode. I practically shoved Helena out to get some air, but she didn't mind. She was just as relieved to be free of our minivan prison.

Aidan came back, dangling a key.

Off to our motel room prison now.

I wished Caelius would die already.

"We're over there, number 4." Aidan turned to lead the way.

After hearing the number, Dad drove ahead and parked in front of our room.

Exiting the van, he walked over to me. "You got your things?"

Such a dad.

I walked over and pulled a small bag out of the back of the van with all my toiletries. "Got it." Being the only human, I was a little jealous that no one had to brush their teeth like I did. Luckily, my dad had packed everything I needed before we'd even started our cross-country-runaway-from-Caelius-a-thon.

Aidan unlocked the door, then ran off to get the cot.

Walking into the motel room, I tried not to cringe at the carpet. It looked like it hadn't been vacuumed in a century. There were two queen beds, a small desk, a dresser with a television on top, a chair, and a door to the bathroom. Same room, different city.

I'd wanted to get an Airbnb, except I didn't trust my newbie vampire dad to not eat the homeowners. And besides, with everything that had happened in Paris, Airbnb hosts weren't exactly in a trusting mood either.

America still acted like it was immune to a massive attack, despite Paris. But keeping to the smaller towns and cities definitely helped in terms of visibility, although it did feel like we were on the verge of a zombie apocalypse.

Plopping down on the bed, I secretly hoped Caelius's goons would find us soon because this place was a real crap-hole. Carrying a cot over his head, Aidan entered the room and set it down in front of the dresser, making it even more cramped.

"Glad you got that cot." I couldn't help myself.

Aidan shook his head and chuckled. "You're such a dork."

Duncan laughed too. "Lose the cot, lad. I'll compel anyone who looks at us funny."

"I can't return it now. That'll be even weirder." Aidan looked appalled at the thought.

"Oh, for crying out loud." Dad took it and left the motel room, grumbling.

I savored the moment.

Not because it proved my point that we were overcrowded, but because it reminded me so much of how things used to be.

96

In that moment, Aidan was my best friend growing up, and Dad was . . . Dad, rolling his eyes at Aidan being too embarrassed to return anything. He was the adult, and Aidan was the child—a child he'd helped raise, since Aidan had been glued to my side our entire lives. It made me miss those days terribly.

Seeing my expression, Duncan placed a hand on my shoulder. "I can get the cot back for ye, lass, if ye want it that badly."

I shook my head. "No. I was just remembering simpler times."

Duncan seemed to understand completely, his expression turning solemn. "We'll have them again."

A moment later, Dad walked back in with another set of keys. "I got the room next door." Before Aidan could object, Dad nodded toward a closed door I hadn't noticed next to the dresser. "They open up to each other. We can guard two rooms. It'll be fine, Aidan."

He reluctantly nodded, and I leapt into my dad's open arms. "Thanks." I grabbed the key and walked outside, letting myself into the nearly identical room. After opening both adjoining doors, we officially had two whole rooms to hang out in. It was luxury living as far as I was concerned.

I lay down on one of the queen beds and enjoyed being alone, even if it was just for a moment. I knew it wouldn't last long, but it made me feel so much better.

And it lasted for all of three seconds.

"Shea Harper, may I speak with you?" Ur-Nammu walked into the room cautiously. His expression said that he didn't want to bother me, so I knew it must be important.

I sat up on the edge of the bed. "Of course. What do you

need?" I motioned for him to sit on the bed across from me.

He complied and took in a deep breath. "I'm not sure what to do."

That was intense language for Ur-Nammu.

"We're in this together. I'll help any way I can." I tried to put the ancient vampire at ease.

Taking a moment to gather his thoughts, Ur-Nammu finally spoke. "I've been trying to Dream-Walk with Nefertiti since she left. Now that we know Caelius can't hear us, there's no reason why she wouldn't communicate with me." He paused, unsure of how to continue. "I fear the worst."

"You think Caelius *killed* Nefertiti? No way. Wouldn't you *feel* that? And Caelius would want to rub it in our faces. He'd make that public. She's not dead. I'm certain." I wasn't certain, but I couldn't just watch Ur-Nammu suffer like this. We had a complicated relationship at best, but I was certain of one thing: family meant *everything* to him.

"Then maybe she's under his blood control," Ur-Nammu said with a kind of helplessness I completely related to. "It's unlike her. We've always been close. Human or immortal, there was never a time she didn't confide in me. Not in Gutium, not in Egypt."

"Maybe she's gathering intel that will help us defeat Caelius, and she doesn't want him thinking she's Dream-Walking? And if she's being blood-controlled, then we have to assume Lucian is *definitely* being controlled. I just hope I can do something about it," I vented. This whole blood-compelling crap had me more worried than I let on. I knew from what I had accomplished with Helena that I could remove Caelius's shadow, but blood?

Ur-Nammu sat forward, anxious. "I know it's not proper to ask, but will you try to reach Nefertiti? Maybe she's too ashamed to talk to me, or afraid that if I learn that she's in danger, I will try and find out where she is and get myself killed rescuing her."

Ding. Ding. Ding. "Yeah, it's that last one. She would totally think that because it's true, right?" With sudden clarity, I was positive that Nefertiti was keeping her distance from Ur-Nammu on purpose.

His face told me that I was right.

"I can't just leave her there with *him*," he grumbled under his breath.

Shaking my head and commiserating wholeheartedly, I reached over and lightly touched Ur-Nammu's hand to comfort him. "I can't promise anything. Nefertiti and I don't exactly have the greatest of friendships, but I'll try."

Ur-Nammu squeezed my hand. "I appreciate the effort. Thank you, Shea Harper."

"It's just Shea. You don't have to say my last name like I'm some kind of celebrity or something. It's weird." I smiled, teasing him. Although I really shouldn't have complained. Aidan's brothers only called me Vessel. My whole name was a huge improvement.

But Ur-Nammu smiled back. "Thank you again, *Shea*."

Aww. We were having a moment.

I didn't want to spoil it by saying something stupid, so I pulled my hand away and lay back on the bed. "No time like the present."

Ur-Nammu stood up and, with a slight pep to his walk, left my side and began to close the door that joined the rooms. "I'll give you some privacy."

Nodding, I closed my eyes, knowing full well that Aidan and my dad would have that door opened seconds after Ur-Nammu closed it. But I tuned all the background noise out and concentrated on falling asleep anyway. I took deep calming breaths. I'd learned to switch into Dream-Walk mode much quicker than I used to.

Concentrating on Nefertiti, I breathed in and held . . . breathed out and held . . .

Breathed in . . . and . . .

Opening my eyes, I was in the middle of . . . Miami Beach?

I could tell because I could see the famous hotel from the movie *Goldfinger*. What was it called? The Fontainebleau? I'd always wanted to go there, but being a college student, it was way out of my price range. Plus, finding out I was a Vessel and being hunted by what equated to *the devil* kind of put a damper on traveling for pleasure. Besides, Miami was supposedly a cesspool for rebellious vampires. Caelius had sent Ur-Nammu there once to keep the extra murderous ones in line. But still, even being in this dreamscape made me worried that I might get bitten.

I stood on the white sand beach and waited nervously.

This was definitely not a regular dream. I was definitely Dream-Walking.

But with whom?

I sighed in relief when I heard Nefertiti's voice. "It's about time you came."

Turning around, I faced the annoyingly beautiful vampire. "I hadn't realized you were ignoring your own father."

Why did she always bring out my angry side? Oh, right. She was Lucian's ex, and I was extremely jealous of her.

100

"My father would only get himself killed," Nefertiti said with a sigh.

"He's really worried about you. He thought you might be blood-controlled." I chose to lose my attitude.

"Thankfully, Caelius doesn't deem me worthy enough to drink his blood. He's reserving that for your mother and Lucian." Nefertiti's expression turned hard. "He's giving Lucian gallons of it. It's the only thing that will erase you from his memory."

I didn't know if I should be flattered or puke. Luckily, I was in a dreamscape, so if I threw up it would just disappear, but I wanted to curl up and cry for Lucian. What would that much of Caelius's blood do to him?

"My mother too? The tons of blood, I mean?" I didn't want to ask, but I had to know.

Nefertiti shook her head. "No. He only gives her a drop a day. It used to be a drop a week, but the memories of you are powerful." She paused as if what she was about to say next was difficult. "It seems you are well loved."

My feelings were so conflicted I could barely think straight. Lucian and my mother were being force-fed Caelius's blood, but they were so strong that they were fighting it. I hoped I could help somehow. I just needed to be in the same room with them, to touch them, to hug them, to *be* with them.

"I brought you here for a reason." Nefertiti cut my thoughts short.

"You brought *me* here? I'm the one who contacted you." There was my weird defensiveness again.

"Like I said before, I've been waiting for you to Dream-Walk with me for a couple of weeks now. Some of those vampires

Caelius sent were messengers, not assassins. They were the worst of our kind though, so I can't say I'm not happy they were killed. Caelius wants to make a new deal with me and my family, and I have to agree to keep them safe.

"I'll still work as a double agent, but I'm only communicating with *you,* not my father. Caelius knows this. He can't overhear us, but if he really wanted to, he could feed me his blood and make me tell him everything we talk about." Nefertiti paused thoughtfully, then continued. "I doubt Caelius would do this. He abhors giving your mother even a drop. He only wants Lucian to have it. The thought of giving me his blood makes Caelius physically wretch. He hates me because Lucian loved me unconditionally."

She stared at me intensely as she said, "But Caelius hates you more than the Light itself because every fiber of Lucian's soul is entwined with yours."

And from the look on her face, I got the feeling Nefertiti hated me just as much for the same reason.

It didn't give me comfort hearing those words though.

I loved Lucian just as much, if not more, but the reason Caelius was torturing him was *because* of our love. Our love would destroy him. Caelius would rather see him dead than to see him love another. Caelius wanted Lucian all to himself, and that would never happen because of how he and I felt about each other.

Nefertiti didn't wait for my response as she said, "The plan is simple. Caelius wants his Adam and Eve again, but he wants an Eve he can control: me. He's rewritten Lucian's memories so that *you* are responsible for the death of my daughters and his Second-

Borns, including the torture and murder of Gracuri." She let that sink in. Her eyes actually showed sympathy, but her speech did not.

She was all soldier as she continued. "Caelius wants Meky and Sherit returned to me and Lucian so that Caelius can convince Lucian his memories of what you did are real. Ur-Nammu will be exiled but not killed. Caelius *will* kill my father if he sees him again. Are we understood?"

I stood paralyzed.

My heart and brain squeezed in pain.

Lucian's memories of me were *gone*. They'd been replaced with fake ones where I was the enemy who'd killed the people he loved.

He'd never forgive me.

He wouldn't even want to.

Lucian would look at me with hate, and I didn't know if I could survive that.

Nefertiti waved her hand in front of my face to get my attention. "Shea? I need to know that you understand the situation."

I tried to gather my wits, but it was difficult, so I focused on the part of the plan that caused me the least amount of pain. "Meky will never agree to go to Caelius, and why would you want her to? Caelius could kill her or Sherit on a whim. You're willing to risk that?"

"Meky will do as she's told to save her family," Nefertiti said plainly. "And trust me, Caelius keeps his promises. He kept his promise to me for three thousand years."

"Was that before or after he decapitated Merytaten?" I knew

it was harsh, but I couldn't believe she was considering putting Meky and Sherit in danger like that.

"I betrayed Caelius, and the deal was off. It was fair rules of battle. I would have done the same to an enemy who'd broken an agreement," she said.

"Are you being serious right now? Nothing that Caelius does is *fair*. Caelius would have no issues whatsoever killing your daughters and then claiming he was justified. If you think any different, you're delusional." I was angry for Meky and Sherit, but mainly angry at the fact that I was helpless to do anything for anyone.

Nefertiti paused, then eyed me carefully. "I have no choice. If Meky and Sherit don't come, Caelius promises he will kill *all* my daughters. At least this way they have a chance."

"Don't do this! We're going to find a way to kill Caelius, you just have to be patient!" I was taking all my frustration and anger out on Nefertiti, but I couldn't stop myself.

"Patient?" She stayed calm but stern. "I waited and planned for decades before you were even born. We failed. We will always fail. And my children paid the price. I will *not* risk that again. If you have a plan, you will execute it with my daughters safely by my side."

She stepped forward, her stature commanding. "Tell Meky and Sherit to meet here, where we are standing at Miami Beach, in the real world. Miami is Caelius's next conquest. He's preparing to destroy the entire city as he did Paris." Then her expression softened as she said, "Please, Shea, convince my daughters if needed. I can't lose another child to this madness."

I was out of steam. I couldn't argue anymore, so I simply

nodded in agreement.

"And one more thing," Nefertiti said flatly. "I used this connection to figure out where you are, and I'm going to tell Caelius as soon as we end this Dream-Walk, so I suggest you leave quickly."

With a loud clap, I was thrown out of the dreamscape, and my eyes flew open.

Sitting up in bed, I noticed I was alone, but like I had assumed, the door was open.

Hurrying into the other room, I yelled, "We have to get out of here! Nefertiti is telling Caelius where we are!"

"So she *is* being blood-controlled," Ur-Nammu said.

"No. She's her stubborn self, but she's still playing the double agent, so she gave me a heads-up that she planned to tell Caelius where we were." I made sure my eyes met Meky's then Sherit's as I said, "You have to meet her in Miami Beach near the Fontainebleau."

I quickly explained all the details of the conversation I'd had with Nefertiti.

Meky was livid. "She wants us to lie to Lucian and pretend we're one big happy family? No way. This is ridiculous!"

Sherit, on the other hand, didn't seem as upset. "Meky, Mother knows what's best to keep us alive. She's been doing it for over three thousand years now. We need to trust her."

Whirling on her sister, Meky argued, "And you're okay with throwing Shea under the bus? Telling Lucian that Shea killed our sisters and his Second-Borns?" Meky turned to me, shaking her head. "I won't do it, Shea. Don't worry. I have your back."

Aidan looked at his girlfriend with pride and clasped Meky's hand. "I'll keep you safe this time."

"I can keep myself safe, but I love you for being so protective." Meky smiled.

I wanted to keep our group together, but the more I thought about Nefertiti's words, the more I knew she was right.

"Meky, you have to go," I found myself saying.

"Shea, no. I won't," Meky said stubbornly.

"Caelius told your mom he'd kill *all* her children. Sete is already there. I won't be responsible for her death. Lucian would never recover. Plus, I need you there. You're the only one I trust." I hurriedly looked at Sherit. "No offense."

"None taken," Sherit replied back. "My mother and I respect you and everything you've done to try and destroy Caelius, but we have no affection for you. Not like Meky does, apparently." Then Sherit added, "No offense."

"I don't know how anyone could be offended by that," I said sarcastically, but Sherit had proven my point. Meky and I had grown closer since the final battle, and I considered her a true friend. Heck, she was most likely going to marry Aidan, so that practically made us sisters anyway. I turned to Meky one last time. "Please, Meky."

After a long pause, she finally nodded. "All right, I'll go. But if Caelius tries to hurt you, I'm out."

"Deal. Thank you." It wasn't much comfort, but it was a little.

Aidan looked like I'd ripped his heart out, but he didn't argue. He leaned down and gently kissed Meky. It made my heart squeeze in guilt.

Ur-Nammu stepped in. "I'm going with you girls all the same. I know Miami well. I can keep to the shadows as not to be found out by Caelius, but there is nothing you can say or do that will stop me. I'd gladly die if it means your safety. I'll be near if you need me."

Not surprisingly, no one argued because everyone, including Nefertiti (though she'd be reluctant to admit it), knew that no one could stop Ur-Nammu. Nefertiti would be livid, but there was nothing I could do.

Helena glanced at the window. "Caelius's goons will be here soon. We should leave."

"On to the next hotel?" Dad asked, a little too excited to get back into the van for my taste.

"I'd rather use the water in that lake out there and transport us all in a giant wave than go back into that van," I grumbled. "Or maybe air? I could tornado us to the next state? Or if I could master earth I could earthquake us to California? Anything but that horrible van!"

Helena froze.

I was instantly on guard.

From the look on her face, the goons must have arrived.

Duncan noticed too. "Helena? What's wrong? Are they here?"

Helena shook her head. "No. I think I just had an idea of how to destroy Caelius, but it involves Shea mastering all four elements, which means we need a place for her to practice."

Meky raised an eyebrow. "Are you going to use that other contraption you used to talk about, the one you said was too risky and would never work?"

Helena nodded, then explained it to the rest of us. "It's a device I abandoned, but I was mind-controlled at the time. Now that I'm myself again, I think Shea's powers just might do the trick. I have a lab that I'm certain Caelius knows nothing about. In all my years as a vampire, I never visited it once. I must have subconsciously protected it. I would have taken us there earlier, but I didn't want to be forced to destroy it if Caelius found us. It's worth the risk for this now though." Her face brightened at the thought. "This could work!"

I tried to match her enthusiasm with a smile, but my stomach turned at the realization that whatever this device was, it relied on me mastering *all* the elements.

No pressure.

Can I vomit now?

CHAPTER 6
LUCIAN

The Light.

I'd done it.

I'd brought the Vessel to Caelius, and he was free.

But why?

Why would I want him *free*? I'd always used the Vessels to torture Adnachiel. It was strange. I must have gotten bored to the point of madness, because now, looking at his auburn eyes, I questioned my judgment. They were searing into me, alight as if they were on fire like my blood was.

I was radiating power. I could feel it move in waves off of me, vibrating between his body and mine. But his blood fogged my brain like a thick tar pumping through my synapses. I was desperately trying to piece together why I would *willingly* free him, knowing this would be the outcome. He caressed my cheek as a memory pushed through the fog: our bodies intertwined, him lifting us into the air over the fields of Gutium.

I pulled away from his touch. "Why would I do that . . . ?"

He pulled me back toward him, holding me tighter in his arms. He licked his lips and pressed his mouth to the soft spot behind my ear as he spoke. "What is it, darling?"

My body tensed instinctively as he moved his hands up and down my back, finally resting them on my hips and squeezing hard.

"We . . . I *willingly* gave myself to you, in my homeland?"

He licked a long line down my neck, nipping at my collar bone, then sucking it gently, leaving a bruise that healed quickly as he pulled away. With agitation, he glared at the place the mark had been. "Permanence. I want all the things I give and do for you to last, Lucian." He leaned his torso back and locked eyes with me. "Because you're *mine*, after all."

Mine.

It was a powerful word for our kind, and I felt it in every inch of my body as it yielded to him. It yearned to be held a while longer. I ached for Caelius. "It's your blood. That's why I'm like this."

He bit the side of his lip, scrutinizing my features. "We've gone over this, my sweet. After you freed me in the last battle with the Vessel, she almost killed you. I had no choice but to feed you my blood. It was to save your life, just as I did in Egypt when you were killed by the Pharaoh, just as I promised when you were a boy in Gutium. I was and will always be your salvation. I've wanted you for so long. Can't you *feel* it now, the knowledge that we will *always* belong together?"

I did.

There was no way I *couldn't* feel him, his desire, his obsession, his body. Right now he was my world, but he had broken me enough times in the cave before he'd been free for me to understand what his blood was doing. I knew this wasn't real; this was a fevered intoxication created and controlled by him alone. However, understanding my situation and being able to resist him were two different things.

"I don't . . ." I couldn't look away from his eyes. It sickened me, but I *wanted* him to be the one who gave me the answers. I *wanted* him to be my salvation, my lover, my everything. I tried to choke down the yearning, but it was impossible. "What's happening to me?"

He smirked, looking over my body. "It's been a few days, and you haven't let me leave this bed. Even now the look of desire, the longing for me to fill your loins, it's enough to drive even a being like me into heat."

I swallowed hard, realizing that we were indeed in bed. His body was just as naked as my own; we were meshed, flesh against flesh with our legs intertwined.

"How did I get here?" I meant that in more ways than one. I didn't even know what city we were in. By the look of the bedding and room, I was wrapped in his arms in some high-priced hotel.

This had to be the effect of his blood, blood he had happily given to save my life. In the cave, he'd spoken of it for centuries like it was holy. It was something he would never give to any human swine, yet he was feeding so much of it to me that I *yearned* for it.

It didn't make sense. I was long since healed from the damage of the Vessel. I didn't *need* it. I had to wean myself off of him or risk losing myself to his control completely. As it was, I had

111

no memory, only his words that elicited images that *must* be memories. But they were foggy and incomplete.

Scattered.

Like I was.

The only thing that felt familiar was this feeling of dissolving like paper in water. It was like a black emptiness was hollowing out something important inside of me. What was it that I was clinging to besides him? Wasn't there anyone else? Where were my children, my Second-Borns?

Gracuri would answer me honestly. He was a part of the world, enough to know what was going on outside of Caelius's control. I could trust him. I could contact David, Duncan, or Bohe . . . no. Bohe I could trust, but he was secluded, and it was better for him that he stayed that way. He was safe from all of this. My chest ached with a strange sensation at thinking of my children. Where were they now? Why couldn't I *feel* them? It was as if our strings had been cut. Was Caelius's blood strong enough to break the maker-bond between me and my children?

The ache persisted. Was this loss? Guilt? Sorrow? How many days had it *really* been since I last knew what was real and what was Caelius?

He pulled my chin up, steadying my darting eyes. "Rest assured, I will repeat what happened as many times as you need me to. But first, let's get you dressed. Like a good god, I have a present for my obedient son."

I instinctively leaned forward and kissed his lips, a moan escaping my mouth.

He laughed, flicking his tongue against mine before pulling back. "Not that kind of *present,* darling." He was enthralled, his

112

body limp and relaxed. He looked almost as drunk as I felt. But there was something else behind his affectionate gaze, something under the surface I couldn't scratch no matter how many times I clawed his back as he sank his hips into mine. His restlessness to reveal what was buried matched my desire to find it. What was I looking for? What was he hiding?

He looked over my body as a painter would his masterpiece, touching the fading bruises and teeth indentations. "I was gentle this time, wasn't I? I stayed flesh for you. I didn't do anything you didn't like."

I laughed outright, then caught myself, choking back my outburst. It was true that he hadn't taken me in shadow form, but that didn't mean an immortal body had been any more forgiving.

He smiled nonetheless. "It was gentle for *me*, I suppose. I am a god, you know."

He scanned my face, that same strange look overtaking his features. "Where are you really, La-Narru? Will you ever come to me again by choice?"

I looked at the tossed sheets and dented bed frame. "I'm here with you now, aren't I?"

He touched my face, letting his hand rest at my cheek. "Do you remember meeting me for the first time yet?"

"Uh . . . yes. I—"

"Don't placate me, boy." His hand dropped, and he averted his eyes. Those eyes, the same ones that had looked up at me with such hope a moment ago, were now tinted with bitterness. "We went over this last time I was deep inside you, and yet you've forgotten. This is a *real* memory, it happened, so why can't you pull it from the recesses of your mind? It's so important. Why

113

can't you remember me?"

I fumbled, unable to follow yet yearning to please him all the same. "I'm sorry, tell me again—"

"Before Nefertiti laid her *tainted* lips on you, before you lost your mother to sickness, you loved me. *I* was your first." His voice grew distant as he looked out our bedroom window.

"I don't know the age in human years, but you were young." He turned his face to meet mine. There it was again; the longing I thought would be satiated after days in bed still burned when I saw the deep auburn of his eyes.

"I had been in human form for some time. And it bored me. It was a little wager, an experiment between me and the Light. This planet had its time, just like every world, but the Light protected it, extended it past reason and balance, and I couldn't fathom why. The Light offered a deal: I could experience what it was like to be alive, just this once. And I was . . . disappointed."

I winced, and my jaw hardened under his tender touch. "Of course you were disappointed." That felt true on every level. No matter what state I was in now, it would never be enough to quench his eternal needs.

He pulled my head up and placed a small kiss on my mouth, nibbling on my lower lip before he pulled back. "Until I met you." He licked the side of my face, the salty sweetness that must have been my skin, enthralling him further.

"Darkness in human form is still not human, after all. And you could sense it right away." He stroked his hand gently down my frame. "You were awestruck. The things that you said to me, I often replay the moment in my mind. The words that you *can't remember*, I will never forget."

"Is . . . is that when I called you God?" His eyes searched everywhere but my own. Then he leaned his face closer so that he was all that filled my gaze.

"Yes. You asked if I was a god. And I said that I could be *your* god." He pulled away as I grimaced. "Are you embarrassed?"

"N-no." I couldn't fathom the child part of me that would be so foolish. But before the wars we had been raised to believe in gods, and in that ignorance I had enticed a being of Darkness.

He looked away again. The uneasiness that had settled earlier sank further into my skin. All of this stuttering and placating. It was similar to the behavior I'd exhibited when I'd been *forced*, when he had broken me in the past. But this was different. This time he wanted more—

"La-Narru."

My eyes shot up. I still hated hearing him call me by my Gutian name.

"The meaning of your birth name in your native tongue couldn't be more true. However, it's the custom of *your* people to be given a new name after you've proven yourself as a warrior to the gods, though your father never gave you the honor after your Harrowing. When you asked me to take you, to save your life under Nefertiti's window so that you could see her again, did I not honor you in your own tradition by naming you Lucian? By claiming you as my own? I let you live a mortal life, unhindered by my touch, until it came to its natural end. Then your life was *mine*. It's what you asked for as a child: that in death we would join, that you could be with me again, your *god*. You promised. Have I not . . . have I not given you everything you've asked for?"

My mouth fell open. Incensed, I tried to grasp his words.

115

"Everything I've asked for? I would have never asked for this—"

"Careful." He hardened his jaw as if holding his rage in place.

I softened my tone. "I don't remember. I only remember the night of the Harrowing. I'm sure I was too young to understand what my words meant."

He rolled his neck, stretching his shoulders and straightening his back. "Why is the feeling of vulnerability now growing alongside disgust?" He stood tall. I struggled to rise next to him but fell to the floor, my legs weak from his passions.

"I want to help you up, to hold you again. At the same time, my mouth is filled with bile." He coughed, reaching for me and lifting me to my feet all the same.

"I wasted my one chance, my one time being human, on you, *boy*. Look at us now, all because of some stupid promise I made to you by that river." He laughed, the sound full and rich and bitter. "The Light's little dogs never would have imprisoned me if I hadn't broken that single arbitrary rule to save you. I was never supposed to take a life. And now there is no escaping it; what's done is done. Because of *you* I suffered all of this time in mortal form, caged for *thousands* of years. Now I will set this world on fire as my revenge. I will destroy everything you've loved . . . just to have what you promised me in Gutium."

His fingernails grew instinctually and pierced my arms.

"I don't understand. I'm yours! How else can I prove it to you?" I fumbled, fearing what his threat meant. I had nothing left to lose, but Caelius was inventive, and I had my Second-Borns to think of. "I only want to please you." It sickened me, but it was true enough. His blood pulsed inside me with every word he spoke.

116

He let me go and sighed. "Of course you do . . . *now*. But this isn't the way I wanted it. When you willingly offered yourself to me, I thought you were finally keeping your word, that you at last returned my feelings, but it was a lie spoken for *their* sake."

"What lie? For whom? What do you mean?" I couldn't remember what he was talking about.

"Never mind that, little one. Power. Control. Forcing you to my will. That is something I know well. And now, out of the cage, I can do it completely and make you *mine* for good. None of this 'willing acceptance of love.' If you're not going to *give* it to me freely, then I'm going to take it, darling."

He kissed me long and deep, then pulled back. "Don't worry your mind with these things. I'm just talking to myself, working things out, as it were. You just relax into my presence, and enjoy my fevered touches like you have been. You are clay now. Trust the hands of your sculptor; I have your best interest at heart. That is why I prepared this gift for you."

He dressed me slowly, fitting me in a silk Hanfu with a bright yellow sash. It was beautiful.

He watched me closely as I studied the fabric. "Is this the gift? It feels familiar somehow."

"This isn't the gift. This is just a Hanfu I've cleaned for you, sweetheart." His gaze was resolute. "You liked it, so we took it off the dead body of a boy. He never would have looked as handsome as you wearing it. No harm done, right?" There it was again, that look in his eyes, like he was masking something important. "And the yellow sash I picked up anew. It sounds like a wedding rhyme, doesn't it? Something borrowed, something new, something yellow . . ." He brushed his thumb by my eyes.

117

"Something blue." He smiled, but his teeth were clenched in anticipation. "Do you like it? Is it not agreeable?"

I couldn't explain the warm affection I felt for this Hanfu. "It feels . . . like it's *mine*." It felt like it had been pressed up against me, held in my arms, like it was something precious I couldn't put words to. "It's like it belonged to me before, but I have no memory of it. I lost it."

I lost it.

My own words struck the growing ache in my heart.

The feeling of loss.

That was familiar too.

Caelius took in a long breath. "No memory, huh? Think hard, dear one." He waited. His eyes were now cold and calculating. The quick shift from affection to distaste was jarring. As the moments passed, my mouth felt dry. Was this some kind of test? Was I *supposed* to remember something?

I searched, but it came up empty, like a gaping hole had been dug out of my mind with a rusted spade. The only thing remaining was a nameless ache.

Still, he leaned closer, like a cobra gazing down at a cornered mouse, the black in his irises opening like slits, threatening to overcome the vermilion.

"Like the memory from childhood. *Should* I remember something?" I whined. "I'm sorry, Father, I don't . . " I looked up at him in desperation. I felt like that lost mouse, wanting nothing more than to be comforted by his hands, even if he was the hunter who had brought me here.

I felt so alone.

Without my memories to anchor me, the pain of the past

118

felt more present. The death of my tribe, the loss of Nefertiti and Moses . . . the loss of Adnachiel.

He sighed, elated. "Of course you don't remember. It was just some material you liked off of a dead boy, nothing important."

He seemed pleased, but I hated it. I had my past, a past where I hadn't been subservient to Caelius. A past full of betrayal and torment. A past that I had always wanted to forget but now clung to like it was precious milk, feeding my life's purpose. And I could remember all of it, every detail. Everything except this last *year*. The question kept repeating: How had I gone from hating Caelius and keeping him in his cage to lying in his lap like some schoolboy in the arms of his first love?

"My present awaits." Caelius fiddled with the yellow sash, tying the bow at my back a little tighter. "You can come in now. This will be the *fourth* time, but hopefully I'll get the reaction I'm looking for." His tone was cold as his gaze shifted to the door, but it warmed considerably when he wrapped his arms around my waist and whispered into my ear. "I think you're ready this time, darling."

"Fourth time for what?" I squirmed in his grip.

He released me and sat on the bed candidly, his eyes again intent on the doorway.

A figure stepped through.

I blinked, then fell to my knees.

"Impossible," I muttered. "You're *dead*! I killed you myself!"

Her gaze flickered to Caelius in a flash of contempt before returning to me and softening. There were lines on the sides of her eyes, grooves that the black eyeliner couldn't hide. There was a weariness there I had never seen in Nefertiti in all of our days in

Gutium, nor in all of the long nights in Egypt.

She walked toward me, then knelt at my feet.

"It is I, my love."

Caelius sneered at her words, but I couldn't take my eyes off of her. I pressed my head into her shoulder. My body ached to weep into her, to believe that this wasn't some blood-induced dream. Tears tumbled down her back, the wet falling on her skin like it had in the endless dunes of the Libyan desert. Every tear that had evaporated in the sand had screamed her name. And now in her arms, I found myself doing the same. "Nefari! You're alive," I wept.

Through the weeping she spoke, but I couldn't hear her. I clung to her as I had when Onack had whipped my back as a boy, when I'd lost my mother, when I had eaten ash and she had saved me from my father . . . and myself.

Finally, there was another name besides Caelius in the dark. "You're really here, aren't you, Nefari? *Please* be real. I don't want to be alone anymore."

"Of course I'm here beside you, La-Narru. For ours is a proud people," she said. In her voice I heard a hesitancy that was also unknown to me. "We are etched into the existence of all things. Are we not then bound by love and fate? Do you think that anything could truly smite the Gutian tribe?" Her grip tightened around my back, almost painfully. To hear our Gutian code referenced so easily through Nefari's lips—as if it had always been there, as if time had not eroded it away—was a dream, a dream I didn't want to wake from.

"How? Besides your father, I thought I was the last Gutian left," I whispered, my chest convulsing. The girl I had kissed by the river in our childhood, the girl I had made love to by the Nile, the daughter of Ur-Nammu, future leader of Gutium, the wife of the Pharaoh, my everything, she was *alive*.

This must be it.

Even as my blood pulsed for Caelius, a part of me resisted with everything I had left. A part of me was reaching for *something*. It was as if I were clawing like an animal trying to dig itself out of a stone cave, buried deep in the black. This must've been the name, the memory I'd been looking for in the nothingness: Nefari.

"It's you. It has to be you." I clung to her arms. "It's always been you."

I held on to that resolution.

And it brought me peace.

This must have been what I'd been missing in the year gap.

I realized now why I had been so desperate to remember.

"Nefari. My love. Jewel among stones, my morning star. How could I have forgotten your resurrection?"

I held her for so long, I lost track of time.

The longer I clung to her, however, the more that strange hollowness crept in. Was this just the effect from Caelius's blood? It was small at first, but eventually it groaned like an expansive crack with wind whistling through.

I held her tighter, trying to fill in the gap, ignoring the emerging sensation. This *must've* been what I'd been searching for. All I'd ever wanted was Nefertiti alive and in my arms again.

Now I had it.

Caelius had given me my dream.

Caelius was my savior.

I felt a surge of affection for him that quickly shifted to anger.

"Wait." I pulled back from her embrace. "I don't remember what happened this past year. Explain to me how this is possible." I glared at Caelius. "When I brought her to you, you said she was *dead*, that my kiss had killed her because male vampires cannot turn females. You said there was nothing to be done!" As anger rolled off my lips, his blood pulsed inside of me, aching for any explanation that wasn't betrayal.

"I was able to save her, true enough, but she was weak and in a deathlike sleep. I wasn't able to turn her fully until I was more powerful and free from the cage." Caelius knelt down behind me, wrapping his arms around my stomach. "We've been over this, dear one. Last year I restored her and revealed her to you the instant I was free."

He stroked my hair with one hand, his other tightening around my waist. "Why do you think I so fervently asked you to bring me a Vessel? I wanted to revive her, to bring you two together. As I've always said, you mean everything to me. It's all for you."

I blinked.

His words seemed habitual, as if repeated. I *had* heard this before. He had in fact told me. But wasn't this the first time? "I drank the sands of Egypt in grief. Why didn't you at least tell me she was *alive*? I suffered for so long!" I looked at Nefertiti's flawless skin, the deep purple of her eyes—a color that had pained me every time I'd seen it after her death. *That* was familiar. It was more familiar and trustworthy than Caelius's words in my ear.

His lips pressed against my hair as he whispered, "It's all for you. At least remember *that*."

Her hands cupped my cheeks, pulling my head away from

Caelius. The feel of her—that I knew more than any thought in my own brain. "Nefari." My lips trembled. "Love of my life." I leaned forward and kissed her. It was nothing like the aching need of Caelius's blood, the possession that forced me to crave him. My heart yearned in a way that only Nefertiti had ever made it yearn. In the way a boy loves a girl. *She* was and would always be my first true love.

My only love.

The name I had been looking for in the dark.

Nefari.

I closed my eyes.

I could feel her resistance under my mouth—a slight pause before giving herself over completely—and I did the same. I was swimming in the deep sea of our lifelong bond, letting it lift the dregs of Caelius's blood from my mind. *This* I knew.

This was home.

Gutium.

Our code.

Our family.

An image pulsed through my mind: her children crying out, being ripped apart.

Mutilated.

My eyes flashed open.

Caelius pulled me back from the embrace, his voice agitated. "Why did I wait, you asked?" He turned my chin to face him, relieved to have my full attention. He shifted my shoulders, pulling me out of her arms. "You would have been helpless, watching her sleep. Better to think her dead, to grieve and go on living, in case you never procured a Vessel. But that's in the past.

Now she's here, a gift for you, a gift from the *god* who cares for you more than any man or woman ever could." He bit his thumb and ran the red over my teeth.

My blood churned. I swallowed, licking my incisors, a fever overtaking my internal rhythm.

"Yes," I said involuntarily.

Yes.

His words made a kind of sense, a sense that might have infuriated me if I wasn't so enamored with every sound his mouth made. His blood was inside of me, calling to go back to its home. It was unlike any home I'd had in childhood. The home inside his body, the creation drawing back to its maker, was all-consuming.

I felt my will crumble.

I nodded in compliance, as if my words weren't enough, and he smiled. It was a dull smile, but he pulled me farther away from Nefertiti's arms and deeper into his.

"Her children. A memory . . ." I spoke slowly, not sure of what answer I wanted. "They were . . . killed in front of us?"

His smile shifted quickly, a hard line overtaking his lips.

"And?"

"A gruesome death. But they died in Egypt a long time ago, didn't they? I watched over them."

"You are so close to . . . remembering, my sweet." He took a deep breath. "Let me go over everything a few more times; we'll perfect it. By the time I'm done, you'll remember everything fully." He pressed a sigh into my neck as he kissed my nape. "Leave, *hag*. I'll call you in, and we'll do this again tomorrow."

She rose silently. Her mouth opened as if to speak, but it hung there, unable. Finally she closed it, speaking through her teeth. "As you wish, Father." She left as quickly as she had entered.

"What's going on? Why can't she stay?" I panicked. I tried to reach for her, but his grip constricted. I was nothing more than a mouse coiled in his arms. "What have you done to us, Caelius?"

He played with his nail, pressing it against my wrist in an idle threat "*Caelius*, you say. How quickly we revert to old bad habits, La-Narru. I believe the word you were looking for was Father or *God*." He pressed the nail into my skin until blood covered the tip. "Because the sight of her kissing you is so revolting, I nearly ripped her apart, just like I did her children and yours. That's why we'll do it over until it's *perfect*. But next time, she's not to kiss you—not unless she wants me to go against our new deal. With her affections removed, this time I'll be able to keep my composure and answer you properly."

"What? You ripped apart her children and mine?" I thrashed in his arms.

Brainwashing.

That's what he was doing.

And somehow he'd brought Nefertiti back from the dead to do it.

What kind of hell was I really trapped in?

"It's okay, my sweet."

I clawed at his skin but still couldn't move.

He licked the blood moving down my wrist and moaned. "I haven't drunk from you this whole time. I've been gentle, and you're being so stubborn." He bit his lip and smeared it along my filleted wrist. The wound closed instantly, but his blood mixing with mine filled me with desire. My tense body relaxed instantly.

He nuzzled his head into mine. "We'll do this until you get

it right. I'll change some things, make a few tweaks here and there to make sure the blame falls on the proper channels. You are *so* close. Although, I won't regret spending more time in bed with you, rewriting your mind. The sex is amazing, and you're so defenseless like this." He cupped my face in his hands, affection overtaking his venomous features.

Tears rolled down my face, as if my body knew something my mind couldn't grasp. "Stop this. Stop this madness, Caelius. No matter how many times you brainwash me, I'll never be yours!"

There it was.

As my lips trembled, a name escaped the blackness.

Shea.

"What a fun word." Caelius smiled to himself. "Brainwashing. A washing of the brain. Yes. As your *god*, I am cleansing it of all the clutter and trash. I'm cleansing it of the *lesser* beings you've clung to like a child clings to his filthy worn-out blanket. All that would make you miserable and keep you from being mine, I will expunge from your existence. Be thankful I am leaving Nefertiti . . . for now."

He cut his wrist and shoved blood into my mouth. My arms instantly fell limp at my sides. I was already at the place where I could not physically resist his control. My mouth lapped up the red as if it was natural, as if I had been starved and aching for it. How long had it taken to become like this?

The name that had risen to the surface vanished, and with its absence, the hollowness returned.

No.

I just had it.

Who was it?

126

They were important.

I closed my eyes as he poured and poured, an ocean of Caelius swimming in my veins as he whispered into my ear.

What was I looking for?

Blackness.

Nefertiti . . .

A woman.

No.

The Light.

Yes.

I did it.

I brought the Vessel to Caelius, and now he's free.

He saved me from her; she tried to kill me.

I'm in his arms.

Caelius.

My god, my everything.

Caelius.

The name that will save me from the dark.

Caelius.

***

Light filtered in through the window.

I sat with Meky and Setepenre by my side, staring into the beautiful eyes of my world: Nefertiti.

I sighed in both contentment and pain. The Vessel had murdered her innocent children. She and Adnachiel had killed *all* of my Second-Borns except Ur-Nammu, who was nowhere to be found. They'd even killed Gracuri, who'd been so adept at hiding.

I understood Ashgar and Gunnhild, but they'd slaughtered Bohe, David, and Duncan, the kindest and most evolved of our kind. They wouldn't have hurt anyone. They'd been living off of animals for decades. How could that dog, Adnachiel, kill beings who were so . . . so much more human than the mortals alive today?

That *beast*.

I scowled.

What was I thinking? If he could kill Moses, he could kill anyone without remorse.

So why now? Why had he finally chosen to spare a Vessel? He had failed his mission and let her live, which had unlocked Caelius, and now he was traveling with her, trying to kill all of us off. It was definitely a new move. Instead of sacrificing his queen, he was keeping her close and going after my king. Maybe he was tired of playing the pawn. But to be desperate enough to kill the innocent . . .

To think, at one time I'd considered him my brother. I hadn't known then what a merciless liar he was. I should have known by the knife in the back of his sibling Halfdan. Still, him helping the Vessel murder Nefertiti's children was a new low I had not thought him capable of. They were vampires, but they were blameless and had never spilled human blood.

How the righteous had fallen.

I looked at Meky and Sherit as I played with Setepenre's hair. She leaned against my shoulder with a contented sigh. They were the last of the Gutian tribe now, and I would give my life to protect them. I squeezed her tight. She was *mine*. My child. She'd been hidden by Ur-Nammu, and when she'd come of age, she'd been half-changed and left asleep with her sisters and the body of their mother. Caelius had turned them all fully when he'd escaped the prison.

I had barely gotten to spend any time with the other girls before the Vessel and that dog had slaughtered them. What was worse was that it was time I couldn't remember spending. That truth ached in me. As a mortal, I had helped raise them by the Nile. But I had missed so much of their lives, and now I would never have the chance to be the father I had always wanted to be to them.

It was Ur-Nammu who had insisted upon hiding Nefertiti and the children from me. How could he have been so selfish? Even though Nefertiti hadn't been fully restored, just knowing she was alive would have eased much of my suffering. He was to blame for this ache I was feeling now.

Caelius had tried to convince him otherwise, but as their grandfather, Ur-Nammu had said it was his right to decide. I'd been betrayed and lied to. I couldn't believe it, but it *felt* real and burned down into my gut. Ur-Nammu had *lied* to me for so long. And now that it was all out in the open, now that we had lost so much to the Vessel, he was hiding like a coward, unable to face his own shame.

I clutched onto my daughter, eyeing the other two girls.

Caelius had plans for us to rule the world, but for now he wanted me to spend time with him and my family, to fully heal from the Vessel's attack. I didn't know where we were exactly: a forest overlooking a lake in a beautiful cabin somewhere. Surrounded by family and nature, I felt more Gutian these past few days than the vampire I had become over the centuries. It was peaceful and empty, simple, almost like I was human again.

I sighed, but it hitched in my throat. It was peaceful, wasn't it? Was that the right word? Why did I have to repeat that to myself every day? Why did I feel such unrest?

It must've been the *Vessel*. I couldn't stop thinking about her. She was out there somewhere, even now, looking for us.

Hunting us.

I almost laughed. I had hunted every Vessel since the dawn of Vessels. And now this one, a woman, had almost defeated me? Was this karma? At the time Caelius had been freed, he'd been weak and unable to consume her soul and restore himself completely. To face off against even a half-powered Caelius with only the *beast* at her side . . .

She must be the strongest Vessel ever made.

The frustrating part was that I didn't remember how she'd done it. Caelius had said the shock of it—the physical damage and loss of the children and my Second-Borns—must have been too much for me to process fully, that even his blood couldn't restore my memory completely.

Still, he had saved me.

Caelius.

As if the thought of him had summoned his ghost, he stepped behind me, squeezing my shoulders.

Setepenre looked up at him affectionately, and I cast my eyes to Nefertiti. She stared out at the lake. She, Sherit, and Meky barely met my gaze these days. I understood. I had failed to protect our family from the Vessel. Shame flooded my body. I wouldn't fail them again. I would rid the world of the Beast and the Vessel, then Nefertiti would fall back into my arms, and I could raise the remainder of our family properly, like I had in

Egypt.

I stared at Nefari with longing, my cheeks flushing like they had when I'd been a boy in Gutium.

Caelius leaned down, nibbling my ear. "Don't blush on account of me." His voice was whimsical, pleased.

I jerked my head from him.

He had used his blood to save me, but Caelius's blood was nothing to play with. He had given me a large amount, and I knew all too well from my own children that even one drop was enough to bring on infatuation, an affection that lasted an age. That one drop gave them immortality and slavery all at once.

Now that some time had passed and my memories were somewhat restored, I was out of the fog his blood had induced. I felt more myself. I straightened my back, shrugging his hands from my shoulders.

"What is it you want, Father?"

He pulled the chair next to me closer and plopped down. He rested his head against the back side of his hand. "You, of course."

"Stop it," I growled.

He licked his lips. "I miss the Lucian that was like a puppy, suckling on my blood," he bemoaned to himself.

I swallowed, feeling a tremble shake through me.

Setepenre leaned up, looking at Caelius. "But he's healed now, Grandfather. He doesn't need your blood." Her voice was sweet and innocent, a smile lifting her sculpted cheeks.

Now Nefertiti and Meky turned to me, but their eyes fell on Caelius alone.

He licked his lips again. "True enough." He reached over and patted Sete's head, eyeing me like dinner. "Besides, you became quite boring, darling. I like it when you come to me of your own volition, tasting of that old rebellious fire we used to share."

"You'll taste nothing." I scowled.

I was fully aware that I'd repeatedly slept with Caelius in my blood-drunken haze. He had taken advantage of the situation and relished in it. Those memories were etched in my soul like a brand I couldn't carve out: his hips against mine, his tongue in my mouth.

I shuddered.

It would never happen again. As it was, I couldn't call him by his name. Everything in me wanted to call him *God.* I knew that he must have repeated that word over and over. "Father" was all I could muster, and even that sickened me. "I'll serve you, I'll burn this worthless world to a husk if that's what you want, but make no mistake, I do it for the sake of my family, not you."

"But your family is *my* family, dear one." Caelius laughed. It was a cold dead thing, lacking whimsy and the airy nature of most of his jaunts. "Children are so difficult, aren't they, Molly?"

"I don't know what you mean." She fidgeted with her hands, stepping from the doorway.

I had hardly noticed her. Apparently Nefertiti and I had turned her in hopes of dissuading the Vessel. But the Vessel didn't care, so Caelius had wiped Molly's memories in order to protect her from the pain of having to battle her own daughter. It was a secret we were supposed to keep for Molly's sake.

Just who was this Vessel really? What kind of woman would willingly kill her own mother just because she was a vampire? It was as if being a vampire was a crime in and of itself. She was probably dogmatic, the religious sort. Good and evil, black and white, drawing rigid lines like I'd seen humans draw across centuries, lines that always ended in massacres. Every generation claimed that some other faction of human was *evil*. What would the world do now that they knew there were vampires?

I thought of Bohe and Gracuri, of Duncan, David, and all the good men who'd *still* been good men even after the change. They hadn't been perfect, they'd killed on occasion, but people didn't go around obliterating all things with sharp teeth that killed in nature. What would the world be like without sharks, lions, bears, alligators? What right did she have to decide what was *divine* and what was unholy? What right did she have to kill my kind without question?

I looked down at the Hanfu I was wearing.

She had killed them all in one swoop, more or less. All their deaths felt fresh, but none so raw as Bohe's. He'd practically been a monk.

I bet he didn't even fight back. I bet Duncan and David didn't either.

I shifted nervously. And what of Gracuri? The smile I had hoped would one day return to his lips was something I would never see again. What kind of monster was she to rob the world of such men?

In truth, I'd thought Gracuri's end would come from Caelius. He hated him, that much I knew. Caelius would have killed him *slowly*. Although . . .

I looked back at him. There was something in his eyes lately, something I had never seen in the cage: a sort of affection. It was like the seeds of love that could grow in any other person, but in someone as corrupt as him, they just remained seeds. They were scattered throughout his irises, visible if I looked long enough.

Scattered.

That was familiar.

Still, his eyes had changed.

He had changed.

A timeless being of Darkness was evolving.

He looked deep into my eyes, stroking my cheek with the back of his hand.

"I'm bored, darling. Let's destroy Miami together."

I swallowed.

Vacation was over.

Chapter 7
Shea

Duncan was floating above me in a gust of wind I had taken control of, and Aidan was buried knee-deep in the ground.

Neither one of them could move.

It was epic.

I was pretty impressed with myself.

We were right outside Helena's secret fortress. It looked like a simple one-room cabin on top of a cliff, but really it was a maze of rooms built deep into the mountains.

"Shea!" Helena shouted from the front doorway. "What did you do to my floors?"

Oops. Earlier I had experimented with using my earth powers indoors and ripped up the wood flooring of the cabin, creating a hole looking down into the room below, hence why we were outside at the present moment.

"But hey, look, she's mastered earth." Aidan came to my defense.

"I can fix it. Don't worry." I hoped I wasn't lying. "I just wanted to come out here since I was on a roll. Hang on."

With a simple thought, I maneuvered the dirt surrounding Aidan and raised him out of the ground, then controlled the earth to seal it back up.

I was about to walk back into the cabin with Aidan when I heard a friendly voice behind me.

"As much as I love flyin', I'm wonderin' if you'd let me down now, lass," Duncan said with a laugh.

Embarrassed, I turned around and lowered the Scotsman safely to the ground. I found it so cute that Duncan called me lass. Of course, he called every woman that, but still. And equally adorable was when he called my dad lad. Jeff Harper was hundreds of years younger than Duncan, even though he *looked* twenty years older, so it was extra amusing to see Dad treated like a youngster. And if I was being honest, I was pretty sure Dad liked being one of the youngest in our group too.

Walking inside the small cabin, I saw the giant hole I had created and cringed. I could see the room beneath it through the opening, but the hole itself was a mess of cement, wood, and dirt.

Now to try and fix it.

I could do this.

Concentrating on the wood itself—the grains, the knots, the inkling of life left inside what used to be a giant oak tree—I envisioned the floor repairing itself. Then I added the rocks and the dried water from the broken cement, weaving in and out until . . .

Well.

At least it wasn't a hole anymore.

It was a mangled mess of wood with a little bit of gray cement mixed in, but it was solid.

I turned to face Helena's wrath, but she was actually leaning on her hip and smiling. "Good job. Not pretty, but impressive work."

"Oh, cool, thanks," I said in relief.

It had been just the five of us for a couple of weeks now: me, Dad, Aidan, Duncan, and Helena. The more time passed, the more I worried about Lucian and my mom, not to mention Ur-Nammu, who had gone off the radar completely. But if Caelius was feeding Lucian his blood and wiping all memory of me, what could I really do? I just hoped there'd be a sliver of recognition. I had seen it in my mom when she'd confessed Caelius's inability to Dream-Walk. But I kept my longing to myself, afraid that if I expressed any emotion about mom remembering me, I would jinx it.

I asked Helena, "How's it going on that device, or invention, or whatever it is that might stop Caelius?"

Helena's expression was distracted, which was pretty normal for her, but she forced a smile. "Slower than I'd like, but I feel like we'll be able to do some testing in a couple of days. You're doing a wonderful job training."

I couldn't tell if she actually meant that or if she was trying to be encouraging. Either way, I'd take it.

Looking awkwardly at the mangled mess of concrete and wood, I said, "I should probably practice a bit more."

Nodding, Helena walked toward her lab table. "Good idea. Just try and keep this place in one piece." Without another word, she pulled her hair back and began working on what appeared to be gears and electronics. I couldn't really tell.

One thing I knew: Helena was a mad genius. It was a shame that she hadn't been recognized in her own time. It made me wonder how many other brilliant women in history had never received the accolades they deserved.

I looked out the window and took a moment to appreciate my surroundings. Helena's "lair" was a cabin in the middle of the Colorado mountains. Seeing glimpses of the range through the bay window in the distance was breathtaking. Crooks and large peaks let in the perfect purple glow of magic hour. It never failed to amaze me.

It had taken quite a hike to get here, though I'd been able to practice my wind moves to help myself up a few tricky cliff walls. Vampires and angels didn't have that problem. Dad, Duncan, and Helena had kind of zoomed up the walls, while Aidan had tried out the new wings his brothers had given him. It was strange seeing Aidan fly, though I couldn't actually *see* his wings. For some reason they were invisible to me since I was part human. As a Vessel, I'd hoped seeing angel wings would be a perk, but nope. Aidan had just looked like me, kind of hovering in midair until we reached the top of the cliff face. So anticlimactic.

The cabin itself was simple in build—four walls, a couple windows and doors—but it was what was inside that made it special. It was like stepping onto a movie set about Nikola Tesla with the amount of what I referred to as Helena's "invention stuff." There were giant electricity conductors, moving gears from the size of a nickel to the size of a small car, beakers, Bunsen burners, wooden tables, and bookshelves full of both ancient books with no authors and newer books by modern scientists like Neil deGrasse Tyson (I may have thumbed through a couple of those), Stephen Hawking, and Carl Sagan.

And that was just the top floor! A staircase led down to more rooms and more staircases with gears and inventions that Helena probably hadn't touched in years. I only explored four or five levels down, but Helena said she had built rooms going at least a mile deep.

Honestly, I didn't want to leave.

It was cozy.

Sometimes isolation was perfect for avoiding reality.

I had my dad. I had my Aidan.

Even Duncan and Helena were becoming fast friends.

And staying here, in a kind of reality-denial, helped ease the aching guilt of the thousands of innocents who had been killed by Caelius. I couldn't erase that entirely. What if Lucian and my mother were murdering people against their will? Could I forgive them? Could they forgive themselves? I had no answers, so I stayed in my protective bubble here at Helena's lair.

Aidan nudged me affectionately. "You and Duncan got this? I'm going to try and contact my brothers and see if they have any new information."

I nodded, turning to Duncan. "If you're okay with it?"

Duncan's smile was contagious. "Of course I'll help ye. Fire's next, right? We should probably head outside again so we don't burn the building down."

"Good plan."

I walked outside with Duncan, and the cold breeze hit my face. It was stuffy inside the cabin. Some of the rooms deeper down in the lair were cooler, but there was nothing like fresh mountain air. Even though it was still fall, being this high up in the mountains, it might as well have been the arctic.

As much as I liked the breeze, I'd get chilled fast. It didn't help that I'd been born and raised in Arizona. My body definitely couldn't handle the cold very well. The vampires couldn't care less, and Aidan said he was cold, but I didn't believe him for a second. He was just looking out for me, which was why he kept the fireplace going in the upstairs room twenty-four seven.

"What do ye have in mind for me, lass? Burn a hole in my chest?" Duncan winked.

"Are you seriously making a joke of when I seared a hole in Lucian? It was by accident, by the way." I shook my head.

Laughing, Duncan replied, "Aye, Gracuri told me of that one. Scared me at first telling, but now that I know ye, I'd be honored if ye laser beamed me through ma ribs."

"I'm pretty sure it hurt. Like *really* hurt. Let's try sticks, in a very safe fire pit, that won't burn down the forest."

"Your decision, lass, but I'm volunteering if ye need it," Duncan said, almost too cheerfully.

Walking over to the fire pit at the side of the house, I sat down on the bench facing it. Duncan sat next to me, concerned. "What is it? Ye thinking of Lucian and your mum again? We'll get 'em back. I swear it to ye."

I didn't want to talk about it.

It only reminded me of how little control I had in my life right now.

"You haven't had any blood since we got here. Are you going to be okay?" I knew I was evading the subject of Lucian and my mom, but I really was curious. Duncan hadn't eaten anything since this trip had started.

"Ah." Duncan leaned back on the bench. "I don't drink from anyone alive. I don't drink animal blood either. I've got no stomach fer it."

"Wait, what?" I was shocked at his admission. "You can't digest it?"

Duncan threw his head back and laughed. "Nae, I can drink it just fine, I just choose not to." He paused, then added, "It's what drove Lucian and me apart. He never understood."

"So you don't drink humans or animals?" I couldn't process what he was telling me. Finally, I replied, "That's so noble. I kind of want to hug you right now. But how do you survive?"

"Much like Nefertiti and her children must've. Hearin' their stories about Caelius not wantin' them to kill anyone and only eating leftovers, I only drank from the dead. At least back then anyway. But now I drink from blood bags. Fer the last hundred years or so." He smiled. "I'm a Second-Born. I'm powerful enough to live off of air for four to five weeks at least."

"Wow." I had no words. A vampire who didn't want to feed off of humans or animals. It made me wonder if there were more vampires like Duncan. Did that make him a vegan vampire? It made me feel an intense affection for him that I couldn't explain. Then something he'd said finally registered in my brain. "What did you mean when you said it's what drove you and Lucian apart?" I didn't really want to ask, but I had to. "Is it because he wanted you to kill?"

Sighing heavily, Duncan nodded. "When I first met Lucian, he had come straight off the docks in Edinburgh, and I admit, there was somethin' about him that caught ma eye. He had an aura 'bout him. I could tell he had some great stories to tell. And since ma favorite thing is tellin' stories, I steered straight to him and started tellin' him how I had just defeated a savage twenty-foot brown bear that had torn apart ma village." Duncan nudged me with a smile. "It was a complete lie, o' course, but Lucian actually smiled, and it was the most magnificent sight I'd ever seen." He paused, as if remembering that single moment.

I completely related. Lucian's smile was epic, probably because it was such a rarity. But I liked thinking of Duncan amusing Lucian. It somehow made me feel better about everything that was happening.

Continuing, Duncan said, "Tha two of us were inseparable after that. He'd always be askin' for more tall tales, and since it was my favorite pastime, I'd oblige. We went on like that for a good three months, all through summer. But the fall was on us, and King James IV called on all Scotsmen to battle the British. I decided to fight like all men of my time did." Duncan's eyes looked to the mountaintops, his usual jovial demeanor turned somber. "Lucian wanted to fight too, and tha two of us joined the thirty thousand strong and marched to the Battle of Flodden. It was horrific. I can see it as clearly in my mind's eye as if it happened yesterday.

"Lucian destroyed twenty men right before ma eyes in less than a second. Scots or Brits, he just tore open their flesh and moved on to the next. He was a vampire. I dinnae even know such monsters existed." Duncan looked as if he were reliving every second of his past.

"I froze. I dinnae know what to do. I saw Lucian rip ma own countrymen to pieces. They were as terrified as I was, but since they'd seen me in Lucian's company the last few months, they thought I was with him. Before I knew it, I had been stabbed straight through with a broadsword." Duncan stopped. I could see that as difficult as it had been to tell his story thus far, what was coming next was far worse. I almost didn't want to hear it. I had heard enough of Lucian's monstrous behavior in his past to last five lifetimes. But I *needed* to hear it. I needed to hear about the kind of vampire Lucian used to be because Caelius had probably turned him back into that very monster.

Duncan continued. "Lucian screamed to high heaven when he saw me drop to the ground. I'm admitting to ya now, lass, I wanted to die. I wanted to pretend that what I'd just seen was battlefield hallucinations and that I could be reunited with ma mum in Heaven." He nudged me to break the mood a bit. "Ma mum was famous for her feasts, and I expected a right good one when I arrived at the pearly gates." Then he took a deep breath and said, "Lucian turned me instead."

I looked at him, and his expression of true regret and grief gave me a sudden chill.

Turning his face toward the mountains again, Duncan shook his head. "I had so much of Lucian's blood in ma system I couldn't think clearly. With the thousands of men surrounding me, I only saw one. It was as if Lucian were an angel come down to Earth to make me his undying servant. And I wanted to please him with every fiber of what soul I had left." He shrugged and looked at me. "It was the blood, of course. Lucian's blood is as potent as it gets, next to Caelius's, and if he would have told me to slit my own throat, I would have done it happily. That's how much control a maker's blood has on their children."

"You didn't want to be a vampire," I said, already knowing the answer from the look on Duncan's face.

He shook his head. "I truly wish I had died that day." Duncan managed a melancholy smile. "I really did want to see ma mum. I still want to."

"I'm sorry." I didn't know what else to say. My heart ached for him. So far, all I'd seen was the happy-go-lucky Duncan who was so much like Aidan it had been comical. To see this side of him gave me a reality check into how unreal my life had become since I'd found out I was the Vessel.

After a moment, Duncan continued. "Lucian's bloodlust was still high, and once he had turned me, or what he'd thought was 'saving' me, he told me to 'drink until I was full.' " There was a catch in Duncan's voice, the memory was so painful.

I instinctively grabbed his hand and held it. "Oh my God, Duncan. I . . ." I had no words. I knew what was coming. I just wished it was another one of Duncan's tall tales.

Squeezing my hand for support, Duncan plowed forward. "Like you know from your da, new vampires dinnae have much control. I killed my entire clan before I knew what was happening. The guilt of what I'd done overpowered Lucian's blood, and I fell to my knees, sobbing. Lucian was enjoying the slaughter too much to notice. When he had killed almost ten thousand men, he finally saw me, alone in the battlefield, surrounded by ma family and friends who I had murdered with my own hands and who I had . . . fed off of." That last admission hurt him the most. "Lucian ran up to me, and the look I must have given him stopped him dead in his tracks. I'd never seen a man look so . . . broken.

"He knew then what he had done, and he knew I'd never forgive myself. He tried to take the entire blame, saying he had 'forced' me to kill those men, but blood control or not, *I* killed them. *Me.*"

The silence between us was deafening.

I knew that even monster-Lucian wouldn't have been able to stomach Duncan's devastation at killing his friends and family.

"I haven't killed a living soul since, unless you count other vampires. I've killed a lot of those, especially the ones who kill for sport." Duncan pulled his hand away.

"And you and Lucian? What happened after that?" I asked.

"I pushed him away until he finally left. I hated what I was. I refused to drink blood. I thought I could starve myself to death, but it only made me motionless and caused excruciating pain. I deserved it though. I was lying in a cave, mummified, a hundred and fifty years after the battle, writhing in pain that was only fitting for what I'd done, when Lucian appeared.

"Lucian carried a large stag on his shoulders and told me he hadn't killed it, that I could smell the gunpowder from the bullet that had killed the animal. The hunters had abandoned the corpse, and it would go to waste." Duncan turned to me with a sad smile. "He was trying to make it okay for me to drink. Lucian understood that I'd never take another life again, and he wanted me to stop torturing myself. I nodded as much as my head could move, and he gently placed the enormous stag next to me." Duncan finally laughed. "I'll spare ye the details of how messy that eating session was, but it brought me back to myself. I was able to feed from people and animals who were already dead after that, and that allowed me to live with myself."

Becoming contemplative again, Duncan added, "Lucian and I didn't see much of each other after that. He wanted to stay the monster he pretended to be, though I could tell he longed to live like me." Patting my shoulder affectionately, Duncan said, "Your love is what brought him back. He's not a devil anymore, and that's all because of ye."

I didn't want to say that Lucian probably *was* that old monster again—not after everything Duncan had just told me.

"I go to those Highlands every year and say ma prayers to the souls I took that day. That's where Caelius snagged me. Everything else you're up to date on." Duncan gave me a supportive smile. "I just thought ye should know ma history with Lucian. I'm the last son he made besides yeer father, and I think there's a reason fer it. We only knew each other fer a short while when I was human, but I'd do anythin' fer him, and him fer me. That's still true enough."

I knew it too. I may have been the catalyst that'd brought Lucian back from being a monster, but Duncan had been one of the seeds.

"It's cold out here." I concentrated on the sticks in the fire pit, and they instantly lit into a roaring fire. I turned to Duncan, surprised, and we both smiled.

"Look at you, lass. Caelius should fear ye."

My smile faded slightly. "Even if I master everything, I'm still no match for Caelius."

"Don't ye worry about that. Helena is makin' some kind of Caelius-death-contraption, and she needs *ye* to power it." He waved at the fire. "And in less than a couple weeks, yeer already making bonfires with yeer thoughts. I'd say our team is doing pretty well fer itself."

As if he were the sound of doom, Aidan poked his head out of the cabin door. "You guys better get in here."

"Uh-oh." Duncan said what I was thinking.

I stood up and walked toward the door.

Aidan noticed the fire and said with an appreciative grin, "Nice one." Then he added, "Better put it out though."

I focused on the fire, and just to playfully show off in front of Aidan, I snapped my fingers, and the fire snuffed out.

As I reached the door, he smiled. "Really? You going to snap every time you put out a fire now? Because you know the fire went out like three seconds *after* you snapped."

Laughing, I smacked him in the chest. "Shut it."

Inside, Helena and Dad were hovering over a small television that rested on one of the worktables. Like with Paris, a demolished city was showing on every piece of news footage, the captions reading: *Miami destroyed. Demons or aliens? Countless death toll. The whole world is under attack.*

The world was ending.

And I was snapping fire on and off with my fingers.

The footage put everything back in perspective.

I may have been training, and Helena may have been perfecting this device no one knew anything about, but it felt like we were hiding. It felt like we were allowing millions of innocent people to die.

I needed to do something.

"This is horrible," I finally uttered.

No one responded. What could they say?

I needed to Dream-Walk. I needed to connect with *someone*

147

in the loop. I needed to know what I could do because sitting around in a cabin wasn't working for me.

"I'm really tired. I'm going to lie down for a bit," I lied. But no one suspected anything. They all gave me looks of approval and words of encouragement.

Walking over to the small cot that was my bed, I lay down and closed my eyes.

***

"Good, you're here." Nefertiti's voice came out of the dark.

Sights and sounds swirled around me until we were standing on the same beach in Miami as before. But instead of the beautiful Fontainebleau behind her, it was only burnt ruins.

Before I could speak or ask questions, Nefertiti said, "How long has it been since you've slept? I've been waiting here for you for two days." She seemed angry.

Thinking about it, I realized I hadn't slept much in the last week.

Nefertiti stood there, not speaking. I could tell she was having a full-on inner battle with herself. About what, I had no idea, and frankly, it kind of worried me.

Thinking the worst, I asked, "Is Ur-Nammu . . . okay?"

Nefertiti looked even more upset that I'd brought up her father, which made my stomach sink. But she answered, "I told you to stop him from coming, but that aside, he's fine. He's been watching from a distance. We Dream-Walk when we can."

"Then what's wrong?" I swallowed hard.

Finally, she said, "I need to meet with you in person. Just

you though. No one else. You can't tell anyone. I know it sounds bad, but it's the only way." Nefertiti walked up to me, her eyes pleading. "Lucian needs you, Shea. If you don't come, it may be too late for him."

The pain I felt was desperate. "Where?"

Relief glimmered in her eyes. "Here. I can sneak out during the day. Can you be here by tomorrow?"

"I can't exactly fly like you." The frustration was real. I'd barely been able to lift myself up the small cliff faces using wind. What did she expect me to do, tornado myself to Miami?

"Where can you get to by tomorrow?"

Thinking it through, I could "wind" myself down most of the mountains, grab our van, and drive at least a few hundred miles from where we were. I hoped it was enough to not give away the others' location.

"Santa Fe?" I offered.

"I'll be there. Tomorrow at 4:00 p.m." Nefertiti popped out of the dreamscape, and I was yanked awake.

Staring at the others watching the television, I knew I had to meet Nefertiti to save Lucian. I had to keep it secret. And I had to do it alone.

Aidan would be pissed.

CHAPTER 8
LUCIAN

New Mexico.

Santa Fe was beautiful when it was spoken of in songs and poetry, idealizing the Spanish colonists that settled there in 1610. It was then glorified, like a husk for dead cowboys, in cinema with every new generation's exploratory epiphanies on the exaggerated life of the old West. In reality though, despite the commercialism of most "historical" sites, there was still something mysterious, adventurous even, in the look of the place.

I remembered the city appearing old, even when it was first made—old and worn out like I was. The lingering scent of dried spices used to remind me of the early settlers. They'd been full of hope, and so many of them had ended up as rotting corpses whose bones had been bleached white buried under the sands of the desert sun.

The Pueblo-style architecture and crooked streets often led to adobe cathedrals and old churches; one specific chapel in Loretto had become invaluable to me because of Helena. Santa Fe was not my favorite place, not since I'd thought she'd died.

Its history was laced with slavery, oppression, war, and heat. Deserts.

Why was it *always* the desert?

Did fate have a sense of humor? Did it enjoy bringing me to these places again and again? I was never myself under its sweltering unyielding rays. It was as if the eye of Light itself was mocking my pain, watching me toil and suffer as I had in Egypt. In truth, if I were to describe the life I'd lived after leaving the fertile mountains of Gutium as a young man, I would say I'd left on a sea of gods and had washed up on the shore of a desolate, burning world, hungry and alone. It was much like the story of Eden. That was what had become of my life: starving in the desert. I'd been landlocked from an oasis that had once carried a people, now erased from history and out of reach forever. My homeland.

Until now.

Now I had been reunited with Nefari and our children.

They were what was left of my people.

They were my everything.

Then why?

Why was this happening again, and in the desert, no less?

I held on to the piece of my rib cage threatening to fall off. I pressed it, bone to bone, and gritted my teeth. Gluing the broken fragments together with marrow and muscle, rather than having to grow the chunk back completely, was one of the first lessons I'd learned as an immortal. My body was mangled from shielding Nefertiti and the children, but I didn't care about the pain. I was glad I'd taken the blows for them. I slowed my breathing, letting my blood heal what it could. I straightened up, cracking my shoulder back into its socket, surveying the damage.

Santa Fe, and the staircase I had once sculpted here with my own hands, was . . . gone.

I looked at the Vessel as Caelius pinned it down. A being so puny had held its own against all of us. It gave my foggy memories more validation. This *thing* must have killed them all.

I stared at her.

There was something familiar about the heat and the way the sun reflected off of her wavy blond hair.

Shea Harper.

It was not a name that should invoke fear, but in our previous battle, it had no doubt been on the lips of Nefertiti's children and my own as they breathed their last.

I moved closer.

She was small framed but curvy in all the right places, and her hazel eyes bored into mine with an ache I couldn't comprehend. A thirst bellowed in me like it always had since I'd left the mountains of Gutium. Even though Nefari was by my side, staring at the Vessel made me feel landlocked and far from home.

I finally bridged the gap between us.

"Don't do this! Lucian, you have to fight him! I love you!" She spoke the words as if they had been said before, but they were foreign to me.

I cringed as Caelius laughed. It was a laugh that filled the empty spaces where the rubble of adobe homes lay in waste at our feet. "She thinks because she is a female that she can seduce you, boy." His eyes lingered on my frame, the wound over my ribs already mending.

I let my laugh follow his; it was a small sound chasing an echo. "As if I could be charmed by someone who *murdered* my family."

Caelius's smile faded. "Yes. That's right," he whispered in a tone that was more befitting a church. Maybe it was the ruins of them surrounding us that made his words seem like a silent prayer of remorse. "How could you ever forgive someone who had done that?" He trailed off as if the sentiment wasn't for me, but a reflection for himself.

"I couldn't. My will is not so weak." I puffed my chest, hole and all. It was a childish habit I had picked up from my father. Although, when Onack had broadened his chest and spoken, it was affronting like a lion, a roar that called for submission. It worked with humans, but as a statement against Caelius, it was laughable.

He motioned toward the Vessel, and the strange feeling that had crept up as I stared into her pleading eyes faded with one recollection: she had killed them, mutilating Nefari's children and my Second-Borns.

"You're a monster." I spat, and it landed on her stomach.

I watched it move up and down with her jagged breaths.

There was a small scar there.

Had I kissed that stomach?

I wet my mouth as if the nectar of her skin had been there before. Maybe I had, in battle somehow? That didn't make sense, yet in this desert I thirsted for the Vessel like she was water on dry land.

I averted my eyes, looking around at the battle we had just

survived. We were all panting like mad and more exhausted than we'd ever been in human form, but since I'd taken most of the blows, everyone else was relatively intact. Sadly, Santa Fe wasn't.

Caelius kept our battle in the middle of this city. "Two birds with one Vessel," he'd mocked. Destroying her and the human ants of New Mexico was a joint bliss for him.

I didn't mind the people that couldn't evacuate being fodder, but the buildings themselves, that was a real shame. All of that history I had seen grown around itself like an unkempt garden was a sort of living thing in its own right. That mud and clay, the rustic beauty of it, was now sticking up in jutted broken columns, much like the bleached bones it had once covered. Soon even that would be eaten away by the sun until there was nothing left, like the decimated steps I'd made for Helena.

Our battle, the force of our bodies and the Vessel's elements, had laid waste to what was now the ghost of Santa Fe. In this modern age, would settlers even bother rebuilding it? It would never look the same if they did. And given that Caelius was going to rule the world, I doubted that humans would be allowed to build cities again, let alone churches. Most likely the larger cities would be ravaged, and the smaller would be reduced to farms for human blood. I cringed, thinking of what was going to become of this "new world" Caelius envisioned for us.

I glanced over his body; he didn't have a single mark on him. He healed much faster than the rest of us. Even at half power, he was stronger than I could have imagined while I'd mocked him from the other side of his cage.

He held the Vessel down patiently as she chatted away. Her mouth grew dry from shouting. Each plea was more ridiculous than the last. It was an obvious string of lies meant to confuse me. Finally she stopped, almost hoarse, and shifted her gaze to Nefertiti. Again her pleading went on for some time, words like, "How could you betray me? We could have saved them all *together*," and so on. It fell flat on Nefari's ears, as it had my own.

What was she thinking, that her Vessel mind-control would work on us as it had my Second-Borns? She was powerful but not stronger than all of us together. If memory served, she had separated us and attacked by using the element of surprise. She had even, once, with Adnachiel, tried to broker some kind of treaty—another trap, of course. This Vessel was as clever as she was deceptive.

We had the upper hand now. We had caught her *alone* and off guard. Even so, she must have thought she could take us and was now shocked at her predicament. Caelius remarked how she was stronger than the last time. Her vain belief in her growing power had been her final mistake. If she was a religious zealot then she should have known the words best: pride comes before a fall. What arrogance, to think we would be unprepared this time.

Nefertiti shifted her gaze away from us and turned her back to the Vessel. Surprisingly, Meky did the same, glaring daggers at her mother. It was unusual. The Nefertiti I remembered, the warrior, would have been the first to sink her hands into Shea Harper's chest and rip out her heart. It would have been payment for the lives of her daughters. And Meky? She hadn't fought the Vessel at all. She'd stayed on the sidelines, frozen as Nefari had fought harder, almost *for her*. Had Nefertiti been trying to protect her from injury? Then why the strange unspoken fury between them? Were they fighting again?

155

Everything had been off since we'd left the cabin. Sherit was obviously obedient to Nefari, without the fury between them that Meky displayed, but even she seemed distant now. Destroying Miami hadn't brought us any closer together, as Caelius had promised. Although, he had thoroughly enjoyed himself in the slaughter. It was visible by the bounce in his step that had remained until Santa Fe.

The only child who had let her guard down had been Setepenre. She'd fought by my side and relished in conquest as I had in the days of old, before I'd lost the taste for it. I was thankful for her attachment to me, but not her viciousness. In my absence, what had she grown into under Caelius's influence? Had I been there for her, had I known, I would have made different choices. I'd missed so much of her life, and slaughtering the world and the Vessel was not how I wanted to reconnect. Still, once all of this was done, Caelius would let us rule the humans like masters over sheep. If I wanted to give her the world, I had to accept that this was one way of doing it.

Once the Vessel was dead, we'd have peaceful days again like we'd had in the cabin. I'd make sure of it. Then the rest of the girls would come back to me. Maybe they would call me Father again, like they had by the Nile when we'd all still been human.

I breathed in deep.

I remembered all of Nefari's children embracing me in some underground lair preparing for battle. Each of them had spoken the Gutian code, their hands reaching for me across the darkness, clinging to my back. It was a moment I held on to, a clear image in the fog of my scattered memories. It must have been just before the Vessel had murdered them. Their love and oaths still burned like hot coals in the pit of my stomach.

I will etch them into the existence of all things. Their memory, I will not lose again, and I will take care of the loved ones who remain. I will be the Gutian father they deserve.

I looked at Sherit and Sete. They were resting at a distance from where we were, keeping Molly restrained, on Caelius's orders. I wasn't surprised. Caelius had said she'd tried to *kill* the Vessel while we were battling. I hadn't seen it myself, but by the way she was thrashing, I believed it. Killing her was not the plan. Maybe that was why Nefari had turned away; she was fighting back the urge herself.

We needed to *subdue* the Vessel, and just as Caelius had predicted, once she used all of her powers, she was spent and quite helpless. It was a relief and something to catalog, that even a being like her had limits, although the knowledge was useless now. Once Caelius was done, she was going to be the *last* Vessel. What use was it to record the weaknesses of a dying species? I looked down on her like she was the last dodo.

"I thought you were stronger than this. I'm disappointed." I pressed the toe of my white shoe into her rib, feeling the dissatisfaction in her failure as if it were my own. "Do you recognize these? They were Gracuri's shoes. Caelius saved them for me after you *slaughtered* him." I looked deep into her eyes, the ache of his loss trembling down my spine. "He wasn't perfect, but he was precious like *all* of my sacred children. And you decapitated them like *trash*."

"I didn't kill them, Caelius did! Lucian, you have to believe me—"

Caelius covered her mouth. "Oh, this one likes to tell stories

157

as much as your Duncan."

I flinched when he said his name, but I didn't know why. In the short time Caelius was free and my Second-Borns were alive, he had met him. He'd told me as much. That must have been enough time to know what Duncan was like.

Still, for him to speak of my son like we shared the knowledge of who he was disgusted me even now. Duncan *hated* Caelius. There were only a few of my children, the warmongers, who would have given anything to see Caelius off his leash, to kill and participate in the end of the world. But Ashgar and Gunnhild were dead, along with those who would have wanted to save it, like Bohe and David, Gracuri and Duncan. In her ignorance, she had killed her best defense against us.

Caelius nudged his foot next to my own as Shea struggled weakly in his arms. "Have a good long look at your enemy, darling. Thoughts? Hatred? What are you *feeling* in those deep turquoise eyes, my sweet? Share with Papa."

I scowled. His tone was gleeful, but there was hardly any red in his eyes; they were consumed in black. Maybe it was being so close to the Vessel, and his long-held dream of being restored to full power, that made him like this. It was all he'd wanted for so long. That must've been why the darkness was emanating off of him in powerful waves. But those waves were directed at me, not Shea Harper, the Vessel crippled in his arms.

What was he doubting?

My loyalty.

I leaned down to her face, sneering up at him. "Because it took me so long to bring you one of these *things*—is that why you're not doing it yourself? Is that why you want *me* to drain her? Do you doubt my devotion?"

Without a moment's breath, he said, "Yes." It was plain and colorless. But what followed was loaded and heavy. "You made me wait," he shot back, the black around him expanding. "I've been waiting for *you* all this time. You failed your tasks and broke your promises. Now prove that you are *mine* and mine alone. That you serve me, if nothing else."

My tongue flicked at the roof of my mouth. It was dry. Everything was so arid and surreal. Staring at her fear-driven eyes, in that moment she looked not like a Vessel but like a young woman. More than that, she looked *innocent*.

I hesitated.

I had seen innocence taken enough to know the feeling of it. I had choked it down myself when I'd turned my Second-Borns. It had been taken from me that night outside Nefari's window by the very Darkness asking me to do it again now.

"I didn't fail you, Caelius." I refocused, ignoring her seemingly pure gaze. "I brought her and freed you from your cage, didn't I?" I moved closer. "Late, I'll give you that, but still I succeeded."

Caelius leaned his head back in shock, the red finally returning to his eyes. "Of course." He gathered his thoughts before speaking again. The blackness emanating off of him calmed and dissipated into the clay and dust at our feet.

"But you failed with every Vessel before that, and you allowed her to kill so many of our kind. They were invaluable to you, and because of that they were invaluable to me. Am I really asking too much of you, sweetheart?" His voice attempted to warm, but there was still a growing agitation behind it. "I know, as a rebellious boy, you hate these kinds of tests, but I'm being more than fair here."

He paused again, looking at the pink skin covering my rib cage, and there it was, that peculiar look he wore recently, as if a demon like him could feel real concern. "I don't want to endanger you unnecessarily." His voice warmed further. "I can–" He paused. It was strange to see Darkness unsure of itself, even for a moment. "I can let her go. We don't have to do this right now."

I blinked in shock. "What?"

"I used to think she was important. Being trapped in that cage for so long led me to false delusions. But she's not important. The Vessel never was. *You* are." He placed both her wrists into one of his hands and held them above her head. "We'll let her go until you're ready to obey my simple request." Reaching out his other hand, he stroked my face. "What do you think, precious? Should we try this again at a later date? When you're ready?"

I chewed my bottom lip, sinking deeper into his auburn gaze. Something about his words bothered me, particularly the words, "try this again." I didn't know why, but they filled me with an inescapable terror. "What game is this? You *need* her so that you can be restored!" I tried to mask my feelings with words that seared out of me like hot pokers ready to gouge those red eyes out. "I know it's all that matters to you. Don't pretend you'll let her go just to mock me—"

"Ask me now, and I will." His eyes locked on mine, steady and unwavering. All the doubt dissipated like the black that had been around him. I bit the inside of my mouth, hard. There was a threat beneath that gaze–a control, a passionate obsession to have and consume. If I was thirsty and lost in the desert, Caelius was the desert itself. How much more did *he* ache for the things he thought he needed than I?

He leaned forward, his black shadow falling over Shea's body, blocking her from my sight. "If you are too fragile from your last defeat, we will wait and try again. If you recall, I am very good at waiting, my sweet. And for you, I will wait for all of time, until you're ready."

There was another long moment between us. Was this Caelius's twisted form of devotion? Did he really care about my rehab? As if I was so crippled by her that I needed the patience of a snake cloaked in black. And his *waiting* would strike me, not her. I would again be filled with the venom of his blood. I knew there was no true absolution for those who failed him.

I ripped myself from his mesmerizing gaze as he moved his hand from my cheek and leaned back, revealing the Vessel. She had stopped thrashing and was now staring at me, as if she hoped I would ask him to release her.

No.

I looked longer at her face.

It wasn't as if she *hoped*; there wasn't a shred of doubt in her eyes that I would do just that, that I would tell him I wasn't ready. Was my shattered state so apparent, even to our enemy?

Nefertiti and Meky turned back toward us, their eyes burning into the back of my skull.

Indignation boiled inside me. If Gunnhild were alive today, he'd kill me himself. Weakness could not be tolerated. I had made that one truth palatable for him over the cruel years we'd spent together eradicating the Vikings. And still, he had fallen for Ashgar. And still, he'd had that one exploitable weakness.

161

It was strange that they'd been killed separately. At least that was what I'd been told, but there was no way Gunnhild would have let that happen. He was too intelligent to be fooled so easily by the Vessel, and he hadn't been more than three feet from Ashgar in over a century. Ever since I'd told him to keep his enemies close but his weaknesses even closer, he'd never left Ashgar's side. He had taken my words as a threat, even though I'd made it clear that I would allow him this *one* love. After all, I had turned Ashgar for *him*. Besides, what benefit was there in killing my own children?

I took a deep breath. Killing my chosen, there was nothing that could push me to such madness, even if Gunnhild wanted my head. I couldn't even kill Gracuri in Thebes when I'd been commanded to by Caelius himself. Then why was I hesitating to kill this Vessel? She was nothing to me. She was not *mine*.

I looked deeper into her eyes. It wasn't the desert flowers filling the air with sweetness that was making me so uneasy–it was her skin, the scent of her sweat. It was throwing me off. I knew I was strong enough to obey Caelius. The problem was my body, not my mind. My mind raged at what she'd done, screamed for justice, for penance, for her head on a spike.

Head on a spike . . . now that *felt* familiar.

There it was again, that cognitive dissonance between what I knew and what I felt. The problem was, I *felt* no hate for the Vessel, even after all she'd done. Maybe Caelius was right: I was too broken. Was I mournfully numb from the loss of the children, and was that preventing me from accessing the full range of my emotions? My mind gave me that answer, and it made sense, it fit with the small flashes of images that I could recall in the black hole my memory had become. But my *body* wasn't listening.

I sighed, heavy and low. This circular battle within was getting me nowhere. I had to trust my mind. My instincts and my body, they could be controlled by the Vessel. Maybe this was part of her allure—this helplessness, her intoxicating aroma, the way her body moved, the way my fingertips desired to slide along her pale skin, even with Nefertiti standing so close by, watching. This familiar feeling between us could be *fabricated*, and Nefertiti wouldn't lie to me, not the warrior queen of Gutium, not the power behind the Pharaoh of Egypt, not my childhood friend and love, Nefari. *She* was true. She was real. I had to depend on that.

I looked up, pleading into her purple eyes. Instead of a fearless affirmation, a death sentence, her gaze looked as dejected and uncertain as I felt. I swallowed. My saliva was thick with a thirst only the desert could produce. Nefertiti had lied to the Pharaoh all those years in Egypt, but that was only so that *we* could be together. She would never lie to *me*, right? I had known her since birth. We were more than lovers. I looked at Setepenre in the distance. It had been Ur-Nammu who had kept everything a secret; *he* had kept them hidden. Ur-Nammu was the liar. The Vessel was the murderer. I needed to remember these simple truths.

But there it was again, that inescapable hollow feeling, as if my words and thoughts weren't connecting to my core self. I clenched my hands into fists. It didn't matter. I'd be damned if I let the Vessel, or Caelius, see me broken. I'd be damned if Nefertiti looked on me again with pity, as she had when I'd been a slave at her feet. I was the first and only son of Onack the Great.

163

I was just as much a leader of the Gutian people as she was. I wouldn't abandon my heritage again, and I wouldn't fail her like I'd failed to protect her daughters in our last battle. My thrashed body and splintered bones should've been proof enough of that.

Now that felt real, the ache caused by my failure to protect them.

"What exactly do you want from me, Caelius?"

"Caelius." His eyes grew dark again. "Try on Father. Or my favorite, which you have yet to master: God."

I stared at him blankly. "Enjoying yourself?"

He licked his lips, tracing the outline of my frame with his eyes. "When you were cradled in my arms, you called me both."

"Stop it," I said with disdain.

He smiled, pressing a hand over the Vessel's mouth as she again rallied to speak. "What do I want? I want you to *feed* on this little light bulb whore. I want you to make her weak enough that my hand can easily pop in and take out her tiny, insignificant soul." He pressed his body closer to hers as her limbs fell limp, the fight leaving them.

I felt that too, the hate at seeing his skin against hers.

Was this possessiveness because I had hunted her and vampires were notoriously proprietorial of their prey? I wouldn't put it past myself. I at least had some memory of the hunt: locusts, a dorm in Arizona, a hall monitor, and then . . . then . . . only blackness and words remained. The words in my mind said that I had destroyed the dorm and taken her to Caelius right away. It was strange that the journey to Caelius was just *gone*. How badly had I been injured in our last battle to have forgotten a *year*?

I did remember a moment of her in his cage though, his skin

164

pressing against hers.

"Disgusting," I uttered.

Caelius smiled. "I agree. The blood of a Vessel will taste like swine compared to mine."

I blinked. *He* was disgusting. The word had slipped out, and it'd been meant for him alone, though I wasn't sure why. He wasn't altogether wrong; her blood would be sour after ingesting the blood of my maker for . . . weeks? Months? He still never gave me a clear estimate when I asked. Who knew how long I had been coddled, helpless in his arms.

Disgusting.

"I've got ahold of her, and she's weak enough so she can't turn her blood into light. It should be *easy* for you, darling, unless you are still unwell." He paused again. "Lucian, if this is making you feel . . . uncertain, I can take us back to the cabin and mend you more thoroughly. My arms do miss your weight, my pet."

I instantly pressed my lips against her neck.

Like hell I would let him drown me in his blood and exploit the fever it induced.

Like hell I would make Nefertiti and her children watch what a subservient worm I became after every feeding.

No.

I needed to prove to him, to all of them, that I was fine, that I would never need his blood again. I had to break the cycle of control he had over me. Even if every cell in my body was fighting to stop, to not hurt the Vessel, I had to resist it. I couldn't be broken like this, not when they needed me the most. I looked again at Nefertiti and her daughters. If Caelius wanted me to prove myself, if that was what it would take for him to

165

stop force-feeding me, then I'd gladly accept the challenge. I had to be there for my family now, what was left of it.

My teeth grazed her supple neck, and she flinched.

I've only been a man with Shea. Never a vampire. I will never feed from her. The words floated to the surface of my mind but were drowned out just as quickly as they'd come.

What was that?

Was the Vessel trying to manipulate me in a desperate attempt at salvation? Did she think such cheap parlor tricks would win against *the* First-Born of Caelius?

I sunk my teeth in deep.

It was sweeter than honey.

I felt both the tensed shock of her body and the relaxed palm of Caelius's hand against my back.

"I'm so glad," he said calmly, resting his chin on my head as I fed feverishly, lapping up her blood like nectar. "I am the only one, Lucian. She is *nothing* to you. You doing this for me means everything." He paused, relishing the moment. "Forgiveness is important to your kind, isn't it? I forgive you then. I forgive you for all of it. Let's never be apart again." He nuzzled his head against mine.

I drank as fast as I could. I just wanted this to be over. I wasn't doing this for *him*.

What?

I choked, swallowing down more of her sweet blood.

What was this?

Tears were streaming down my face.

I heard Nefertiti gasp at the sight. The pain in my chest felt raw, like the Vessel had singed a hole through my rib cage, but I was intact. I drank faster, trying to bury the feelings spinning like a hurricane at the center of my heart. I felt out of control.

Loss.

So much loss.

The grief was inescapable.

Why was drinking her making me feel like I had lost the most precious thing in this world? It didn't make sense. *Nefari* was my world. This Vessel was nothing.

"Okay, Lucian. That's enough, dear one." Caelius stroked my back, tugging on my Hanfu.

I clung to her with my teeth, wrapping my arms tight around her waist.

"I said that's enough, boy." He pulled the fabric harder, his tone threatening.

I couldn't stop; I wouldn't stop.

She was *mine.*

The word growled in me, deep, like a hunger that would never be satiated, like an ocean breeze moving over the desert, calling the sailor *home.*

"Mine!" I shouted through my clenched blood-soaked teeth.

I pushed him back, yanking her free from his grip.

Then I felt it.

I'd had the same feeling in Pompeii when I'd drunk the Vessel then. It was as if I were starting to pull at her soul, drawing it out like Caelius had planned to do for himself.

Did I even have that power?

"Enough!" Caelius threw me back with such force I heard the sound barrier snap in my wake.

My body smashed into the earth like a meteor, the crater

surrounding it filling up with a mushroom cloud of dirt. Through the haze I heard Meky's voice. "You should be ashamed to call yourself Gutian!"

"Meky!" I stood up quickly, coughing out the grit choking my lungs dry. "Where are you? I'm sorry! I'll fix it!" I tried to see her through the cloud, but it was too thick. She was right—what was I doing? The Vessel was *mine*? Was I intentionally trying to piss Caelius off and get us all killed? I should've been ashamed; I'd humiliated myself in front of them, no more Gutian than some rabid newly turned vampire.

"Wait, don't!" Nefertiti called through the storm cloud of silt, and I ran toward the sound.

"Nefari!" When I arrived, Caelius had a hole burning in the side of his skull like a fist made of fire had punched through it.

"What happened?" I shouted, looking around desperately.

Meky and the Vessel were *gone*.

Nefari fell to her knees, pleading at Caelius's feet. Caelius glared at Nefertiti before kicking her off and shifting his one remaining bloodred eye to me. His teeth grew, splitting his gums, drool pooling at the tips. "You failed. That's what happened."

CHAPTER 9
SHEA

"**P**lease wake up. Please, please wake up." Meky's voice was filled with worry. "I'm so sorry. I'm such an idiot for putting up with that charade for so long. I didn't even know what was happening until we arrived. If I'd have known, I would have warned you, I swear . . ." Meky trailed off, obviously not knowing if she was talking to an unconscious person or not.

I tried to open my eyes or move any part of my body, but I couldn't.

After blasting one last firebomb at Caelius's face, which had felt really good, I'd found myself whisked away by Meky, then I'd blacked out. But like a giant boulder to the brain, all the memories of what had just happened hit me with terrible impact.

I moaned. It was all I could do.

But it was enough to hear a huge sigh of relief from Meky. "Oh, thank the gods! Shea. Shea, can you hear me?"

Moan number two. It was meant to be a yes, but nope,

couldn't quite form words yet.

"I've got to get us to Aidan and the others. They'll be able to help you. I just don't know how." The desperation in her voice was heartbreaking.

I didn't blame Meky at all. I didn't even blame Nefertiti, though she was the one who'd lured me into the trap. I blamed Caelius.

I'd had to fight them all, though thankfully, Meky had steered clear. She'd even body-slammed her mother and sister a time or two when they had come close to attacking. Lucian had been too busy focusing on me to even notice, or if he had, it hadn't seemed to register as odd.

What was scary about the whole thing was the fact that even his view of the fight was distorted. Every time I'd tried to hit Caelius, he would shadow-yank one of the girls in front of him as a shield. Then Lucian would jump in front of said girl, and I'd end up blowing a hole in *him*.

Lucian had thought he was saving Nefertiti and the others from *me*! As much as I was furious at Nefertiti, I hadn't wanted to hurt her. I knew she was only doing this to save her daughters. And poor Sherit. I'd blasted her four or five times when Lucian wasn't there in time. Only Sete had been into the fight. She'd kept coming after me like she was a cat and I was the laser. I'd had to use some serious wind power to keep her away, but I hadn't tried to hurt her either.

The only shining light from that horrible confrontation was my mom. When Sete had pinned me down at one point, Mom had yanked her off me like the poor girl was a rag doll. Then my mother had looked me in the eye and said, "Shea? *My* Shea."

Sete and Sherit had pulled her off of me and kept her restrained for the rest of the fight.

But I'd seen it in my mother's eyes: love.

She'd remembered me.

I knew it wouldn't last long. No doubt Caelius was giving her blood even as I had these thoughts, but it gave me hope.

Lucian, on the other hand . . .

I thought I'd prepared myself to see him brainwashed, but nothing could have prepared me for what I'd seen.

When he wasn't attacking, he'd looked at me with a blankness that had made my knees weak with pain. I'd tried so hard to get to him, to remind him of our connection, of our love for each other, but . . . there was nothing.

Not even when I first met him in Arizona and he'd only seen me as a Vessel had he looked at me like that. His expression had been so full of emptiness, it made me wish I had the power of a thousand suns to destroy Caelius.

And when Lucian drained me . . .

He'd just kept drinking and drinking.

It was Caelius who had stopped him.

He would have killed me.

The Lucian I knew was gone.

I felt so helpless.

Oh! A finger. I could move my finger.

I hated that I was completely incapacitated because of Lucian drinking from me. He had promised he never would, even when I had given him permission at the sundial. He had been so burned, I'd wanted to help heal him, but he had refused.

If he ever did remember the truth again, he'd never forgive

171

himself.

"Meky." My voice was back, but it was gravelly from screaming.

My eyes opened. I was leaning up against a tree in a dense forest of pines. Meky stood in front of me, her expression full of concern and shame. Kneeling down, she touched my arm gently. "I told my mother what I thought of her and her little scheme to trap you. I swear I didn't know, Shea. She disgraces the Gutian name."

I found the strength to clutch Meky's hand. "Please, don't blame her. She just lost your sisters; she can't bear to lose any more of you. She'd do anything for you. You know that." I didn't know where my sudden defense of Nefertiti had come from, but I knew I spoke the truth. If sacrificing me saved her daughters, she would do it without question. *I* could never trust her again, but Meky could.

"You're seriously too nice. It's probably all that Light flowing through your veins. She was over the line, and she knew it. But at least Lucian seems to be fighting his blood control, so that's a positive, right?" Meky had a glimmer of optimism in her tone.

"How was drinking my blood and almost killing me 'fighting his blood control'?" I asked incredulously.

"You didn't see him?"

"Kind of hard when his teeth were in my neck." I tried not to sound too wounded. It still hurt to think about Lucian wanting to drain me like that.

Meky squeezed my hand and smiled at me. "Shea, he was crying the whole time, as in, waterfalls. His soul is fighting to remember, even if his brain can't because Caelius is shoving his blood down his throat."

"But Caelius was the one who stopped him. Lucian kept going." I wanted to hold on to the shred of hope Meky was giving me. If he had cried while drinking me, then he remembered on some level who I was and what I meant to him.

"I don't think Caelius liked it when Lucian claimed you. His own ego made him pull Lucian off. Let's just say screaming 'mine' probably means another brainwashing session for Lucian." Meky tilted her head to the side and sighed. "Plus, I'm pretty sure Lucian tapped into your soul like he did in Pompeii with the third Vessel. It brought Aidan's brothers in to protect the poor guy, and then Aidan had to . . . you know . . ."

"Kill the Vessel? Don't remind me. I still get aches from where *I* was stabbed." I thought about what Meky was telling me for a moment, then said, "My soul, huh? So Caelius threw him off of me because he was jealous and afraid Lucian would eat his power-up pack?"

"Yeah," Meky confirmed. "I wouldn't have let Lucian kill you, Shea. I was already running toward you when Caelius threw Lucian off. I'm just grateful you had one last fireball in you, or I'm pretty sure Caelius would have popped my head off when I got there."

I knew she was right. Caelius wouldn't have hesitated if I hadn't distracted him with a face-bomb, and I would have been blamed, yet again, for killing one of Nefertiti's children.

Meky continued. "When you blew his head half off, I took you and ran. Ur-Nammu came after me to make sure I was okay, but now he's back to spying on Mom and my sisters. He's being a coward too, letting doubt make the decisions for him. I'm

173

seriously the only one who's even acting like a Gutian."

Standing up once more in frustration, Meky shook her head, then put her hands out as if displaying the trees like a prize. "Welcome to the Black Hills National Forest in South Dakota. I ran until I was sure we weren't being followed. That could change very quickly though, so we need to get to Aidan and the others."

"Agreed. I need to Dream-Walk and tell them where we are. I've done it with Aidan before, so hopefully he'll be ready for me." Taking a deep breath, I paused. My strength wasn't getting much better. "I don't know if I have the mojo to do this."

Meky sat down across from me. "Your Vessel powers are tapped, so it's going to take a while. Just try and see what happens. If you can't do it, I'll keep us moving toward the cabin. I'm not going to let anything happen to you."

I felt a burst of affection for Meky. Nodding, I closed my eyes. "Here goes nothing."

It wasn't difficult to fall asleep, as exhausted as I was. It was nice that my brain was so used to Dream-Walking that I ended up standing next to the swing set in the backyard of the house I'd grown up in. I remembered Dream-Walking with Lucian here, back when we barely knew each other. It was somehow comforting and devastating rolled into one. Still, being back home, I felt relieved. Aidan and I had hung out on this swing set every summer, all the way through high school.

"Aidan? Are you here?" I called out.

"Shea! Is that you, or am I having a weird dream about our backyard?" My *dad's* voice came from behind me.

Surprised, I turned around and saw Jeff Harper, the best dad anyone could ask for. He pulled me into a hug. Whether it was a dream to him or not, he was obviously terrified, not knowing where I'd gone and what had happened to me.

Gently pulling away, I kept our hands clasped together as if I were a little girl that still needed her daddy.

And I was.

I *really* needed him now more than ever.

"It's really me. I'm Dream-Walking with you," I said. "I thought for sure it would be Aidan that would show up because I've done this with him before, but obviously my brain decided I needed to see you instead. I could really use some 'Dad' time right about now."

My father framed my face with his free hand and looked at me as if I were the most beautiful creature in the world. Such a dad. "Thank *God* you're okay." His expression quickly turned worried as he pulled his hand away from my face. "You *are* okay, aren't you?"

"Yes. I'm all right. Meky saved me. Nefertiti lured me into a trap, and I fell for it like the naive sap I am," I grumbled.

"Don't apologize for being a trusting person; it's what makes you better than everyone."

"Everyone? Really, Dad?" I smiled at his unwavering devotion to me. It made me feel safe. And a little bit better about what I had just been through with Lucian.

"Yes, *everyone* in the entire universe. You're the best there is." He smiled at me as he squeezed my hand with affection. Then he sighed. "So Nefertiti is definitely bad news, huh?"

I shook my head. "No. She was just protecting her daughters, but that fact alone now makes her untrustworthy." I tried to stop the catch in my voice, but I couldn't when I said, "Lucian thinks

I killed his family. He hates me, Dad. As in really, really *hates* me."

Dad pulled me in for another hug, and I took it as my cue to cry my Dream-Walking eyes out. I knew I wasn't really there in physical form, but it felt good to let it out anyway. After I regained my composure, I took a step back, realizing I hadn't told him about Mom.

"Dad, Mom recognized me. She said, '*My* Shea' and tried to protect me from being attacked by Setepenre."

His face brightened at the possibility. "We have to get her away from Caelius. She'll remember everything on her own if we can just get her alone. I know it."

"Or if we can restrain her in the vicinity of Aidan like we did with you, he can fix her." I really hoped it was possible, but I didn't think Caelius would let me near my mother after witnessing her momentary lapse in judgement.

My father placed his hands on my upper arms to steady me. "First things first. Where are you two? We need to come get you."

Duh, that was the whole purpose of this Dream-Walking session. I had been so happy to see my dad, I had almost forgotten. "Black Hills National Forest, South Dakota. I can't be any more specific than that."

"Don't need to." He took his hands away and tapped his nose. "Super smeller now. Just need to be within thirty miles or so, and I'll find you."

"Super smeller?" I groaned. "Dad, you're such a dork."

"The first vampire-dork in existence. I'll take it. Maybe I should start thinking of some good 'dad' jokes for the ride back to the cabin." He laughed.

"Nothing would make me happier," I teased. But I actually meant it. My dad may have been a Second-Born vampire, but he was still my dad. "Just hurry. Caelius has probably sent a goon squad to attack us, and I'm weak. I'm going to need some time to regain my strength."

His expression turned serious at that. "We'll leave as soon as I open my eyes." Reaching down, he kissed my forehead. "I love you to the moon and back, Shea."

"I love you too, Dad."

I opened my eyes, and Meky was staring at me expectantly.

I allayed her tension immediately. "They're coming."

With a sigh of relief, her posture relaxed a bit. "I'm trying not to be mad at my mother, but I can't help it. She's never been weak, and she's always stood up for what was right. She never let fear rule her."

"Maybe she'll come around. You rescuing me might have woken her up a bit." I tried to comfort her.

"I doubt it. She's too stubborn." Meky made a face of disgust. "Let her have Sherit and Sete. Sherit was always a follower, and Sete . . . she's always belonged to Caelius." She shrugged. "Which basically has made her a mean girl her whole life."

"She's probably never had the chance to really be herself or even know who she is, not if Caelius influenced her." Was I defending the brat who'd almost killed me? I just didn't want Meky to hate her family. "I mean, look at my mom. She's pretty horrible because of Caelius, but back when she had her memories, she was just my mom. She was the kindest person you'd ever meet. We just need to destroy Caelius, then you can decide if you hate your sisters or not."

177

"I guess. It's just easier for me to be angry," Meky confessed.

"I get that. I'm angry too." I really was. I simply didn't know what to do with it.

My eyes grew heavy again. I wasn't healing fast enough, and Dream-Walking had drained me even more. "I think I need to rest for a bit."

"Of course. They should be here soon. I'll carry you if you're still asleep."

"Thanks," I said as I closed my eyes. My exhaustion was too deep to stay conscious.

Just as I was drifting off, I swore I heard the flapping of giant wings . . .

***

"Shea?"

Was that . . . ?

"Mom?" I opened my eyes. I was standing in a swirl of colors, as if I had jumped into a child's painting.

I was Dream-Walking, I knew that right away, but where was I?

And had I imagined hearing my mother's voice?

I tried to give the environment shape, turn it into a forest or my old backyard, but the spinning blobs of color continued to swirl instead.

I knew then that I wasn't controlling this Dream-Walk. Someone else was. Someone who didn't know much about it, or at least couldn't seem to figure out how to make a real-life setting.

"Shea?"

Definitely my mom. But where was she?

"Mom, I'm here. Can you hear my voice?" I called out to the whirlwind of blues and pinks flying in front of me.

"Yes." Her voice sounded relieved. "Yes, I can hear you. I can't see you though."

"Just concentrate on me as hard as you can. Think about our house. Our life. Our—" My voice caught in my throat. It was painful to even think about how perfect life had been growing up. I really took it for granted. I had two amazing parents that, frankly, I didn't know if I deserved.

The colors began to take shape and form into furniture until I stood in my childhood bedroom. Everything was decorated as it was when I was eight. *Harry Potter* posters adorned almost every wall. There was even a small poster of *Twilight* I didn't remember having. Ironic much? A four-poster canopy bed was in the corner, and a small rolltop desk sat across from it.

"Mom?" I tried again.

Molly Harper materialized in front of me, sitting on the edge of the mattress with her hands in her lap. Looking up at me, I could see the confusion in her eyes. "Is this real? Is this your room?"

I nodded, not wanting to spook her. "I was in love with Ron Weasley." I motioned to the posters and the fact that most of them were of Rupert Grint.

Mom actually smiled at that, then looked as if she were trying very hard to remember something. "We named our cat Weasley because she was orange."

I sat down next to her, and she flinched slightly. I scooted away so there was at least a foot between us. "Yeah, you'd call

179

her your little gingerbread because you thought she was so sweet when she'd sleep on your chest."

Tears rolled down her face. "I remember that."

I was too scared to say anything that would cause her to leave. A long silence passed.

Finally, she said, "It comes to me in flashes. I used to tell Grandfather whenever I had one, then he'd give me a drop of his blood, and it would go away. I craved that at first. I didn't want to remember. It was too painful."

"But now?" I asked tentatively.

"Now I don't tell him because . . ." She turned to me, unsure. "Because I *want* to remember. I can feel it, this overwhelming sensation, and it fills me up like nothing ever could. At first I thought it was love for Grandfather, but it isn't." Mom paused, a frown deepening her brow. "I don't think I like him very much at all." Shaking her head, she continued. "When I saw Sete attack you, I realized all that love is . . . is for you. Isn't it?"

I felt like her words would burst my heart on impact. It was almost too much to hope for. I was terrified that this was a trick, a horrible joke that Caelius had put my mother up to, but her eyes . . . they looked sincere.

"I love you, Mom." I decided I'd go with honesty. If she was faking it, these words would make her break character and attack.

But she simply said, "I love you too, my little girl."

I swallowed down the intensity of emotions that threatened to drown me. "If Caelius finds out . . . he'll erase this from your mind. You won't remember any of it. Or me."

Mom's eyes brightened when she said, "Shea, I'm evolving somehow. He already gave me a drop of his blood after the fight. It did nothing. I remembered everything, and I didn't feel bonded to him or the false sense of love that his blood normally gives me."

"You're saying his blood control isn't working on you anymore?" I asked, doubtful.

"I think so. I don't know. Maybe if he was giving me the amount he gave Lucian it would work, but the one drop? It doesn't affect me at all anymore." She was actually smiling, proud of this new power.

"It must have something to do with you being a child of both Lucian and Nefertiti, or maybe it's because you're my mother." I began to work through it out loud.

"Mother of the Vessel, daughter of the First-Borns." Mom repeated my sentiment with a nod of agreement. "I don't know what I am, but I know above all, I'm your mother, and I never want to forget that again. My soul and mind are filled with you, Shea. The most important thing I've ever done in my life is being your mom. I will kill Grandfather myself if I have to. Blood or not."

"Oh, Mom." I couldn't control myself. I leaned over and hugged her desperately. She embraced me back with even more intensity. "I don't ever want to leave here."

I could hear her crying openly. "I don't either."

I pulled out of our embrace, desperate. "Can you escape? Can you get to us? We can protect you! Mom, I need you. I need you to be safe from Caelius and his blood."

Mom's face became pained. "Shea, I can't. I can't be with you yet. Grandfather is so much stronger than you suspect. He could squash all of you with the snap of his fingers. He's

181

choosing not to because of his obsession with Lucian. Lucian is all Grandfather cares about. He's trying to reshape Lucian's thoughts and memories over and over until he gets it perfect."

Pausing a moment, Mom made sure our eyes were locked when she said, "Lucian fights for the memories of you like nothing I've ever seen. His will is so strong, it's what made me determined to start remembering. If he loved you that much . . . and you kept begging me to remember that I was your mother . . . I just had to know for sure." She shook her head with sadness. "Shea, Lucian has remembered you so many times despite the amount of blood Grandfather feeds him. Still, I'm afraid he may never recover from this."

Not what I wanted to hear, but I knew I needed to. It only made me more motivated to save Lucian, and the only way to do that was to kill Caelius.

"But why do you have to stay? Why can't you find us and fight with us?" I asked. I could hear the panic in my voice.

Mom took one of my hands and held it in hers. "My fight is being by Grandfather's side. He has to believe I'm his alone. I don't know what his plans are, but I have to find out for *you*. If you want the chance to destroy him, you need as much information as you can get, and I'm the one who can get it for you."

"It's too dangerous. He'll know you're lying. He'll kill you." Now that I had a shred of my mother back, I couldn't let her go. It hurt too much to even contemplate.

Mom smiled. "Oh, Shea. Grandfather is completely clueless. He's probably the original narcissist, and you know how I handled Ms. Thompkins from the school board."

Comparing Ms. Thompkins to Caelius actually brought a

smile to my face as well. She was the worst. She was a classic narcissist, didn't care one iota for the kids, and only wanted to push her agenda with the school. That had basically equated to making everyone else do her job while she sat back and collected a paycheck for doing nothing. The stories of how my mom had manipulated Ms. Thompkins into actually working and doing great things for the schools was legendary. If Mom could do the same with Caelius, we might actually learn something useful.

It just scared me to think of her putting herself in danger like that.

"What if he—"

"Trust me, Shea. He's been holed up for thousands of years; he's completely vulnerable to modern-day manipulation."

I remembered that after Caelius killed Gracuri, I had made some things up about what Lucian had said about him. Caelius had gone nuts. It had been pretty easy too. I'd been trying to enrage Caelius, and he had fallen for it hook, line, and sinker.

If Mom thought she could handle Caelius, I had to trust her.

I nodded slowly. "But if you think for a second he's figured you out, you have to promise me you'll run."

"I will." Sighing, she said, "If I see you again in person, I might not be able to stop myself from going with you anyway, or die trying."

"Don't say that. We will all come out of this *alive*." As I said it, I wondered if it was true. A deep dark knot in my stomach threatened to overwhelm me, but I pushed it down.

Squeezing my hand with affection, she looked at me as if it were the last time. "You're healing now, I can feel it. I can feel you, my beautiful daughter. It's time to wake up."

A surge of warmth filled every cell in my body as I jolted awake. Bright lights and rainbow reflections blinded me as I blinked. I felt like I was back with Lucian in his small house; he had used crystals to heal me after Aidan had stabbed me. But as my eyes adjusted, I saw that I was in Helena's cabin again.

Someone turned off the lights, and I saw Dad, Aidan, Meky, Helena, and Duncan enter the room with hopeful looks.

"There she is. Welcome back, lass." Duncan smiled.

My mom had been right—I was healing. The refracted light had restored me just like it had at Lucian's home.

"I'm okay." I sat up.

Helena looked me over like I was a patient. "Back when I was human, Lucian asked me to find a way to heal with light. I didn't know then that he wanted this knowledge to heal creatures of Light."

Aidan nodded. "Lucian wanted to torture the Vessel, then heal them, then torture them again, knowing how much it would hurt me."

Duncan placed a hand on Aidan's shoulder. "I would've given him a right kick in the arse if I had known you then, brother."

Brother was new. And my heart really loved it.

"I Dream-Walked with my mom. She remembers me now," I said in a small voice, as if I couldn't quite believe it myself.

Dad clasped my hand and squeezed it. "Is she coming to find us? Will she come home?"

I shook my head. "No. She thinks she can find out more for

us if she stays." I hated saying it out loud.

Dad nodded, though I could tell he was heartbroken. But he tried to stay positive as he told me, "Helena is so close to finding a way to destroy Caelius, Shea."

I turned to Helena, hope surging through me.

Helena nodded. "There's just one missing ingredient, but I know I'll figure it out. I just need a little more time."

"I'm not sure we have it. Caelius will find this place soon."

"I've gotten everything I need from the cabin. The rest needs to happen here." Helena pointed to her head. "The missing link is right in front of me, I know it. I just need to percolate for a bit."

"It's not me?" I asked. The whole assumption was if I learned enough of my powers, I'd be able to juice up one of her contraptions to kill Caelius.

"That's the thing. It *is* you and it *isn't*. I can't explain it. I need to think about it more." Helena looked as if her mind was racing.

Aidan took my hand from my dad and helped me to my feet. "In the meantime, you need a bath."

I looked down and was finally able to see what he meant. My clothes were practically in shreds. There was dirt caked on my skin, and I was pretty sure there were leaves and blood in my hair from the big fight with Caelius.

Gross.

"A bath sounds nice," I said.

"Good, because you really do stink." He smiled.

Aidan's joking made me suddenly feel normal, and I was grateful for it. I grabbed him before he could pull his hand away and hugged him tightly, making sure I rubbed as much dirt on him as possible.

Laughing, he tried to push me away, but I just held tighter. "What's the matter? You don't want to hug me? But I missed you so much."

After a moment of struggle, he finally gave in to the hug, despite my odor. He looked down at me with his gentle eyes and said, "Don't run away like that again, okay?"

I let go of him and nodded solemnly. "I never will."

And I meant it.

I'd never make that mistake again.

CHAPTER 10
LUCIAN

You should be ashamed to call yourself Gutian!

Those words echoed through me as Caelius pulled his body off of mine. He stood up next to the bed. The sun shone on his skin, and it glistened from our mixed sweat, making him shine like the god he was. I worshiped him more than Nefertiti, more than anyone. It sickened me how he had pounded that truth into every muscle of my body, every cell in my veins, until I'd screamed for him alone.

I wiped the red from my lips. Despite swallowing a gallon of blood, I was still thirsty. Caelius's feedings *always* left me hungry for more. He obliged the tremors of my aching need by giving me all I desired . . . at first. It was my body, not my will, that had responded so readily. Now that he had both at his disposal, he gave me just enough blood to keep me begging shamelessly for more. Still, it was just enough that I wouldn't go through total withdrawal and recover. Addicted. That was how he wanted me, and although part of me knew his game, knew what this was . . . every other part worshiped him.

My legs trembled, unable to stand from the long hours of being bent into submission. He hadn't let me leave this bed for over a month, or had it been longer? Time ran together like the pulsing of his blood in my veins. I hadn't seen my family for so long, only *our* bedroom. No matter how hard I screamed, no one else dared enter. My world consisted solely of Caelius now—his words, his next "fun" idea for us to try out.

He looked down at me and smiled, reaching his hand around my neck.

"My adorable pet," he mused, squeezing my throat.

I was bound by angelic chains, but I was drunk enough with his blood that he could tie and keep me in any fashion he liked. I wondered how much of this was really punishing me for disobedience. He seemed more like a convict that had just escaped prison and the first and only thing that drove him was lust.

I blamed the Vessel for this. I'd been off of his blood, and my mind had just started to clear, but my failure to obey Caelius had forced me right back into his arms. Meky's words as she left were never truer than in this moment; I wasn't Gutian—I was Caelius's plaything.

I felt the restraints cutting into the bruises on my wrists as he pulled my hair, my spine arching painfully. I winced but said nothing. Despite my addiction, if I could keep his focus on punishing me and not the others, I would gladly take the brunt of Caelius's twisted sense of justice. The thought dwindled as I mocked my current state—as if I had any pride left, as if I could resist him now, even if I wanted to.

I squirmed as he twisted my body against the chains. "Uncomfortable, pet?" He released my hair and pulled me by the neck, lifting my lips to his.

"Please," I gasped.

I shifted my weight restlessly. The boy who had sworn never to beg for anything after his mother's death was pleading–as if I was the *pet* he so called me. "More blood," I panted.

He leaned forward and cut his thumb, shoving the red tip into my mouth.

My head jerked up in anticipation as my lips curled around my thumb, licking the crimson in a blissful agony that was the definition of being with Caelius.

He jerked his finger out suddenly. "Please, what?"

"Please, *God*, it's not enough! I need more!"

His eyes flashed to mine, and as mixed as I felt, he looked the same.

"I like it when you call me God." There was a spark of pleasure as he thrusted his thumb farther into my mouth, cutting it on my elongated fangs. "As insincere as it is." And there was the stab of pain.

"No," I moaned instinctively. "Your wrist, like before." I suckled, but the few drops escaping his thumb weren't enough.

He didn't yield.

He toyed with me for another hour after that.

He released my chains when he was finished, and we panted in each other's arms. He cradled my head to his chest, weaving my dark hair through his pale fingertips. I looked up at him with an adoration my body *felt*, but the longer this went on, the more

189

I realized that I was just under his control. And the more aware I was of his influence, the longer these sessions became. In the end, all I was aware of now was that I'd lost myself.

I'd had questions in the beginning. Why was I crying when I drank the Vessel? Why did her name sound like salvation, and Caelius never used it, like it was a curse? Why couldn't I remember that *name* in the darkness? What really happened in the year I lost?

All those questions were like stories erased from a chalkboard; they were abstract numbers and letters, scribbled mathematical theories that were half-formed and impractical in real life. All that was real, was now, and right now I had to be obedient to Caelius to protect my family.

Questions about the Vessel were meaningless while stuck in purgatory with only penance and no release. Even my lips couldn't form the words to ask him to stop. They only begged for *more*. This wasn't purgatory at all, but hell itself. I should have known that by the *thirst*.

He kissed my forehead, and I practically purred.

"Good boy." He patted my hair, nuzzling his face against mine.

I looked briefly at the door.

Salvation wasn't coming.

I could hear her voice just beyond it, but Nefertiti didn't interfere. I was glad she kept her distance; Caelius was too powerful. It did make me see her in a different light, however. Nefari was not the woman I had fallen in love with back in Gutium. She was broken and compromised like I was. I couldn't trust her after all, no more than I could trust myself and my fractured memories. My one constant, my morning star, my jewel among stones . . . had fallen.

Caelius could've been lying about everything, and most likely he was.

But that didn't matter.

What mattered was survival, *their* survival: the remnants of the Gutian tribe. However, Meky was right; I didn't deserve to be called a part of that tribe anymore. Our code—a code that had been engraved across our tapestries, woven into our minds, spoken like a nursery hymn over every child in Gutium—was more meaningless text erased on the chalkboard that had become my mind. And it left me . . . empty.

In all my years hating Adnachiel and the Vessel, hating myself and what I'd become, I'd never felt so despicable as I did now. This baseless devotion to a master that made me call him God, the humiliation of it–if it weren't for my family, I would kill myself while there was still a self left to kill. Even that desire, over time, would be consumed by Caelius and his ravenous hunger to devour all that I was and could be.

The sad thing was, his shallow ache for complete devotion actually robbed him of what he truly wanted: the real me he had renamed in earnest. The more I dissolved into him, the more I realized he'd made that mistake too. Calling me Lucian, making me "new," changing me, it all only added to the pain so evident in his eyes. He was bleeding out his own pleasure with every ounce of blood poured down my throat.

The more I became his, the less he wanted what I was becoming.

Pleasure and pain.

191

He was stuck in the same hell I was, only he didn't know it.

Could the devil even know he was in hell? Maybe that was what kept him there. He would never want to admit that, in defeating me completely, he had defeated himself and torn what was precious out of his own hands.

Now, looking up at him with such devotion, I was really *Lucian*, the one he had made. I was no longer looking at him as I always had, as La-Narru.

Meky was right.

Everything Gutian about me was dead.

***

"What kind of *god* would I be if I didn't believe in second chances?" Caelius laughed to himself. "Or, in your case, a thousand chances." He laughed again, but this time it was full of resentment. "I've never tried so hard for anything in all my existence. I've swallowed galaxies more willing than you." He frowned, looking up toward the ceiling. "Kids. Am I right, Light? They're the *worst*."

When his gaze met mine, I felt nothing but subservience.

He did that often now, talking to the Light as if they were old familiar rivals.

I crossed my hands in front of my chest, touching the silk that covered it. It was nice, wearing clothes again.

"Come now, pet, it's time." He paraded me out into the living room like some sort of finished masterpiece.

Having spent the sole of my time in the bedroom, I hadn't realized we were back at the cabin. All the girls were silent; not even Setepenre met my gaze. They were no doubt devastated because Meky was missing. She'd been taken by the Vessel I had failed to give over to Caelius.

"Now we will all *try again*." He moved his fingers through my hair, eyeing the bruise around my neck. I flinched as his hands moved to his side. I could still feel them at my throat, and in that, choking me during sex had served its purpose well. I would always feel them now, like a collar reminding me whom I belonged to. He wanted permanence on a body that could heal from wounds, and he'd found a way to do it. Even as the purple began turning cream, the others could tell just as readily that he had indelibly marked me as *his*, whether the bruising was still visible or not. Nefertiti made no motion to bring me comfort, as she had upon our first reunion. She stood by the window, as cold and distant as the mud sculptures I'd made of her in Egypt.

Caelius leaned forward. "I believe in second chances, so I'm going to—"

"Grandfather . . ." Finally Sete's gaze lifted as she scanned my body, eyeing the visible cuts outside the Hanfu. It was the same garment he had dressed me in before. There was something comforting about it being close to my skin, as if it were alive somehow, as if I weren't so achingly alone, standing at the center of what should've been my family. I had become alien to them in my absence, consumed by long nights pinned under the weight of my new god.

Setepenre swallowed, looking over my wounds one last time before shifting her eyes to Caelius. "I understand wanting to punish *us* for the Vessel escaping, but . . . you took all of your punishment out on my father, and for so long. In the beginning he was screaming for days, begging you to stop. After that, he was moaning and . . . and we could all smell how much blood you were giving him, but he's not even injured. I mean, he's injured now, but that's from *you*, not the Vessel. It just seems unnecessary, cruel even."

Her face twisted, as if Caelius's behavior was shocking. "I don't understand. Aren't we a *family*?" She turned her chair, facing him. "You used to read me bedtime stories from the human world. You said we'd be like *that*. You said it would be perfect, like a dream. This doesn't match what you promised when you were imprisoned, saying that my real father and I would finally be reunited at last."

I had thought it impossible for the room to become quieter, but after she spoke it was like we'd flown to the moon. Fear pulsed through Nefertiti so fervently that I could taste it on my own lips. Sete had confidence in her voice, as if she believed she could talk to Caelius so casually, as if she didn't completely fear him like the rest of us. "What you're doing now is nothing like those fairy tales. If anything, you're acting like the villain—"

Stop! I reached into her mind and shouted that one word over and over.

She stuttered as she met my sharp gaze, ending her deadly progression of syntax.

"But—"

I shook my head at her as Caelius stepped forward, palatable rage emanating off of his limbs. He raised his hand to strike, but I quickly laced my arms around his waist, pulling him against my chest. I rested my head on the nape of his neck, as if I weren't terrified. "You're wrong, Setepenre. It is *my* job and my responsibility to handle the Vessel. I failed. None of you would have even been there had I done my job centuries ago. The blame is mine alone to bear. The consequences are mine alone to reap."

Caelius leaned back into my arms. "As if I, a god, would break a promise to you Sete. Only a human would think something so idiotic. All of you, you're the promise breakers. The whole lot of you. Maybe it's a Gutian thing," he taunted.

Nefertiti's subtle tell of biting the inside of her cheek when she was upset wasn't subtle anymore. The left side was sunken in, as if she'd had it for breakfast. I couldn't blame her; they all looked gutted from the remark. Caelius, in short, was calling our homeland a tribe of liars.

Reaching up, he patted my head, our devastation cooling his rage. "What a good pet *you* are though, finally taking responsibility for your failures."

"Have mercy. She doesn't understand the complexity of the situation." I held him tighter.

"Agreed. A momentary lapse on her part . . . and mine." He stroked my arm and winked at Sete, as if that were an apology for almost smacking her head off.

Nefertiti's eyes were still down, but she scowled deeper. Her shoulders sagged with relief at Sete's safety and what I could only guess was shame. I had to guess because I'd never seen her look the way she did now. It wasn't in my catalog of Nefari emotions. This wasn't a "tell" she had developed over time that only I knew. This was something I hadn't seen, not even as a slave in Egypt.

This was *defeat*.

"But Grandfather, don't you think—"

"Enough." I spoke before Caelius had the chance. Openly

195

defying him, doubting his choices, talking back: those were all things of the past that could have been done and survived, if barely, from the other side of his cage. This was different. He was free now, and she didn't need to learn what that shift meant. My body should have been proof enough for the both of us. "Caelius knows exactly what he's doing. He's not a villain; he's our savior. Anything on the contrary is blasphemy. Let it rest, Setepenre. Not. Another. Word."

She looked surprised, as if I, above everyone else, should have joined her in protesting my treatment.

As if I would be that selfish.

She was still mine to protect. Even if she felt undermined, even if in the end she hated me for it, it didn't matter. It was a father's greatest desire to shield his children from all the ugliness of the world, and right now that ugly was leaning against me, fiddling with the sash around my waist. For a brief moment, I was glad that Onack had died in battle. To see his son like this . . . would have killed him.

"Good, *very* good, pet. Better than expected even. But be careful throwing my name around. You know what to call me." He pulled the sash tighter and then grinned, taking a long moment to stare at each of their disgusted faces before continuing. "Now as I was saying before I was so rudely interrupted, I believe in second chances." He moved out of my arms and stepped behind me. Pulling my waist against his hips, he wrapped his hands around my shoulders as he spoke into my ear. "I'm going to let Lucian try again, if he thinks he's ready."

"I'm ready!" I yelled instinctually.

"Oh, such eagerness," Caelius growled, his breath hot against

196

my neck.

"Are you *really* ready, puppy?" he whispered. "Or do you need more *training*?" A vampire could hear a whisper a mile away. He wanted everyone in the room to see the intimacy of his lips pressed into my skin, his ownership clear.

"Yes, I'm ready!" It almost sounded like a bark, the way it exploded from my lips.

"Yes, *what*?" His grip tightened.

"Yes, *God*."

They cringed together, as if one breath had moved around the room and touched all of their skin. And technically it had. Caelius's breath was moving, activating his blood that now lived in all of us, blood that lived in *every* vampire in the world thanks to me because I'd turned humans who then turned more humans. I had the arrogance and ignorance to call them children, but in reality, *I* was the child. Broken, lost, and suddenly immortal, even then Caelius had me by the throat, when all along I had thought myself a man and not a dog. I was playing Caelius's game the instant I turned Ur-Nammu.

No.

It was when I lay in his arms dying in Egypt and he asked if I wanted salvation for *her*: Nefari. The moment I agreed, I had unknowingly forfeited my eternal freedom.

He squeezed my shoulders, pinning me up against him like the master he was.

That same Nefari wouldn't even look at me now. I scanned the room. Setepenre, Sherit, and Molly were all staring at the floor. I was glad Meky wasn't here, so she too wouldn't see me like this.

197

In all my years as a slave, I had never been so broken down by a master. A whip could crack the flesh and spill blood, but it could not infect it with intention; that alone was left up to willpower. I had seen many slaves turn on their own kind, giving up information and sinking rebellions before they started, just to be spared the rod themselves. They would claim they had *no choice*, but in the end, as slaves, that was all we ever had. At that time, I had never compromised my Gutian integrity. Not once had I begged. Not once had I revealed anything. Even as the Pharaoh beat me to death, I'd protected what I loved. I'd protected *her*.

In Gutium, I'd left, but only after my father cried that he would surely fail in battle if I were by his side, dooming our entire village. I was all he'd had left to fight for, so he'd sent me away. That mistake had created in me the desire to never run from battle again. In fact, after I was turned, I ran *toward* war.

I vowed to never abandon my principles and pride, not for all the tears in the world, not even for the ones I loved, which was why I'd kept my Second-Borns at such a distance. Yet here I stood, giving up myself and my dignity for family. A family that, by the looks on their faces, would've rather seen me dead than Caelius's sock puppet. Was this worse than betraying them, like the slaves of old? Was this equal to my fleeing of Gutium the first time? Wasn't I doing the right thing? Wasn't this brave in its own right?

"I will not fail you this time, God. I give you my word as a—" I couldn't bring myself to say Gutian. I couldn't envision Onack the Great looking at me as if I were his son. This *thing* I'd become was more dog than man. I wasn't La-Narru anymore—

198

this last feeding of Caelius's blood had made sure of that.

I was Lucian.

Now and forever.

"I swear on my life."

Caelius clicked his tongue. "It's something precious to me, however, that life is not *yours* to swear on and lose. Remember, it's *mine*. And that life is the only reason I have for staying flesh." He nibbled the side of my neck, nuzzling his nose in the back of my ear. "Your vows excite me all the same," he whispered.

He pulled his head back and looked at the others. "But we will all formulate a plan and try again together, as a *family*. I'll supervise, of course, and this time you *will* drain her without those pathetic tears, stop when I command, and hand that meat-sack over to me so I can take her whore of a soul. *Understood?*"

"Yes." I didn't hesitate. "You know best. I'll do whatever you want."

He released me, then sat at the table, looking casually at the rest of them. "Well, family!" Their eyes were on him in an instant. "I *said* we'll make a plan together, didn't I?" He patted Setepenre's head, as if this approach would somehow appease her.

He slid his hand to the chair next to him, tapping his index finger on it. I rushed over and sat, quickly obeying the small command. He stared at Nefari and Sherit. "Sit." Only Nefertiti paused. And when she did, Caelius ran his hand through Setepenre's hair. "I keep them safe, don't I? The least you can do is obey without hesitation." She instantly sat in the chair across from me. It was strange, seeing the pride of Egypt afraid. Not in battle or beside the Pharaoh had she ever shown such fear.

No.

That didn't feel right. When her daughters died, she must have been afraid then, but I couldn't place it. I could still hear her screams though, the sounds her body made as they were torn apart in front of her. The Vessel had made her less Gutian in that moment, just as Caelius had done to me.

She was hollowed out, and it showed.

"Now." Caelius casually carved a light bulb onto the table with his pinky. He then ripped it apart with his long nails, cutting the table savagely as they grew thick, splitting his fingertips until they oozed dark blood. When he stopped, his eyes were black and filled with wrath. "Let's all be good little children and kill that slut once and for all, shall we?"

***

This was the first night Caelius let me sleep in the living room with my family. For the past few weeks he'd been giving me less blood. I was "dieting," as he liked to call it. The sex that followed lasted for a few hours; it wasn't an all-day affair like it had been. His hope was that, in time, I would be ready to drink the Vessel and give her over to him with nothing of the strange possessiveness that had overtaken me before. He explained that his blood "healing" wasn't supposed to be a punishment, but to undo the mind control and power the Vessel had over me.

Even though the pain and hunger was unlike anything I had experienced, I was thankful that some of my senses were finally returning. I could question and think, at least somewhat, for myself again. I thought about the task ahead. I found it odd that, simply because she was a woman, she was able to possess such control over a First-Born like me. Not in all my years hunting the Vessels had I ever encountered something so devastating.

Was she really *just* a Vessel? Was there nothing more to it? I shook my head, drawing a hand through my dark hair. I was always thinking about her. If Caelius knew that, he'd never let me leave his side. Just how strong was her mind control? I balled my hands into fists. All that mattered now was that I captured her for Caelius.

I couldn't wait.

He was going to fatten me up and then starve me like he was now until he thought I was ready. He had only given me a few drops today, but the lust in his eyes was insatiable. He was going to drown me in red soon, then pull out again. Each time he would give me less and less blood than the previous time. Each time the hunger for his return would grow, and that was exactly what he wanted: for me to spend the rest of my life *craving* him.

The way Caelius had looked at me this morning, like I was the oasis trapped inside his desert, didn't give me any confidence in an immediate time frame for this "plan" to be executed. When I asked *when*, he'd responded, "You're so close. We have a plan, but we are immortal, so we have time, darling. I need you to be foolproof. I want you to get this *right*. It will mean a lot to me, and to you too, in the end."

Was making me "foolproof" more important than him becoming whole? I had known of his obsession with me in the cage, but this was to a new extreme. How many times would he break my legs so I couldn't run away, mend them, and then break them again? I wasn't myself anymore. My personality and rebellious nature felt like a distant dream, much to Caelius's displeasure. He remarked how he wanted the *old* Lucian back, but perfected: the old Lucian, but subservient and infatuated with him. That was like taking the ingredients out of a soup, then complaining there was no flavor. It wasn't broth anymore, just boiled water, and that was what I'd become under his "care": empty.

Empty, but smart enough to know that I needed to redeem myself, not in his eyes, but in the eyes of my girls. Even though I was allowed to socialize with them again, they wouldn't look at me. Even Setepenre had distanced herself after I'd reprimanded her in front of Caelius. It was for her own safety, but she took it as a personal attack.

I sighed.

It was quiet at the cabin as the days passed, but not like it had been before. Before I could have stayed there forever, but now their distant eyes made my body sweat with the overwhelming feeling of failure and shame. If I brought Caelius the Vessel and did as he asked, he would have no need to feed me *period*. Without his blood, if I was still in there somewhere, maybe I could regain myself like I had done in the past. At least enough of myself to protect what I had left . . . which was dwindling before my eyes.

I thought of Meky.

The Vessel had taken her right in front of us, but not even Nefertiti was making a move to rescue her. Was the fight so gone from Nefari that she'd given up on her own daughter? We couldn't wait for me to be "ready" in Caelius's eyes; he didn't care about Meky. While he was force-feeding me, I had all but forgotten about her myself. Only her words that I wasn't Gutian had remained. Once his dosage had lessened, her image, her laugh, all of it came rushing back. What in Caelius's name were we doing just sitting here?

What?

I caught my own thoughts.

In *Caelius's* name?

My shoulders sagged in defeat. He had really become my god. I had so much of him still inside of me, I could feel his body against mine, his hands forever around my throat. I coughed. I was so *thirsty* . . .

I had to get out of here.

If sucking down that Vessel and bringing her to him would end this hell, if it would save Meky, then what was I waiting for? I had already taken the worst of Caelius's punishment. I knew what was coming if I failed him again: his words, his touch, hollowing me out, sculpting my flesh into something made for him alone. If that was what I was *now*, what did I really have to lose? And if I died trying, it might be a relief to the girls, no longer having to look at how pathetic I'd become. In truth, I couldn't feel any worse than I felt now, but if the Vessel hurt Meky while we were all just sitting here, I'd never forgive myself.

I went to the terrace overlooking the lake. The moon was hidden out of sight. It was the blackest night I'd seen since we'd been here, but it still had stars, unlike the blackness inside Caelius, the vacuum of nothingness.

I looked back at Nefari. Those Egyptian lines on her eyes faded in the soft light as she clung to Sherit, rocking her in her arms. Sherit didn't resist her mother. She stayed silent as Nefari spoke to her in both Egyptian and Gutian. It was a mangled mesh of words and phrases, and among them was, "You're all I have left now." Even though I was hollow, I was alive enough to feel her loss. To see the great Nefertiti broken like this, it must truly have been the end of the world.

I sighed, looking back at Caelius's bedroom. The door was shut. I knew he was giving Molly a drop of blood. "One drop to console her," he had said earnestly. But ever since she'd stood up to him, Sete had been asked to join them inside, and afterward she would reek of Caelius too. Was he drugging her as well? A fury rose in me, then sank like a rat drowning in water.

With every breath I felt subservient to him. I had to finish this and get my mind back, no matter the cost. When I returned I vowed I would find a way to protect her. I would convince him that Sete didn't need *any* of his blood . . . that I would take her share, if that's what he wanted, as long as she was free from him.

I licked my lips.

That's what *I* wanted.

More.

More of his blood.

I should take all *of it.*

I shook my head again. Even my love of Sete was getting clouded by hunger. And to think, I had spent all those years calling Adnachiel a dog. I ran my tongue along the growing tips of my incisors. Only Caelius could satiate this hunger now.

The Vessel.

An image emerged of her long locks streaming like liquid gold, bouncing down her shoulders in the sunlight. It was wet and wild, and her soft cheeks were flushed like she had just gotten out of the bath.

The image was so clear, but I couldn't place the memory.

All of that gold flickered deep in my mind, and for a brief moment I forgot my ravenous emptiness and called out to her.

Shea . . . where are you?

It felt like a strange light was weaving through my mind, like an unconscious part of me was pulling something through.

It burned.

It burned until the only words left on my lips were "Help me."

CHAPTER 11
SHEA

As I stepped out of the claw-foot tub, which had probably been made in the late 1800s, I almost slipped on the wood floor. It wasn't my normal clumsiness; it felt like something had tugged me forward. Grabbing the towel from the hook hanging on the wall of Helena's never-ending fortress of rooms, I felt it again.

Okay, it was full-out *yanking* now.

I looked around and hugged my body. I wasn't actually moving, so what was I *feeling*? Quickly throwing on my jeans and T-shirt, I reached for the door to find the rest of the clan to tell them about the weird sensation, though I had no idea how I'd explain it. *Hey guys, I know I'm not moving, but I swear I'm being pulled somewhere. Weird? Crazy? Insane?*

All of the above. Ugh.

I hesitated as I turned the knob, not sure if it was a good idea to get them riled up about something that may be nothing.

Maybe I should see if it goes away?

It could've been magnetic something or other because I was made of Light and we were all locked in a multilevel laboratory created by a real-life mad scientist.

Yeah, that had to be it.

I opened the door.

My Dream-Walking form was fully yanked out, and I watched in horror as my physical body dropped to the floor, unconscious. Suddenly I was grateful I had gotten dressed. Nothing like having someone walk in with me splayed out naked on the floor. Why was my mind even going there? Probably because I was terrified that I couldn't break free from whoever was pulling me out of my body.

It had to be Caelius.

If I could breathe, I would have tried to take deep breaths to calm myself. I needed to figure out a game plan, but what could I do? Caelius was Darkness. Maybe this was how he would devour my soul and come into full power. If he could separate my spirit from my physical form, then I'd no longer be a threat. I couldn't connect to the Light without my body. Maybe he just had to suck my soul out and drink it, as if the air itself was his straw.

I instinctually ducked my head as I passed each floor, helplessly flying through the levels of Helena's lair. I didn't see anyone as I finally pushed through the top of the cabin and into the sky. I tried to fight, but there was nothing to fight. It was just me being yanked to my inevitable oblivion. My mind squeezed with a powerlessness that sent surges of terror through me.

Until the pull began to feel *familiar*.

Warm almost.

Like home.

I knew with a sudden certainty that Caelius wasn't the one pulling me toward him.

It was *Lucian*.

My heart soared in anticipation as I flew past rivers, valleys, and mountains. Maybe he had broken free and was scared and alone. Maybe he needed the *essence* of me in this form to be strong, to fight Caelius's control.

I pushed myself into the stream and flew faster. I was even more sure now. I could feel him. I knew his spirit as if it were my own. I was so close. I leapt forward blindly, my surroundings a blur from the speed I was soaring.

Without warning, everything was suddenly black.

Um.

"Lucian?" I cried out.

Could he hear me? Was this really him? Had my desire for him clouded my reason, and had I just walked into Caelius's trap? I desperately wanted Lucian to call my name, to let me know he wasn't gone forever. The scenery around me shifted and moved until I was standing in the middle of a desolate wasteland.

Paris.

I recognized the twisted, mangled form of the broken Eiffel Tower in the distance. There was no sign of life anywhere, only abandoned cars and destroyed buildings lying in piles of rubble. Even the cobblestone streets had been ripped and torn to pieces, scattered across the broken soil like extracted teeth in a bowl. It was horrifying. What once had been a beautiful city, bright in its long history, was utterly destroyed. There was no recovering from this; there was nothing to rebuild. There was only dirt and crushed stones.

Suddenly Lucian was standing next to me.

Even though I was Dream-Walking and my physical form wasn't really here, it felt as if my heart had leapt into my throat. I turned to him, desperate. "Lucian! Are you fighting Caelius? Are you in Paris?" I rambled at his still form. He didn't respond to my voice. He stared straight ahead, as if soaking in every detail of the demolished city.

I had to reach him. He obviously brought me here for a reason, but why couldn't he see me? I stood, waving my hand in front of his saddened eyes. "Lucian! It's me, Shea. I love you. I love you." My voice broke. What else could I say?

"I love you," I whispered, no longer able to speak without falling apart.

His expression was anguished, as if seeing what he and Caelius had done to the people and this beautiful city was too much to bear. Then he reached down and picked up a small pink barrette made for a young child, and a tear fell down his cheek.

"Lucian," I said helplessly.

A shuffling from behind caused me to whirl around, and my brain froze in shock. Another Lucian stood there, *watching* the one that had just picked up the barrette. But the new Lucian's eyes were empty, blank, as if he couldn't comprehend his own existence.

I turned to this Lucian and tried again. "Can you hear me? What is this?"

No response.

Terror raced through me as Caelius walked toward the Lucian with the barrette. I turned to run but then noticed he wasn't paying me any attention.

I was in a memory.

Lucian's memory.

Caelius grabbed the pink barrette out of Lucian's hand and tossed it aside. "Why aren't you celebrating our victory? Instead you come here and wallow over a child's hair thing."

"A child *you* killed," Lucian choked out.

Caelius shrugged. "I killed lots of children. And *you* killed lots of men. And lots of women. That's why I want to celebrate." Caelius scowled. "You're ruining my excellent mood with this nonsense." Then he sighed heavily. "I thought I could take you out of our bedroom, to test you, but it seems you're still as headstrong as ever. No mind. I'll erase all this from your memories anyway." Taking Lucian's hand, he nodded. "Come on, back to the angel bones for you."

The Lucian behind me stepped forward and now stood next to me. I looked up expectantly. If this was a memory, then the Lucian watching was the *real* one, the one who needed to see this for some reason. And whether he knew it or not, his subconscious had yanked me into his mind too, and we were visiting the memory of the aftermath of Paris falling. Since he didn't have the power to Dream-Walk, that may have been why everything was so strange and he wasn't able to interact with me.

Cautiously, I took the real Lucian's limp hand. "Why are we seeing this? What does it mean?"

Nothing.

I might as well have been talking to one of the bricks on the ground.

Then hope filled me. His eyes and expression were blank, but Lucian's grip tightened, his fingers lacing through mine. I had to break through, and this was a good start.

The scenery swirled and shifted again. We were going somewhere different: a new memory. I kept my hand firmly in place. There was no way I was letting Lucian go, not when I was so close to reaching him.

As the scenery took shape, I recognized it immediately.

We were in our villa just outside of Paris.

If my dream self could've blushed, I would have. The memory we had stepped into was of Lucian and me making love. This memory was burned into my brain. It was our first day in the villa, and we hadn't been able to get enough of each other.

Feeling Lucian's hand gripped in mine as we watched ourselves getting busy was . . . intense? Weird? Uncomfortable? But pushing aside my own embarrassment, I realized Lucian was remembering this moment for a reason. Insecurities ruled my life, so to see that Lucian had held on to this memory at all made my heart soar.

It was actually beautiful in a non-porny kind of way. We almost looked like we had been fused together, blending into each other. The intensity was probably making my actual body, lying on the floor of Helena's bathroom, sweat.

That would be embarrassing.

I looked away from our past selves and stared up at the Lucian next to me. He gave no indication of knowing I was there or that *he* was there. If he hadn't been squeezing the life out of my astral fingers, I wouldn't have known if this was really happening.

With a loud boom, we were no longer standing in the bedroom of our villa.

We were standing on what was left of it: smoldering, burning heaps of ash for as far as the eye could see, mixed in with blackened lumps of what used to be walls and furniture. The only reason I knew we were still at the villa was because a charred corner of the bed frame was burning on the ground in front of us.

Past Lucian returned and flew to the ground, alone, viewing the charred ruins with devastation. This was the first place Caelius must have destroyed. Past Lucian looked more like himself than the one squeezing my hand, who showed no emotion at all.

I was broken.

Seriously broken.

I tried to get through to him again. "It doesn't matter if Caelius destroyed our villa. It was us being *together* that made that time magical. We can do that anywhere."

Again, no reaction.

But he didn't let go of me.

The ash began to swirl, and I knew we were headed to a new location. When the memory came into focus, we were standing on a floor covered in dried reeds of grass. It was some kind of one-room hut. House? Definitely a living abode with mud for walls and a thatched roof. There was a bench that looked like it was also used as a bed against the wall. It framed a stone trough that could hold a fire, but it was burnt out, an empty cauldron hanging useless above it. A few rabbits hung from the walls, abandoned and already rotting.

Two identical twins caught my eye. They were dead, lying next to each other on the ground. One had a large knife wound on his back that was covered in dried blood; the other had red streaking down his hand.

It was Aidan.

He had just stabbed the Vessel: his brother, Halfdan, I thought his name was. Sadly, I couldn't remember Aidan's name during this lifetime, mainly because he'd always been Aidan to me. Now, seeing the real person he had been, I felt like I was dishonoring his memory.

The door opened, and Meky walked inside. I wanted to run up to her and hug her, but I knew she wasn't really there, just a memory. Past Lucian was in this house somewhere, watching, or we wouldn't have been able to see this.

Meky didn't seem to notice as she raced to Aidan's corpse. Her beauty was just as perfect back then as it was today, her long locks of hair falling over Aidan's body as she cried. My heart ached for her. I knew how she felt about Aidan, but seeing her like this was devastating to watch.

"You Moors are tougher to kill than I thought." Lucian walked out from the corner of the room that had been cast in shadow. "I won't make that mistake a second time."

Meky's head flipped up to face him, furious. At this point I knew Meky well enough to know that anyone with an ounce of sanity should run away as fast as they could, but the Lucian of the past didn't know who she really was. Or *what* she was. So instead, he leapt at Meky, teeth bared.

He didn't reach her.

He was thrown back so hard his body crashed through the mud walls and landed violently on the ground. But it wasn't Meky who had tossed him as if he were a twig . . . it was Nefertiti.

And she was a seething storm of beauty and rage.

Lucian raced back inside the house, then stopped dead in his tracks at seeing the woman he used to love standing before him filled with hatred. Shock drove him to his knees, eyes wide with disbelief. "It can't be. What trick is this? Did Adnachiel's dogs conjure you to torture me?"

Nefertiti walked like a huntress as she approached him, her voice furious. "It is no conjuring! You broke your promise to me! To the Gutian code! You beat Meky to a pulp; you could have killed her!"

Lucian couldn't comprehend the sudden accusations. His eyes immediately turned to Meky, who sat next to Aidan's body, holding his hand.

"No." His voice was a horrified whisper.

"Yes." Nefertiti's was like ice, her expression set in unwavering anger.

"My love? Is it really you?" His voice cracked with emotion.

My love? Awkward. Of course I knew they had a love story for the ages, but it was so long ago, my mind could almost look past it. But seeing it in front of me as if it were happening now made me feel out of place, like I'd never really had a chance with Lucian, like I was a distraction for when he and Nefertiti reunited, just like Caelius had wanted.

Leave it to me to turn this into a personal attack on my self-esteem. I needed to stop my introspection and watch, to remember everything. Lucian's subconscious was stuck in these memories, while his conscious mind was controlled by Caelius's blood when he was awake. Where we stood now was the part of his brain that was repressed but untouched by Caelius, so he had to be trying to remember these moments for a reason.

"Don't speak to me of love when you almost killed my daughter!" Nefertiti was having none of it. When it came to her girls, not even Lucian was exempt. "And besides, I see what you do to the ones you love!" She eyed Aidan's corpse.

Lucian's face went blank as he really heard her words. He looked over at Aidan with Meky leaning over him. Instead of the anger and betrayal he always seemed to show toward Aidan, it was replaced by . . . shame?

Meky stood up and said softly to her mother, "You know I'd never let anyone destroy me." Then she seemed on the verge of tears as she said to Lucian, "*Physically.*"

Ouch.

Talk about guilt.

I knew him enough to know how much that hurt. Past Lucian lost all pretenses of the monster I'd just witnessed. He was *my* Lucian, brokenhearted at what he had done. Lost. Wracked with emotion.

He stayed on his knees, placing his hands over his face from the pain. It seemed to be all hitting him at once, as if he didn't know how to react to what was happening around him. That was when Nefertiti's expression finally softened. In that moment, I think she saw the boy and the man she'd fallen in love with. Going to her knees to face him, Nefertiti gently took his hands away from his face.

Their eyes met, and if I wasn't completely and totally in love with Lucian, I'd almost have been rooting for them to kiss.

But no. Not that mature.

Please don't kiss. Please don't kiss. Please don't kiss.

I hoped the Lucian holding my hand couldn't hear my thoughts. I looked up, but he stared at the memory as if he didn't even know he was there.

215

Past Lucian spoke. "I can't believe it's really you." He glanced at Meky, though his eyes were so full of guilt he could barely stay focused on her. "Your daughters, are they all . . . ?"

"Vampires? Yes. Caelius made me, and I was able to make them." Nefertiti brushed her hand over his cheek. Lucian took her hand and kissed it.

"My Nefari. My love. My morning star. I thought you were dead, and now you've returned?" He grew stronger in his conviction. "Whatever the reason, I'll never leave your side again."

Nefertiti looked as if she was going to kiss him, but another man entered the house.

Ur-Nammu.

"Daughter, stop," he commanded. He looked scared. I knew that fear—I'd seen it many times. He was afraid for the lives of his family, and he'd do anything to save them. *Anything.*

Nefertiti stood and turned to her father. "We could run. Caelius is stuck in his prison. He can't hurt us."

"You know that's not true. His shadow form has more reach than his physical form. We live by his will alone. Don't think it otherwise, or we'll all be killed, and your daughters will be first; that much he assured me of before he sent me here."

Nefertiti seemed on the verge of protest, but after a moment, she slowly nodded.

Ur-Nammu stepped up to Lucian and lifted a metal flask. "A drop of Caelius's blood is in here. It's enough to make you forget that you saw us."

"No! I will not go back now that I have seen that they're alive. I held her dead in my arms. I drank the sands of Egypt and still couldn't escape the pain. I won't go back to ignorance! The ache of her loss is unbearable. I can't." Lucian looked desperate.

And he was.

He needed to hold on to the piece of him that was good. He'd been living in loss and vengeance for so long, I could see that just a tiny shred of hope had changed him instantly.

Ur-Nammu grabbed his arm with his free hand. "Lucian, if you ever cared for Nefertiti and her daughters, then you must do this. If you don't, it means their *true death*. You know Caelius. He will punish them to great lengths before he kills them. He'll forgive this one misstep, because you tried to kill Meky, but their existence *must* remain a secret, as per his and Nefari's original agreement."

"I can't," Lucian begged. "I need her. I need Aidan. I need all of them. I'm so alone, Ur-Nammu. Ever since . . ever since I left Gutium as a boy . . . ever since my mother died . . . I can't lose them again."

"Yet lose them you must, or they will *suffer*. I won't make you. You must choose to; it's what Caelius asked. A willing choice guarantees that you won't remember, because at the core of it, you know it's to protect the ones you love," Ur-Nammu said with authority.

He was invoking that damn Gutian code again. My heart ached, but I was selfishly relieved to see Lucian nod in agreement. Caelius's threat was real, and I'd seen firsthand what breaking Nefertiti's agreement had cost her.

"It's her children. If Nefari agrees . . . who am I to protest?"

"I'm sorry, La-Narru. I will find a way to free us—I promise. But the risk right now is too great." Nefertiti's eyes were pained.

217

"I love you."

He choked down tears. "And I you. I trust you with my life. If this is the only way to protect all of you . . . give me the blood." He stared at Nefertiti and Meky, as if their eyes would soften the blow of what he had to do next. "Know that even though I will think you dead, you will always be *alive* in my heart. I will cherish you through the ages, even if it's in grief alone."

Ur-Nammu opened the flask and handed it to him. He drank the drop quickly, like pulling off a Band-Aid. Then his eyes went blank, much like the current Lucian who stood next to me.

Ur-Nammu spoke the words that would make Lucian forget everything he had just seen. He then prompted him to bring the next Vessel in, as per Caelius's command. Well, I knew *that* hadn't happened. Past Lucian had obviously fought that part of the compulsion five hundred years later with a Vessel named Brummel, I thought it was.

The scenery shifted again, and we were headed into another memory. I wondered how many of these he was going to take me to. I needed to keep track, to remember as many details as I could.

Everything turned yellow and brown until we stood on the cliff face of a jagged canyon overlooking a dry, cracked desert. Even though I didn't recognize the people, I knew exactly what we were witnessing.

And holy crap, I was seeing Moses. *The* Moses! Even though this moment was intense, I couldn't help but be awed. The Bible had always felt like fiction to me, but learning what I had from Lucian, I knew that it was actually a variation of the truth, but it *was* the truth. Moses was real, and he'd been a Vessel—the first

Vessel.

And I was the last.

It was a circle that immediately made my brain freeze. I was a part of something so huge that if I had been in my corporeal form I would have barfed.

Moses.

A Vessel like *me*.

Could Lucian be remembering this for that very symmetry?

I needed to know why we were here.

Events unfolded in front of us almost too quickly to follow. An old man ran up the craggy rocks that made up the cliff face to reach Moses's side. I didn't need any introduction. He had a different face, but I'd know those eyes anywhere: Aidan.

"I can't let Lucian take you to Caelius. He'll free him, and it'll be the end of everything." Aidan's face was wracked with guilt. I knew that guilt. It was the same expression he'd had right before he stabbed me.

Past Lucian landed in front of them, hearing every word Aidan had just said. "Adnachiel? What is this? After all these years together, why would I betray you and take Moses to Caelius? Brother, I don't understand." His eyes showed his shock. "Have I not proven what you mean to me? I love you both. This is madness. Come, let us sit. We'll sort this out *together*. Isn't that what we always do? You taught us that, Moses." He extended his hand out to them, a slight tremble in his fingertips. "Let us make good on his teachings now, brother."

"Don't lie, Lucian! Caelius is your father and Darkness incarnate! And Moses and I are the Light," Aidan said, panicked. "I know what you've planned, and I can't let you free him! All of this was a lie! You used us for your own gain!"

With frightening speed, Ur-Nammu ran up to the trio. "It's time to bring in the Vessel, Lucian."

Moses was hurt and betrayed as he looked at Lucian. "My brother, what is this?"

Lucian growled at Ur-Nammu. "Go back to Caelius! I will not betray them!"

Aidan froze in doubt. Even though I knew what had happened, I almost thought he'd change his mind.

Ur-Nammu said, "We've waited too long! The Vessel must be taken to Caelius. We already discussed this, and you agreed!"

"That's not true!" Seeing Aidan's expression turn to one of resolve, Lucian panicked. I could see that he was scared that Aidan would make the wrong decision. He raced forward and grabbed Moses, flying into the air.

I knew it was to save him.

But man, did he look guilty now.

I could see Aidan lifting his chest, his face sad but determined. He leapt after them.

The Lucian who held my hand squeezed tighter as we flew with the memory. I searched his face for a sign of anything, but there was still nothing, just a vacant stare as we both watched the most horrifying thing I'd ever seen.

Aidan caught up to them and grabbed Moses's arm, trying to wrestle him back from Lucian. Moses cried out to Aidan, "Brother, you must do it! He has betrayed us! We can't release Caelius; he will destroy the world!"

Past Lucian was devastated. That this was what they thought of him broke him apart. He released Moses to Aidan. "Listen to me . . . I'm not a monster. I want only to live by your side in *peace*, like we have done. We freed a people together. Do you not believe in the truth of who I am?" he cried.

Then Moses's expression changed, the realization hitting him as he saw the sincerity in Lucian's eyes. "Brother?"

Lucian nodded, desperate for them to believe him. "I would *never* hurt you."

Moses's face filled with shame. "Forgive my weakness. Fear overcame the wisdom of my heart." He turned to Aidan, eyes once again alight with faith. "Adnachiel, he won't betray us. I was wrong to doubt our oath!" Moses yelled over the wind.

Tears streamed down Aidan's face. He wanted so badly to believe, just like he had wanted to with me. But he'd been created to protect the Light and the Earth itself. "I can't take that risk."

"Aidan—"

With a quick thrust, Aidan stabbed Moses straight through the heart.

Both their bodies fell from the sky, crashing to the hard ground below with a loud crunch of bones.

Past Lucian screamed in agony, and it tore my insides apart. The pain was so intense I almost let go of the Lucian next to me, but I held on tighter instead. I hoped that on some level he could feel me, that I was there with him, sharing this heart-crushing moment.

He'd lost both his brothers that day.

For no reason.

The scenery changed again, and I was grateful. I didn't want to see him cry over their bodies like I knew he had.

But when everything came into focus, I was shocked at what

221

memory we were in.

We were back in the ruins of my dorm building. I had pushed my hand into Lucian's chest, searing a hole in its center. Past Lucian said with sadness, "I couldn't save them." Now, knowing what Lucian had felt, I knew he'd been talking about Moses and Aidan.

When we were in Paris, he'd confessed that he'd been so relieved I was alive he didn't care that I'd punched a hole in his chest. It had been the moment he knew he loved me, though he hadn't been able to admit that yet.

I watched as I destroyed the rubble holding Aidan down.

Past Lucian tried to warn me. "Wait, Shea, you don't understand. He's not who you think he is. He'll kill you . . . I won't let anyone touch you. Just come with me. I know I'm a monster. I know what I've done . . ."

Lucian had terrified me, but now I knew he had been telling the truth. It was so sad that with Moses he hadn't been the monster he so easily confessed to being with me. Then he'd uttered his biblical threats toward Aidan, followed by the words I would never forget. "Shea Harper is *mine!*"

The Lucian holding my hand let go. I tried to grab for it again but froze when his eyes were suddenly alive and awake.

"Help me," he whispered.

***

I woke up on the bathroom floor, as if I had been rubber-banded back into my body. I coughed, choking on unbidden tears. I couldn't control anything—my body, my emotions, my brain. It

222

overwhelmed me to the point of deep sobs.

And suddenly I felt Aidan's arms wrap around me. "Shea, what is it? Are you okay? What happened?"

I managed to pull myself together for only a moment as I sputtered, "Aidan . . . he . . . needs us."

Shock and sadness covered every feature on Aidan's face. He nodded slowly, then held me against his chest. "We will save him, Shea. I promise you."

CHAPTER 12
LUCIAN

I awoke from a strange mental fog and was back in the living room of the cabin. What had just happened? One minute I was here, the next everything had gone black. I looked at the clock in the corner of the room; I'd lost an hour. I'd never experienced a blackout like that before. The light and burning I'd felt before it started when I was thinking about the Vessel dissipated once I'd regained consciousness. And what was left in its wake was emptiness accompanied by an unshakable ache.

I wanted to drown that ache in Caelius's blood.

I clenched my fists, steadying myself, shaking the experience from my mind and replacing it with an urgency I felt boil up inside: I needed to escape. I leaned away from the visibility of the doorway. Aside from my strange lapse in time, I had been waiting for this moment. They were all finally preoccupied at the same time. It was now or never. I had to make my move.

Without a moment's hesitation, I leapt into the night. It

didn't matter where I flew first; I just had to create some distance between Caelius's presence and my physical body.

It was agony.

It felt like my skin was being pulled apart by a million hooks linking me to him. Every part of me screamed to go back, to fall into his arms like a puppy suckling milk.

I *needed* Caelius.

I needed my *savior.*

I cringed at my state and flew faster.

I tried to think only of Adnachiel, and it felt good. This was something familiar. *This* I remembered: hunting that beast and the searing feelings of betrayal his memory induced. To feel anything so deeply again, even pain, was bliss to me now. I longed for the recollection of Moses to pull me from apathy. I was reaching into the nothing for a hand, even a hand that I despised.

"Come back to me, Aidan," I whispered.

His scent was easy enough to find. Now that I was hopped-up on Caelius's blood, I could visibly *see* his Light trail. It was no wonder Caelius had said he could find them whenever he wanted, that it really was just about me being "ready." I tried not to think of him, the taste of my maker calling me to his feet.

I was so *thirsty.*

Just a few drops would be enough, wouldn't it?

I gritted my teeth, trying to shift my focus. That angel-beast, where was he going? Following a trail of heavenly light felt familiar somehow, even though this was a power I'd not possessed before. The image of Gracuri and a pile of dead bodies at our feet flashed like a quick bolt of lightning through my mind. Then, just as quickly, that image was replaced with Caelius.

225

My pace quickened.

Every time my mind went back to Caelius, I tried to refocus on Adnachiel's scent, his boyish nature, the way he had gutted our brother, Moses. It was strange—the more I thought of him, the more bizarre images would blink into my mind. Just as strange, however, was their immediate deletion, as if they'd never existed. Was I so fractured that my thoughts were like a shaken jigsaw puzzle? So it wasn't just the girls that made me feel out of place; even alone I felt disjointed.

It was all right though.

Caelius's blood would sort me out.

I sighed again, flying hard enough to break the sound barrier.

"We are not looking for *Caelius's blood*, we are looking for *Adnachiel*," I reminded myself over and over until I caught the mistake. I trembled, feeling a grip tighten around my throat. Caelius had so infected my subconscious that I now called myself "we." I shivered again, racing harder toward Aidan.

When I landed, I gasped for breath and leaned against a tall cedar tree. His trail had finally met the Vessel's and Meky's in South Dakota, and I'd followed it to this end here in Colorado. I winced, noticing that most of my skin was stripped off. Even an immortal's body wasn't meant to move that fast; after all, my original form was still flesh and bone. As it was, I felt like my body was barely containing the new strength Caelius's blood allowed. If *I* felt like this, how was Caelius's power not ripping his mortal body to shreds? Was he in pain like I was?

I stopped myself again.

We don't need to think about Caelius. Remember why we're here.

I took a quick breath. The cool air helped fight the pain as skin slowly grew back, but nothing helped the *hunger*. I crushed a large rock under my foot as a bird began to sing in the trees behind me.

Music.

I'd forgotten that it even existed outside of Caelius's bedroom.

I tried to think of my favorite songs across the ages. Words of men made from strings of beats. Harps and pianos, drums and electric guitars. Even remembering lyrics felt religious and holy. I was so relieved—relieved and terrified at how far gone I was.

I looked up at the snowcapped mountains. They were beautiful and untouched by man. It made me feel clean in a way I hadn't been. Even washed, bathed, and wrapped in the white sheets and walls of our bedroom, I'd still been filthy. Caelius's touch and the eyes of my disapproving family had assured me of that. I stared at the gently falling snowflakes in the distance. It was comforting to see that it wasn't only Caelius's blood that made the world anew.

I looked around at the adjacent mountains. Nestled in the center valley, Aidan's trail had led me to this peak. In contrast, the mountains surrounding it were giants. This was the smallest point, hidden in the center, dwarfed by the others like David had been, surrounded by Goliath and his armies.

I smiled with the recollection. Goliath had been quite the man in his day, but he was powerless once he had fallen in love with David. I rested my hand against the sharp edge of a rock at the mountain's base. In my experience and observations throughout history, it was not faith that could move mountains, but love. Of course, love could also take magnificent giants and bring them to their knees. I cringed as the rock I was leaning into

227

cut my hand.

Blood.

Was such a thing more powerful than love itself? I looked past the red and stared up at the tiny mountain being overshadowed by the others. How had my friend David been so brave, and Goliath so foolish?

My friend.

It was something David had always called me, even at the end. He hadn't been as charming as Moses, but he'd had that way about him, inviting in even the worst among us and calling them companions, forging allies instead of enemies. He'd used that same language with Goliath, who'd only been called a giant, a *beast.*

If ever there were soul mates, they were proof enough. But in the end, Goliath chose David over immortality, and David chose his people over Goliath. The betrayal and regret that followed had hollowed out the warmth in David's eyes as the years passed. He never loved again: not his children, not his wives, not the kingdom he had won after the war. He never forgot that, as Goliath breathed his last, the only words left on his lips had been "I love you."

My friend.

Had I been a true friend, I would have killed him to end his suffering. At one point he'd begged me to, but even then I'd ensured that no harm came to him, that he fully lived his immortality, crushed by the weight of the choices he'd made in his youth. It was part promise, part punishment for what he'd done: choosing political victory over love. It was only in the last hundred years that I regretted keeping my promise to Goliath:

to protect David until the end. Who was I, Lucian the Merciful? I should have killed him the day Goliath died. In the wake of all I'd lost, I should have known that even a coward deserved that mercy.

I turned my gaze to the soft white above me. At least my past was still mine. It didn't belong to Caelius, no matter how painful it was. The reality that David, along with all my other sons, was now gone pained me further. That pain made me crave the comfort of Caelius's blood like a fever.

Wash away Goliath and his David. Wash away the promise of love and its inevitable betrayal. Wash away all my sins and mistakes. If I am yours, I do not have to be my own. I do not have to be responsible for my failures.

I groaned as the thirst grew.

Caelius.

My salvation.

I closed my hand over my mouth, trying to push back my jutting fangs. Their eyes . . .

I tried to remember the icy look of Nefari and our girls. I held on to it. Even with all I'd lost, I still had something to protect: a family worth fighting for. I couldn't give in to oblivion like Goliath, who'd only had his David.

I needed to end this.

I squinted. The Light trails led to a large house at the peak. It was visible and open once you passed the outer mountains. The way through the ice caps would be treacherous if you couldn't fly. I, however, could just jet up and grab her. It was an exciting thought, the Vessel snatched so quickly in my arms, but they would see me clear as day through those endless glass windows adorning the cabin.

I clenched my teeth, letting my eagerness be replaced by rationality; with a Vessel this powerful, I couldn't let her know I was coming. I had to sneak in through the center and take her before anyone could respond. I needed every advantage, and surprise was a good one. Surprise had taken down kings, even the great Caesar. He was another interesting man, another giant that fell because of his love of Brutus.

I paused. Why was I even thinking about the past by pondering love's betrayals? What was it about the Vessel that brought on such worthless recollections?

I need her.

That sentiment alone struck me in a strange way.

Let's rephrase.

We need her dead.

I stared at the large stones around me, collecting myself.

There had to be another way in.

The treetops waving in the breeze cast fragmented light across the rocks, and an unnatural glint caught my eye. The boulders had been moved and put back in place. I ran my hand along the hairline cracks. The seams were flawless; not even my kind would have noticed. But I wasn't just some vampire, not anymore, thanks to Caelius. These misplaced stones were a hidden door, most likely an emergency exit if things at the top went south. I smiled. Only one scientist I knew of would be this clever: Helena.

Caelius had said the Vessel might have brainwashed her and kept her alive to use against us, but to not hold out hope. With her aiding them, however, Adnachiel had procured himself a rather ingenious advantage. I sighed with relief. "Helena, you're alive," I whispered. Touching the grainy surface, I searched for a small hole. Shadowed by a large bulging rock, I slipped my finger into the crack underneath it.

Just as I had thought, there were small gears hidden inside. A key could be lost or forged, but this was a code, a pattern. Having to turn the cogs with the tip of your finger until they locked into the correct sequence was ingenious.

It was just like the prototype she had been working on when we first met. She hadn't yet known of my full capabilities as a vampire, that my sight was enhanced enough to see through the spaces in her metal "do not touch" boxes. Trying to hide any of her work from me had been fruitless, but it was just like someone so brilliant to miss a calculation; she hadn't taken into consideration how long I had known her before we became friends. I knew more about Helena than I'd ever confessed, though I'd come close to telling her such in Loretto.

I smiled as gears moved and the boulders parted. She had an affinity for lemniscates—all the shapes in her machinery reflected it in their designs. In that way, she was an easy code to crack. I stepped inside, and immediately the rock door sealed behind me, not that I would be going out that way. Past this point, there was no going back for me.

My eyes adjusted to the dark until I saw perfectly. I was inside a small tunnel with equations scribbled along the sides. No doubt she'd had ideas flash in her mind as she was coming and going. Wood pulp was nonessential to geniuses: their world was made of paper.

I looked closer. The writing was old, forgotten. Something must have happened to make her abandon this lab. My smile faded. The Vessel was using her, making her reveal her sacred places like they were hideouts and not something to be cherished.

My hands balled into fists. I'd had a place where I had kept all of my keepsakes: trinkets accrued over centuries. It was a long lonely life being immortal, but that refuge had been like an anchor to my sanity against the storms. I had even stored Nefertiti's necklace there. I'd searched all of Pompeii for that tribute, and where was it now? If I could offer that necklace to Nefari again—like I had as a boy, then as a man in Egypt—perhaps she would look at me like she used to.

The Vessel had done all of this. I didn't know how that light bulb had found my hiding place, but she had destroyed it completely, as she would do to Helena and her lab once she was done with her. I couldn't let that happen.

I moved forward.

The narrow hallway let out into a large circular room. It was hollowed out, like a cyclone had dipped down into the center of the mountain. The walls were covered in moss. I looked closer. Under the carpet of wet green were cyclical lacerations in the stone, each an inch thick and perfectly equidistant from the other.

I was wrong; this was nothing as unpredictable as the wind. This was symmetry carved out by a machine with large claws. Of course Helena would invent something to hollow out the base of a mountain. Even as a human, I had thought her mind unstoppable. People that judged scientists as technical and not creative had never met a *real* scientist like her. She was the embodiment of both.

Distinct patterned dots of light filled the entire cavern and made it look like a classic pointillism painting. It reflected her tastes. She admired Georges Seurat's work. When I stole the original *A Sunday Afternoon on the Island of La Grande Jatte* as a gift for her birthday, she'd been livid. At the same time, she'd made no demands for me to return it. In fact, it was the first thing she would unpack every time she moved to a new lab.

When she was stuck on a particularly hard equation, she would get close enough to the painting that her nose almost touched it. She'd remark that anything without objectivity became impossible for the observer to see clearly. Then she would lean back and look at the painting again, watching as all of the dots started to form a larger image. When she would do this, I always took it as an invitation, and sure enough, I would provide the wanted distraction, and sure enough, when she returned, physically worn out and wild, she'd solve the problem within minutes. We worked well together in that way.

She could have changed the world if she had been given the chance. In her generation, they'd been too sexist to see her infinite possibility, and now, as the world was, science didn't matter—not in this transformed planet Caelius was envisioning.

Blood, teeth, and servitude were the new reality.

I moved toward the center where there was a singular helix-shaped staircase that led upward. I could see now that the light at the top moved its way down by refracting off of polished stones. I stopped and marveled. More than a pointillist painting, the bottom chamber was colored like the stained glass reflections of an old Catholic church. I never thought I'd see it again, not after Caelius had destroyed it, but sure enough, the staircase itself mirrored the one at Loretto Chapel in Santa Fe. The nuns there

233

had called it the "miracle stair," saying it had been built by St. Joseph himself. It had become a legend to the faithful.

I smiled, waving my hand through the specks of color as I touched the staircase. Had the nuns known Joseph, they wouldn't have called him a saint. Now *that* was a man who could drink. Still, he was always honest, which was why I'd brought Helena to New Mexico, just before I *thought* she'd died.

I was going to confess who the saint had been, but I fell short, seeing her come alive. She'd marveled at the arithmetic and artistry of the carpenter, who had used crude tools and no electricity to complete such a masterpiece. The nuns had filled her head with stories of a saint coming in the night hours, and for once she'd listened and hadn't argued science over faith. And for once, I'd listened and hadn't argued either.

Even as a drunk, Joseph had been a better man than me; at least his legend could inspire belief. She'd confessed to me then that her father had abandoned her once in that very monastery as a child, that she herself had witnessed the miracle and had some faint memory of the man.

In truth, there'd been no miracle. In that era, they took in too many orphans who needed food and schooling. The nuns had been desperate for space and needed a second floor. Children were forced to stay outside in shifts, suffering the blistering heat or the unrelenting cold depending on the season. I had no love for Catholicism, but after wandering the streets, a child covered in mud had asked fervently for my help. She either hadn't noticed the bloodstains on my shirt or didn't care.

When I shrugged her off, she pleaded on bended knees, gripping my shins, refusing to let go.

I asked for her age and name and was surprised that she was younger than I had been when I'd lost my mother. She was just a little thing, and still she was so determined. She spat her name like it had only ever been spoken as a curse. She said it was Helena, but it should have been *Henry*. I knew what she meant. At that time there were plenty of households that only wanted boys, so much so that they abandoned their own children in merciless places like Loretto.

The Gutian Harrowing had allowed young ones to prove themselves, despite their gender, but these children were thought worthless by *birth*. As I stared at her muddied hands and fierce eyes, I was sure that she would have passed the terrifying nights alone. She would have made it home and been honored and renamed, given a place in my tribe as a warrior.

Yet there she stood, proving herself worthy to no one, with blistered hands and raw cheeks.

It pulled on my old rumblings as a Gutian, and I agreed to help her, despite what I was.

Even the nuns didn't acknowledge Helena; instead they said I was sent by God. It made me laugh, the idea that God would send a devil to do his work. All the same, it was a welcome challenge at first. As a boy I had enjoyed crafting things with my hands. I had been so caught up in destruction as a vampire that I hadn't tested my new capabilities as an immortal. Sure enough, without needing sleep, I had designed and constructed the staircase in a matter of days. It had been easy. Too easy.

I hadn't felt the old satisfaction I had as a child, laboring to create beauty. The only pleasure I took from it was the look on Helena's face once it was completed. Despite the nuns' appreciation, it was her gratitude alone that I cherished. She polished the stairs daily like they were precious to her, and eventually, that made them precious to me.

Then her father came.

Without so much as a thanks to the nuns who had raised her for *three years*, he dragged her screaming back to the wealthy mansion he'd ejected her from. Some stranger with a birth certificate, that's all he was, yet that paper gave him power over her life.

I could have stopped him. I wanted to, but I was what I was.

A vampire couldn't raise a child.

I watched as her rags were exchanged for dresses hemmed in gold. I listened as she sang the songs from the church, like a sad canary, out her open window at night. Once she even called for me, the Carpenter Saint of the Loretto Chapel. I had thought my presence hidden then, but she spoke my name all the same, believing that I was always out there somewhere, creating miracles for her little church in the shadows.

I couldn't bring myself to answer her call.

I was no saint.

Eventually she stopped singing, and I couldn't bear to watch her grow into the shape of her father's delusions. I left her side, as I had left so many others in a long line of abandoned heartstrings. I scoffed at my recollection. Lucian the Merciful, indeed. I had been a coward, afraid to raise and lose a child like I'd lost Nefertiti's. At the chapel, rumors that Joseph had built the stairs took hold, and I didn't care. Without her, those steps were just empty planks of wood. Time passed, and I put her out of my mind along with the whole of New Mexico.

Then by accident, over a decade later, I tried to kill her.

I was roaming the sleek cobblestone streets in London and got hungry. I let myself into an estate that was lit up like a candy shop. I decided that a fluffy little debutante in a dress was just the right amount of fatty blood that I needed to tide me over until I reached the next continent.

When I stepped in, I knew immediately that it was just the kind of party I hated: an upper-class young woman was making her first appearance in *fashionable* society. It was a fancy butcher's shop, and she was the piece of meat for sale. The wealthy suitors were already surrounding her, making their assessments. They might as well have opened her mouth to check her teeth. One of them leaned in close when she was laughing, and I had no doubt he was doing just that.

I decided then to save the pretty young thing from a life of servitude by wetting my appetite and cutting the pearls at her neck off with my teeth. But she outwitted me; with wild eyes and muddy hands, she'd fought me back. I was dumbstruck by the memory of a child in Loretto with eyes just as fierce: Helena. She had grown in the shadow of her father into something magnificent.

She had taken my pause as an opportunity to strike the final blow. Had I been a murderer like Jack the Ripper, she would have won. But my skull healed, and I came back for her the next night, this time offering companionship.

As the years passed, she accepted what I was and our friendship deepened. Secretly, I'd vowed never to leave her side again, but I still longed for her to know me, to remember, so I took her to the chapel. To my disappointment, as awed as she was by the sight, her memory was blurry, and she barely remembered the nuns' names, let alone the saint.

Or so I'd thought at the time.

I cast my eyes upward. Was I again looking for some kind of redemption for not telling her when I had the chance, in this handmade church of Helena's? Had my influence left such an impact that she'd subconsciously built this staircase, a replica of Loretto's? I had never confessed to being the saint from her childhood, and now that staircase was dust, along with what had been Santa Fe.

I looked at the thin steps spiraling above me with no central support beam. It was a beautiful stretched-out nautilus, like the perfect sequences found in nature. Many had remarked that my design defied physics, but really, the only thing keeping it afloat was math.

My smile returned. She'd done well. I gazed at its perfection and simplicity. Beautiful things were like that: infinitely intellectually complex but simple in a fundamentally endearing way.

That was Helena.

All this time I'd thought she was dead, but she had been asleep next to Nefertiti and her children. She was another "loving" surprise kept secret until they could be turned fully and released from the prisons of their dreams. But the prince that awakened them had been a monster of Darkness, and the kiss had been a vicious life-sucking crunch to the neck. Their transformation was more in line with *Grimms' Fairy Tales* than the popularized version of *Sleeping Beauty*. Even Duncan with his silver tongue wouldn't have created such a hopeless story.

She deserved better. Perhaps if she did remember meeting me as a child, she would have cursed the day she asked for that staircase. It had been free, but the cost had been her eternal servitude to Caelius.

Muffled voices pulled me from my thoughts.

The sounds were moving down the stairs, losing dialect and tone as they absorbed into the moss and scattered along the stones. However, one word did manage to filter through: friend.

There that word was again. As with David, it had been important to Helena. I sighed, feeling the heavy weight of it. I had failed many friends in my lifetime, but I had to save Helena, even if she belonged to the Vessel now.

I fought back a growl.

My Second-Borns had been brainwashed before being butchered, David among them. But once the Vessel was *dead*, her control would leave Helena, and I could convince Caelius to spare her. It would no doubt take time to undo the damage to her mind, but it would be a welcome relief to have her by my side again. I had lost all of my chosen Second-Borns, and my family was small now, thanks to the Vessel. Helena was precious. I had to do this for her as much as I had to do it for Nefari.

I moved noiselessly up the stairs, hovering over the steps. To my surprise, the staircase branched off like the base of a tree trunk. Small bridges extended to more doors. Some were open, revealing bedrooms or labs. Some were closed with massive locks and sheets of metal drilled into them. Experiments gone wrong, maybe? If I had time, curiosity would have prompted me to open those doors. As it was, I had to be ready. I needed to harden myself and prepare for battle. I had to think of the beast.

My smile grew.

The thought of seeing Adnachiel filled me with relief.

I caught the sensation and crushed it.

Relief?

How far gone was I that the sight of that beast should bring me *relief?* Maybe it was the familiarity of torturing him that calmed my mind. If thinking of Helena had softened me, that angel, in contrast, should've filled me with the desire to fight. I shook my head, trying to refocus. The Vessel was too powerful, and I couldn't fail. Caelius would continue to do the unspeakable to my body and mind if I came back empty-handed.

He would give me blood.

I licked my lips.

So much blood . . .

Thinking of Helena had distracted me from feeling just how *thirsty* I was.

I moved closer to the top, where the light was coming in.

The final door.

I shattered it with one quick punch and ran into the room that held them. The wood splintered and fell down on everyone in the room like rain. Power surged through me in waves, radiating down my spine. I hadn't used my juiced-up body for anything other than Caelius's pleasures, but now that I was moving on my own accord, I could *feel* the difference in strength. I was more powerful than I had ever been.

My body moved in a flash like lightning. I snatched the Vessel and Meky in an instant and smashed through the walls, flying high into the endless blue outside. I made my way quickly to the thing my blood longed for: Caelius. I *needed* to get back to him, even if our flesh peeled off in the process.

I flew faster.

With this kind of speed, I was confident that Adnachiel would never catch up. Not even with his ability to hover midair could he compete with flight like this. Nothing could.

They both struggled in my arms, shouting, but it was Meky's words that slowed my pace. "What the hell are you doing, Lucian? Let me go! Put us both down this instant!"

I looked at her face; her eyes were furious. "I-I'm sorry I failed you before, Meky. But I'll take the Vessel and make it right. Let me at least have the honor of your rescue." She was so disgusted with me that she didn't even want me to save her.

"Are you insane? *I* saved Shea! I wasn't kidnapped! Caelius is lying to you, Lucian. Wake up!" Meky screamed, squeezing my arms with all her might.

"What are you talking about—" I heard a crack in the sound barrier as huge white wings surrounded me, then something yanked the girls from my arms. Before I could move, I was flung to the earth. I landed on my face. It caved in with the force. For a moment I was blind, rolling on the ground like a worm as my bones and eyeballs hung out.

What was that?

I scratched at my bright red skin. It burned like my body was being eaten by fire ants. Healing was always a painful process, but it seemed more intense now that I was fattened up with Caelius's venom. I clawed and clawed until my face finally returned along with my vision. I panted, weary from the effort.

"Beast?" I stared at his soft features. "What . . . what's happened to you? How did you get your wing back?" I blinked

241

as my eyelids grew into place. Adnachiel's wings were extended. They were vast and magnificent, shining like glory itself. His whole body looked blessed and more kissed by the sun than ever. I was awestruck until I saw that he was cradling both Meky and the Vessel in his arms, as if they belonged to *him*, as if a creature like that deserved to even *touch* them.

I brushed the dirt off my Hanfu. "Impossible. You haven't been able to fly since you killed Moses. You're earthbound, you dog." I cracked my neck, preparing for the fight. "Did that Vessel restore your wings somehow? Does she know that your true form is *ugly*, covered in eyes and animals? Does she know that you're as ugly inside as out, that you gutted all the other Vessels along with Moses and—"

"I know." She moved out of his arms and took a step toward me.

"Shea." He spoke desperately, his hand wrapping around her wrist.

"I know, Aidan, it's okay." She pushed his hand away, and he growled like the dog he was.

"*Aidan?*" I laughed out loud. "So you have the same name that you wore back when you killed Moses. It was the last word on his lips as he died in disbelief at your betrayal."

Adnachiel scowled. "Caelius let you keep the painful memories of your past, just not anything recent. I mean, you really don't remember having us swallowed by a whale? That was pretty epic. It was a first for me at least." He shifted his gaze to the ground and moved his hand down his muscled arm in the insecure way he used to when we first met. "We're over all of that now. I apologized, and you forgave . . . well, you said . . . that we were *brothers* again." When his eyes found mine, they were sad, dimming some of the glory his body was emanating.

What was that, guilt?

Pity?

I blinked, again dumbfounded. Aidan was a lot of things, but he wasn't nonsensical; a *whale*? What kind of lunacy was he referring to? "We'll *never* be brothers again. You saw to that with Moses and every Vessel thereafter," I hissed. None of this mattered. "I don't have time for this. Whatever game you're playing, it's not going to work."

"Okay, just stop," the Vessel said. She stared at me with a strange look of longing. "How can you not remember? You let me into your mind! You sucked me into your memories and asked me to help you! Isn't that why you're really here? Some part of you ran to me, I know it!"

"Are you talking about Dream-Walking? With *you?* That's not even a power I possess!" I didn't know what kind of mind game she was playing, but she was obviously misinformed. "Even the dog knows that, Vessel. How moronic can you be? In a game of wits, it's obvious you'd lose. I won't fall for your childish deceptions."

"It wasn't Dream-Walking; you took me into some of your memories! Maybe your subconscious is more powerful because you're hopped-up on Caelius juice—it literally grabbed me! I still don't know why you picked those specific moments, but maybe we could figure it out . . . together." She reached her hand out for me to take.

I stepped toward the Vessel, then stepped back, shocked at my body's obedience. What kind of power was she using?

Adnachiel pulled her back, placing himself between us. "I should be the one to offer peace. I'm sorry, but we really are here for you—"

"I don't mind going *through* you to get to them, Beast. Don't forget, I know who you really are, and she is no safer behind you than in front."

Adnachiel clenched his jaw. "Listen to Shea. Some part of your brain reached out to her and asked for her help. Brother, listen like I should have before Moses—"

"Don't you dare call me brother!" I lunged forward but stopped before contact.

My nails were so close to the skin at Aidan's throat, a slip of paper couldn't pass through. Meky stood between us, her face inches from mine, her arms pushing me back. "It's not him you'll have to go through, Lucian! It's me!" She struggled with all her might to hold me in place, but it barely felt like butterfly wings touching my skin. "I won't let you hurt him! I love him!"

My eyes widened in surprise. "You don't mean that!" Meky in love with the beast? It wasn't possible. "You have to trust me; the Vessel has *brainwashed* you. She's created stories as elaborate as the old fables I used to read to you and your sisters in Egypt. It's all fabrication. You have to trust me, trust what your heart *knows* to be true—"

"Look who's talking." She smacked my outstretched hands away and laughed, but it wasn't with any of the joy she used to have when I would braid her hair by the Nile, back when we'd *both* been human. "Caelius has turned you into his pet and rewritten your memories. Lucian, you are on *our* side! We're working together to kill Caelius. Doesn't that *feel* familiar?"

It felt like a bomb had gone off in my mind.

My ears buzzed. She was still talking, but her words were drowned out. All that remained was a pulse—a dark, devouring pulse repeating words into my brain, pounding it into my body. The pulse spoke the truth. The Vessel was brainwashing *them*. It had killed her sisters. Meky was deceived. Her words were lies created by the Vessel's power.

I had to get back to Caelius, my savior.

I needed his blood to protect me from her manipulation.

I shook my head, everything coming back into focus as my mind reeled at the sight; out of breath, traveling on land, stood Helena.

"Lucian, stop! Listen to reason," she panted, tucking in her loosened shirt. "Should I be offended that you only took Shea and Meky?"

I staggered. "Helena, I can't express in words how glad I am that you're alive. I . . . will always care about you." I stumbled forward, wanting to reach for her. "I can't." It took all my willpower to keep myself glued in place. "You have to understand. I will save you too, once the Vessel is dead, but I can't bring you back now. Caelius will *kill* you, if not out of jealousy, then because of what you've done."

That's right, the voice in my head whispered. "You created some kind of invention to harness the Light and used it against us." I shook my head, grabbing my chest. An invention to harness the Light; now that *felt* true. "Once I've proven myself to Caelius, I will plead to him and Nefertiti on your behalf. It's not your fault that her daughters died—you were being used. You are still . . . my friend. I will save you and your lab from this Vessel, I promise. I know it's too late, now that Santa Fe is destroyed, but I'll finally tell you about the staircase in the Loretto Chapel. We can save that church in our memories, if nothing else."

Her hair was pulled back, which meant she had been working. She swayed nervously from foot to foot, her eyes darting back and forth, calculating just as she had as a human. Finally, she rested her hand on one hip. The movement was so familiar that it put me at ease.

I straightened my back and hardened my resolve.

This was part of the trap.

The Vessel was trying to disarm me by shielding herself with the bodies of the people I cared for. She wanted me to hesitate. She was just waiting for the right opening to attack.

"Lucian," Helena said. She pulled the tie from her hair and slowly untangled the braid. My mouth fell open, but I didn't respond. Seeing her tresses fall free like they had decades ago when we were riding horseback across the plains felt more recent than nostalgic. "I need you to listen to the science of it."

I chuckled. "Still trying to convince a vampire in a world of chaos that there are irrefutable laws and facts? Oh, Helena, if you weren't brainwashed, I would . . ." How was I going to finish that sentence?

I would embrace you like I did before and tell you everything.

It was all I could do to not grab her in my arms.

"In the last battle, you were on the Vessel's side," she said quickly. "The device I made was meant to harness your power and hers, to kill *Caelius*, but he had warped my mind with his Darkness, his shadow. Consciously, I was a puppet, but subconsciously the true me still existed, even if it was buried, and I sabotaged his plan to absorb the Vessel's soul. I know deep inside, the true you still exists too. You brought Shea into your memories. A part of you knows exactly what happened. You just have to find it."

"Enough!" I motioned for Meky to move. "I don't want to hurt you, but I can knock you out and bring you back. Your mother is worried to death—"

"My mother is a traitor! Listen to Helena! She knows you!"

"The Meky I know would never speak ill of Nefari," I snarled.

Meky's hands balled into fists. "The Nefari *I* know would never sacrifice La-Narru. She wouldn't act from a place of fear or loss. She's given up her Gutian code; she thinks she's protecting what she loves, but you can't protect what you love by destroying it. She was letting Caelius *destroy* you, and that was destroying the rest of us. She's not worthy of being called Gutian anymore."

Her words burned down my throat as I swallowed. "So neither your mother nor I are Gutian to you." I paused, letting the callus wash over me. "So be it."

"Lucian, that's not what I meant—"

I moved to grab Meky, but Helena stepped between us, thickening the shield around the Vessel.

"I was barely able to resist Caelius!" Helena interrupted, just as brave and socially awkward as the mortal she once was. "I can't imagine, scientifically, the miracle it will take for you to resist his blood. But I know a drug addict when I see one. You're stronger, sure, but look how *thin* you are. Look at the dark circles under your eyes. You're barely hanging on. Lucian, he's *killing* you . . ." Helena's voice trailed off. It was rare to see her unable to complete a thought because of emotion.

247

Rare and unwarranted.

Caelius had *healed* me, and I was stronger than ever. I hadn't seen a mirror, but there was no way I looked as bad as she was implying. Most likely, I was as radiant as Adnachiel.

"The lass is right, brother. Look at ye. Ye reek as bad as a dead spawnin' fish upriver. Of course, Caelius be the body layin' eggs, and ye the body dying. Not the sort a story I got planned for ye."

"How?" I ran forward and grabbed him instinctually. "Duncan!" I pulled him into my arms. "You're alive! I thought you were dead like the others!"

"O' course! It'll take a better tale than that to kill ol' Duncan. I guess that worthless bucket o' black dinnae think to remake a memory of me livin' since he dinnae know it. There ye go! I'm alive, and he dinnae have the chance to get to that part in yeer brain! That's proof, brother!" He hugged me back, hardy and strong as he laughed. The sound of it vibrated through my chest. I relaxed a little into his warmth.

On drunken mornings on grassy hills, we'd laughed and embraced like this. There were long nights and tall tales. There was an endless summer where we looked at stars while walking down cliffs to the ocean. He spoke of magic, lore, and fairies, and I listened. His mind was as endless and as deep as those stars, and he could have created whole universes had he the power of a god and not a man.

But he'd been a man before the war.

Before I'd turned him into something he hated.

Before he hated me.

He patted my back. "There, there, brother. I'm here with ye now. Ye saved me in tha caves when I was lost, longin' fer death.

248

Ye brought me a dead animal, remember? I'll save ye now that yeer lost. Come with me. This Shea, she means tha world to ye, even though ye dinnae remember. She's who ye want to protect from that dobber, Caelius. Not tha other way around."

I slunk out of his tight grip and stepped back. "I see. Another shield has arrived to aid her." I looked back at those hazel eyes alight with the power of a Vessel.

Behind me, another familiar voice called out. "Hey, sorry I'm late. You guys are a little faster than me." Jeff Harper moved a hand down his shirt, straightening it with embarrassment. His eyes looked up and down my body, and he smiled. "H-hey. It's been a long time, Father. I mean, Lucian. Sorry." He laughed to himself awkwardly. "The father thing is weird, especially since you're with my daughter."

I looked at him with disdain. "I only turned you in hopes that the Vessel would join us and not doggedly despise vampires like the religious Light-worshiping zealot she is. I am not, nor have I ever been, *with* her."

Jeff threw up his hands. "Hey now, that's my daughter, and we've never been particularly religious in our household, so that's totally uncalled-for. Surprising for a couple raising the Light though, right?"

I scowled. "How candid."

"Yeah." He walked toward Shea. He moved with an ease in his own skin, even though he was newly turned. "It's good to see you though. Helena's right, you look rough, but you're still very handsome. I mean, you know, the blood you gave me really creates like an, uh, infatuation, right? So if I'm being weird, that's totally why." He blushed a little. Surprisingly, the Vessel's face looked just as mortified as I felt. "No, I'm just, what I'm saying is if you drank Caelius's blood, you probably worship the guy by now. Think about it."

"I do." I spoke without hesitation. My devotion to him wasn't something I could resist. Helena's words seemed to make some sense in that respect. *I know deep inside, the true you still exists too.* A small part of me still knew that Caelius was poison, but the rest of me wanted him like a drowning human wanted air.

"Caelius is my salvation." I spoke as if his hand was still on my throat. In truth, I could feel it there, even as far away from him as I was.

"No, Lucian, that can't be true," Adnachiel said from behind them.

My eyes momentarily locked with his, but he didn't make a move. It bothered me, this whole situation. Why hadn't he tried to kill her? He'd killed *every* Vessel throughout time. When it came down to saving them or saving the world, he always chose his *true* family: the Light. What had made him change his mind? Was she controlling him as well? And if she was this powerful, how had I succeeded in bringing her to Caelius in the first place?

I shook the thoughts from my head.

This was what she wanted, to throw me off-balance so that she could kill me or make me her puppet like the others. Was this why Caelius wanted to pump me with his blood until I was ready? Did he know how effective her manipulative tactics would be?

None of this mattered in the long run.

Caelius was free now, whether the light bulb was alive or not.

The rules had changed.

I looked at all of them like they were strangers. The relief I'd felt at Duncan being alive faded. They were the Vessel's pawns now. "There must be some part of all of you that knows you're being manipulated. The Vessel killed all the other Second-Borns, Duncan. She killed your *sisters,* Meky. You both at least feel *that,* do you not?"

Duncan shook his head. "Yeer so stubborn, in right or in wrong. Ye killed some of yeer own children to save her, and Caelius drank the other lot like ale. Drank me right in front of ye. With yeer own eyes, ye cried for me. It was ye cryin' over my body, that's why some of the devil's blood fell in ma mouth, and I'm alive now because of it."

"Your accent gets thick when you're nervous. I bet she can't control that, but it's a tell. You're good at making up stories, and she's using that to her advantage, Duncan." I sighed. "Even you must understand how ludicrous this all sounds."

"I can't help my accent–I always get excited when yeer around. Come now, lost lamb. What are we gonna do? Won't you let me save ye? Please. I'm sorry for pushin' ye away all this time and never saying it; I still love ye, Lucian. I can't forget what ye did, but I can forgive it." He reached out his hand.

Crazier than his words was the fact that I reached back to him before yanking my hand away. What was I thinking? First she'd used Helena, now Duncan. Just how powerful was this Vessel at mind control? I moved farther back.

"How dare you use him to speak of love." I glared at the Vessel before my gaze met Duncan's and softened. "Don't worry, once she's dead and your free will returns, I won't hold you to anything you're saying. I know you *hate* me, and it must be killing you, having to choke out words otherwise."

Duncan's hand remained outstretched as he shook his head and sighed.

Meky reached out her hand as well. "He ripped through his mortal flesh, the Darkness in him trying to contort into a more suitable *physical* form, with spikes and blood for eyes. He had black claws and huge teeth that ate—" Her face twisted in horror and grief. "How can you not remember the sight of it?" She shivered, haunted by the fake memory.

I had seen something similar in the caves, when he would take me and bend me to his will in shadow form. I had felt the horror she spoke of. It was nightmarish and not something I could forget. I shook my head again. All of this could be fabricated by the Vessel. No doubt she knew the various forms of Darkness.

Why was I even listening to them? By now Caelius had figured out that I was gone. I couldn't fail. No matter how much I wanted it, I couldn't be forced to drink gallons of his blood again. I needed to stay clean, for my family.

My dry tongue moved along my teeth. It didn't matter how *thirsty* I was, he could always do something worse if I failed. He could have me watch as he tortured the children, especially Setepenre because she was *mine*.

They all stepped around me and inched in.

This was the trap I had known she was setting. The Vessel called them all to her. She was controlling their minds, and because of my fondness for these familiar faces I had allowed myself to be surrounded.

She was smarter than Adnachiel, I'd give her that: using Meky as a shield, using Helena and Duncan to sway me and keep me raw. I had played chess with the beast for centuries, but this was pure exploitation, to use family and friends. It was something *I* would have done, not Aidan. How had she caused such an angel to turn against all that he valued when my torment over the centuries had not?

For that alone, she needed to die.

I lunged forward and knocked Meky down. I'd have to come back for her. I punched Adnachiel in the chest, angling it so he flew into Jeff and Duncan. Caelius's blood had allowed me to hit harder than I had expected. They soared so far out of sight, their scent trails were masked with debris from fallen trees and mountains.

Helena wrapped her arms around Meky and shot me a defiant look, as if I would go after her and risk injuring them both. "I lied to you." Helena's voice was resolute. "When you took me to Loretto Chapel, I acted like I didn't remember. But I never forgot you or what you did for me, Lucian. *Please* don't leave me again."

I paused. My heart felt crushed. I wanted nothing more than to take her then and there. "I can't." It pained me, and I saw her then as the child she once was, calling my name out her window. "I'm sorry for abandoning you then and for what your life has become because of me. But you're not safe until this is over. I *promise* I'll come back for you when she's dead and your mind is clear. We'll talk about everything. I'll make it right somehow. Trust me this one time, my friend, and I will never leave your side again. I . . . love you."

I leapt into the sky with the Vessel pressed against my hips, her head resting on my chest. I had to leave my feelings unresolved at Helena's feet. I hoped she would understand once this was all over.

I flew backward as fast and as hard as I could, shielding the Vessel's body from the ripping force of the wind. Meky had slowed my pace, and Adnachiel had used the element of surprise, but it wouldn't work twice. There was no way, even if that beast had functioning wings, that he could catch me, as strong as I was now. The only *thing* that could was probably Caelius himself. I winced at the thought. I had to get back to the cabin before he lost his temper, before he accused me of taking Shea for myself.

That was not what this was.

I grimaced.

Why did that idea feel so familiar, as if it were a real possibility? I shrugged it off. Whatever rebellious leftovers were still cooking in my brain, Caelius had baked most of that out in heated hours of blood and lust. I would make sure he questioned *nothing*. I would drink this light bulb down enough for him to get her tiny, insignificant soul.

Then we will be fed.

We are so thirsty.

The Vessel's voice wheezed, not able to reach past the frequency of the wind and muffled further still by the pounding of my frantic heartbeat. Then I felt it, wet and sticky. I stopped midair, pulling her back.

"I threw up," she moaned pitifully.

"Obviously," I retorted in disgust.

She looked dizzy and pale, as if she might do it again. I pulled her farther from my torso, holding her at arm's length, her legs dangling like wet noodles.

She looked down, and fear replaced nausea. "Oh my God,

we're so high! Lucian, I can't fly yet. I've barely mastered enough wind to hover, like, a few feet off the ground, if that!" She wiggled her legs, clutching my arms. She jostled herself enough that my grip loosened, and just as she had predicted, she fell. It was comical really.

My grip wasn't as tight as it should have been. Why had I been holding such a repulsive thing so gingerly? I'd even cradled her head against my chest to protect her from the wind. Just as troubling was the fact that she'd thrown up so easily, like she was a regular human, unaccustomed to moving at high speeds. *This* was the Vessel that had defeated Caelius, that had defeated *all* of us?

Pathetic.

I watched as she flailed helplessly. The panic must have made her forget herself, unless she was still weak from the last battle or the strain of manipulating all of those vampires below us. How could she use such powerful suggestions and not have mastered enough wind to fly?

Her voice reached me in an instant.

She was screaming my name.

As if it meant something to her.

As if I would *willingly* save her.

As it was, she was falling into an active volcano. She had chosen the perfect spot to throw up. Had she no sense of self-preservation, to vomit over something like this when she couldn't fly? Caelius was right—humans were idiots.

We should let her get burned a little, maybe lose her legs in the heat.

She didn't need to be intact for Caelius to get her soul.

The idea instantly filled me with an unexplainable fury, as if I would punish an entire volcano if it dared touch her.

What was this, jealousy?

It was the same possessive anger I'd felt before, when my teeth wouldn't let go of her neck.

That same word tried to vie for importance: *mine*.

What was she to me? The Vessels were just mindless little puppets created by the Light to—

"Lucian, help me!"

An image burned through my mind hotter than the magma that would dare singe her beautiful long hair: the same words had been on her lips as Aidan held a bloody Enochian blade, like he had with Moses. Her gut was lanced, her hand reaching toward me . . .

Something snapped.

Before my mind could stop my movements, I was clutching her in my arms, kissing her like she was some sort of homecoming to a boy lost in the desert. My mouth took hers in again and again as I lifted us higher into the air. But as high as I went, I couldn't escape the heat. I burned for *her*, and with every gasp of breath, with every moan, I felt satiated in a way that oceans of Caelius's blood could not. When I finally released her lips, I looked at her long and hard.

"Sh-Shea?"

Something flickered, so raw and bare it terrified me. "Is it your name I've been trying to find? I've been so . . . so *thirsty*. Ever since I left Gutium, all these centuries wandering in the sand . . ."

The look in her eyes as tears rolled down her cheeks was

overwhelming. "Lucian, you saved me." Love, whole and completely unfabricated, was what I saw there; that was what I felt in her arms.

And I let her go.

It was a while before she started screaming again.

I watched as that name I had called her drifted just as far out of reach as her body.

What had I done?

Why had I *kissed* the Vessel and said such delirious things?

Why did that name mean *anything* to me?

I reached for the memory again, but it was already turning black.

Her name.

The feel of her lips on mine.

I hovered midair, frozen, my blood at war with my heart.

She fell closer to the flame.

She screamed as the heat started to scorch her body.

What did she matter?

She was nothing.

Nothing like I was.

The name calling me home was . . .

Caelius.

It was Caelius who was always by my side.

With him, I was never alone.

Caelius was my savior.

My everything.

Caelius was the name I was searching for in the dark.

CHAPTER 13
SHEA

I was going to die.

The heat from the lava was already blistering my skin as I plummeted downward toward its embrace. Where the heck were we? Hawaii? Lucian had flown far and fast.

I needed to protect myself from the magma. I had to dig deep and tap into my fire element, or I was going to die or be burned beyond recognition. I didn't even think Helena's rainbow light show could heal me from being swallowed by molten lava.

I was concentrating so hard I didn't notice Lucian diving down toward me.

My heart leapt into my throat.

Did he . . . ?

Was he . . . ?

Nope.

He stopped as if a giant hand had halted him midair.

And suddenly I was filled with a rage so deep I couldn't see straight.

Before I knew what I was doing, I connected to the fire inside the liquid magma as if it were an extension of my own body. I pulled on the wind to separate me from the burning substance, and it answered my call like it was my loving savior.

And it was.

Floating above the lava, I stared at Lucian, anger filling my veins, fire itself reaching into my blood.

Caelius did this.

Caelius turned *my* Lucian into his broken plaything.

No.

I was never going to let that happen again.

Lucian would detox from Caelius's blood whether he wanted to or not.

Our eyes met as I moved closer to his body. He hovered midair, trapped in indecision. I could see the conflict brewing behind his beautiful teal eyes. He had kissed me. I knew *my* Lucian was still in there somewhere. He had reached out to me through his memories, though his conscious mind was still clueless. His lips had parted mine like they had the first time in Arizona. It had been instinct, but it had come from his *soul*, from the Lucian who had clasped my hand desperately in his memory.

I had to believe that.

Otherwise . . .

Lucian would be lost to me forever, and there was no way I would let that happen.

The problem was, I needed to trap him before his super-vampire reflexes kicked in, which meant I needed to distract him.

I kept my mental hold on the lava, ready to strike, while I

used the wind to float face-to-face. Lucian was still frozen in a mixture of shock and anguish. I didn't even think he knew the anguish was there, it was so deeply shoved down by Caelius's blood control.

"Oh, Lucian," I said out aloud, staring at his cold eyes.

"Are we going to fight?" he asked. Though his tone was fierce, his body looked worn and tired.

"What has Caelius done to you?" I couldn't hide the catch in my voice. It was excruciating to see him like this, like a feral animal that desperately wanted to be loved but snapped at anyone who tried to come near it.

"He's made me stronger. He's made me whole. He is my salvation. He is my god, Shea." He stopped himself when he said my name, as if he was surprised that he had uttered the word. "Wait, that name . . . it's gone again."

I knew for certain Lucian was still in there. I just needed to connect to him. "Caelius has taken *everything* from you, not just me, Lucian, but your whole family—"

"I have my family!" he interrupted with rage.

"Not really though," I answered calmly. "Nefertiti isn't the same, right? And Sherit? She's such a sweet and loving girl; when was the last time you saw her laugh? Or smile even?"

I could see my words were reaching him. Lucian was struggling internally. He was so exhausted, he couldn't even hide it anymore. "They're just angry . . . at you . . . *you* took their sisters away . . ." Lucian said this like a mantra, something he'd practiced over and over.

More mind control.

"And what about Paris? Why do you think Caelius destroyed

260

that villa just outside the city *first?*" I used the memory Lucian had shown me to try and reach him.

"Because . . ." Lucian began.

He didn't have an answer, so I gave him the truth. "Because it was where we stayed after our first battle with Caelius. We made love every day, and our lives were perfect, just like you showed me in your memories. Caelius needed to destroy it *first* because he needed you to forget me, to forget that we love each other more than we could have dreamed. And I do love you, Lucian. Even when you look at me with hate, I love you even more because I know how hard you're fighting to hold on to . . . us."

He didn't speak.

He didn't move.

He just hovered like a statue.

For a moment, I was afraid I'd broken him completely.

Finally he said, in a dull lifeless voice, "Caelius is my everything now. I'm bringing you back to him. Then this will all be over."

I controlled the wind to move closer to Lucian until we were only inches from each other. I knew it was dangerous, but I had lava awaiting my command. My stomach churned, but I had to keep him away from Caelius's blood. I remembered the night in Paris when he told me the torture he'd gone through, buried in ash and lava after fighting Aidan's brothers in Pompeii. I was about to do the same thing to him.

He might never forgive me, but I can't see any other way.

Lucian was too strong to subdue otherwise, unless I could break Caelius's hold on him first. Maybe Caelius had used a combo of blood and shadow control. If I could just touch Lucian

261

long enough to see inside his mind, I could remove at least some of Caelius's power. Maybe it would be enough for Lucian to free himself.

I had to try.

"You saved me. When two of your Second-Borns tried to take me to Caelius, *you* killed them to protect me, and when Aidan stabbed me here"—I lifted up my shirt to show him the scar—"I asked for your help, and you didn't hesitate. You smashed a boulder on Aidan's body and took me to your home where you healed me with light."

I couldn't help but notice the brief smile at the mention of smashing Aidan with a boulder. I didn't know if that was a good sign or a bad one, but I continued. "And we made love for the first time in that house. It was intense and magical and all the things that musicians write songs and poets write poetry about." I gently held his hand. "*Us.*"

"Mine," he mumbled in a daze.

Not what I was hoping for, but at least it was some kind of memory of the two of us.

I slowly tightened my grip on his hand.

And . . .

I closed my eyes and used Dream-Walking to push my Light inside Lucian's body like I had with Helena. What I saw inside of Lucian made me want to scream in anguish and horror. Black swirled everywhere I could see. Where tiny pricks of light would rise, it would be snuffed out before it had a chance to grow.

Lucian's soul was being devoured whole by Caelius's Darkness.

Even though I was inside Lucian's head through Dream-Walking, I could feel his outside body trying to pull away from me. It wasn't him that wanted to retreat—it was the Darkness knowing the Light was there to extinguish it. Helena's body had reacted in the same way.

I used my power to yank the lava up and hold Lucian in place, only covering his legs and hips. I could hear him scream from the agony, and my heart broke at the sound, knowing I was the one responsible for it. Not wanting him to suffer any more than he had to, I did something I had never done before.

I called on all four elements at the same time.

A surge of power raced through me as I pulled water from the nearby ocean, dirt and rocks from the volcano itself, air from the wind, and fire from the lava. With my mind, I knit a layer of protection between Lucian's skin and the molten magma itself. It was made with water to cool and harden the lava, and dirt to pack Lucian in tight so he could heal but not escape.

Since I was still inside his head, I could only *hear* that my barrier of protection worked because he had stopped screaming in pain.

In fact, he was absolutely still.

I nearly cried when I realized . . .

Lucian *wanted* me to destroy the Darkness inside him. That tiny bit of him that had reached out to me through his memories was letting me do this.

He may have been consciously fighting with his brain because of Caelius's control, but his body was reacting on instinct, like it had when he cried while drinking my blood. His *body* knew me and would always know me, even if his thoughts battled it out with Darkness.

Quickly, I used my Dream-Walking form to chase every

shadow I could find. Just as Helena's shadows had been etched with words and instructions of how she was supposed to act and react, so were Lucian's. The difference was, Helena had one set of instructions, whereas Lucian had *thousands*.

It was terrifying and overwhelming, but I had to fight for him.

I couldn't destroy Caelius's blood control, but I could destroy his shadow. How much of that would bring back Lucian's memories, I had no idea. These instructions could be behavioral and have nothing to do with memories and feelings, but I knew I still had to clean house. Lucian's mind would never heal if he was constantly contending with both blood *and* shadow control.

Encasing him in lava would dry him out of his blood addiction, but destroying the shadow control?

Well, to put it like Lucian would: destroying the shadow control was *mine*.

Pushing my Light through Lucian's veins must have been excruciating like it had been for Helena, but he kept quiet regardless. One after the other, I destroyed the hidden pockets of Darkness. I had no idea how long it took, but it felt like hours until I finally snuffed out the last shadow.

There was light again.

Caelius's blood was still swarming around like deadly wasps inside Lucian's body, but the shadow control was gone and some of Lucian's precious soul was returned to him.

Pulling out of Lucian's mind, I opened my eyes.

He stared at me, still holding on, though his hand was red and burned from where I had entered with my Light.

I couldn't read him; it was almost as if he was in some kind of coma.

I stared into his blank eyes.

"Lucian?" I wasn't sure what to do or say.

He didn't respond.

He just kept staring at me, expressionless.

"Lucian? Are you okay?" I was starting to feel like I may have broken him for real this time.

"You're so beautiful when you sleep." The words came out, but there was still no life in his eyes.

"Lucian?" I choked off my forming tears.

He pulled me in tight and bit into my neck viciously, drinking with savage desperation. On instinct, I turned my blood into Light. Lucian didn't let go, the pain not seeming to affect him at all. I knew then that Caelius's blood control was too strong to overcome. Even eradicating the Darkness wasn't enough to wake him up.

It was finally time to detox.

I barely felt the heat even though I was connected with fire. Something had changed inside of me when I used all four elements at the same time; I knew now that I was one with each, making them a part of who I was. I had complete control.

Pulling more lava up, but making sure the water and dirt kept him free from pain, I made it reach up and cover his back and then his head so I could yank myself free. I saw a glimpse of his tear-filled eyes before quickly encasing him in the liquid magma. When I was done, a mountain of dried lava stood in front of me, forming a peak.

"That will hold him for a while." Aidan's voice rose up beside me. "You did the right thing."

I nodded, not wanting to say anything.

I was exhausted and devastated.

Aidan drew me into his arms so that I wouldn't have to use wind to levitate anymore. "We found a safe house, but honestly, if he can follow our Light trails, I don't think any place is *safe* anymore."

I leaned my head against his shoulder and let him carry me as he flew across the ocean and toward the mainland. A deep depression rose inside of me, to the point where I couldn't even cry. Only sleep felt like a reasonable solution. I closed my eyes but was haunted by Lucian's empty expression as he'd said, *You're so beautiful when you sleep.*

***

"Shea?"

I opened my eyes.

I was standing in the doorway back in my old room from childhood.

My mother sat on the edge of the bed as she had before, but upon seeing me pop into the room, she quickly stood up and embraced me.

"Oh, Shea, I was so worried. I thought Lucian had gone to *kill* you."

"Mom, he's so broken." I could barely form words. All I felt was pain.

"Did you . . . ? It would be okay if you did. I wouldn't judge you for it." Mom said the words, but I knew the bonds between

266

maker and vampire were strong. It only showed how much she loved me, that she would forgive me even if I had killed Lucian.

"No, Mom. I could never kill him. I'd die first." Dramatic, but it was how I felt.

We both sat down on the bed, keeping our hands clasped.

"Lucian hasn't returned yet. Caelius will only hold out for a day, maybe two, then he'll come for you, and I just . . . I don't think he can be stopped." I could tell that was difficult for her to say. The Molly Harper I knew would never tell me I wasn't capable of something. To her, anything was possible, and that went double when it came to me. So for her to say that she didn't think I had a chance of stopping Caelius shook me to my core.

"Helena said she's close to figuring something out." That sounded way lamer than I'd intended.

"And you trust this Helena?" My mom actually sounded . . . hopeful?

"I guess. I don't really know her that well, but she's super smart, and she was the one who rigged that necklace . . . where she pretty much juiced up Caelius . . ." I wasn't exactly instilling confidence about Helena's capabilities at this point. "Anyway, she moves around her lab, tinkering with things and saying 'ah-ha,' and 'maybe if I . . .' She never really finishes those sentences though. I dunno."

Mom smiled. "You make her sound like Doc Brown from *Back to the Future*."

I smiled back. "Yeah, she is kind of like that. And hey, if he can invent a time machine, maybe she can invent a way to kill Caelius. She has a device already, it's just the powering-up part she's having trouble with." I shrugged optimistically. "Originally she thought I could be the one to power it if I mastered all four elements, but then she seemed to think there was something else she was missing. But, Mom, I actually used all four elements at the exact same time. I've never done that before. When I wake up, maybe it'll help Helena somehow."

"Shea! That's huge!" My mom's eyes widened with pride as she squeezed my hand. "That could mean the difference."

"You think so?" I asked. It felt like when I was a little girl and Mom had encouraged me to try out for the gymnastics team. It had been a total failure. I fell off the balance beam with stunning impact, landing flat on the mat with an on-land belly flop. Before that, Mom and Dad had been cheering in the stands like I was Simone Biles. Until I fell. Then I had two mother hens racing to get to me. Actually, make that three; the third, Aidan, got there first. Where had my wind power been then? Huh? Stupid late-blooming superpowers.

Mom shook her head as if I amazed her. "You are truly special, Shea. I'm just so honored that I was the one chosen to be your mother. You're the Vessel; I still can't wrap my head around it. From the way Grandfather describes it, you were made of burning sunshine that was meant to destroy everything he loves. But he talks about the Light itself sometimes as if they were friends once, as if they shared some kind of bond that no one could ever fathom or understand. When he talks like that, I think . . . my daughter is made from that Light. *My* daughter." Her hands squeezed mine tighter.

"Thanks, Mom. It is weird, isn't it? We had such a normal life. Now look at us." I casually glanced around to indicate that we were Dream-Walking in my old room again. "A Vessel and a vampire mother."

Mom put her head down in what seemed like shame. "I hate that I'm a vampire. I can feel the Light inside me too, and I fight with the Darkness every day. It's so difficult sometimes."

"You can feel Light in you?" I asked, curious. Now that my mom was "normal" enough to talk to, I found that I wanted to know as much as I could about what she was going through. She really was an anomaly: the mother of a Vessel and Lucian and Nefertiti's vampire baby.

"I haven't told anyone, not even Grandfather."

"Could you not call Caelius that? It makes it . . . weird. And I hate him with every fiber of being, so there's that too." I tried to be delicate but couldn't.

Mom nodded. "Of course. I don't even know I'm doing it, to be honest. It's probably that drop of blood that keeps me in check. I want to hate Grandfa—Caelius . . . like you do, but I see such sadness and desperation in him. I-it must be the blood," she said, almost embarrassed.

"No, I'm sorry. You just don't know him like I do." I didn't really want to make her feel bad, especially since we had such little time together, but it was difficult not to when I knew she had witnessed all the horrible things Caelius had done to Lucian and to the world.

I decided to change the subject. "So, the Light, when did you notice it?"

"Right away. I just didn't know what it was. As a vampire I can feel it like a foreign substance pumping through my veins. It doesn't hurt exactly, but it doesn't feel natural either. I never told Caelius about it because, this is going to sound weird, the

Light wouldn't let me. In the beginning when I thought only of Caelius, I wanted to tell him everything, but I physically couldn't. Every time I tried, nothing would come out of my mouth."

"That's crazy," I said in wonder. "I guess it makes sense that you'd still have some of the Light in you, since you gave birth to me."

Mom suddenly sat up straight, as if hearing something. "Grandfather is having a tirade. I have to get back. Maybe Lucian has returned."

"I doubt it," I said guiltily. "I kind of encased him in lava to, you know, detox. And I destroyed all of Caelius's shadow control. Does the shadow go back to him? Do you think Caelius knows?"

Mom looked uncertain. "I don't know how it works, but that sounds likely. Don't worry, I won't tell Grandfather anything. I have to go now though. I don't want him to suspect me." She kissed my forehead and popped out of the room before I could utter a goodbye.

Taking a deep breath, I woke myself up.

***

I had the feeling of déjà vu as I opened my eyes to rainbow light.

"All right, all right, enough with the healing stuff." I sat up in bed as the lights snuffed out.

Like before, Dad, Aidan, Meky, Helena, and Duncan were all huddled around me like I was their dying patient.

"I'm okay. I swear. Helicopter parents much?" I teased, but it honestly felt good to know how much everyone cared about me.

"Dinnae expect that smash-and-grab by dear ol' Lucian, if I'm being honest," Duncan said. "I'm just glad yeer in one piece."

"Really. I'm better. I Dream-Walked with my mom again. She thinks Caelius will come after us if Lucian doesn't return in a day or two, so we have to be ready." I proceeded to tell them the entirety of the conversations I'd had with Lucian and my mom.

Helena was the first to speak. She looked like her mind was racing. "Your mother has a piece of the Light inside of her? Maybe we could use that. I don't know."

"Do you think it's important?" I asked. All eyes were now staring at Helena.

The scientist began to pace, nodding her head and, like my mom had observed, looking very much like Doc Brown.

"Maybe, but I'm thinking more about the fact that you used all four elements at once." Helena turned to us with a giant smile, which was completely out of character for her. "I think that may be the answer."

Dad said, "You mean . . . ?"

Helena nodded. "Shea mastering each element separately wasn't enough, but being able to use them all simultaneously as if they were one . . . I think we just found the way to kill Caelius for good."

No one spoke.

We didn't have to.

It felt *right*.

I just hoped Caelius didn't kill any more innocent people before then.

I really did hate that guy.

CHAPTER 14
LUCIAN

I was entombed like the Pharaohs I'd despised in Egypt.

The irony was laughable.

I wasn't adorned with gold for my passage down the Nile, however. There was nothing but dirt. Another suitable irony considering my relationship with it. It seemed I was destined for things like this.

What have I done.

I let out a long breath.

Finally, the word "we" was gone.

I could feel how empty the space outside of my tomb was.

The Vessel was gone too.

I felt filled with her and the absence of her at the same time. Her scent was in all the elements, wrapped around me like an embrace, but she herself had left with that beast, Adnachiel. His words about her doing the "right thing" seared hot like the magma that had burned my legs. She'd tricked me into lowering my defenses, then captured me like this. She and that dog deserved each other. He'd tricked me too once. I'd come to rely on that kindness in his eyes, like it meant something, but he had only been out for his own gain. He was selfish in the way he defended the world—selfish, untrustworthy, and yet . . . the Vessel hadn't let me burn, just as Aidan had saved my life from his brothers in Pompeii by burying me.

Was it that same kindness, however, that left me alone in my agony now?

That was familiar.

I knew loneliness well.

Maybe they were *holding hands* while laughing at their triumph over me.

A flash filled my mind: Shea holding my hand, walking through the ruins of Paris, standing next to Aidan as he betrayed me and Moses. I shook my head. It was like a memory, but it was something else. Maybe the Vessel's manipulation? She was powerful, after all.

"Where are you now?" I hissed. "Why didn't you finish me off?"

Maybe she and Aidan were pressed against each other in comfort, pitying themselves for knowing such a monster. I clenched my fists. I didn't want to acknowledge the spark of extreme jealousy that thought produced.

In a moment of desperation, I'd let her do it: burn Caelius's shadow out of my soul. Now that my mind was clearer, it made sense. Why wouldn't I allow her Light to chase him out? As "healing" as he claimed his blood was, and as much of this year was still a mystery, I still had my memories of the past. I had been bent by that same shadow when he was in the cage. I'd been tortured enough times by its ravishing to know what it felt like when it was still inside of me.

The pain of her chasing it had been like having my intestines slowly pulled out by rolling them on a spit over a fire; it had been pure agony. I'd endured because, as much as my blood wanted to serve him, I owed it to my family to be more than Caelius's dog.

I didn't do it for her.

I didn't do it . . .

Even as that thought arose, I felt its falsehood.

I did do it for her.

I swallowed hard.

Why?

The image of her sleeping peacefully, like a beautiful pearl wrapped in the sheets of my bed, sprung to mind again but left just as quickly. If I wasn't so tightly encased, I would have physically shook the thought from my head as I'd done before. " 'Why' doesn't matter right now, nor do these strange images."

I had failed.

Right now, Caelius was no doubt aware of my absence.

Right now, my family was in *danger*.

I growled, guttural and real.

As exhausted as I was from her burning my insides, the absence of the shadow made me feel much stronger. Even though I'd cried again, it had been wise to drink her blood to repair myself. Who knew how long it would have taken my body to recover from her bleeding the Darkness out had I not. I didn't have the luxury of time that she apparently thought *she* had, while resting in the comfort of Aidan's arms like a coddled child who had everything and everyone at her feet.

As if she were precious simply by being.

I growled again and this time acknowledged that it was indeed jealousy.

But of whom?

The Vessel or Aidan?

I thought of the beast. They really were perfect for each other. Everything came so easily to him. He was immortal and lived countless human lives without having to feed on blood. He'd been born to protect the Light, born next to the divine creator of all things. He was loved by the Vessels, his brothers, and loved by his god. The only pain in his side was me.

And I'd been born a worm, tortured and played with by Darkness itself. That precious Light of his did nothing to protect me because I was not its *angel*. I was nothing more than another human it had abandoned to some game with Caelius. I was not gifted with divine purpose, but the Darkness had carved one out of my soul. I was left to struggle, caught in his web, with potter's hands forced to bathe in blood, the poetry in me drying up in the rage of an unfair and unwanted existence.

"Only you." The words rang through me, and my tongue felt swollen against the roof of my mouth. "Only you. You are all I've wanted since I became flesh. You are my *everything*. Let me be your god, and I will give you this world and any other that you like." Caelius's whispers at night, as he pressed long kisses into my neck, were a twisted sort of comfort.

It was unlike the comfort I felt when I kissed Shea.

My eye twitched comparing the two in such sharp contrast.

With her it felt . . . even her blood was . . . truly healing, like

275

an oasis on dry land.

With Caelius, every action was carefully planned, all so that he could increase his control over me.

His embrace, no matter how thorough, always left me *thirsty*.

If she was an oasis, he was the desert itself.

He would force my submission.

He would *make* me obedient.

I laughed, feeling my body quake in the encased magma. Wasn't this force as well, and where was she? Was she by my side, or now that she had stopped the *vampire* from bringing her to Caelius, was she done with me? All of that affection, was it just a powerful manipulation like Caelius had warned me against?

Still . . . images kept creeping up in my mind, then dissolving: we were on a bed in Paris, my hands moving across that small scar on her stomach, the taste of her sweat, haunting, like it was telling me all of her secrets. There were moments of clarity reaching through to the joy and pleasure of loving her, not through the suffering and pain of my past.

Her scent was like a balm that lingered even now, provoking such musings.

And yet, where is she?

I growled again.

If she was *mine*, why was I alone?

I hardened myself.

These memories, sorting them, feeling anything toward *my* enemy, was a mistake.

Caelius was more powerful than all of us combined. More powerful than Shea Harper.

That I *felt*, and with that came an image so savage and unholy

I gasped, sucking in the dirt around my face: Nefertiti's children were ripped apart, devoured by giant fangs. The Darkness exploded from Caelius's human form, searching for a way to extend its power out, holding us all like tiny flies clutched in his engorged claws.

Death and failure. I broke into a cold sweat. Was this the *detox* the Vessel had wanted? Were these images even real? My body shook.

There was something else . . .

An offering.

I'd offered myself at the end of the last battle, to save them.

To save *her*.

The bones of my shoulders sagged into the meat of muscle, unable to lower into the stones around me. I paused for a long breath, wetting my bottom lip with my teeth as my eyes darted back and forth in the black.

If this was true . . .

Then *united* we had already failed.

What choice did I have but to go back to him, to save Nefertiti?

I winced.

Nefari, her cries as her children were killed in front of her, and her embrace now, the hollowness of her gaze . . . the commander of Gutian armies, the great ruler of Egypt, had finally been brought to complete ruin, as had the son of Onack the Great.

"Is that what you believe? Were all of our deaths for nothing then?"

My breath hitched with the familiar voice. I searched in the darkness the Vessel had concealed me in. Was it really him?

"Do you plan on forgetting all of us? Will you desecrate our memories by becoming Caelius's puppet?"

I flexed my muscles. It couldn't be.

The excitement made my teeth grow large enough to split my gums as I shouted, "Bohe! You're alive! Thank the gods! Thank your gods! I never thought I'd see you again!"

I struggled against the elemental prison, extending my claws and tearing at the earth between me and the magma. I had to get out of here. I had to aid him. It was better that Caelius didn't know he was still alive. "I'll keep you safe! Just wait a moment! We'll go back to your lonely mountain, together! I'll hide you until I sort things out!" I clawed frantically, clumping handfuls of dirt.

Bohe was *alive*.

"I don't blame you for resigning yourself to your fate, La-Narru. When I was mortal I had done just that, knowing that I could never win against those who sought the power of my throne. I was used willingly because I thought it guaranteed my protection, that I would, at the very least, live. And I did. I led a horrible defaced life because of it."

I clawed, ripping my teeth into the earth. I swallowed it, creating space around my head. That was all I needed, a few inches to shatter this small mountain whole. "It's all right, just wait a moment longer!"

"I fell prey to that same weakness again under Caelius's torture." Bohe's tone was low, saddened. "Even after all that time as a monk, he made me lose myself."

I was used to swallowing dirt, having drunk the sands of Egypt. I chewed and slashed, his words pulsing both ferocity and urgency through my veins. "I don't know what Caelius has done to you, but I will protect you from him as soon as I break free! He won't lay another hand on you; it's me he wants!" I snapped at the earth and shifted my weight, feeling power surge in my muscles. His face, his voice—I felt like I could see them through the darkness, as if they weren't form but light, pulling me toward him.

"But you were never like that, were you, my friend?"

I froze.

No.

Stop.

A memory was trying to push through.

Something so agonizing that I wanted to rip my skin and scream.

Bohe's dead body was tied to mine with a yellow sash. He'd been wearing the same Hanfu I was now, before Caelius removed it. He was pressed against me, as cold and hollow as Caelius's gaze that watched my every reaction.

My mouth fell open, breathless, as I squeezed my claws into fists full of dirt. The garments around me now, I had been wearing them like a blanket of familiar comfort, and the familiarity was because they had adorned Bohe before he died in my arms.

The images couldn't be real.

Bohe was alive.

I thought the Vessel had killed him, but if he was here . . .

"Bohe, I'll save you! I saved you from death once before; I can do it again! Just wait for me!"

"For all the things that you are, Lucian . . . *you* don't give up. You think yourself a coward for abandoning your people in

Gutium, a weight I always saw you carry, a deeper scar than the lashes of slavery that cover your body. But you were obeying your father. *That* was not *this*."

Emotion welled up inside of me. I had to cover the pain his words were unearthing. I struggled, hearing the cracks of magma as well as my bones as I started throwing my body against it.

Still, the image kept returning.

His lifeless form had been tied to me for *days* as I'd wept and prayed for his safe passage into the afterlife.

"It's not true! If I'm speaking to you now, the memory is *wrong*. You're alive, aren't you? Please be alive." I winced at the sound of desperation in my own voice. The memory was *wrong*. "You're alive."

"You have fought lifetimes over. You are a fighter, but it doesn't have to be in the way of Nefertiti or your father, Onack. Fight like La-Narru fights. Lucian was *his* name for you, wasn't it? Have you forgotten what your name means in Gutian? Have you forgotten who you really are? Son of Anna-Steen. Poet. Friend. We have *all* loved you. Will you forget the way we died as you have forgotten yourself?"

I stopped moving and leaned against the dirt and magma for support.

My eyes flooded wet and hot.

"No. You're *not* dead. Please, Bohe. You're here with me now, aren't you?" It was a desperate question, and it quivered as it left my lips.

"Just as your mother never left your after she died, even as you spent years in the desert wandering, thinking yourself lost and alone, I will never leave you. None of us will. Do you not see, even here, covered in Darkness, that the Light is with you, that our love is *here*, La-Narru?

"Even Gracuri waits for you in the form of a boy, laughing by the river where you first met."

I clutched my chest. Gracuri's words echoed in my ears: *I'm sorry, Father. I didn't want Caelius to use me against you . . . Always remember what I said to you when we first met in Thebes. I will always feel that way about you, Lucian. Please don't blame your—*

Caelius.

He was wearing Gracuri's shoes and holding his head on a spike.

"Rest assured, La-Narru. He smiles like he used to, and he still believes that you were his salvation. He will wait with his hand outstretched for yours; that was the deal you made when you returned to him every year before Thebes, and he is still honoring it. He will *always* wait for you to return to him, in death as he did in life."

I couldn't breathe.

What was this?

Was I hallucinating? Dying?

"He can't still think that after how many times I failed him, after I rejected his confession of love." The pain was too much to bear. "Stop this madness, Bohe." I slumped farther. "I'll save you."

"Gunnhild and Ashgar can love without fear now, and they do just that. They don't blame you; instead they wish for you to think of them with favor. All they've ever wanted is your approval. Will you continue to hide your fondness for them, even now? Will you not give them rest?"

281

"No! I didn't . . . hide my fondness . . ." Was that what I'd been doing this whole time, safeguarding those closest to me by keeping them at arm's length? "I was protecting them."

"David still calls you what he whispered on his deathbed: *my friend.* Can you not hear his voice when the moon is full like it was then? Can you truly not hear him calling you? He waits beside the mountain Goliath, hand in hand, their love offered to you as well."

I turned my head away from the voice. "I . . . I don't. I don't hear anything. I don't feel *anything.* Just Darkness and loss."

"And what of me? I have been speaking to you this whole time. Will you deny my voice as well? Will you call me a waking dream like you have to other ghosts from your past?"

I opened my mouth, but nothing came out.

"You spoke to me in my own tongue, a Gutian blessing. You said you loved me. You asked that my soul find the light. You said you would carry me with you *always.* Have you easily forgotten such loyal words?"

My eyes darted.

I wouldn't.

I would never willingly forget anything between us. I cherished him. "Bohe, I—"

"I rest with your family because you gave me that gift in your blessings at death, and I *chose* yours over mine. I will always choose you, as you chose me in life. Will you reject me now, your *Bohe?*"

Another image flashed through my mind.

The dejected look on Bohe's face as Caelius toyed with his hair, the guilty feeling accompanying it as I tried to explain myself; my mind filled with the memory of his mother trying to abort him and how that was just the start in a life that would make him feel unwanted by all who touched him.

I tried to turn my face back toward the voice, reaching out to it, clawing handfuls of dirt. "No, Bohe, I'm sorry. I would never reject you. I just don't know—"

"Nefari's daughters and your parents wanted you to remember that no matter what happens in this life, you are always Gutian. You still have a home. You are not without a tribe. I like the words of your kin. They taught me something precious in my stay with them. Will you hear it?"

I felt like he had stabbed me in the chest.

I had felt orphaned when my mother died, and twice over when Nefari told me of the slaughtered fields of Gutium in Egypt. What right did I have to still belong to any of them? "Bohe . . . stop."

"The code of your people is right. United, we beat with *one* heart. Because you offered me a place with your own, what's yours is now mine, so I can say with certainty, the flame that is *our* people cannot be stamped out of time. We are etched into the existence of *all* things. And love is truly the soul of all that's worth fighting for. Have you forgotten those simple truths, La-Narru?"

"No." I closed my eyes. "Yes." I gasped for breath. "I don't know. Everything's so confusing. I'm sorry." I felt like the hollowness was filling in and flooding, like I would drown in this sarcophagus, swimming in the ache of my tears.

"Our memories of you and the love we shared have only grown in our deaths. And they live on."

I made fists. "What are you saying?"

"You aren't and never were *alone*."

My body shook. I closed my eyes, as if it would shield me from his truths. The sweat at my palms mixed with dirt. I wanted to bury my eyes in that mud, to rip them out as Gracuri had done in Thebes.

"They can live inside of you, my dearest friend. You carry your home on your back like the World Turtle. You are not lost, for you are fused with all of our histories and stories, our rich cultures and memories. Duncan would like that, wouldn't he? Even though he's still living, will you deny him as well? You think your life has been a failure surrounded by loss, but loss is an illusion, a *lie* of the Darkness, a lie the Darkness itself believes, for it is the opposite of the Light. In truth, Caelius clings to you because he is afraid of being alone."

His voice was a whisper now, but it didn't take away from the power of his words.

"You studied too much in the mountains, Bohe. You've become wise." I laughed, or at least tried to through the ache in my chest. "Is this why you can speak to me, because you were the only one of my children that became enlightened?"

"We are *all* here. You are not alone."

I clenched my teeth.

"Fight him. But fight him the way La-Narru would. Not as a singularity, but held by the love of your people. *All* your people."

The cracks in the magma began to fill with a strange sort of light, a light that grew externally as it grew inside of me.

"Can you feel it now, what has always been here? What will always be here for you?"

"Yes," I muttered.

Love.

It was all I could feel emanating from that light. It beckoned me back to who I'd been as a boy, summoning a call from a childlike self within. For the first moment in a long life, I felt clear, like the clarity after a long walk in the fog of heat from the illusions of the desert.

I grabbed my chest, feeling a tidal wave, an ocean inside of me that had been kept at bay for too long. I had been afraid of these emotions. I had thought they would destroy me after my mother died, when my small hands had turned to fists that held her burned body. This whole time I'd been eating the ash of all that I had loved and lost . . . this whole time I'd been grieving. So I'd run, from everything and everyone, only to arrive at the center of my grief again and again.

When my father said that Anna-Steen's death had killed him and not her, it was in that moment that the lie had formed; loving me had a *cost*. Love was fragile and easily burned, and my existence was nothing more than kerosene, my very breath fire, turning the ones I held close to embers in my hands.

I'd become afraid, afraid of myself and terrified in the loneliness that followed. With every century the lie had become a self-fulfilling prophecy, and it burned. My small hands, still covered in ash, had turned into the hands of a man.

But she'd been with me this whole time, my mother, Anna-Steen.

And so was Gracuri.

Gunnhild and Ashgar.

David.

Bohe.

The girls, my father, my tribe.

They were all *here*, the family I was born with, and the one I had created and loved, with those same desperate hands.

"Fight. And remember who you are. Remember we are *all* Gutium now." Bohe's voice faded, and I felt his presence lift, but it didn't fill me with hopelessness as it might have before. His love, all of their love, was with me.

I wasn't alone anymore.

I didn't need Caelius's twisted devotion to stave off my childhood fears of abandonment.

I shattered the mountain in half, erupting from the tip like a geyser. As the pieces fell to the earth, I felt the lies fall with them, and I flew with the lightness of a boy.

I gasped, sucking in air.

Ever since my mother died, I had been unconsciously holding my breath.

I smiled, finally feeling the warmth of her love as I had known, so long ago, as an innocent child of the mountains.

The lies I had believed had stolen her from me twice.

I flew like a lightning bolt, cracking the sky open.

I landed, my heart and the ground thudding together, at Caelius's feet.

"I finally understand how to save you. You don't have to do any of this. It was all a lie!" I yelled into the cloud of dirt that surrounded my landing.

We stared at each other as the dust slowly cleared. As it did, his blazing red eyes came into sharp focus. I looked around, suddenly realizing that it was pitch-black, a darker night than all I had seen on the desert plains of Egypt while wrapped in death.

Just as it had then, with the dark came uncertainty. It struck me as quickly and deeply as the truth had moments before.

I looked around again, feeling that sensation of being lost.

"Bohe?" I called out into the black, but there was no answer.

Caelius's brow furrowed with the name. "Lucian." He stepped forward, reaching for my hand. "You seem *confused*. Are you unharmed?"

I stepped back. The presence, the light that had surrounded me, was gone, and I was standing in front of the absence of, as if it couldn't follow me into this place—as if Light and Darkness canceled each other out. A fear, visceral and instinctive, moved through me. Empowered with truth, I had felt strong enough to stop him myself, but now that I felt my mortality sinking in with every heavy breath as his eyes bored into mine, I questioned my sanity. Perhaps I had lost my mind after all, trapped in that tiny mountain.

I swallowed.

The trees rustled behind him as Nefertiti and Molly stepped out.

We were in a forest halfway between the cabin and where Shea had encased me.

I swallowed again, stepping back. "You were coming for me?"

He moved closer, his hand still extended. "Of course, darling. Why wouldn't I?"

There it was.

In the way his words curved when he said "darling." Uncertainty, fear, loneliness—it was all there smothered in his breath. I had seen glimpses of it before, lingering in his gaze, but with Bohe's wisdom still ringing in my ears like the gongs at a funeral pyre, I knew the lie that those emotions held.

"More so than anyone, I know your loneliness." I convinced myself to step toward the Darkness, toward his outstretched hand.

He froze in place. "Is that so, boy?"

"It aches in you, like it's a void that can't be filled." I stepped closer.

He smiled, a cruel wry thing, a defense to cover what was momentarily exposed. "I think you can *fill* it just fine."

He snatched my hand and pulled me into his embrace. His mouth was wet, his kiss hasty and forced. I pushed back, but it was no use. My physical strength couldn't match his. I was like a wilting flower in the arms of stone, but I didn't have to fight in the ways of Onack or Nefertiti.

When he pulled back, he sighed, relief filling his gaze. "I was worried that I had lost you, but you came back to me of your own free will." He buried his head in the nape of my neck, rubbing his face against the place where his deep bruises had bored into me like a dog collar. "You came back."

I clenched my teeth, pulling my head back, trying to create some space between us. "You're not going to punish me then?"

He straightened us both up, trying to mask his elation. "Oh, what a good suggestion." He laughed.

"Caelius, I came back to tell you the truth. Listen, I know why you're doing this—"

"Caelius?" The softness in his gaze disappeared, replaced by the monster I had seen tear through cities, engorged with death and rage—the monster that had truly killed Nefertiti's children.

My eyes searched for her. She was staring at the ground. I had never known this Nefari, the one that would not meet me head-on with honesty and pride. I sighed with an inward knowing; fear could destroy even the brightest of stars.

"I believe you were calling me *God* when we last touched." He ran his hand down my side, lingering in the space between every rib.

I growled in anger. "*Don't.*"

He scoffed and seized my shoulders, breaking the bones underneath his grip with the force.

"Grandfather, stop!"

I must have looked surprised and my face matched his as we stared at Molly.

"What's this now, *child*?"

She hesitated, then shifted against her heels, steadying herself. Nefertiti's eyes met mine with relief, as if she had been holding back and finally someone was brave enough to speak in her place.

"You thought the Vessel might have killed him. You've been inconsolable this whole time. Why are you acting like this? I'm sure Father left for a good reason, and now that he's back, our family is reunited." She folded her hands in front of her in a nonthreatening gesture. "I'm just saying, shouldn't we *celebrate* that he's safe and he returned to you? You don't . . . you don't have to *hurt* him. We're all tired of it. Let's just be a family. Isn't that what you really want?"

To my surprise, he released me.

He moved as if he were going to rush Molly and snap her neck.

But he didn't.

He looked up, as if contemplating. "A *family*." He tilted his head toward me. "Why did you leave me?"

"To prove myself, to return the Vessel to you." It was quick and moved like a flood out of my mouth, fear already hastening my tone. I was surprised at how whole I had felt minutes ago, and how that wholeness felt like it was bleeding out of me with every breath of the black air emanating around him. His fear was my fear, and it was powerful.

He looked me up and down. "You failed, I imagine. As you always do."

I thought for a moment. I wanted to keep confronting him, to tell him there was another way, but maybe that was something gradual I could do over time, maybe facing him now would only result in my torture and continued brainwashing. As it was, the few pieces of memory that I had regained were like images of stained glass, each separated by missing information like a line of black grout. At least they couldn't be disregarded as false anymore, and among them, one thing was certain: Caelius had to be stopped.

"I'm sorry," I said. "She trapped me in lava. The instant I broke free, I flew back to you. I wanted to do it myself, to prove to all of you that I deserved your . . . affections."

He smirked at the word, then thought for a moment longer. "You've always been like that, even as a boy, rushing off to do things on your own. You're so obsessed with *proving* your worth. In all honesty, I shouldn't have been surprised, but there I was, like a fool whose lover had run off in the morning." He growled, but there was no threat to it this time. "Nefertiti, I'll return your children to you, since no harm was done."

"You'll what?" I looked at her, but her eyes were fixed on

Caelius.

"I told you I hadn't betrayed you. There was no need to bind them in the first place!"

He growled again, and this time it was hungry and horrifying, the threat palpable in the air itself.

Nefari instantly bowed her head in reverence. "What I meant to say was thank you, Father. Thank you." She lowered her head inches from her ankles.

It was disgusting to see, and I hated stomaching it.

"I'll go get them for you, Grandfather!" Molly leapt into the air, and as quickly as she left, she was thrown down.

I raced to Nefertiti, protecting her instinctively in my arms.

Molly looked startled as Caelius wrapped his hands around her shoulders, lifting her back up. "Tut, tut, Molly. You're not going anywhere. That was quite an independent speech you gave earlier. I think you and I need to spend a little more time together. After I have some alone time with Lucian, that is."

Molly nodded in compliance as Nefertiti's arms tightened around my waist.

Time together meant more blood.

"I'm not strong enough to ask you to leave, to damn the consequences. But that's exactly what you should do." Nefari's voice was barely a whisper, light enough that a distracted Caelius might not hear her plea.

"I won't leave you like I did in Gutium. I won't abandon the girls either." I held on to her, hoping to hold on to myself. I had to keep this oasis I had found inside of me alive, even as Caelius wrapped us in the black pulsing from his body.

A feeling came over me as I clung to her. We had done this

once as children. By the fire on a dark night like this one, when our fathers spoke of the Great Unknown and the endlessness of existence, when they spoke of monsters and gods, she had clung to me. It was as if our arms were a tether, the only thing keeping us from being sucked into the abyss of night. And here again, staring at Caelius, we were tethered, but it wasn't her arms I longed for. This wasn't the safety and reassurance of a love that would last through all of time, the promise to stand against Darkness as our Gutian code had reassured us of; I didn't feel that from Nefari anymore.

She had broken our tethered oaths with every whip mark on my back in Egypt, even before Caelius had taken me as his own. Even now, as I held her close, I knew I couldn't trust her. She had forfeited my life to that very Darkness we had sworn to protect each other from. As he fed on me and his will became my own, she had let go, and I was sucked into that abyss.

Our chord had snapped.

I thought of Shea.

I didn't know why, but it was her I longed for now. I wanted to feel her soft breath against me as she slept in my arms. We could ignore the Darkness like it wasn't reality, but a nightmare we could awaken from just as easily as a dream. The image made me wish that I was a man and not a vampire, so that I could sleep with the same peace that covered her resting face.

Images and the sound of Shea's words called to me. They pressed, like a thumb, against the inside of my ribs in the opposite places Caelius had touched, like the other side of a coin: love versus fear. I felt a pressure build in my brain, like at any moment it would pop and I'd remember everything, if only I could get away from this Darkness.

You are not alone.

As Nefertiti clung to my back, I was more certain that the ghost of Bohe had spoken the truth; it wasn't just her arms embracing me, steadying me against the Dark.

They are all with me.

I clung to that realization, squeezing her tighter.

I wouldn't run anymore.

I was fortified by love, and I would fight the Darkness *my way.*

I just needed to find out what that way was.

I just needed a little more time.

"Egypt." Caelius turned to me, his eyes ablaze. "My darling, I will give you Egypt."

Nefertiti's grip left mine, and she stepped away from me, her gaze unable to meet Caelius's. Her body instantly obeyed his silent order to not touch what belonged to *him* and him alone.

"What is there in Egypt?" My voice was low. I was uncertain how to play this new hand.

He released Molly. "Don't make me repeat my movements. Stay put." She nodded, and he walked toward me.

He pulled his hand through my hair, his fingers tracing the outline of my face. They felt cool, but they started a burning within: his blood. His blood was still inside me, and it was calling back to itself. I was still his possession in that way, a claim he had wrought as deep as my bones, but not my soul. I could reach that at least, thanks to Shea's "detox."

Thanks to all of them.

"I hate it because it's where I was imprisoned, but you hate it too, don't you, my sweet?" He fondly kissed my neck in the same spot he had first bit me when I was turned. It was a spot he often touched tenderly after sex, pointing out that very fact. "They made you a *slave* in the desert. That place scarred your precious back and destroyed your people. The Egyptians slaughtered your father like a *stuck pig*."

I cringed thinking of the heat and long days enslaved by the same Egyptians that had burned my village and tribe to ash. On the deathbed of my people's slaughter, Akhenaten had taken Nefari as his living prize of conquest. At first she'd been his slave, then his wife. I'd had to watch as the love of my life was impregnated over and over again, then paraded around like some spoil of war. My only offering to her was my slavery, to never leave her side, and even that was stolen with my demise. The death I'd suffered at the hands of the Pharaoh was as brutal as my father's had been, my bones crushed and my back bloodied by a thousand gashes. Egypt had been my personal hell before Caelius.

"That was a long time ago." The words were soft and broken, as my heart had been then. "I'm past it." I sighed. "You should move past it too. That's what I came back to help you with. To move on."

"They still worship him, you know."

The thought started to mask the tenderness of love with dark rage, a rage that was fueled by Caelius's blood pounding in step with my heartbeat. "Akhenaten?"

"They worship *all* like him, as if being Pharaoh was some *divine right*. Kids these days even think it's *cool*. Should we show them, darling? Should we show them what a nameless boy from the mountains can really do?" He smiled, and I felt something wicked fill my face as my teeth grew. "A boy not written in their sacred texts, or even mentioned once in the glyphs of Akhenaten's tomb, could be their demise. Let us unite and destroy a place that has marred your life since you were a boy." He ran his hands down my arms, then rested them against my palms, clasping tight. "As a thanks for your return, I will help you kill your ghosts."

"Wait." I struggled. I was already losing myself; his persuasions and presence were so powerful they unmoored me.

He smirked. "Let us go as a family. Let us unite and watch the living and entombed lords of this world shake in fear. I want you as my *equal*, Lucian. Convince me that's what you are, then we'll talk all you like about this *loneliness* you speak of." He squeezed my hands. "Do this with me, and I'll even let the fact that my shadow is gone from you slide."

I swallowed as he pulled me closer, then licked the side of my neck like sampling a delicacy.

He yanked my hair back and thrust his wrist against my elongated incisors.

Blood.

It poured into me as he tightened his hand around my throat.

"Did you think I wouldn't notice what that *whore* did to you, pet?"

CHAPTER 15
SHEA

Now that we had a plan, I felt rejuvenated and ready to fight.

Whoa.

Strike that.

A sudden wave of weakness washed through my body.

I lay back down. Maybe I needed to rest a little.

No one seemed to notice as they talked fervently about the new revelation of me using all four elements.

I wanted to tell someone about my abrupt change, maybe get some more light therapy from Helena, but I couldn't seem to form words. My mind could barely focus on my surroundings. Everything sounded muffled. I couldn't even tell where I was anymore; my vision started to blur.

That was when I realized with clarity . . . I wasn't recovering.

Using all four elements was supposed to bring me to my true self, my true power. Wasn't it? So why did it feel like I was breaking apart from the inside out? I tried again to speak, to ask for help, to do *anything*, but I could no longer move.

A giant gush of light burst from my hand, rising upward like a beacon of white fire, then immediately snuffed out.

That couldn't be good.

They were all paying attention to me now.

Aidan's voice sounded in my ear, his face inches from mine. "Shea? Can you hear me? Say something!" His tone was desperate.

I knew exactly how he felt. I couldn't calm him because I couldn't freaking move anything.

"What's happening to her?" Aidan screamed.

Helena answered, but her voice was so distant I could barely hear her.

Stand closer, woman!

It sounded like she said, "I have no idea," which pretty much summed up my life right about now.

I wished I could say something, but what would I say?

I didn't know what was wrong with me.

And I was scared.

So yeah.

Help?

That was all I had.

Another burst of light flew out of my right thigh, rising like the other one before, then blinking out of existence.

What was happening to me?

Aidan's voice was next to my ear again. "We're going to try and induce sleep, see if Dream-Walking can snap you out of . . . whatever this is. Helena thinks it might have something to do with you using all four elements at once. Maybe it's some kind of consequence for using that much power?" He paused, his voice shaken. "I really hope you can hear me."

I can hear you!

No words came out.

I tried to calm my mind, to help whatever kind of "inducement" they had planned for me. Knowing Helena, it was probably some kind of device or tonic. Either way, I was glad I couldn't see all that well because whatever it was would most likely freak me out.

Then I heard my father's voice, soft and reassuring.

He began reading *The Lion, the Witch and the Wardrobe* by C.S. Lewis. It was the book he always read to me before bed when I was a little girl. We read the whole series in third grade, and it had been pure magic. After that, I would beg him to read the first book whenever I had trouble sleeping. I was embarrassed to admit it, but Dad had read me this book through high school.

I didn't need any of Helena's contraptions to help me fall asleep. It was just going to be my father being his true self, not a vampire, just a dad reading to his daughter. If I'd been capable of crying, I would have. I listened to the words he spoke. They were so familiar that I knew them by heart. They made me feel like I was . . . home.

I could move!

Overjoyed, I did a quick jumping jack, then noticed I was standing in the living room of my *parents'* house.

I was Dream-Walking.

Well, at least I could move in my head.

I'd take it.

"Shoot. I thought we'd end up in Narnia for sure," Dad said as he materialized in front of me.

I hugged him tightly, then pulled away smiling. "I don't think Dream-Walking works that way, Dad, but trust me when I say being back home is better than Narnia right now."

His face was wracked with concern. "Are you okay? What's happening to you?"

I shook my head. "I have no idea. I used my powers, got really tired, then felt fine and excited to attack Caelius, then suddenly I lay down and couldn't move or speak, with light bursting from random parts of my body! My guess is as good as yours."

"What's happening to you?" Mom suddenly appeared in the living room with us, eyes wide with worry.

Dad whirled around to face her. When their eyes met, it was like watching a romance movie. Normally, I'd make hurling noises at my parents' obvious love for each other, but at this moment, it was the best thing ever.

I quickly assuaged my mother's fears. "I'm fine. Please kiss, or hug, or something. I promise I won't be grossed out."

They both smiled at me like they used to when they thought I'd said something witty, and for just a second, everything felt completely normal. I wanted to hold on to that sensation for as long as I could. "Normal" had such a bad rap as being boring or uneventful. What was wrong with normal? Nothing. Absolutely nothing.

Embracing each other, my parents kissed passionately. This was their first reunion with both their memories restored. They weren't the wiped robots that Aidan's brothers had left behind. They were Jeff and Molly Harper: a father and mother with a lifetime of experiences we'd made as a family.

They eventually parted, and Mom reached over, grabbing me

by the hand, pulling me in for a group hug. It was wonderful.

Parting enough so that she could see my face properly, she placed her hand under my chin and forced me to make eye contact with her, just as she had done when I was a child and she wanted a truthful answer. I'd hated it then; I loved it now.

Mom said, "Spit it out. What's happening?"

"I swear I don't know. I used all four elements to bury Lucian so he'd be safe, and suddenly I was exploding light and couldn't move," I explained lamely.

Mom released her hand and turned to Dad. "Does anyone from your group know what this is? Is Shea going to be all right?"

The look on Dad's face made me feel guilty for being so candid. "We have no idea what it is. Helena's trying to figure it out," he replied.

Mom nodded. "Good. I hope you two haven't misplaced your faith in her, but I trust you." Then her expression turned grave. "Caelius is attacking Egypt as we speak. I told him I needed to rest for a moment, but I have to get back soon. He's being very possessive of all of us. I think he suspects we'd leave him if we could, which is absolutely true. Luckily, he's too obsessed with forcing Lucian to *worship* him right now that he let me have a few minutes without them."

My heart sank into my stomach. "Lucian broke free of the lava?" It hadn't been enough time to rid himself of Caelius's control. With one sentence, everything I had sacrificed to save Lucian was for nothing. My powers, my inability to move, all of it was so that Lucian would never have to go back to Caelius and be his slave again. Now they were apparently destroying one of the oldest civilizations still left on the planet. Yay, Caelius.

Realizing what her words meant, Mom's arms were around me again. "Oh, honey, I'm so sorry. If it means anything, I could feel a physical change in Lucian when he came back to us. Whatever you did helped him regain some of his old self. He's fighting so hard." She stopped herself, not sure if she should continue. I couldn't see the expression on my face, but if it was anything like how I felt, it was pretty bad.

"I just thought if he could get a few days away from Caelius's blood, maybe he would remember . . ." I didn't know what else to say. I had failed. I had probably made it worse. Lucian's torture would be maddening now that he had some of his sanity back. What had I done? I just wished he would pull me into a memory again. Maybe I could help him in that way. Maybe I could figure out what those experiences meant.

My mother kept her arms around me in support. I hadn't realized how much I had missed this kind of contact with her until it was gone. Just having her near me, fully my mom again, was everything.

"Don't regret what you did. Lucian is better for it," she said.

"But you guys are ravaging Egypt right now. How is he better if he's *hurting* people?" I didn't want to think about the fact that Lucian and my mother had most likely *murdered* for Caelius's sake. How could I forgive that? How could I forgive anything? Depression overwhelmed me. Was this how family members of serial killers felt? On one hand, you loved them—on the other, they *killed* people.

My mom allayed my fears. "Oh, honey, we're not killing anyone—none of us, not even Nefertiti. And Lucian is destroying pyramids, tombs, and any structure he can get his hands on.

He doesn't even seem to see the people around him, which is a good thing. We're making Caelius believe we're killing, but we're draining people to unconsciousness. There's lots of blood everywhere, but no one is dying from *our* hands. Caelius's victims are another issue. We can't stop him. I know it sounds awful, but now that I'm truly *awake*, I will never harm another living soul again. I promise you that." She spoke the last sentence while staring at me directly.

I believed her, mainly because I wanted to, but also because she was my mother and she had never lied to me before.

As if hearing something in the distance, Mom turned her head, listening. "I have to get back."

Dad touched her arm, and I realized he had been simply watching the two of us the entire time. He looked like he had been basking. Dad was definitely a basker.

Mom held our hands, one in each of hers. "I'll try to break free, but I don't know if it's possible. Being a spy is pointless now. It's now or never. I'll return to you or die trying."

"We'll come to you," I said.

Even Dad's eyebrows rose. "Shea, we don't even know what's wrong with you."

Shaking my head, I said with confidence, "This ends now. Helena said she was close to finding a way to turn Caelius back into his shadow form, and whatever's happening with me, shooting out powerful beams of light, can only help." I had no idea if that was true, but somewhere down deep, it felt right.

Mom didn't look pleased, but she nodded. "If Helena finds a way, let's end this and be a family again."

"It's happening." My confidence didn't waver.

Smiling at me, Mom kissed my cheek, then kissed Dad. "I love you both."

And with that, she was gone.

Turning to my father, I held both of his hands. "Let's get back."

Dad stared at me, eyes crinkled in worry. To him nothing had changed; I was still in a semicoma, but something inside of me had awoken.

Seeing my mother, knowing she and Lucian were in danger, knowing that Caelius needed to be stopped . . . I was finally ready.

And it was time.

Closing my eyes, I squeezed my dad's hands with determination.

***

My eyes opened.

I was in a hotel room sitting on a chair.

I could move.

I could see and talk.

"I'm good," I assured them. Then I turned to Helena. "It's time."

To my surprise, her expression showed that she agreed. "It's your powers *united*, Shea. All four elements, that's the key. No gadgets, no inventions, just pure Light and the energy of the Earth itself should be enough."

"Yes." I nodded. It was as if we were the only two in the room. I could feel the intensity behind her words. As much as exploding Light out of various parts of my body was terrifying, I also knew that it had the potential to free us from Caelius.

"I can control it now." That was a total lie, but I hoped to figure it out by the time we got to Caelius. I needed them all to believe me, otherwise they wouldn't agree to go. I was being reckless, but I couldn't stand a second more of Lucian and my mom being held captive.

I physically and mentally couldn't take it, and the world couldn't either.

Too many innocents had died already.

Caelius needed to be stopped before any more people were killed.

Aidan faced me, forcing me to focus on him and not Helena. "Are you sure, Shea? *How* can you control it?"

Freaking Aidan with his direct questions! I managed to muster up my confidence. "I can't explain it, but I can control it, just trust me."

He stared at me, trying to read my body language.

I remained determined.

Finally, he relented and agreed. "I will always trust you, Shea. I'm in."

Meky was the first to respond after Aidan. "I'm *definitely* in."

Duncan echoed Meky. "Ye know where I stand. 'Til tha end."

"May the Force be with us."

Dad, seriously? It was so "him" that I had to laugh. Aidan joined in, and soon we were all smiling despite the terrifying confrontation we were about to run straight toward.

"Aidan, you take Shea. The rest of us will run," Helena said.

Our smiles faded as we fully realized what we were about to do.

It was fitting that I was going to be flown in by an angel when I was about to fight the devil on Earth.

I just hoped we'd *all* survive this time.

***

Soaring over Egypt was a nightmare. I felt as if I were watching a horror movie where the bad guy had destroyed one of the seven wonders of the world. The pyramids were *gone*, flattened to the ground in crumbles of stone and sand, along with every other ancient structure that used to exist. Knowing that Lucian had been responsible for most of it made my heart hurt. Seeing living history being destroyed was both terrifying and incredibly sad, though I knew Lucian had lived at that time and he was finally getting vengeance on the symbols he had helped build while he was a slave.

Now that the large monuments were ruins, it was easy to see where the action was happening. Large clouds of dust and dirt flew in every direction, along with streaks of red. There may have been a city here before, but it was gone. Nothing but desert and blood remained.

I kept reminding myself of what Mom had said, but as many people as they spared, thousands of others were dying anyway because of Caelius.

It made me sick.

I had to end this.

Through the chaos and hovering midair, Aidan looked at me with his usual concerned expression, then said, "Are you *sure* you can do this?"

No. Not at all.

"Yes. I'm sure."

Aidan nodded, and we made our descent onto the sands of Egypt.

Caelius and the others didn't even notice; they were in full destruction mode.

I needed to make myself seen.

But I also needed to clear out all the dust and debris to get an idea of what we were truly up against.

Here went nothing.

Taking a deep breath, I called on each element: water, fire, earth, and air. Water burst in giant crashing waves from the mighty Nile. The blood in its waters erupted with it, and the force looked like some kind of biblical red sea. I focused on fire next. There were millions of tiny sparks from where the desert sun burned into the sand so deeply that they almost acted like embers. I tapped into each overheated grain of sand and lit the debris around it using fire. I shook the earth violently, forcing everyone to stop in their tracks. And then I connected to the winds and blew the sand, ash, and dirt away from where Caelius stood.

Standing in the remains of the mighty pyramids and the civilization that had grown close to them was devastating. Everything was gone. All of it.

Now that I had Caelius's full attention, I wiped the elements away so all that remained was . . .

Silence.

Only the whimpering of the injured people could be heard.

My eyes met Caelius's.

He looked at me with deep hatred.

Behind him stood Lucian, my mom, Nefertiti, Sherit, and Setepenre. They stared at me with hope mixed with fear, like they were yearning for me to free them.

I wouldn't let them down.

Mustering up the courage, I walked closer. "It's time, Caelius. It's over."

He laughed. "Time for what, little Vessel? Time for your death?" He motioned for Lucian to stand next to him, and he immediately obeyed.

"Kill this one, Lucian. I don't want her dirty little soul anymore. I'm powerful enough without it. I only *need* you. Now that I have rewarded you with Egypt, prove to me that I'm the only one and destroy this hollow skeleton of your past," Caelius ordered, though his voice was soft, almost loving.

Lucian didn't move; he simply watched me with calculating eyes.

Was he still in there?

Did taking away the shadow inside of him help?

Caelius didn't like the hesitation. He turned his head so that his eyes met Lucian's. "Do this for me, boy, and all is forgiven. I will never doubt you again."

I hated that I could see conflict on Lucian's face. Darkness itself had swallowed him whole, and yet I could see that he was fighting its grip on him. I wanted to run over and physically separate Caelius's blood from Lucian's body.

But I couldn't.

I had to end this first.

Without warning, a burst of light shot out of my shoulder, almost reaching the clouds, then snuffed out.

I tried to look as if I had done it on purpose, but I almost collapsed from the force of it.

Maybe I didn't have this whole Light thing under control after all.

My vision blurred slightly, but after blinking a few times, I was *almost* able to see clearly.

Okay, not clearly, but at least I could still tell people apart.

I needed to get it together or Caelius would win.

Again.

"Will you look at that, darling?" Caelius's laughter broke the quiet.

Aidan's hand rested on my arm, and I turned to him. "Did you do that on purpose, Shea?"

"Yes," I lied. I was really getting this lying thing down. I just didn't want Aidan to pull me away this time, and I knew that was exactly what he would do if he thought I was in any danger.

Helena, Duncan, Dad, and Meky all arrived at the same time. They looked strong, refreshed, and ready to fight. I was proud to stand with them. This was the team. We were the ones who would take Darkness down once and for all.

Then one other arrived.

Ur-Nammu.

He gave me a small nod. "I've been watching and following my daughter and granddaughters as they have been serving that *thing*. I did nothing out of fear for my family's lives, but I can tolerate Lucian's and their abuse no longer. I stand with you, Shea Harper. As the sole surviving leader of Gutium, I am honor bound to take a stand against Darkness. I am a Gutian, and I will die as one."

Caelius stopped laughing for a brief moment as he viewed Ur-Nammu with disgust. "That can be arranged." He sighed, exasperated. "Ur-Nammu, a backbone can't be grown overnight. You've lived like a weasel since the day you were turned."

I wanted to punch Caelius in the face and hug Ur-Nammu at the same time.

But I could see it in the way Ur-Nammu held himself. He was there to fight with us to the bitter end. We had our differences in the past, but we'd resolved them, and having another father figure here made me feel safer, like everything would be all right.

But everything wasn't going to be all right unless I destroyed Caelius, who was laughing again.

Again. I really wanted to know what was so funny. When evil people laughed, it was usually because they knew something the good guys didn't.

And that scared me.

I was yanked forward by an invisible force and came face-to-face with Caelius.

Aidan leapt to my defense, but as he took flight a long shadowy arm grew out of Caelius's body and pinned him to the ground.

More sinewy tendrils of black smoke flowed out of Caelius like a creature from my deepest nightmares. Arms of smoke grabbed hold of every person for as far as the eye could see, tightening and squeezing them into submission. And it wasn't just my rescue team; it was Mom, Nefertiti, Sherit, and Sete as well. Even the humans were pinned down by his shadows, dead and almost-dead alike.

Caelius's trust was gone.

He didn't want to risk any surprise attacks, even from his own army.

Okay.

Definitely up to me now.

Staring into his hot red eyes was more terrifying than it had ever been, probably because he was a bit on the blurry side, but also because there was a black shadow moving and swirling around his entire body. I was finally seeing Caelius for what he truly was: the thing that made monsters themselves.

Lucian stood close to him, arm in arm, the black smoke almost caressing him. His eyes looked me over as if he wasn't quite sure what to do with me.

And could Caelius stop laughing already?

It was *really* annoying.

Finally the manic cackling stopped.

He placed his hand gently on my chin.

I swatted him away, which only entertained him more.

"You have no idea what they've done to you, do you?" he asked, knowing full well that I had no clue what he was talking about.

I didn't answer; I didn't have a good enough lie to back me up.

When enough time passed, Caelius chuckled again in an irritatingly satisfied way. "Aidan's precious brothers decided you were *disposable*."

What now?

I spoke, but my voice was shakier than I wanted it to be. "They made me *strong*."

"Oh yes, they definitely did that. I'm guessing you were supposed to be cautious and wait to fight me. They didn't count on you using their little Light-bomb to trap Lucian in magma while you chased out my shadow. You used all four of your elements too early; now your power is waning, and you're going to disintegrate right before our very eyes. Not even your soul will be left, little light bulb." Caelius's smile was cruel, and he was the happiest I'd ever seen him. "Looks like you won't have to lift a finger after all, darling. Her fate is already sealed." He moved his hand down Lucian's side.

No.

They wouldn't do that.

Would they?

"He's a liar, Shea!" Aidan yelled behind me as the shadow pinned him to the ground.

Caelius's gaze quickly turned to Aidan. "You think so much of your brothers, but they know you better than you know yourself. You'd never let anything happen to *this* Vessel, you've proven that much. But to them, she's just a carrier of Light, a weapon to be used to force me back into shadow form. They don't care if she dies and loses her soul. They only want the balance back where *they* think it belongs. Do you deny it? As a protector of the Light, wouldn't you do the same if you were in their position, *angel?*"

I looked at Aidan; his face was full of doubt.

And I knew at that moment that Caelius was telling the truth.

Aidan's brothers had over-juiced me to rid the world of

311

Caelius; they didn't care if my soul survived. It was probably why they kept calling me Vessel instead of Shea and why they never told Aidan their plans because he'd never agree to it.

And I had ruined it.

I'd tapped into my powers too early when trying to stop Lucian from burning in the lava, and now I didn't have enough juice to do the job I was meant to.

Or maybe I did.

Maybe if I gave everything, even my soul, I could force all the Light inside of me to consume Caelius. Then he'd be forced to turn back into his shadow form and leave his human body behind forever. It would be the only way he could save himself. I had to try. I had to save the ones I loved. I was just a Vessel, made for the purpose of restoring balance to the universe. At least I'd die for a *reason*.

Facing Caelius, I took a deep breath. This was happening.

I saw a flicker of fear in Caelius's eyes.

Good.

I wanted him to be scared for once.

Drawing the elements to me, I . . . fell forward as a wrenching pain hit my body.

Looking down, I saw Caelius's arm sticking through my stomach.

He had stabbed me with his own hand!

I couldn't connect to any element; the pain was too overwhelming.

I was going to die like this, and I wasn't going to be able to take Caelius with me.

I had failed *again*, miserably.

I turned to Lucian. I wanted the last thing that I saw on this Earth to be him. Whether he remembered me or not, his love had changed my life, changed who I was. It had made me into someone who would sacrifice herself for the greater good.

Our eyes locked.

And there he was.

My Lucian.

Fully himself.

Looking at me with the intensity of a thousand suns.

His eyes moved toward Caelius.

And he was seriously pissed.

CHAPTER 16
LUCIAN

The wholeness I felt from the Vessel trapping me in lava and stripping the Darkness from my soul, locked into place when I realized that she might actually *die*.

Shea Harper.

Finally, I understood.

That was the name I had been searching for in the dark.

I had tried to hold on to it before Caelius's brainwashing consumed me completely.

And finally here it was again, rising to the surface like a powerful force of light, burning my blood until I felt it boil up inside of me. I was weakened by the corruption of that tainted blood, but I was stronger than Caelius knew. My mind was fortified by the love of Bohe and all of my people. Now that Shea was here, I could feel them reaching for me again, like a horde fighting to push back the lies of Caelius's sequestered void. Their love was here for me now, in the shadow of my poisoned heart.

That truth was *powerful.*

More powerful than Caelius.

Even a solitary candle could dissipate darkness.

And that was what Shea was: a light.

My light.

How dare he even *touch* something so precious.

I growled, and in a sudden fit of rage I wrenched Caelius's arm back and threw him across the desert. Had the pyramids still been standing, he would have pierced right through them on his way to Libya.

I looked into Shea's eyes as she collapsed into my arms, red making its way down her parted mouth. The others, pinned back by Caelius's shadows, had been released when his body went flying. They ran to our side. I could feel their hot, untrusting gaze against my back, but I didn't care. Their judgment and the pulsing obedience commanding my heart's loyalty to Caelius could do nothing to control the feeling that a life without her would be more of a true death than I had ever known.

I pressed her forehead into my chest. Her scent filled my senses and, like a flood, memories rushed forward, overwhelming me. With every new memory came an adjoining agony. Faces screamed through my mind like wailing banshees, furious at the insolence of how I had forgotten their importance.

I had killed Gunnhild and Ashgar to save Shea.

I clenched my teeth.

I killed my own children with my own two hands. That was something I'd never wanted; no matter how callous I'd become over the centuries, they were still mine to protect. I lifted my hand as it shook, now covered in Shea's blood. I had done it for *her*, hadn't I?

He had killed the others.

Duncan had been sucked dry, and although I never saw David's demise, I was sure it was agony because Caelius had brutally tortured Gracuri and Bohe right in front of me. How could I have forgotten their deaths? I was still wearing the Hanfu Bohe had bled out in, while Caelius wore Gracuri's shoes on the days it pleased him. When he wasn't wearing them, or making me wear them, he kept them on a *spike* outside the cabin.

This was a sick joke.

It couldn't be real.

I squeezed Shea tighter to my chest as a more terrifying impression pulled through. This wasn't the first time. The words "try again" repeated from Caelius's lips like there was still a chain around my neck. How many times had I remembered, only to have his blood make me forget everything again?

Caelius's betrayal seared in me, but my betrayal of memory to the ones I loved scorched hotter. It was against the code of Gutium; it was our duty to burn the ones passed into the existence of all things. It was a brand we carried until our own death was carved out, in turn, by those left behind. No matter the pain remembering had wrought over the centuries, it was a tradition I had never broken . . . until now.

I thought of my father on the hills of Gutium, his people slaughtered at his feet, his body pierced with spears like a "stuck pig," as Caelius had called him. Onack the Great came to such an unworthy end, and he had spared me of it. Only now, as every new pointed memory pierced through, the code of our people erased, did I feel that I was indeed my father's son.

But for Onack, the devastation was glory as he proved his right as our leader and fought for love. The things Caelius allowed, and the things he took from me, weren't in the name of love, but were in the absence of it. All of my torment over the centuries was for *his* pleasure, just to show that I was a slave in more ways than Akhenaten's whip had ever made me. There was no honor in it, and only in defeat was I like my father.

Defeat . . .

I remembered our last battle and how Caelius had torn Nefari's children apart.

Maybe it was that moment, as I committed another betrayal of our code, that had led me to this place now. I had fought for the ones I loved, but in the end I had *surrendered* to save them— something my father would have never done. Was this fate's cruel sense of irony, to lead me to the same choice again? Was it only Gutian to know such ruin?

I looked at the faces of those surrounding us.

They were here again, in no better state than before.

We would lose.

I wept into Shea's back.

My mind flashed with the memory of a different desert. It was Arizona and, despite my mission, I was falling in love with the Vessel. Her pale blond hair and light hazel eyes healed me in a way that blood never could. Memories of Paris and our nights together rose and lifted the veil that had blinded me, the compulsion finally overcome.

My body tensed as I remembered *everything*: the entire year I had lost.

Shea Harper wasn't just the name I'd been searching for in

the dark; hers was the name I would always search for, until the end of time.

She was my soul mate.

A part of me knew that in the first moment we met.

A part of me would *always* know her.

My lips moved against the nape of her neck. If she were a vampire, I would offer her every drop of my tainted blood, anything to heal her. But it was because she was not that she was able to bring me so fervently home. As with every time I met her, it was her humanness that had returned mine.

"I'm so sorry, Shea. Please . . . I will fight Caelius myself."

Leave here.

Run.

"As long as you are alive, I can keep fighting." I pushed my hands through her thick hair. "If you are by my side and anything more happens to you, I will surely die. You are all I have left. Please *hide*." It struck me, the arrows of memory twisting further. These were, in essence, the words my father spoke the night before battle, begging me to leave Gutium. All this time I had resented that he'd asked me to leave, and now that his bones were no more than ash, like my mother's, I finally understood his love.

I'm sorry, Father. Forgive me as I now forgive you.

I couldn't look at her face.

The dishonor of all of it.

I had fed off of her.

I had hurt her.

The one person I had sworn never to be a vampire with—just a man.

318

And now I was begging her like my father, as if I still had any right to call on the loyalty of our love.

The only other woman I had longed to be mortal with offered me support. Nefertiti reached down and placed her hand on my back. "It's all right, La-Narru. You didn't have a choice."

I recoiled from her touch. Now that all of my memories were alive again, I rejected her pale platitude of comfort. "I *remember*, Nefari. It was you, not Ur-Nammu, who lied to me."

She was silent, and in her silence grew the rage of a thousand lifetimes.

"You should have killed me when I *asked*—when I was chained, before we fought him the *first* time! I told you he would use me against her. He used me against *all* of you. You shouldn't have let me become Caelius's lapdog. You promised in Gutium; we both did. 'Death over servitude.' It is the Gutian way, and you robbed me of that birthright."

Her hand dropped. Her voice was jagged, more like stones scraping together than words. "I thought we both agreed in Egypt. That was a part of our people's code we'd have to leave behind to survive, along with our life together in the mountains."

"Don't rewrite history as if I wasn't there. *You* asked me to vow to live on; *you* wanted to survive. And when death finally did come for me outside your window, *you* gave me over to Caelius and had me turned . . . then left me in the wake of mourning your loss."

"I know," she whispered. Nefertiti had once spoken with authority in this very place. Her confident words had flooded over an entire people—her *new* people—after Gutium's demise. She'd ruled alongside Akhenaten and had even commanded his armies from behind the throne. Her natural ability to adapt and lead had not been inhibited by her new station. True to her Gutian name, Nefari had shone bright through oppression. She'd been a morning star, a jewel among stones.

Now she felt to me like a burning coal embedded in my stomach, a constant ache that I had returned to again and again, unable to move past.

"How many times have I been tortured because you couldn't let me die in peace? How many thousands of years have I hung on because your last words in Egypt asked me to deny my right of death over servitude?" My tone was steady, unlike her breath, which became more jagged with every word I spoke.

Rulers across nations had come to see the Pharaoh's prized wife, whose eloquence had given her a reputation, an adoration even amongst the slaves. After she made us vow to live, the mere whisper of her name—even as my bare feet pressed mud into hay and whips lashed my back—had persuaded me to fight on. Her speeches from high above the palace reached me, even there, in the squalors of hell.

I withstood torn flesh and broken bones because I knew with that same powerful mouth she would whisper the sweetest of lullabies to her children and kiss promises into my neck in the moonlit nights along the Nile.

Promises she never fulfilled.

I wanted to bury it, along with any love I had for her— choke it down like I had the sands of Egypt when I'd grieved for lifetimes over her loss.

Now, holding Shea in my arms, stabbed by Caelius because Nefertiti would not end me, all of the betrayals I had suffered by loving her since Gutium linked together.

"I knew this would happen; you should have let me go. I may understand *why* you've done what you have over the ages, but you broke me in the process, Nefari. And without Shea, I can't . . ." I clung to Shea's body, tormented like a man possessed by grief itself.

Nefertiti stepped back as if I had lanced her gut.

"Please," I whispered into Shea's hair. "Tell me what to do. I'll do anything." I didn't want to know a world without her light. There was no sacrifice I wouldn't give. "Death over servitude," I whispered. "If that's all I can offer you, I will. My life for yours, a million times over. I can't begin to apologize for what I've done to you."

She breathed in deep, running her face along my chest. I felt the wetness of tears. She was clinging to me–she had been this whole time, in both thought and action. She hadn't let me go.

I clung back in desperation. "I tried, Shea. I tried to hold on to you too. But I was so lost."

"Lucian, I know." She squeezed, and there was a fierceness in her grip, despite her mortal wound. "I love you." Her words were sobs, and they broke my already splintered heart. "It's okay, I'm just glad you're back."

How could she respond so easily?

No punishment.

No resentment.

She was better than I was. Her love was pure and unselfish; it was unlike anything I had experienced with Caelius. His affection came with conditions; it had to be constantly earned, proven, and above all else, it came with a *price*.

Like the very thought of him conjured the demon itself, smoke filled the air.

Caelius was furious.

I could already feel the agony he was going to burn into me as black started covering my skin.

"Lucian, let go!" Shea shouted.

I clung tighter. "I won't lose you again!"

If Caelius wanted her, he'd have to kill me, and I would die as my father had, with my people at my back.

"I said let go!" she screamed, struggling in my arms.

The smell filling the air around us was grotesque.

I waited for his hand to grab my throat, but it didn't come.

I looked up briefly.

Caelius was still far off, sauntering back at a slow pace. Even as flames rose around me, I could see that his face was downcast, looking more like a kicked child than Darkness. Defeat weighed his shoulders down in a way I had not seen, even in the thousands of years he was caged. His red eyes were staring at the sand. Instantly, I understood what I was seeing. I too had looked at that same Egyptian sand with such bitter heartbreak once.

Now we both had.

I for Nefari, and he for me.

He must have finally realized that the love I had for Shea was more powerful than his control and that I would *never* belong to him. It was a death of expectation—the agony of an unquenchable desire left unfulfilled.

It hurt.

I knew well enough.

It *burned*.

"I said let go!" Shea pushed back in my arms.

I looked down.

The smoke wasn't coming from Caelius; it was coming from me.

He wasn't the one burning me up from the inside. *She* was.

Shea's skin was starting to emanate light.

Everyone had been screaming, their hands trying to pull me back, but I hadn't noticed. I had been so lost in my returned memories—my agonizing over Nefari, Caelius, and Shea—that it'd been as if the whole world had fallen away.

I looked up in a blur at the desperate faces around us. They yanked at my limbs, trying to distance Shea from my body. Their voices were a mix of her same sentiment.

"Let go!" they shouted over and over.

I grabbed her shoulders, hard.

I wouldn't let her go again.

Not for anyone.

Everyone was forced to retreat, shielding their gazes and bodies from the fire consuming us.

Through their desperate cries, I held on tighter, wrenching her back into my arms.

Her eyes met mine as my skin burned with a holy flame I had experienced once before, when I had clung to her after she had charged her powers with Akhenaten's sundial.

Except this was worse.

Much worse.

I fought back screams of anguish.

"Shea, are you all right?" My words were almost a screech alongside the sound of my skin frying like bacon. "What's

323

happening? What did Caelius mean about Aidan's brothers and your soul? Are you overpowered? Is this the sundial again?"

Her smile made my insides burn hotter than my skin. "You *remember*."

I missed her. I would *always* miss her. "Shea . . . *I love you*."

She nodded. "I love you too."

She took in a deep breath, then tried to jerk herself out of my arms.

"No!" I squeezed, blisters covering my hands. "Stay with me, tell me what to do to save you!"

"Just let go." She paused, looking at my burns as if they hurt her more than me. "This whole time you've been fighting a long fight. Deep inside you've been doing everything to hold on to me—I *know* that now. Even when you were lost, you still couldn't kill me. You pulled me into your memories when you were at your worst. You still felt it: *our connection*."

I kissed her; my longing and my scorching lips ached.

She lingered for a moment, then shoved me away. "It really is time. Please understand, I have to do this. You have to let me go. This world, all the people . . . *you*, Lucian, are worth dying for. You have given up your life and so much more. Don't you think I love you just as much as you love me?" She took in a quick gasp. "I'm sorry, but it's my turn to die."

My body flipped back as hers burst with light, healing the gaping hole in her stomach. I fell into the sand, skidding face-first down a dune. Choking on the dirt and brushing it off of my skinned cheeks, I coughed as I stood up, screaming out her name. "Shea!"

She was already hovering in the air, her whole body aflame

324

like the sun.

I squinted, unable to make out her face. "No, Shea, please, wait! Let this whole world burn, and me with it! Just live! You're all that's worth fighting for!" I clawed at the sliding dune like a worm trying to make my way back to her, but the waves of power pulsing off of her body kept forcing me back.

Then gears and the fierce beating of wings sounded behind me.

I turned and saw everyone fighting Caelius. His moment of melancholy had passed, and he was *savage*. But to my surprise, he wasn't the only one.

Aidan blasted him with light, fighting him from the air without restraint, his wings creating whirlwinds in their wake. I stumbled forward with the residual force of it, caught between his power and Shea's. He looked now as he had just before he'd stabbed Moses. His grief and confusion were evident as much on his face as in his shrieking war cries. After all these centuries, his agony finally matched my own. He loved Shea as much as I did, and his brothers' betrayal, to that end, was a shock to him alone. I knew what they were like after Ashliel was abandoned to the pit. Now so did he, as he threw heavy fists and wings at Caelius.

For all my years spent hating him, not once would I have wished to see him as he was now. Despite the weight of my torment through the decades, and even though his build was enormous like Gracuri's, Aidan had bolstered a careless lightness about him. It was like he was a caged bird with hollow bones that still remembered how to sing. I saw none of that lightness now; he had changed. He was finally flying again, but he was without the holy dignity and righteousness he'd always held.

325

He looked heavy as stone.

The sound of gears that followed after him belonged to Helena. She was using a device that flung bottled concoctions into the air. Some landed hard hits, exploding in glass and colored vapors that boiled Caelius's skin; others were brushed off, as if she were throwing pebbles into the ocean. Looking at her slumped stance, I realized that Helena had changed too.

She looked more bitter and unsure since our last battle, where she had been unknowingly brainwashed by the very being she stood toe to toe with now. That kind of self-doubt, even for a levelheaded scientist, was detrimental, and it showed.

Her hair was pulled back and filthy from hands that were smeared with the blackness of lubricated gears as she forced them into place. The delight of seeing her creations work was replaced with frustration and the fear of failure. The last time I had seen her this haunted was when she'd been isolated by her abusive family. Back then she believed their lies: that she would never belong in this world, that an intelligent woman had no place in it and was powerless against the force of a society ruled by men.

Nefertiti was quickly by her side. She must have caught the same gaze I had because she shouted, "Are you a man that you should give up so easily? Where is your pride as a woman of science? Have you abandoned reason for defeat?" In that brief moment, I could see that their time together as the years passed meant more than I'd initially understood.

Helena's resolve hardened along with Nefari's.

They had become friends, like Helena and I had a hundred years ago.

"Science never yields to weaker minds," Helena said through

clenched teeth. "A belief in absolutes is weakness; failure is the true path to success. A will to keep *trying* is the only real measurable outcome of greatness." She parroted the words, words I had heard her repeat to herself millions of times in the lab. That sort of ritualistic affirmation paid off; it steadied her now when she was at her lowest.

Nefertiti nodded, pleased, and kissed her hard on the lips in a quick moment of passion. When she pulled back and gazed into Helena's stunned eyes, she cupped her face as gently as she had her children's. "I believe in you, Helena."

I was shocked. Nefari only believed in the capabilities of her own hands. She had never once said those words to me, or to *anyone*, but they flew from her lips just as fluidly as the embrace had. Perhaps she had become *more* than friends with Helena, as I had with those I'd turned in the past.

Ur-Nammu stepped beside Nefari as Meky and Sherit joined them. He extended his hands, and for a moment the girls all linked together. It was painful to see what would be the last unified Gutian front in history. When they released one another, they all attacked Caelius with fists and teeth, tearing bone and hair in handfuls.

I wasn't sure if it was Helena's kiss that had awoken her, but finally the fire had returned to Nefari's gaze. The drawn black lines around her eyes were smeared and imperfect, but now they resembled war paint as the ink ran down her cheeks. She looked more the leader of Gutium than the queen of Egypt, and I was glad for it: to see her return to herself here, at what would truly be her end. She knew it, and now so did I. There was no forgiveness or plan that would make Caelius spare her this time.

I hadn't realized the resentment I had been harboring toward her until the careless words had spilled from my lips. In truth, I hated that she hadn't left with me in Gutium, on the eve before they battled Egypt. I hated that she hadn't run away with me in secret, escaping Akhenaten with the girls. I hated that she'd hidden with Caelius while I was tormented by his obsessions, all the while grieving her. I had lived a life of longing. I hated that I'd always waited for her, but she'd never come. And now that I had finally disowned our love, I would lose her again, as I always lost Nefari.

Still, at the end, despite the fear that Caelius would slaughter more of her daughters, I had finally seen her return to the image I had held of her as a child and desperately clung to as a man. It was an image that had never changed, even though she had.

She paused and looked at me.

No, not at me; she looked past me.

I turned and saw Setepenre frozen in place. She couldn't bring herself to raise a hand to Caelius, but she didn't help him fight her family's unified attacks either. Even as he called for her, her eyes stayed down, refusing to meet his gaze. She had finally seen enough in the past few months with the degradation of her family to doubt all that she had been raised to believe as his granddaughter.

She left his side, beginning a slow walk of isolation in the very desert she had grown up in. Her shadow was lit by the sun as she gazed back at me, then she silently disappeared, like a mirage leaving nothing but waves of heated sand.

It was a judicious choice, but then again, she was a part of Nefertiti and had no doubt inherited the diplomacy from her mother. For that, I was glad. There was solace in thinking that once we were all dead, Caelius might just spare her.

I looked at Nefertiti. Her eyes found mine, and for a moment we shared in that relief.

Then Duncan's cries turned our heads. He spat Scottish hymns and chants at Caelius. One was familiar. It was a dark poem he'd made up as a boy to ward off trolls. When we'd crossed the Highlands and he walked over bridges, he would speak it under his breath like placing a holy curse.

He now looked like the young man I had met coming off the boat in Scotland. He spat his troll-ward at Caelius, sinking in heavy hits reminiscent of his days as a street boxer. There was glee in the way he moved, a bounce in his step. He'd always loved a good fight, but I had robbed him of it when I made him mine and slaughtered his kinsman, expecting him to do the same. His love for battle had ended that day, along with his life.

At least his stories remained, and *this* was one he would have told with fervor. This was a death he wanted: a fight in the blaze of glory against the devil himself. It was a tale worth telling, unlike his death before: being drained and left without a grave like the nameless dead in war.

In fact, his rise from a second death and then coming here to save the world was worthy of the *Iliad*. Gracuri would have liked to hear Duncan's interpretation of his own death, as he used to listen with awe in amphitheaters playing Greek stories battling gods with men. They had become friends over the years. He would have sat, leaning off the edge of his seat, the boyishness in his demeanor apparent, while Duncan spoke in earnest, his hands waving about with the telling. There was no doubt that

Gracuri would have fought by our side without hesitation. So many of them would have. All I had to do was ask, and they would have followed me to this glorious end. Instead I'd isolated myself, and them in the process, thinking that I was alone.

It was painful realizing I was surrounded by so much love but that I hadn't seen it. I labeled it as petty things like lust and amusement. At times, I'd even been afraid to call them *friends*, but that, and so much more, was what they had been to me. This whole time they'd been sending me messages in a bottle carried on an ocean of acceptance, while I'd shut my heart away inside a solitary desert of loss. If anything, it was my fear of loss that had kept me losing the ones that I had come to love.

It had kept me thirsty and aching with insatiable hunger.

A hunger that not even Caelius, with all of his blood, could fill. He said that swine weren't worthy of a single drop and guarded it from everyone but me, like it was holy. I watched as they tore him apart, that same blood now strewn carelessly across the sands like a giant inkblot test.

Molly and Jeff moved around Duncan, bobbing in unison. They were so close to each other. I noticed they were holding hands as they attacked with fervency, as if their lives depended on it. But they didn't.

It was *her* life.

I struggled in place, still held at bay by the force of her mounting power.

Why weren't they trying to *stop* Shea like I was?

Then it finally sank in.

I knew exactly what they were doing.

"All of our lives rather than yours!" I shouted up at her.

"That's what we're all saying, Shea!" She hadn't made a move yet because they were blocking Caelius with their attacks. "If we can stop him ourselves, you don't have to do this! We won't give you up! Not to the Light, nor to the Darkness! Power down, and let's do this *together!*"

I ran away from her, toward Caelius.

My people's creed wasn't wrong; love was a powerful force.

It was stronger than his Darkness, stronger than the lies I'd been living my whole life.

Light exploded past me.

It landed on Caelius's body, blasting everyone around him back. He shrieked—a sound in all my years I'd never heard him make. A ghastly sound.

And I wanted to scream with him.

Shea was doing it anyway, despite everyone's efforts.

Instantly, a shadow with enormous limbs sprung out from his diminished frame, reaching its claws for the Light.

Shea didn't relent.

I turned and ran the other direction, back toward her. "Stop!" If I had to sacrifice myself, I would. I didn't matter. As long as she was alive, my soul could rest at peace. But there would be no peace for me left if she died and her soul disintegrated.

As I made my way to her, the light emanating from her chest began to sputter like the backfire of an old truck.

She fell.

I caught her in my arms before she touched the ground. The light pulsing on her skin faded until she was dull and weak, her breath jagged. Her skin shifted between translucent and a sickening gray. It was like she was dissolving in my arms, turning

331

to ash like my mother had . . . like everyone I loved.

"It wasn't enough." Tears rolled down her cheeks as her body flickered in and out of existence.

"No matter the outcome, you will *always* be enough, Shea Harper." I clung to the ghost of her. "Please, stay with me . . . or take me into oblivion with you. Don't leave me here." I had said similar words to Anna-Steen on her deathbed. My hands felt just as small and helpless now as they had been then.

She ran her hand through my hair, but it felt formless, like a gust of wind. "I have *more*. There's more Light inside of me," she whimpered. "Help me, Lucian. Give me the strength to finish this for all of us."

I stared at her beautiful hazel eyes. She had awakened so much that had been dead and forgotten, filling it with light so it could finally start to heal.

"No." I pulled her fiercely into my lap. "I have given up everything and everyone I have loved, one way or another, out of arrogance or fear. I have made so many mistakes; I can see that now. Don't ask me again. I won't give you up as well—"

"But, Lucian!" She took in a long pained breath, her eyes still fixed on mine. "Ours is a proud people."

The breath I gasped in shock mirrored hers and quivered like she had reached her hand into my stomach, as Caelius had just done to her.

"Shea, don't—"

"We are many, but united we beat with *one* heart." She pressed her hand to my chest as it phased in and out. It was cold, unlike the warm desert wind at my back.

"No. I won't help you lose your soul, no matter what you

say."

"Though we fall—"

I winced. How many of my people had spoken these very words before death, their slaughtered bones piled by Onack's?

"We will *never fail* because we have given ourselves over to glory."

I pressed my forehead against hers. This wasn't fair. "Stop. That damn Gutian code, it's just words made up by dead men."

"To fight for those we *love*." She breathed in deep, but it puffed out in an uneven wave. "And though our bones may brittle with time, and life may wear and kill the tenderness of affection, the burning heart, the flame that is *our* people and what we stand for, cannot be stamped out of time. They are more than words, Lucian, and they were created by your *father*."

"Shea, please—" I held on to the hand at my chest. I could feel it, the warmth in her touch slowly returning.

"We are etched into the very existence of all things, you and I."

"Please don't leave me. I don't want to be alone again," I muttered, but even as I said the word "alone," something shifted inside of me—a stirring, as if the old weight it carried, the old lie, was leaving.

"You are not alone because we are and *forever* will be a people who fight for what we love. And love"—tears steamed down her porcelain face as she choked out the last words—"love is the *soul* of all that's worth fighting for."

Her words rang out alongside the laughter of my mother, Anna-Steen. It was warm and strong like my father's arms had been when he'd carried me on his back, alive and happy. The words of our code were true and wise like Bohe under a waterfall as he meditated. They were soft and wild like the curls in Gracuri's hair as he waited by the river for my return. The voices of all of those in my past began mixing with hers in the Light as her body started to regain its color, warming the skin of my forehead and melting my heart under her touch.

She laughed to herself. It was light and kind as it had been in Paris, before all of this. "Ur-Nammu taught me."

I squeezed the hand at my chest that was now fully solid again.

"He said as an elder it was his right to allow me into the tribe of Gutium. He said he'd forgotten that it wasn't just about blood. He talked about his wife and your mother, how they *became* Gutian. Then we argued and made up." She laughed again. "He's seriously super stubborn. Still, I get to live and die by your code now, just like the rest of the Gutians." She smiled to herself, her mind resolute.

"Lucian, that's what love is; it's all the same. I see that now more than ever. All the people of the world are *my people and your people*, and we are all singing the same song, we are all shouting this same code, aren't we? We are not alone standing against the Darkness. You feel it too, don't you? I know I'm connected to the Light right now, but I know you hear them calling you, calling *us*. That's why I have to do this, because they are *all* our people. The whole world is Gutium."

My mouth opened, but nothing came out.

How had I forgotten the people Onack had taken in? Most of the elders alongside him had come from conquered tribes. People had been integrated as equals from all parts of the world

334

for generations, long before Onack and Ur-Nammu unified and created the code of *our* people.

Had Nefertiti's children been any less Gutian by having the blood of the Pharaoh? All of my Second-Borns were from different generations and cultures. Had blood ever really mattered when it came to *love* or *family*?

I looked back at the fight still raging behind us. They were all tearing at Caelius's grotesque spider body, which had been torn open by her Light.

Blood.

I closed my eyes, sighing.

I couldn't deny the truth she had discovered. I had been close to understanding similar truths while buried in her magma. Ur-Nammu was wise like my father and must have discovered it for himself while in exile.

Being Gutian was *never* about blood.

Another lie woven in the Darkness was broken.

I had been willing to let the whole world burn for Shea.

But she was right.

Only now did I fully understand what Bohe had meant when he said, "Remember we are *all* Gutium now."

A hand grabbed my shoulder.

It might as well have been my neck.

Caelius.

My late-blooming revelations didn't matter now.

It was too late.

How could Shea's words, how could any of their words, reach me if I was consumed again in his Darkness? I still felt his blood burning, threatening to overpower my every breath.

The hand squeezed.

I closed my eyes and did the only thing I could think of to protect her. I used all the strength I had left and pulled her into my mind, like she said I'd done before unconsciously.

Everything went black.

CHAPTER 17
SHEA

I was back on the craggy cliff face with Aidan, Moses, and Lucian. It was the aftermath of Aidan's betrayal, the part I didn't want to see. Aidan and Moses were dead, stabbed and crunched by the fall.

But what I saw in front of me wasn't what Lucian had always said happened. He had hated Aidan for killing Moses, so much so he wreaked havoc on the world for three thousand years to punish him. Lucian always talked about how he had held Moses after Aidan killed them both. Though it was true that he held Moses's hand, it was actually Aidan he held in his arms.

And his cries. I knew I wasn't there physically, but I felt my heart squeeze with agony at the sound and sight. I never knew how much Lucian loved Aidan until this moment. And his betrayal was so much deeper than stabbing their fellow brother. Aidan had taken his own life. And that had almost killed Lucian.

"Shea," Lucian said.

I looked up at him. He stood beside me, holding my hand just like last time, but unlike before, Lucian was *awake* and truly present.

Turning away from the scene was a blessing; it was too difficult to watch.

"You always told me it was Moses you held." I motioned.

"That was how I remembered it." Lucian seemed surprised at witnessing the truth in front of us.

He stared at his past self crying over Aidan's body, holding him close.

"I loved them both, but it was Aidan who brought me out of the tailspin of losing Nefertiti. We were *brothers* then. You know him. You know his spirit. He helped me . . . he changed me . . . then he took it all away, and I was more alone than before."

Lucian turned to me, a deep sadness in his eyes. "What he showed me in that brief moment was that, even though I trusted him completely, he didn't trust me. He must have always been wondering, in the back of his mind, if I would betray him and take the Vessel to Caelius.

"It only took a few words of doubt from Ur-Nammu, and Aidan was willing to die and kill Moses. My hate and anger grew with each year that passed. I longed to show him that he had created the exact monster he'd believed me to be.

"So I hunted and cornered him, each time giving him the choice: to believe in me or in the monster. I never had any intention of taking those early Vessels to Caelius. Even after Moses." Lucian shook his head. "And each time, he chose to see Lucian the Monster. And each time, my agony grew with his." He ran his hand through his hair in anguish. "Why are we seeing

338

this now? What purpose do I gain by remembering the pain of this moment?"

As if to answer, the scenery changed to the memory where I seared a hole in Lucian's chest in my old dorm building.

In our last excursion to memory lane, these two memories had been shown in this order as well. It had to mean something, but what did it have to do with what was happening outside of his mind? And did it *really* matter? We were in our final battle. Aidan's brothers had given me the power to send Caelius back into Darkness. We needed to get back!

"Lucian, our physical bodies are in the battle of our lives. We can't stay here and relive your worst memories," I said. "I know you think you can somehow save me this way, but you can't. You know what I have to do."

Lucian didn't respond, he just stared at his past self where a small smile of relief crossed his face when he realized that I was alive. "That was the moment I knew I loved you."

Squeezing his hand harder, I responded gently, "I know, Lucian, you've told me that before."

He looked down at me, wonder in his eyes. "You don't understand. After Aidan, I never thought I'd love again."

"But you loved Gracuri and Duncan and all your Second-Borns to some degree, right?" I was trying to make sense of what was happening and how it could be important to the battle at hand.

"Yes, I have loved. But it wasn't the same as this. I had no hope for true love, for true happiness. There were times when my strength would falter and I'd let myself slip into false hope that I could love again. That was when I'd turn someone."

As Lucian said this, the background changed to Gracuri covered in blood with dead bodies all around him, eyes gouged out. It was gruesome, and I had to look away from the sight.

Lucian's voice was steady as he said, "But look where that hope would get me. I met beings capable of the very love I desired, and I turned them into beasts. It was a cursed cycle I knew I'd never break."

I could see the scenery changing again at my feet. I looked up, and we were in a cave. A skeleton rested against the wall as Lucian walked in carrying a large deer. Then the skeleton moved, and I knew right away that it was Duncan, desiccated, as he'd said he was when he told me this story.

Lucian dropped the deer at his feet.

"Duncan reminded me of Aidan. I didn't consciously see it at the time. I pushed my emotions down, but there was no denying his spirit was pure like Aidan's had been. The carefree way he laughed, his smile, it was so close. Then I turned him, and in his bloodlust he killed all his clansmen and family. I broke him, Shea. Broke the very thing I loved most about him. When I saw him there, almost dead, refusing to give in and drink human blood, I knew: Aidan had been right. I was the evil one, the monster. And he was right to distrust me."

In a flash, we were back at the cliff face with Lucian holding Aidan's body with one hand while holding Moses's hand with the other.

Just as quickly, we were back at the dorm building, my hand burning through his body, but his small smile was real.

Back and forth, back and forth on a loop, switching every few seconds. It made me dizzy.

"I can't seem to stop this," Lucian confessed, a tinge of fear in his voice.

"It must mean something," I said, trying to see how these two moments tied together. "But Lucian, how will this help us fight Caelius, even if you do figure it out?" My mind was racing. My mother and father were fighting as we stood trapped in Lucian's mind. I couldn't see how anything we discovered here would help us.

"I think I'm beginning to understand. Even if you lost your soul, you can't just force Caelius to leave his earthbound body by torturing him with Light. He could withstand that for eternity. We have to find a way to *convince* him. It has to be his choice." Lucian's face was animated, almost desperate.

And I realized in that moment he was right.

If Lucian thought we could find the answers in his memories, then I trusted him wholeheartedly.

"Okay," I said, pulling our clasped hands to my lips and kissing him gently. "We can do this." I tried to focus on each memory as it flashed by, but they switched too quickly for me to see any details. "Is there any way you can freeze the Moses memory?"

With some effort, Lucian halted the background so we were now staring at what was essentially a 3D photo of the scene. It was much easier to analyze this way, not having to see Lucian sob in agony in real time.

So what were we missing?

"Let's look at this objectively." I put on my detective hat, as much as I could anyway. "Your mind wants you to remember something about this moment."

"My pain? My love? My betrayal?" Lucian said in anguished tones.

He was way too close to this. I'd have to be the one to help him navigate through. "All those things, but the fact that you rewrote history in your waking life has to mean something. Why would you blank out that it was Aidan you held?"

"Too painful," he said.

But I ran with the seed of an idea. "Too painful because you began to think he was right in not trusting you, and because you felt that he was able to see you as a monster before you even knew you were a monster." Oops. I hadn't meant it like that.

Lucian didn't seem to notice, which just showed we both had serious self-esteem issues. Mine were looking far less scarring than his at the moment.

"I remember losing hope that I'd ever be able to love again." He looked at me, eyes helpless. "That was the strongest feeling I had after it all happened. It was the same feeling when my mother died."

"I feel like we're close, but that's not quite it. How would losing hope for finding love again convince Caelius to go back to shadow form?" I wondered aloud.

Lucian shrugged. "I don't know."

Nodding, I asked, "Can you show me searing that hole in your chest now?"

A small smile reached his face, and he touched my cheek with his free hand, sending shivers down my spine. How was he able to do that when my body wasn't even there? Seriously!

A 3D freeze-frame of my hand inside his chest, glowing from the Light melting his skin and bone, appeared.

Ew.

We both stared at his obvious expression of relief.

"And this is when I got my hope back that I could love again," he said.

"I don't think you're wrong. I just think we're *looking* at it wrong." I tried not to get frustrated. Losing hope and then gaining hope was huge, I felt that, but Caelius wouldn't care about that. He only cared about Lucian; he meant *everything* to Caelius. He was willing to destroy all life as we knew it just for the slight chance that Lucian would be with him.

We all knew that wasn't going to happen.

I stopped looking at past Lucian's expression and started watching my own past self's face. What had I been thinking at that moment? I tried to remember.

Then it hit me.

"At that moment, when I saw what I had done, my whole body ached with regret and loss," I said.

Lucian turned to me, surprised. "But you hated me back then."

"No, I never hated you. I didn't understand you. I was angry with you, but I never hated you. And when you tried to hurt Aidan, I acted without thinking and did . . . *that*." I nodded to the frozen scene of melted-chest. "I thought I had killed you. And it almost killed *me*."

Lucian stared at me, then looked back at the memory.

"Lucian?" The ideas were forming in my head like puzzle pieces coming together. "Do you think it wasn't that you were afraid you'd never find love again, but that you felt no one would ever love *you* again?" Before he could answer, I continued. "And

343

this moment wasn't you realizing you were capable of loving again, but it was seeing the regret and horror in my eyes, and you knew . . ." My voice caught from emotion, but I pushed forward. "You knew that *I* loved you."

Lucian's eyes found mine, and he pulled me into his chest. "I would never have presumed, not back then."

"But you can see it, here, in this memory. *I* can see it. My whole face, my eyes—I loved you, and you saw a glimpse of it, not daring to believe it, turning it into your own obsession." The words felt right. I was onto something.

Lucian pulled back. Taking both hands and cupping my face, he looked at me as if I were the only thing that existed in his world. "Yes. Even when Gracuri or my other children expressed their love, I never believed it because they had my blood in their veins. I never gave them the chance to love me when they were human, so I never knew if their love was real or not. And I never believed it was. And if Aidan was willing to die and kill Moses with only a few words from Ur-Nammu, it meant he never really loved me either." I was about to argue, but Lucian stopped me, continuing. "I know that's not true now, but back then it was my only truth and why I turned so bitterly against him."

"This is it, Lucian. This is the connection we need to convince Caelius to give up his physical form. All he wants is for you to *love* him, and he can't seem to force you to do it. You know how he feels. For thousands of years you believed you were unworthy of love because of what Aidan did to Moses, and you relived it every five hundred years until you met me." I pulled his head down to mine so we were forehead to forehead. "And I love you with every fiber of my being. I truly love you. Even knowing and seeing all the horrible things you've done, I still love you."

"I love you more than my life, but I can't love Caelius. I can never love Caelius. I'll never be able to give him what he wants." Lucian seemed panicked.

"You can't love him because he tries to force you to, but if he can see that sacrifice is the key to your heart, he might let go." I knew I was right, but I also knew what I had to do to get Caelius into a position to actually hear Lucian out.

Lucian instantly saw it in my eyes. "No. I'll try to talk to him, but we don't need you to sacrifice yourself. I can do it without you."

Tears came to my eyes. "You know that's not true. You need me to lock him down, and the only way to do that is the Light-bomb Aidan's brothers armed me with."

"But your soul will evaporate!" Lucian screamed, unable to hold back.

I was terrified but resolved. I nodded. "Yes, but it'll be worth it."

"Not for me! Not for anyone who knows you! I can't, Shea. I can't!" Lucian looked like a caged animal.

Our surroundings changed again, and we were standing in the empty bedroom of our villa in Paris. "We can stay here for a long time. No matter what happens outside, we'll be safe. Not even Caelius can fully reach us. You know this from before when you collapsed after the sundial, and I leapt into the vacuum of your mind. My memories of us in Paris are the one thing the Darkness can't dissolve completely."

"Lucian," I whispered. "We can't."

"But we can!" he insisted. "I'm keeping you here. You're *mine*, and I won't let you go. I won't lose you!"

"And now who do you sound like?" I said, knowing it would hurt, but also knowing he'd see more clearly how he'd be able to connect to Caelius.

Lucian flinched, and my heart nearly broke, then he said softly, "I'll die without you."

I reached up and brought him down to my lips, kissing him with all the love and passion I had in me. Pulling away with tears streaming down my face, I said, "Then we'll die together, saving the ones we love."

"I will love you forever." Lucian kissed me again.

"I will love you forever," I repeated.

It was time.

CHAPTER 18
LUCIAN

When my eyes jerked open, the hand released my shoulder as Molly sat down next to us, the memory over. Her clothes were splattered with the black ink of Caelius's blood. "Don't worry, we have some time. They're still going at it." She motioned behind her. "But that won't be enough to kill him; he's already getting his power back."

Shea was cradled in my arms. She reached past me and grabbed her mother's hand. "That's why I have to finish this, Mom, even if I have to die doing it. We need to give Lucian time to talk to Caelius. I can weaken him, then Lucian can convince him to turn back to his shadow form."

Molly patted me reassuringly before I could retort. "Don't worry, Lucian, it's not the job of the daughter to die before her mother." Her eyes were kind, but her words carried a loving authority I had not heard in thousands of years, not since they'd last been spoken by my own mother on her deathbed. "It's okay.

I know what's best, child."

"Mom, *please*, I have to—"

"Sh." She brushed Shea's cheek, and as she did, it became more solid.

I squeezed Shea's arms; they were fatty and flesh. Her lips regained their pinkish hue. She shook her head no, her eyes locked with Molly's. "Listen to me, Mom, this is serious! This is what I was made for!"

"Sacrifice." Molly took a deep breath. "It's one of the Light's most powerful moves: to sacrifice yourself wholly and completely. That's why it's in the Gutian code, right? It's not just about fighting for those you love." She addressed me, but her eyes stayed on her daughter. "Lucian, you were right to give up last time in order to save them. You weren't disgracing your people, you were honoring them."

She kissed Shea's forehead. "You are so *brave*, my little girl. To think at one time I had you safe in my belly." Tears rolled down her cheeks, and Shea's followed. "And now you are strong enough to sacrifice yourself for the world. My precious, beautiful baby."

Molly looked up at my desperate face. "I'm going to be the one to save her this time."

She gently pushed me aside and pulled Shea out of my arms and into hers, squeezing her tight. She whispered, "It's a mother's job to sacrifice herself for her daughter. It's always been a mother's job. That's what Light is: the mother, the creator of *all*, who loves its children more than anything."

I felt helpless watching as they wept together, and Shea continued to protest in vain.

"Light is the *mother*, you say?" Caelius's voice stopped all of ours. "Then I guess I am the *father*. And what She creates, I will happily destroy." A darkness swept from behind us, followed by the screams of everyone left on the battlefield. They were pierced and pinned down just as Nefertiti's daughters had been in the last battle, before he'd gouged their necks open and sucked out their lives. I could see by the hate spilling off of Caelius's ghastly form that this was all repeating, except this time there would be no one left to tell the tale once he was done.

He rose upward like the base of a spider, lifting above his long clawed legs, hovering in the sky like the god he thought he was. "Besides, what do *you* know of the Light, hag? The Light and I have been together since the dawn of time, and even I don't understand Her. What could you possibly know that I do not?"

I stood up, placing my body between them and Caelius. "Even as a mortal, I know more about the Light than you." That came out wrong.

He leapt into the air, landing over us in an instant. "Careful, boy!" he sneered. "Or the next *makeover* I give you won't be as gentle."

"Love." My voice quivered as I shot a quick, knowing glance to Shea. "I know more about the Light because I know *love*. Tell me, Caelius, what have you been wrestling with this whole time, trying to understand, trying to know for yourself through me?" My voice was shaky, but my determination was resolute. I wasn't sure what Molly had been talking about, how she could sacrifice herself instead of Shea, but if I could persuade him now, Shea wouldn't lose her soul. Maybe my words would be enough to pin him down. As convincing as she was, I wasn't going to lose her.

He encased us in the coils of his twisted black limbs, pulling me close to his face as he wrapped his other claw around Shea, covering her mouth. His incisors grew as he spoke in heated gasps. "You, mutt-child of *Gutium*! What do *you* know of love? What do *you* know of sacrifice? *I* was willing to give up that Vessel bitch's soul. *I* was willing to give up becoming whole, all so that I could keep you. In all of my existence, I have never chosen to give up power. I have never cared for anything as I have for *you*!"

He was right.

Like the rest of us, he had changed too.

There were so many new emotions he had been trying to hide, but they were evident, even here, as he shook us in his fists. This wasn't the same monster that had pierced his claw through my chest in our last battle. He was holding me so I couldn't move, but he wasn't *hurting* me this time. If anything, even as he squeezed the others tighter, he held me gently.

As angry as his voice sounded, there was something else there, something I'd seen evolve over our time together but hadn't named. In truth, I hadn't *wanted* to name it. I'd explained and written it off because of what he was doing to me then.

But Shea had helped me bring it to light through my memories.

And here it was again.

In this momen, I knew him as I knew myself.

Shea was right.

Caelius wanted to be *loved*.

Perhaps now was the right time, and I could fight *my way*, as Bohe had suggested. Perhaps the nightmare of Shea's death didn't have to be a reality.

Caelius shook me again for emphasis. "The moment I saw

you, La-Narru, by the river in Gutium, the moment you called me God, I *wanted* you, and I can't stop—I've tried. I can't control you or change your affections to return what I feel. It's Shea now, but it was Nefari then. And once I kill Shea, it will be someone else. If you understand the Light more than I, then tell me what I have to do to make you *love* me. Tell me now, and I might spare your precious Vessel's life!"

Fear and loneliness accompanied by an ache to be understood and loved in return—I knew these words well and had spoken them myself over the centuries. I had threatened Moses before Aidan, Gunnhild before Ashgar, Gracuri before Bohe, David before Duncan. On and on, one after another, I had threatened Vessels, angels, and Second-Borns, daring them to love me even though I couldn't love myself. I'd threatened the world, daring it to *make* me understand.

And finally, it had.

"Alone." My lips moved on their own, and his gaze followed the sound, awaiting my answer.

"Finally willing to speak up, darling, now that the offer to spare your whore is on the table!" He laughed painfully to himself. "Of course, always defending your precious *family!*"

"Such isolation and loneliness," I whispered, feeling the words sail like arrows through my own chest.

"How dare you speak as if you know anything of the isolation of *Darkness*." He jerked his head, spit landing on my face.

"I tried to talk to you before, to tell you what I've only recently come to understand. You're not alone, Caelius. Loneliness is a lie, a lie *you* created. In our despair as mortals, we believe that lie when we experience loss. But it's not true, is it? The love I've had and the love of those passed is with me now, even in all of this. They are here by my side. I was *never* alone."

He pulled me to his chest, finally squeezing me as tight as the others. "I told you to be careful. I don't want to hear about your love of swine and their continued obsession with you."

"Or what, you'll kill me?" I scoffed.

He stared at my insolence, dumbfounded; even he was blind to how much he had changed. The Caelius that might have accidentally taken my life in blind fury a year ago was too afraid to lose me, and now I knew why.

His teeth receded as he brought me closer to his face. "What are you offering then?" His eyes sent shivers over my skin as he looked over every inch of it. "Another bargain, perhaps?"

"Would you take it?"

I could see Shea struggling against his grasp, screaming into the fat of his thick spider-arm. She thought it was her turn to die, but I would die a thousand times if it meant the salvation of her soul.

He hesitated, searching my features for a tell. "It would be a lie. I would *know* that this time, boy."

"I think you knew it last time."

He winced, then scowled. "Aren't we cocky?"

I cleared my throat. "Even knowing, would you take the deal? My imprisonment for their freedom—not just Shea's, but the world's."

"I would." There was no hesitation in his voice now. "But you will be fully conscious this time as you give yourself over to me; no blood, no memory wipe, no Nefertiti or Vessel, no games. There will be no one else, just you and me traveling this land for all eternity. I've said this before—you're all I've wanted since I became flesh. *That's* the deal."

I swallowed, realizing what immortality with him would be like: my own unimaginable handcrafted hell. I had created a plan with Shea to convince him to go back to Darkness, but she wanted that plan to include her sacrifice, along with words that could reach him after. But I couldn't sacrifice her, and even though I was a poet as a boy, now my tongue knew nothing of the art. This wasn't the best way, but it was *a way* for them all to live. And that's what mattered most. "If that's what it takes to save them, it's a dea—"

"And that's what you don't understand about sacrifice." Molly's voice was soft, but her authority commanded his attention. "Devotion isn't a *bargain*. It's not something you manipulate and force. If you truly cared for Lucian, you would prioritize his happiness over your own selfish desires. You'd give up your mortal form and go back to being Darkness and let him go because that's what *he* needs."

She sighed. "You've never been a parent. I can't expect you to understand what I mean, but surrendering your power to get what you want is not the same as sacrificing your life. Lucian gave his *life* to save Shea. She tried to do the same. And I would die for my daughter."

Caelius shook his head and laughed, as if the thought was ludicrous. "You would have me *die* to prove myself, *Mother*? How convenient that would be for you and your little Vessel; me dead and all of you holding hands. Don't make me sick."

She pulled her arm out of his grip and cupped his cheek. To my surprise, he let her hold him like that as she spoke. "It's what the Light would do."

"Is it now? Is that what the *Light* and everyone else would do? Do you really believe in that stupid code his fat father Onack made? He was just a man, but I am a *god*! Why should *I* follow such human drivel?" He shook all of us in rage.

When he stopped, his limbs sagged. "This is exhausting. I'm *tired*," he choked out, his voice cracking for the first time. "I'm not *supposed* to be in mortal form, you dumb cow. It's proven . . . difficult. Even I have my limits."

He shifted his eyes back toward mine. "Last chance, boy. Take the deal, or I kill them all in seconds, and you'll be mine anyway."

I gaped. Of course I would take the deal, but Molly, without knowing what Shea and I had discovered, was circling the revelation. I looked at her hopelessly.

Molly nodded, not letting me speak. "I know you're tired, Grandfather. It's okay." Her tone was so motherly, even I felt somewhat reassured by its promise. "It's been hard for you, and there's so much you haven't understood."

"That being said"—he jerked from her embrace—"I am not the *Light*. It's always giving up pieces of itself to save its pathetic little creations. That is not *my* way. By nature it is not. By nature I am the opposite; I am different from everything that is or was. There is Light, and there is Darkness. The one remaining truth is that we are *not* the same. I am not created by the Light. Just as it exists, I am a singularity."

"And yet here you are." She leaned closer. "And yet you took this *bargain*. What were you looking so desperately for in this playground of the Light? What were you trying to understand after eons of being what you've always been? Can't even the

Darkness want to change?"

He paused, and the wind around us grew still, as if it had been sucked out into the vacuum of space. "I don't know."

"That's not true."

I was astounded; Molly Harper was talking to Darkness as if he were a rebellious teenager. She was speaking for me while I gathered my thoughts in her shadow.

"Ever since I became mortal, I've felt strange. I've been searching for . . ."

"Is strange really the word? And searching? Haven't you already found what you were looking for?"

"I thought I found it"—he tilted his head toward me—"when I found him."

"But you couldn't hold on to it?" Her voice was low as she leaned even closer to him. "You considered it worthwhile enough to come here, to suffer in this small form just to understand it."

"I was patient," he spat, "like you're supposed to be with fragile things. I waited. I didn't pluck his life until the humans snipped his string for me. I let him have the experiences he would have had, and after that he was supposed to choose *me*. He *promised* to be mine. He was supposed to be grateful, he was supposed to—"

"Love you."

He froze, blinking at her soft round face.

"Yes, of course."

There was a long pause.

I was still unsure of what to say. For all of the things that I had felt for Caelius, *true* love was never one of them. Even now, I understood him, pitied him even, but I did not *love* him, and

I never would.

I squeezed my fists. This was what I needed to convey, that *my* love didn't matter.

I wasn't what he needed.

How could I make him understand what had taken me thousands of years to realize? How could I reach him, now, when he was vulnerable and open?

This might be my only chance.

I had to follow Molly's lead, as inarticulate as my dry tongue felt. "But love is in everything the Light touches, Caelius, even you!" I shouted, breaking their silent gaze.

When his eyes met mine they were sadder than before, and I could see the tiredness he had spoken of. He looked ancient and weathered, so unlike a pompous lord strutting his arrogant wishes over humanity, over me. "The Light doesn't touch the Darkness, boy, so it is not *in* me." He half smiled, but there was no humor to it, only desire. "As I have been *in* you, I know what I speak of."

"But—" I was thrown off by the lingering lust in his gaze. "I don't know how long you were watching me for, but the morning I met you . . . was the night after my Harrowing, wasn't it?"

He eyed me up and down. "Of course I was there."

I swallowed. I thought that might've been the case; I had watched a fair share of my Second-Borns before turning them.

"So you saw it." I paused, remembering that night vividly. It wasn't uncommon for cultures, even now, to have a rite of passage for boys becoming men. In Gutium, however, it hadn't been gender specific; all children underwent the Harrowing, and that was what I'd been, a *child*. It was worse for me. My mother had just died, and instead of waiting three more years, my father decided that if I was old enough to cause her death, then I was old enough to become a man.

Others had to last a night in the mountains alone, but as the son of our leader I had to survive a week. It was his verdict, and I believed it a fitting punishment for her loss. It was brutal. I had barely learned to speak, let alone hold a bowl, and there I was . . . in the black woods, lost and alone.

He tilted his head, eyeing my scowling face. "It is the reason you called me God and reached for me the next morning, not yet understanding what I was." He looked at me for a long while, pained by his own words. "You were afraid then, as you are now." His eyes saddened further by the truth of his most treasured memory. "You've always been afraid of the dark."

"Yes." I nodded. It was not only an innate fear for all humans, it was something that had terrified me specifically as a child because of the Harrowing. Even so . . . "That last night, I discovered something in the dark before I met you."

His eyes flashed, his interest piqued. This was a conversation he'd never thought of having. "You don't speak of the days surrounding your mother's death often. And your memory of the next morning with me has been all but forgotten." He bit his bottom lip, salivating. "Isn't this a mistake, Lucian?"

He bit harder until there was blood. My teeth grew in anticipation. It was an enticing threat. I watched as it moved from his chin down his neck.

"Think clearly, lover. The more I learn about you, the easier it will be to take you apart later. You know that by now, don't you? I will hold nothing back next time."

"I know." I swallowed, *thirsty*. I had to force my gaze from the red of his blood to that of his eyes. I wouldn't let him stop me from saying what I should have said as a boy, instead of mistakenly calling him God.

"After feeling the fear of night and crying for my mother, I was lost for days. Alone, I lay on my back clutching my stomach, ready to die from the unyielding pains of starvation. It was then that I saw the full light of the moon. It had been there the whole time, but in my terror, I had only looked down, never up. Then as I walked, easily finding the path back home, I also noticed the stars. There were so many, it was overwhelming; I felt . . . that I wasn't alone anymore.

"There are daytime things we forget about in the dark—things we take for granted, things we get too afraid of or blinded by. But I saw it then. I've forgotten it a million times over, just like you have, but the light of those stars, they stood *with me* in the dark. They were *inside* of it, just as they are inside of you."

He sighed, moving his fingers through thick pitch-black hair. "Is that what you think?"

"Yes." I wrung my hands nervously. I needed to drive the point home. "I should have told you then; the Light is not *separate* from you. It's not standing in opposition fighting some ongoing war over territory. It is a part of you, just as you are a part of it. You have never been alone.

"Just as the moon carried me home when I was lost, the Light has been by your side this whole time, *loving* you." I thought of Shea and those I'd turned. I thought of Aidan and Bohe, Gracuri and Duncan, all the people who loved me, but I hadn't been able to see it, all because of a lie . . . the same lie Caelius was caught in.

"Can't you see it in the world it's created? Day and night,

summer and winter, up and down, everything coming in pairs to create and sustain more life that then gives way to death. It didn't strive to make a world *without* you; out of love, it etched you into the existence of all things, just like our Gutian code. It never stopped loving the Darkness who thinks he is alone.

"Without asking you to change, it will *always* love you. Out of all the things that do change, that has remained the same. You are worthy of love, Caelius. The Light knows it more than all of us, paying homage to your existence in everything it touches."

His claw moved from around my waist, craning my head forward to meet his. "That night, I was taken in by *your* light, boy. That's why I spoke with you that next morning. You were radiating something I couldn't touch, and I fell for you—for that something I saw in your gaze. Then you called me God, and I was never the same."

I opened my mouth but hesitated.

He sighed again. Our faces were so close that his hot breath moved over my cheek. "And now you say you were radiating with the knowledge that Light and Darkness are one." He brushed his lips over mine. The blood was dry now, but I had to use all of my strength not to lick it clean.

I jerked my head away.

He wrapped his darkened limb over my mouth as if hiding the temptation from himself as well. Shea and I now matched, our bodies and our voices muted. He leaned back, lowering his legs to the ground and us with him.

He looked up into the sky at the moon blocked by brilliant rays of sun. "Through the mouth of babes, huh, Light?" He glanced at me and chuckled to himself. "And what a *mouth* it is."

He stared back up for a long while, analyzing my words. "To think these humans could forget something you and I have known for all of time." He squeezed all of us a little tighter. "To think that even *I* could forget."

His shoulders slumped. "Do you still shine upon me, even now? Do you not despise me, Light, for all I have taken from you in my forgetting? For all I *will* take, even now that I know?" He readied himself, shifting his eyes from the sky to the sand covering the tops of his feet.

The wind finally returned in the vacuum his powerful emotions had created. It flowed past us and circled him for a fraction of a moment. It was so brief and subtle that if I hadn't been a vampire I would have missed it.

"Is that truly what you believe, Light?" He laughed to himself—the disheartened laugh of the defeated. "That's your answer then? In a small still voice, just like always. Patient. Gentle. Constant." He sighed again, returning his gaze to the sun. "How annoying." He paused. "Not that I don't like it." His chin raised higher toward the blue that veiled the blackened night and its stars. "This whole time, it was *me* then. I was the one who didn't understand *you*, not the other way around."

Slowly he released his hold on all of us, his shape returning to that of a man's. I ran to Shea's weakened body and propped her up in my arms. She clung to me, pulling my Hanfu into a ball at my chest.

"Don't you *ever* think about sacrificing yourself again!" She was trying to yell, but it came out low and hoarse. I held her close, knowing it might be the last time. If anything, Caelius was unpredictable.

He still might kill us all.

And as I thought his name, his gaze met mine.

"You really do love her." His tone was even more deflated. "Even though I offered you immortality, unlimited power, and a seat to rule the world and all we touched . . . if only you'd stay by my side."

I nodded reluctantly, not wanting to provoke him. "I would choose her every time, for all of time."

He stumbled back, as if struck. "Of course you would."

"But the Light chose *you*."

"So it said." He smiled wryly. "But I want to hear it from *your* lips. Tell me again, boy. Tell me in a persuasive way that only a poet born of a warring race could. Tell me of love and loneliness, La-Narru, and this time, and only this time . . . I will listen. So make it *convincing*."

I cleared my throat. It was always unnerving when he spoke my childhood name. I wished that I had kept writing poetry, that I had searched relics over the ages for wisdom like Bohe had, instead of power. I sighed, trying to remember that it was the inarticulate child by the river in Gutium who had won his heart the first time. It was La-Narru he had fallen for, and at the heart of me still lived that boy, no matter how much I had hidden him from the world.

"I'm sorry, Caelius." I held Shea tighter. "Looking back on it now, I can see that I was never meant to be by your side."

He stumbled again. "Gentle now."

I swallowed. "I was always meant to be the *messenger*. You weren't supposed to keep me. You saw the boy but not the message of love that the Light had written for *you* in the stars that night. I think the Light gave you the chance to become flesh so that you could watch us and learn—so that you could embrace each other again."

I took in a sharp breath, trying to steady myself. "The Light risked all of its *favorite* creations by having you come here. It even sent a piece of itself to be carried by a human Vessel so that you wouldn't be alone, trapped and imprisoned forever. It didn't stop you from devouring Aidan's brothers, its beloved angels. It hasn't tried to stop you, has it? Only the free will of its creations has ever stood in your way. And you act as if you're not loved." I scoffed.

Caelius's eyes widened.

"You are more loved than *all* of us." My body began to shake in fury. "You, who are more loved than all of creation, forgot? How absurd. How . . . human." I laughed as Caelius's look of shock grew. "You who have been jealous of *me*. You who are a part of us just as much as the Light. You are loved no matter what you do, no matter how you change or don't." As my resentment grew, I felt something else overshadow it: the same peace I'd felt as a boy staring up at the moon. In truth, there was so much love in the universe, and we were *all* a part of it.

A solitary tear ran down Caelius's face.

I gasped unintentionally at the sight.

He tilted his head, as if rolling the words around. "How very human indeed." He played with a chunk of his hair. "I suppose it is possible that the Light loves me as much as I love *you*." His gaze moved back to the sky. "I feel it reaching, trying to hold me, arms that have been outstretched since the dawn of creation. Arms I ignored, then forgot existed, even in my longing for them." He chuckled to himself. "The prodigal son returns. After all this time, after what I've done and who I am, the Light still cares for Darkness. What an idiot."

He peered into the sky. "It has a better personality than I do. Out of all our games, I suppose it won this one." He reached up and spread his fingers, letting the sunlight fall through them, casting a shadowed hand over his face. "I'll win the next one though."

He lowered his hand and touched his face, moving his thumb along the wet trail at his cheek. "Crying, that's a first for me, even though you weaklings do it all the time." He scoffed even as his voice cracked. "I don't get why it's supposed to be *healing* or why it was created as a function to a mortal body." He sniffed, wiping his nose on his arm. "It's disgusting." He patted his face dry, shaking his head. "It's a strange sort of release, different from destruction, but . . . I suppose I do feel better for having done it."

His gaze met mine. "How cringeworthy and cheesy your little poem was. You should be embarrassed. You spoke less, but it meant more when you were a child. Still . . . despite your failings, I do understand that I am loved and not alone anymore and blah, blah, blah."

This time the weariness I had seen in his gaze faded, as if the fatigue of time itself, the burden of it, was gone for a brief moment. He extended his shadow out to me. I flinched as it patted me on the head. "Don't worry. You did well enough."

He retracted it, then balled his hand into a fist at his chest.

"I know where I'm wanted. I'm ready then. I'll go." He squeezed his fist until the knuckles paled. "And I'll do it for *you*, La-Narru. *I'll* be the god you need this time. Not because of your little speech or the Light's lame confessions."

He unclenched his fist and reached it toward me. "But there's still a price. I can't pop this mortal flesh without the *key*." His nails extended. "I need the Vessel's soul to become whole, to give up this contract and return home. It's why the Light sent her, after all. I'm sorry, my love, but as we all have a purpose, this was always hers."

I followed his outstretched fingertips toward Shea.

My mind was reeling. "No, I won't—"

She kissed me hard. I blinked, staring at her face as she poured her passion into it. She pulled back with the intent of leaving the embrace and stepping forward. I clung to her, not letting her go. "I lost you once."

"We'll be together again someday," Shea said with a small smile as she eyed our entire family. "All of us."

Caelius's nails retracted as Molly stepped between him and her daughter. "I told you, Shea, that's *not* your purpose."

"Mom?" She leaned toward her as I steadied her trembling legs.

"Caelius, *I* am the mother." She walked up to him and took his outstretched hand in hers. "I felt her life in my womb. I held and kissed her tiny fingers in my arms as she cried. I have watched her and loved her all of my life. If she is the Vessel, I am the vessel that held the Vessel. I am the child of your two First-Borns. *I* am the key to bringing you home. That is why her soul broke you out of the cage but has eluded you since. It was never meant for that." She looked at Shea with affection. "I love you."

"Mom, no!" Shea lunged forward, and I followed her.

Caelius's shadow emerged around the ground at our feet and held us in place *easily*. It was only then that I realized just

364

how much he'd been holding back. This whole time he'd been playing a long game, not to win against the Vessel, but to win my affections over time.

He could have effortlessly killed all of us, the whole world in fact, with one flood of his overwhelming power. He was Darkness itself: a force just as vastly immense as the Light.

He stepped toward Molly, then looked again at the sky. "Is this how it is, old friend? I would have *preferred* to take the whore." He talked for a while longer under his breath, as if arguing. He tilted his head toward us. "Although death would be quick for her, taking her mother will elongate her suffering. That's not a bad deal, but I still want the girl."

Molly squeezed his hand. "I know you want her, but I am the mother and it is my place."

"Mom, no! It has to be me, please!" Caelius's shadow covered Shea's mouth. I clung to her as if my insignificant arms were strong enough to save her from the power of his oblivion.

"Fine," he snapped at Molly, then met my desperate gaze with resolution. "It would feel good for a while, but I supposed watching Lucian stumble around miserably for the rest of his days without me being able to comfort him would bother me, even in abstract form." He licked his incisors. As much as he'd tried to fill his words with callousness, to harden the vulnerability he now felt, it was still visible on his face. After all this time, the truth that the Light had been trying to reach him with was already bridging the gap, and he was changing more rapidly than before.

"Come then, *Mother*, give me your little soul, and I'll leave this world . . . forever." He flinched with that last word as if struck by a heavy blow, the weight and weariness returning briefly to his eyes. This time doubt met my gaze as he looked over my body with longing.

"But you won't be going back to who you were before, Caelius." My words rushed in to displace his fears.

"What I am, not *who*, child. I am not human." He shrugged, a smile spreading from one side of his mouth to the other. "And yet a *human*, one that I have tortured to make mine, offers me this simple truth in my final hours as a mortal. Even I'm not foolish enough to turn down such a decadent deal, boy: the Light as company, the memories of our time together, and your words. It's not a bad trade. All I have to do is forfeit this sad flesh-sack." He pinched his own arm in disgust. "It wouldn't have been able to hold me in an appealing form for much longer anyhow, and I wouldn't have wanted you to see me otherwise."

He laughed, and this time it wasn't full of malicious intent or hate; it was hearty and wild—wild like dark nights in the forest with howling animals and strange eyes. Then it struck me: for all of the order and stability of Light, Darkness was the unknown that Light pulled its creations *from*. They were each other's soul mates, one the completion of the other.

I looked at Caelius somewhat anew. Was it thrilling for a being like Light to have something unknown existing beside it? I moved my hand unconsciously through Shea's hair. The unknown parts of her, I wanted to seek all of them out, all of her corners and vast spaces, to know her and lose her, only to know her again, throughout every world and every lifetime.

That was what the Light had felt for Darkness all this time. What would change for Caelius now that he remembered the

Light's affections? What would change for all of us existing inside their eternal dance?

"Think on me, won't you, boy?" Caelius's words penetrated my thoughts, his shadow moving intimately along my spine.

"You said that those who have loved you and passed are with you now. They think of you, and you remember them. You may not have cared for me, but I have always *loved* you. Will you answer this last request, as the child at the base of a mountain who looked at me in wonder and thought me a god?" As wild and untamable as his eyes had been before, they shifted with every word he spoke. They were uncertain, inexperienced, and afraid—the other aspects being in Darkness produced for mankind.

I bit my bottom lip. "I will. I can never forget you, Caelius." For better or worse.

He sighed in relief, then squeezed Molly's hand. "It would have been nice for you to call me *God* one last time, but, things being as they are . . ." He pressed his other palm against Molly's chest. A light emanated and moved like pieces of stardust into his veins. "I will rest in your love for a good long while, old friend. It's been an eternity, hasn't it, since we've embraced Light to Darkness?" Molly's light ceased, and it filled Caelius like white spots sprayed on black canvas. He began lifting into the air as her body fell limp and cold to the earth.

Finally Caelius's shadow released us.

"Mom!" Shea shouted. She ran to her side. I followed her but stopped as Caelius floated between us.

Another trick?

The thought flashed through my mind.

I was foolish to think he would change.

Now he was all-powerful.

Now there would be no stopping him.

I gazed up at him in rage.

But his face . . . his whole body became black and started to fill in with the cosmos above us. He reached down and kissed my lips. As much as it was cold and foreign, his form shifting, there was an abiding tenderness there.

"Goodbye, Lucian. I cannot create life, but you were and will always be the only living thing I loved and named as my own. And like a good puppy, you led me back home to myself and to the Light. For that, I will be forever grateful." His face was evaporating, but I could feel the Cheshire smirk lingering on his lips. His red irises danced like flames, flickering over my skin one last time before he dissolved completely.

And just like that, the being Caelius was no more.

And just like that, balance was restored to the universe: Light and Dark in their *rightful* place.

But now they were no longer separated by an idea that had turned into a lie, that had gained power over the one that had created it and caused the Darkness and the world to suffer in loneliness.

Now they were one, as Shea and I could finally be.

They were together, and all of humanity, all of life, and all of us . . . were finally free.

CHAPTER 19
SHEA

5 YEARS LATER

"**M**ommy, do I have to wear this tie? It makes me choke. Are you *trying* to choke me?"

I stared down at my little boy with his oh-so-serious expression and tried not to laugh. He looked so much like La-Narru it made my heart sing every time I saw him. Even though it had been difficult to get used to at first, I completely understood why Lucian wanted to be called by his birth name, his *true* name. Now I didn't even think about it anymore. He was just my La-Narru, a name that meant "the way home" in his native tongue.

I shook my head at Ash with a smile. "No, I'm not trying to choke you. Go ahead and take it off, but keep your jacket on."

Ash was short for Ashliel. He was named after Aidan's brother, who'd sacrificed himself to trap Caelius in his "human" prison all those years ago. It felt right. We did it for Aidan, and he was honored. Even though I'd been mad at his brothers after our final battle with Caelius for juicing me up with a Light-bomb that would have evaporated my soul, Ashliel had still made the ultimate sacrifice to save humanity. His memory deserved to live on. And it would, through our little boy.

Ash's four-year-old hands happily yanked off the clip-on bow tie at the neck of his adorable little tuxedo. He let out a huge sigh of relief as if I had intentionally tried to choke him.

Dang, he was cute.

I was still amazed that Ash even existed. He was only possible because Helena cured Lucian. A few months after my mother's sacrifice and Caelius's return to Darkness, Helena discovered that vampirism could be eradicated like a disease. One injection of the formula she made destroyed the last of Caelius's blood in a vampire's system, turning them back into a human.

A cure.

An actual cure.

Even a few years later, it still stunned me.

Helena said it wouldn't have been possible if Caelius was still in human form and his blood tied to the mortal world, but as Darkness, it had no solid connection to Earth anymore and therefore could be eliminated. Essentially, in scientific terms, Caelius's blood was a virus and her serum was the cure.

I wished my mother was alive to see it. She would have been cured and a proud grandma to Ash. My heart still hurt thinking of how she had sacrificed her life for everyone, for me. It was easier now that five years had passed, but the wound would bubble up whenever I thought of her. I missed her so much.

As I looked at myself in the mirror in my wedding gown, I wished she was here with me. I could feel her sometimes: her presence, her love. It had taken me a long time to get to this place of peace, and if I was being honest, I wasn't sure I'd ever truly be okay with what had happened, but I was happy in this moment, and I knew she would be too.

It was my wedding day, for crying out loud!

"Why are we the only two stuck in this room? I want to go see Uncle Aidan," Ash complained.

"Are you sure it's Uncle Aidan you want to see?" I teased, knowing full well Ash had a crush on Aidan and Meky's daughter, Lulu. Lulu was only two months older than Ash and pretty much the most beautiful little girl ever. It made perfect sense of course, considering she was half Egyptian princess, half celestial being. Not to mention the fact that she was the sweetest, most mild-tempered child in the history of all children, or at least compared to Ash anyway. Stubborn, willful, and intensely passionate pretty much summed him up, which made him quite a handful at times. Like father, like son.

Ash sighed, his voice sounding a lot older than his actual four years of existence. "You can tease me, Mommy, but I plan on making Lulu my girlfriend. She's the prettiest girl in the whole world, and I love her a lot."

My heart melted. "Well, I didn't know it was so serious. I won't tease you again," I said with as much sincerity as I could muster, though all I really wanted to do was scoop him up in my arms and kiss his cheeks a million times. "And we're here alone because I thought it'd be nice to spend some time with my little boy before you and Grandpa walk me down the aisle."

"I guess, but I'm not that little." Ash looked contemplative, then said, "You look really pretty, Mommy."

"Thank you, sweetie. That means the world to me." I leaned

371

down and kissed the top of his head, and he smiled.

I smoothed out the cream satin fabric as I stood back up and looked in the mirror. I felt like a movie star, wearing a form-fitting dress that trailed out into a long train. I loved how the strapless neckline framed my face and hair but hoped that I wouldn't get cold in the evening. Maybe the long, bouncy waves that Meky had spent hours curling for me would give me some kind of warmth.

There was a knock on the door and through it came Aidan's muffled voice. "I know you said you wanted to be alone, but we have a slight emergency out here."

I nodded to Ash to open the door, and he made a mad dash to the knob, throwing open the door as if he expected to see a fire. "What's the emergency?"

Aidan smiled at Ash's intense expression. "Hold on, little man. I said 'slight' emergency, and I was actually lying. I just wanted to see the bride before she heads down the aisle."

Ash almost looked disappointed but waved his hand out to welcome Aidan into the room.

Aidan's eyes widened when he saw me. "You look stunning."

I hugged him tightly. "Thank you. How's everyone doing out there?"

We separated from our hug, and he laughed. "Well, La-Narru is more excited than I've ever seen him. You did make him wait for five years. He actually smiled for ten minutes straight, if you can believe that."

"I can't. And I didn't make him wait; I just wanted it to be perfect, and sometimes that takes time. But continue," I said with a laugh.

"Meky is trying to organize everyone and everything. I think you picked the perfect wedding coordinator. She's found her calling in life. She says it's just like organizing a battle, but without all the blood." Aidan smiled again.

"I'm sure that's not far from the truth. Though I am a bit worried about the 'leftovers.' " And by "leftovers" I meant the vampires who had eluded Nefertiti and Helena's grasp. The two women had not taken the serum that cured vampirism because they'd made it their new mission to hunt down every vampire on the planet and force-inject them with the cure.

It wasn't surprising that a large portion of vampires didn't want to lose their immortality and super strength. Those of us who'd fought Caelius, however, knew that the vampire "disease" needed to be eradicated, whether the vampires wanted it or not. More importantly, there was a whole faction of vampires that enjoyed killing, loved that they were a predatory species, and only thought of humans as food. They needed to be taken out.

Nefertiti and Helena had volunteered to hunt the last of them down. Helena had invented a device that was able to track Caelius's blood, so they knew there were exactly 234 vampires left in the world, not counting them and Duncan. Duncan desperately wanted to be human again, but his sense of duty was a stronger pull, and he wanted to help turn every last vampire human.

Lucian had called it "self-penance" and tried to talk Duncan out of it, mainly because he felt guilty about turning Duncan in the first place. But Duncan was stubborn, and he wanted to feel as if he had righted his wrongs in this lifetime. Tracking down vampires seemed like the only thing that would satiate his guilt.

Aidan understood the meaning of "leftovers," code for vampires, so Ash wouldn't know what I was talking about. Aidan also understood why I was worried about possible vampires wanting to crash the wedding of Lucian the First-Born. Killing La-Narru would be like winning a trophy to any vampire left.

Aidan shook his head. "My brothers are hiding this church from anyone with Caelius's blood in them. I had to bring Nefertiti, Helena, and Duncan myself or they never would've been able to find it. I'm pretty sure my brothers did this as a thank-you for returning Caelius to Darkness, by the way."

I couldn't trust Aidan's brothers after they duped me into being a Light-bomb for Caelius. "I appreciate the gesture. That was nice of them," I mumbled under my breath.

Picking up on my state of awkwardness, Aidan changed the subject. "Your dad is beside himself with excitement to walk you down the aisle. I don't know if he's happier for you or *La-Narru*."

I playfully punched Aidan in the arm. "He does not still have a crush. Would you stop?" Unfortunately, even though he was human again, my father's feelings were very strong when it came to my future husband.

"Okay, but the way he looks at La-Narru, I'm just saying," Aidan teased. "And Ur-Nammu has been waiting at the front of the church to marry you two for the last hour." Aidan laughed.

"He has not!" I laughed with him, and even Ash cracked a smile.

"I kid you not, the man is prepared," Aidan said in an amused tone. "And the Gutian wedding ceremony is what, two minutes long? It's not like he has much to prepare."

"Oh my God, he's so adorable." I felt nothing but affection

for Ur-Nammu now and saw him as the grandfather I never had, since both sets of grandparents had died before I was even born.

"Yeah, and Lulu is glued to his side. The two are inseparable," Aidan said.

"Lulu? She's at the front of the church?" Ash asked with interest.

Both Aidan and I laughed again. Then I said, "Go on. You can stay up front with Ur-Nammu and Lulu and watch me come down the aisle with Grandpa."

Ash didn't wait for me to change my mind. He raced out of the room toward the main church.

Aidan and I watched him go with smiles plastered on our faces.

We could hear the grunts of Ash tangling up with someone in the hall, then Meky popped her head in the doorway. "You look like a dream."

"Thank you," Aidan said.

"Not you, dork, though you always look like a dream to me." She winked. "We're ready for you, Shea." Meky was beside herself with happiness.

Butterflies threatened to yank themselves out of my stomach and do a tap dance on my head. "I'm ready."

"Yeah you are. Get over here." Meky grabbed my hand and led me out of the room with Aidan trailing behind. She turned her head to him. "When we get up to the altar you'd better do your best man duties. La-Narru needs you. That boy is practically fidgeting out of his suit."

"I will, I promise."

Walking down the long hallway of the church, I had never

felt so happy.

Even though my mom wasn't physically here, I knew she was with me and loving me from afar. I felt it so clearly, my heart was full.

Finally we reached the closed double doors that would lead to the inside of the church. Dad stood there waiting for me, smiling from ear to ear.

He placed his hand on his heart. "You are so beautiful."

I hugged him. "Thanks, Daddy."

Holding me tight, he said, "Your mother would be so proud."

"I feel her here," I said, trying not to cry.

"Me too," Dad said with a slight catch in his voice. Then he pulled back from the embrace, holding his arm out for me. "Shall we?"

I nodded. "We shall."

Meky was in control. She and Aidan stepped in front of us as the best man and maid of honor. They opened both doors, and the music started. It was a song from La-Narru's childhood in Gutium. Nefertiti had hired musicians to record it. It was a simple tune with just flutes and drums. It was both sweet and dramatic, perfect for our wedding.

Meky and Aidan walked down the aisle first.

Then after I counted to ten, like Meky had instructed me to, my dad and I followed after them.

The pews were full on both sides of the church. There were people we'd met in the last five years who knew nothing of our past or what we'd sacrificed to save them. The destruction of the cities that Caelius had wreaked havoc on had been rationalized away as terrorist attacks with super sophisticated weapons that had made the attackers invulnerable. Only a handful of people on Earth knew what really happened, but they just looked like conspiracy theory nuts talking about vampires demolishing cities.

The front row was filled with our family: Duncan, Sete, Sherit, Nefertiti, and Helena.

Setepenre gave me a quick wave and smile. I smiled back. We'd become close over the last couple of years. It was easier for her to talk to me rather than family, and I was a willing ear. After being brainwashed by Caelius for the last three thousand years, she hadn't even known who she was after she got free. It took her a while to understand what had been done to her and to get to know her family, for real this time.

It had been difficult, but Sete was generally a happy person, though I could tell her past life still haunted her. She was still struggling with her relationships with her sisters, mother, and La-Narru, but they were getting there. Ash helped immensely. It was a new relationship for her, and she wanted to be a good role model. The fact that she was here meant the world to me.

Then I saw him.

La-Narru.

His bright turquoise eyes stared at me with the intensity only he was capable of. Being human hadn't changed that part of him at all. He was much lighter in spirit, but the boy would always be intense; that was just who he was—a true artist.

Ash and Lulu held hands while Ur-Nammu waited patiently for me to arrive.

It almost took my breath away, the sight was so beautiful.

I wanted to run up there and give them all a group hug, but I followed the beat of the song and slowly made my way toward the altar. Aidan and Meky made it there first and stood to the side. Aidan gave La-Narru a gentle nudge in the arm for what could only be described as bro-love.

But La-Narru's eyes never left mine. Once his focus was on me, it would take a mountain falling on him to tear his gaze away. I still couldn't believe how lucky I was. To defeat Darkness itself and come out of it alive was a miracle none of us were taking for granted.

I just couldn't believe it had taken us this long to walk down the aisle. After everything that had happened, we were simply happy to be together. Then we'd had Ash and life had become . . . life: finding a home to settle down in, buying furniture, decorating Ash's room (with Ur-Nammu painting ancient protective symbols on the walls, then painting over them thinking we hadn't noticed), and just being *us* for once without murder and mayhem looming over our heads.

It was amazing.

The only thing missing was Mom. That's why I'd waited so long to have the wedding. La-Narru had wanted to do it a few years back, but I just couldn't. It felt wrong somehow, to have a celebration when she couldn't be there with us. A couple of months ago I saw a hummingbird fly into a lupine flower. Hummingbirds were my mom's absolute favorite. She had told me one time that she thought they were messengers from the ones we love that had passed. I'd known then that it was time.

As soon as I gave Meky the word, she was on it, planning this wedding as if she'd been planning weddings her entire life.

It was absolutely perfect. We were in a small chapel in the countryside of France, and the amount of flowers decorating the walls and pews astounded even me. The vaulted ceiling was framed with rich brown wood that was centuries old, and the stained glass windows brought the perfect amount of light into the sanctuary.

My father and I reached the altar, and he turned to me with tears streaming down his face. "I love you, kiddo."

"I love you too, Daddy."

Dad took my hands in his and leaned down, kissing my cheek, then turned to La-Narru. "My little girl is in your hands now, and I couldn't be prouder of the both of you."

My father might not have been a vampire anymore, but his sire bond with La-Narru hadn't seemed to lessen much when he'd become a human again. I didn't mind it. My dad had been a little too overprotective of me and who I dated before I went to college, so it was nice that he wholeheartedly loved La-Narru, even if some of that love had been blood-based.

Dad held my hands up and lowered them into La-Narru's.

As we touched, a thrill surged through my entire body. I knew that would never change. Our connection went beyond anything imaginable, and I wouldn't have it any other way.

Ur-Nammu pulled out a white silk scarf and began wrapping our hands together. It was a little tight for my taste, but this was a Gutian tradition. With each tug and wrap of the scarf, I only felt more bonded to La-Narru.

Ur-Nammu began speaking in Gutian as he worked the scarf. Only a handful of us understood his words. La-Narru had spent the last three years teaching it to me and Ash, and I didn't care that all our new friends had no idea what Ur-Nammu was saying. When they realized how short a Gutian marriage ceremony was, it would make up for not understanding what was being said.

As he wrapped each layer of scarf, then tightened it with a large tug, his words called out to us. They spoke of bonding, loyalty, and love.

Ur-Nammu completed tying the scarf around our hands at the same time he finished his ceremonial words.

"It is done," Ur-Nammu said in English. "These bonds bind your heart, body, and souls together in this life and the next."

That should have been the end of the ceremony, but he sighed and added, "You may kiss the bride." I could tell it pained him to say something so Western, but he managed a smile all the same.

And so did La-Narru.

Realizing he couldn't hold my face because our hands were fastened, he leaned down and our lips met, sending an explosion up my spine. I wanted to grab him, but all we had were our lips, which was probably a good thing considering I'd forgotten we were in a room full of people. I had never felt a purer kiss in my life, and that was saying something, considering how many times I'd kissed this beautiful man. But having our hands bound together, standing in front of everyone we loved, was a snapshot of true happiness.

La-Narru's lips left mine. "Because of you I am whole again. I love you, Shea Harper."

"I love you too, La-Narru, with all my heart and soul." Words didn't do justice as to how I felt.

An eruption of cheers and applause filled the air.

I couldn't believe it.

We were married.

And we were still tied together.

Ur-Nammu began unwrapping the silk scarf from our hands, and I could feel the circulation come back to my fingers. Dang, that man could tie a mean knot.

After he was done, La-Narru kept hold of my hands and brought them to his lips, kissing them gently.

My smile was big enough to slide off my cheeks. "So I guess this means you're officially *mine* now," I teased.

"I was always yours, from the moment you slammed the door in my face at your dorm," he teased back.

Aidan laughed at that. "Best moment ever."

Meky motioned for us to move. "Get down the aisle. Everyone is staring. Besides, you guys have no idea how amazing your reception is going to be. One word: epic."

La-Narru kissed me one last time, and we both went to grab Ash's hand to walk with us as we left the church.

Ash was in the middle of tying his hand to Lulu's with the silk scarf he'd snuck out of Ur-Nammu's pocket. "You're *mine* forever now too, Lulu."

Trying not to laugh at the obvious like-father-like-son moment, La-Narru gently took the scarf away from Ash. "No one is a possession, Ash. Lulu is to be respected and adored. Did you even ask her if she wanted to be yours?"

"No," Ash said solemnly. "But I *do* respect and adore her. That's why I want her."

Lulu looked thoughtful and replied, "It's okay. I love him too."

Ash's smile was so big it made my heart squeeze with cuteness. "*See!*"

Lulu smiled back and took Ash's hand. "But I'm not *yours,*

381

okay? We're equals."

Ash nodded vigorously. "I will love you forever, Lulu."

Ash led Lulu down the aisle, and the two of them giggled at all the elaborate hats the guests were wearing.

La-Narru held his arm out for me to take, and I did so happily.

"You ready to celebrate?" La-Narru smiled.

"For all of time," I said, and we walked out of the church and into the next chapter of our beautiful lives.

EPILOGUE
CAELIUS

So . . . I was Darkness again.

Not that I was complaining. Honestly, the heartwarming moments between me and the Light were nice enough.

For now.

I destroyed a galaxy or two when I first returned, just to blow off steam. It had been painful being human, having my unlimited power confined to weak mortal flesh. Ah, but that flesh knew things that I had not, and the sounds Lucian made when he was mine would ring in my ears brighter than the songs of all creation.

It was a first for me, to love something other than myself, and a creation of the Light no less. It was long ago, so I had forgotten, but I had once loved Light itself in that way. Then jealousy erupted as It expanded past our union and made things out of Us. Jealousy, contradiction, confusion, rage . . . a million other feelings emerged that hadn't existed before, if you could call them *feelings* in the void. They were creations in their own right, though I wouldn't call them *mine*.

Our relationship was hard to define, as we'd both always been. It wasn't easy to know how you felt about something that was so much a part of you, other than to separate from it. But I'd gone too far. I'd gotten lost in the undoing. I'd forgotten that, in stepping away from your dance partner, the next step was to pull them back in. Luckily Light remembered. It was good about things like that.

I understood now why Light created form. To further Its understanding of Itself, and of me, It played this little game with life. And It did it for *us*.

How flattering.

Being human taught me much in a short time.

And now time was a part of everything and not measured by human standards, so I drifted as I always had, keeping balance. As Light created stars, I took the old ones and gave them rest. As things lived vivaciously, I held them quietly as they died. There was a mercy in endings, a gentleness I had forgotten, except when I'd touched Lucian's hair while he slept. It was a gentleness I had wanted for him alone when he had praised me as a god by that river in Gutium, a gentleness that had made me forget myself and remember myself all at the same time.

Now that I was formless, all of that seemed like what humans called a dream. It was a dream I replayed in my memory often, nonetheless. It was not the way of Darkness to hold on to things. If anything, it was my way to constantly let go. But for this memory, this bright spot that was no doubt a dark spot for him, I would hold on to Lucian. For all of my existence, I would remember him. I was Darkness, but I held on.

Was that love?

Before I tortured Bohe, that little mouse had spoken of Yin and Yang: a fascinating human concoction, but not altogether far off. Now that I was reconnected with Light Itself, I had a white circle inside my Yin, just as my connection with the Light added a black spot in Its Yang. I liked Lucian's interpretation better, referencing the moon and the stars, living and moving inside of each other . . . as I had moved inside him.

Cute.

And you act as if you're not loved.

What an adorable face Lucian had made when he realized how much the Light wanted me. Ah, if he was here now I would try and make him show me that face one more time.

Alone and unlovable.

What a wild lie I had created and believed for so long. It was a good one. I knew because it had been easy to believe, and just as easy for the Light to refute. Good lies were like breathing, just like good truths. We were opposite and similar in that way. How bold for the Light to finally destroy something of mine, and such a powerful long-held belief at that.

How ballsy.

I laughed.

I had done horrible things.

I still might do horrible things.

I would still do horrible things.

And the Light would love me, *always*.

I missed having lips. I supposed if I had them, I might have smiled at that.

As it was, I was looking over Earth now.

I visited often, watching them muddle around.

Watching *him*.

I was sure Molly was watching too. She was with the Light now, no doubt blissed-out like all beings on that side were.

Today I could've used some of that bliss. Because today *my* Lucian was marrying that Vessel.

He would have made a better wife to me than a husband to that light bulb. Still . . . their child was *adorable*. If I could do it again, I would keep Ash and Setepenre and raise them as *our* children.

I kept watching. They were all so happy.

I sighed, feeling the Light comfort me in the way that It did.

"I know." I leaned my presence against the moon, making a crater that looked like my human face had. "Now the next time Lucian is lost and looks up at the moon, he'll remember me and what he said about Darkness." I caressed its shape. "No one wants to be forgotten entirely, darling." I embraced the Light, as much as we could embrace without destroying each other completely. "You have churches and synagogues and all of that, you lush. I just want this *one boy*."

"He really is something." We sighed together as the Light spoke in warm waves.

"Oh, don't flatter yourself. How cheesy to say that it was worth all of creation just to make something I liked." I warmed further but still refused to yield. "You know, he was *mine* too, wasn't he? I had my blood *in* him. I remade him a few times over; I even renamed him. Give him to me."

I growled, which was more a tremble in space rippling

through time than an earthly sound.

It made a tidal wave that sunk a populated island.

Oops, was that Japan or Hawaii?

It was the same for Atlantis last time.

Oh well, they'd make up stories and find it amusing later.

I smiled. "I know, I know. All that you have is mine, and all that I have is yours. And they are created out of both of us and so on. But you know what I mean. I'd like to keep him for myself in a less *corporeal* way, but I won't hurt you by leaving your side again."

We spoke often now and at great lengths. We planned things, worked together, fought together, reached the far corners of our beings and touched where we could. And I was changing, and so was the Light.

I wasn't sure what that meant for creation, if it meant anything at all, but integration had been harder when I was human—riddled with feelings of love alongside possessiveness and the need to destroy. Maybe as the Light and I eventually found our rhythm again, creation would as well.

Maybe that is my final gift to you, La-Narru.

The final gift to the humans you love.

That you could set aside the lie of loneliness. That you could feel in your souls the peace of creation, and finally rest like I have, in the joy of eternal balance.

COMING SOON
NOVELLAS :

VESSELS: LUCIAN & AIDAN
THE HUNT: NEFERTITI, HELENA & DUNCAN

Other Books by Hina McCord

Ivory

Love & Dark Series (with Becca C. Smith):
Vessel
First Born
Gutian Code

Other Books by Becca C. Smith

The Riser Saga:
Riser
Reaper
Ripper

The Atlas Series:
Atlas
Grigori Returned
The Underworld

Alexis Tappendorf Series:
Alexis Tappendorf and the Search for Beale's Treasure
Alexis Tappendorf and the Search for Atlantis

The Dream Diaries:
The Dream Diaries
The Dream Diaries: Blood Ties

Love & Dark Series (with Hina McCord):
Vessel
First Born
Gutian Code

SHEA Chapters Written by:
Becca C. Smith

Becca fell in love with storytelling at an early age. The first book she read was *The Lion, The Witch and The Wardrobe* and she's been looking for the door to Narnia ever since! Becca is a passionate reader, consuming anything sci-fi or fantasy. Mix it in with YA and she's a fan for life. So it's no surprise that she writes in these genres as well. When Becca isn't writing, she loves to sew. From *Mortal Instruments* rune pillows, to elaborate *Firefly/Serenity* bags, Becca loves to create!

LUCIAN Chapters Written by:
Hina McCord

Hina McCord is a novelist, aka an avid bullshitter; that's why she lives in L.A. She's been writing for as long as her ancient mind can remember, devouring tales like an anemic vampire roaming the streets in hot-pink heels, always thirsty for more. When she's not writing, she's making steampunk weapons, sewing giant plant-eater Mario plushes, making costumes for some film bloke or cosplayer, and sculpting/casting movie prop replicas while gardening in her urban apartment. Her favorite tools? A soldering iron, a blowtorch, a band saw, a sonic screwdriver, a replicator, and an active imagination.

www.ingramcontent.com/pod-product-compliance
Lightning Source LLC
Chambersburg PA
CBHW060221030726
47499CB00004B/1137